A DESTINY IN DEFIANCE

HEATHER BLANTON

RIVULET PUBLISHING

Cover DESIGN by Ravven

Scripture taken from the HOLY BIBLE,

KING JAMES VERSION - Public Domain

A huge *thank you* to my editor Lisa Coffield and all my awesome beta readers!

Heather Blanton

Please subscribe to my newsletter
by visiting my website
authorheatherblanton.com
to receive updates on my new releases and other fun news.
You'll also receive a FREE e-book—
A Lady in Defiance, The Lost Chapters
just for subscribing!

FOREWORD

Dear Readers,

Isn't it funny how characters seem to develop minds of their own? When I started this book, Hope Clark was going to be my main protagonist. As the story grew, blossomed, developed, life in Defiance happened to my characters, and the Holy Spirit took me in other directions.

Charles and his rivalry—not just with Matthew—but with his own need for control, rose to the top. How does a good man run a bad town? How does he keep his family safe and their lives peaceful if not by brute force? How does he really let go and trust God for the things he used to get himself?

Aren't these questions for us all?

Hope's story is the biggest sub-plot. You should know, she is based on the historical character of Doc Susie Anderson, a legendary physician who made her way alone in the Rockies. A formidable woman who truly loved her vocation and her patients, she traveled the region, helping the sick and dying. Her story is fascinating and I include it at the end of A Destiny in Defiance.

I hope you enjoy riding into Defiance with me once more. There's a lot going on in town...

God bless and happy reading!
Heather

Just as you don't know
the way of the wind
or how bones grow
in a pregnant woman's womb,
so you don't know the work of God,
the maker of everything.

Ecclesiastes 11:5 (ESV)

CHAPTER 1

ick. Tick. Tick.

r. Hope Clark tried to ignore how loudly the Regulator wall clock resonated in her empty office. She surveyed the tiny waiting room, devoid of patients, and sighed. She couldn't go much longer like this. If just one sick person would walk through that door, she felt certain she could win over many, many of the citizens of Denver.

It could all start with one.

As if in answer to prayer, her doorknob turned and slowly the door began to swing open. Hope jolted to attention, touched the stethoscope hanging at her neck to make sure it was still there, and pasted on a smile.

A cumbersome pink hat buried beneath ostrich feathers appeared in the entrance. It led the way for an older, quite rotund woman in a blue velvet dress who peered with suspicion around the room.

"Good morning," Hope said, crossing the room quickly,

before the woman could take in the lack of other patients. "I'm Dr. Clark."

She offered her hand, but the woman's eyes narrowed and she pulled back, as if Hope's greeting was offensive. "Yes. I know who you are."

Spirits sagging, Hope tried not to show her disappointment. Somehow, she knew the woman was not here for a health visit. Floundering, she lowered her hand and smiled. "What can I do for you, Miss...?"

"I'm Mrs. Abbington Chalmers. Perhaps you know my husband? The mayor."

"I am not personally acquainted, but I know of him."

Mrs. Chalmers sniffed, as if the answer didn't surprise her. "I am not here, however, on his behalf. I am here on behalf of the Ladies League of Greater Denver."

Lovely, Hope thought. *Not a patient. Worse. She wants a donation.* "Yes. How can I help you?"

For a moment, Mrs. Chalmers' hauteur wavered. The confidence exuded by her raised chin and squared shoulders faded a bit, or so Hope thought. "Well, it isn't easy to say what I've come here for."

"When I have difficult news for my patients, Mrs. Chalmers, I tell them outright. Beating around the bush can be unnecessarily cruel."

That brought the woman's chin back up. "Right you are. So I shan't beat around the bush, as you say. I've come to tell you, Miss Clark, that you have had no patients and you will not have any."

Hope blinked and wondered if she'd heard correctly. "I'm sorry."

Mrs. Chalmers twirled away in a flurry of ostrich feathers and blue velvet, presenting her back. "Women have their place in the world, Miss Clark."

"Doctor," Hope corrected without thinking.

The woman stiffened, slowly turned back to Hope. Her pudgy face, so round and soft, did not hide the heat in the woman's dull brown eyes, or the disdain in her thinned lips. "I see I need to speak plainly. You upset the balance. Women in Denver and in the rest of the world are happy with their stations in life. We are mothers and caregivers. Helpmeets to our husbands. We run our homes, raise our children, and give our husbands a place to rest from the world. You—'

"Threaten that," Hope interrupted wearily. She had heard all this before but from *men* back in Pennsylvania. The women, for the most part, had been cool and silent regarding her vocation. To hear this nonsense spoken aloud—by a woman—nearly left her speechless. Nearly. "You think I put the idea into your husbands' heads that you're capable of more than birthing babies and hosting cotillions? You prefer the myth that women are the mentally weaker sex. It keeps your credit account at the dress shop open."

Mrs. Chalmers gasped. "How dare you—?"

"With grim purpose and determination is how. I harbor the burning desire to help people, Mrs. Chalmers. I know that I am capable of helping them—possibly even saving their lives—and sitting back on my padded bustle simply will not do."

Mrs. Chalmers snapped her mouth shut and her face flushed. "There are men for that vocation, *Miss* Clark. The letters *M-D* do not make you a doctor."

The verbal slap, so wrong, but so vindictive, stung. Hope knew of course, graduating at the top of her class from Pennsylvania Women's College would mean nothing to this grand dame. Worse, Mrs. Chalmers might see it as a threat, to her way of life, her unchallenged, comfortable existence.

Hope did not want to fight this fight against her own sex. She couldn't believe she had to, especially here in the West where women were reportedly so strong and independent. "I'm sorry you feel this way, Mrs. Chalmers. I strongly believe, however, that women are as cap—"

"You've had no patients." The woman leaned forward a little. "As I said, you will have none. The Ladies League will see to it." Her chin rose higher in triumph. "How long can you hold out, Miss Clark?"

Against every woman in Denver? Hope *was* a doctor, a good one, but she was also at her wit's end...not to mention the end of her bank account.

Mrs. Chalmers moistened her lips and softened her stance a hair. "If you truly want to help people, Miss Clark, why don't you go to, oh, I don't know, India or somewhere. Some place they're desperate for medical care."

Any place Mrs. Chalmers didn't have to worry about bumping into a female doctor on the sidewalk? Well, Hope wasn't about to let this woman defeat her. But that didn't mean she had to fight the battle here in Denver where she was so outnumbered. There were other places in this big, wide world to ply her trade. Yes, some place where the people *were* desperate for medical care. India, however, seemed a touch far. "I'll consider your suggestion, Mrs. Chalmers. Thank you for coming by."

---

*T*he intriguing aroma of human prey mingled pleasantly with the scent of dirt and cedar and the cougar lifted his head. The hope of a meal stirred grumbling in his stomach and he sniffed now with keen interest, whiskers twitching. Led by hunger, he rose from his sun-washed ledge and slipped silently between the rocks, slinking beneath the evergreen branches, staying in the shadows, tracking the peculiar but distinctive odors. Within moments he was hiding atop a boulder, peering down at two humans.

The pair—a woman and a boy—strolled carelessly through the blueberry bushes, plucking the fruit, dropping it in buckets on their arms, eating one now and again. They chattered like magpies and wandered about aimlessly, picking fruit here and there, relaxed, unhurried.

The hunger gnawing at the pit of the cat's stomach grew, but he waited.

And watched.

The boy was similar to the people who had trod these mountains for as long as cats could remember. Dark skinned, his black hair glimmered in the sun like a raven's wings.

The woman was the new breed. She was like the pale-skinned humans who had come here when the cougar had been a cub playing at his mother's feet. She did not wear animal skins or smell of sweat like the Utes and Cheyenne. She smelled of flowers and plants. Her hair was long and light, the color of grass dead from winter cold.

The cat's eyes narrowed. The young one began to wander away from her. Little by little, farther and farther. A step at a time.

The cougar considered his choices, his gaze darting from the child to the woman and back again.

Yes, the boy. Younger. Smaller. Unaware.

Tail twitching, muscles quivering, the cat slithered off the boulder and crept into the base of an evergreen thick with low-lying branches.

---

*N*aomi smiled at the sweet taste of the blueberry, pleased this patch was still producing for so late in the season. She could already smell the pie her sister Rebecca would make. One of these days, Naomi would make a serious effort to become as good a cook as her sisters. She stripped off two berries and dropped them in the basket on her arm. Two Spears, the young Indian boy with her, was not her son by blood, but Naomi loved him as if he were. Just as she loved his father, Charles. For them, she would—should—learn to cook better. She tossed a berry up into the air and caught it in her mouth. Yes, these berries would be for her own pie.

Two Spears laughed at her antics and tossed up two berries, easily catching them both in his mouth.

"Show off," Naomi said.

Grinning, the ten-year-old drifted away, his chest puffed out. He was precious and she was so glad they'd finally gotten past his resentment of being dropped on their doorstep. Well, honestly, the resentment had started before that. His mother, Hopping Bird, had been given back by Charles to her father Chief Ouray, for a remuda of horses—the trade a peaceable way to end the marriage. Charles had not known about the child. Later, Hopping Bird had fallen in love with a violent renegade by the name of One-Who-Cries, who hated Charles almost as much as he hated the entire race of white men.

Unfortunately, Charles had been forced to kill One-Who-Cries about the same time Hopping Bird had died on the White Mountain Reservation. Chief Ouray, tired of losing family to the white man, had shown up the day after Charles' and Naomi's wedding with a very special request: for Charles to raise his grandson.

She shook her head and dropped another four or five berries in the basket. Two Spears had run away it seemed about every third day, but finally, just lately, she thought he was settling in. Charles had been taking the boy out with him to check on the herd, making a real effort to—

No conscious thought shot through Naomi's mind when she saw the cougar leap off the rock. She screamed as it raced toward Two Spears, but she was moving, too. Her own body felt as if lightning had struck her, and the power of it compelled her

6

forward at an uncanny speed. No earth beneath her feet, only electricity.

The cat lunged as Two Spears turned. A supernatural strength and fury arced through Naomi and, with a primal yell bursting from her lungs, she leaped for the boy, knocking him out of the cat's path. The claws meant for him sank into her back, burned like lava as they gouged into her flesh. She hit the ground hard, air whooshing out of her lungs. She tried to turn, but fangs clamped down on her, burrowing into the meat of her shoulder; the claws dug deep and tightened like a vice grip made of needles.

She yowled in agony. Or was it the cat?

Pain, white-hot, vicious, shot down her back, and she could feel her blood soaking her shirt. "Run, Two Spears," she yelled as she tried to fold her arms over her head and neck, to fend off teeth and claws.

Fight or die, something told her. *Oh, God, help me fight.*

Anger and terror mixed in her mind on a primitive level. The need to survive took hold. Naomi had to kill the cat. She jammed her elbow back, connecting with the heavy mass of fur on her back. The cougar shifted. His claws tightened, sunk deeper, but he let go of her shoulder.

Bellowing with rage and terror, she rolled before he could reposition his bite. She hammered the cat's snout as his claws flayed open her back and part of her side. His fangs sunk into her wrist.

Somehow a rock filled her hand and she swung it, connecting with his temple. The cat growled, angry over the hit, but only bit down harder.

"I'm not going to die, I'm not doing to die," she screamed as she hit him again and again—

An explosion rocked the air and the cat suddenly leaped skyward, twisting at a grotesque angle, and then disappeared from Naomi's sight. Unsure of where the cat had gone, she kept swinging the rock over and over, pounding the ground, and screaming, "I'm not going to die. I'm not—"

"Naomi!" Running to her, Charles holstered his gun and folded to his knees. "Naomi," he said again, breathless, as he slid his arms beneath her and lifted her off the ground.

She dropped the rock, saw the blood streaming down her arm, felt the slickness of it as Charles held her close. The fury drained away, leaving her weak, confused. She smiled at her handsome husband, those magnificent dark eyes of his and that perfectly trimmed beard. Oh, how she loved him, and it hurt her to see the fear in his face.

"I'm all right," she whispered. "Just a scratch." She suspected maybe it was a touch more, but the weariness that overcame her then stilled her concerns. She would sleep and when she woke up, everything would be fine.

----

*H*annah lunged to her feet as Charles burst through the door of the doctor's office, a bloody and unconscious Naomi in his arms. The sight of her sister in such a state galvanized Hannah; her heart hammered so hard in her chest, she thought it might bruise her ribs.

Oh, God. "Put her on the bed," she ordered as she grabbed a tray already loaded with a few basic medical supplies. "What happened?" *Dear God, please let her be all right*, she prayed as she rushed after Charles.

"A cougar."

Hannah's stomach lurched at the word. Charles had wrapped Naomi in his own shirt and a saddle blanket, both glistening with blood. He laid her on the bed and carefully peeled back the soaked articles. Hannah stepped in close, ready for the examination, and was pleased to see his effort had stopped much of the blood, but Naomi's torso and left arm were bathed in red.

A quick survey told Hannah they weren't seeing everything. "Here, help me turn her over." Naomi's shirt and camisole hung in bloody shreds. Hannah removed the clothing and flinched at the deep, raw wounds. "Oh," she whispered softly. *Lord, this is work for a surgeon. Help me, oh, please help me.* Tears pooled in her eyes. If only she were a doctor. If only Doc Cook hadn't died. Nevertheless, Naomi was depending on her. Neither of them had a choice. "Look at the depth of those claw marks..."

Charles touched Hannah's shoulder. "We're counting on you, Hannah. You're all she's got right now." His dark eyes pleaded with her to make her whole again. "She's all I've got."

Hannah squared her shoulders, feigning a confidence she didn't feel, and nodded.

CHAPTER 2

*C*harles wasn't sure his legs would carry him out of the examination room. He paused in the doorway, just to make sure. Hannah looked as terrified as he felt, blue eyes round as full moons.

God, You cannot let her die. Hannah's fished a bullet out of a man. Surely she can sew up those wounds...

She's lost so much blood, a voice whispered in a sinister tone.

He refused the dark thought with a jerk of his head. *No, Lord, you can't take her. Guide Hannah's hands.*

"Charles, would you ask Emilio to send Mollie down?"

"Is there anything I can do?" he asked, surprised by the break in his voice.

"No. Mollie knows how to ready certain things I'll need."

"He's outside with Two Spears. I'll send him on to find her."

Outside, Charles was only a little surprised to find Two Spears sniffling on the front porch, the young man Emilio patting his back. Emilio had been with Charles now for some time. Initially doing grunt work around the Iron Horse, while his sister Rose entertained customers, the teenager had wound up becoming an integral part of the McIntyre family. Hispanic, only about eighteen or so, he too, wore his hair long and straight, like Two Spears. And he'd proven himself to be honest and reliable. A good *man* in the making.

"Emilio, Hannah needs Mollie on the double."

"Sí." The young man leaped to his feet. "I'll find her." He hurried to his horse, swung up in the saddle and raced off toward Defiance's main street, only one row of buildings over. Charles waited for the sound of the horse's feet to fade before he dropped down beside Two Spears. He wished for his hat, but for the life of him couldn't recall where he'd left it. A sign of his rattled state of mind. He glanced at Two Spears and considered how much worse his nerves must be.

"She'll be all right," he said, attempting to use his most gentle Southern drawl to shore up the statement with confidence and peace—things which he did not feel at the moment. She was torn and bloody. His stomach clenched at the images. "And I'm glad you're not hurt."

The boy dropped his head to his knees and shook his head. "The cougar should have jumped me. He was coming for me."

Charles dropped his hand on the boy's back. "Naomi...?" He faded off, already knowing what happened.

"She saw him and jumped between us."

Charles shook his head. Exactly what he would have expected his lovely, fearless bride to do. She could have done no less. Probably didn't even think about it.

"She told me to run. At first, I...I..." Two Spears shook his head. "I did nothing, but she was screaming and...and then I picked up a big rock..."

"And I saw you throw it, Two Spears. You did what you could."

"No, no." He sat up straighter, his little brown face contorted with shame, chin quivering. "I am no warrior. I am a coward."

"No, you are not a coward," Charles said firmly. "Don't ever think that of yourself. You tried to help her."

"I will kill that cat and bring back his hide."

"You stay away from up there." Concerned, Charles laid a hand on the boy's neck and gave him a reassuring pat. "I hit him. He's dead already." He'd rushed his shot, but had had no choice at the time. "The buzzards have already picked him clean, so you forget about that cat and stay off the ridge."

The boy offered only silence. Charles firmly clutched his shoulders, turning the child to him. "Give me your good word you won't go after the cat."

Fury twisted Two Spears' features. Scowling, his sable eyes burning, he finally gave his father a short, sharp nod.

---

*N*aomi came awake slowly. Before she opened her eyes, she took in the scent of freshly laundered sheets, the smell of alcohol, and a sharp ache throbbing in her back and shoulder.

Upon further consideration, she decided her left arm didn't feel normal, either. She shifted and realized she was lying on her stomach in the bed. Not her and Charles' bed, though. This mattress was hard and lumpy.

She thought to roll over on to her back, but the attempted motion brought an eruption of more pain from her side and shoulder, and she groaned. Rolling back onto her face, the cougar's scream echoed in her head and she remembered.

Blood-chilling screams, claws, pain...and Charles. She breathed a little easier.

"Was that you, Naomi?"

Hannah's voice. Naomi nodded, tried to speak, but only a hoarse whisper escaped her.

"Here, just a moment." Hannah came alongside the bed, lowered herself to eye level. "You can't lie on your back yet, but you can try to sit up."

Naomi nodded, and Hannah helped her. After much groaning, painful tightness in too many places, she managed to swing her feet over the edge and straighten up. Hannah had a glass of water waiting. The first sip tasted wonderful and awoke a deep thirst. Naomi tried to guzzle it, but Hannah wrestled it away.

"Drink it slowly."

Naomi wanted to argue, but Hannah clearly wasn't going to hand the glass back until Naomi agreed. She nodded and the water returned to her hand. She finished the water in four sips and licked her lips. "Is Two Spears all right?" she asked, pleased her voice was working, though it was a bit raspy.

"Fine."

"What happened to me? Was it the cat?"

"Yes."

"How bad?" When Hannah didn't answer right away, Naomi pinned her with an expectant stare.

"You've got a total of thirty-five stitches."

"Thirty-fi…?" Naomi trailed off. She didn't even want to say the number. "Am I…all right?" She touched her face, worried the cat had done some ugly damage there. She felt something on her cheekbone.

"Only three stitches in your face." Hannah smiled weakly. "I tried to make them tiny."

"Thank you. What aren't you telling me?"

Her sister took a deep, resigned breath. "I don't know that your shoulder will be all right. And you're going to have some pretty good scars."

Naomi let that sink in. Scars weren't ideal. She didn't want Charles to have to look at her mangled body, but maybe, in time, the damage would fade and not be very noticeable.

Hannah poured Naomi another glass of water and then sat down beside her on the bed. "I did the best I could, Naomi. I'm sorry. I'm not even a real nurse."

Naomi didn't sip, thirsty as she was. She lowered the glass to her lap. "I know you did the best you could. I'll never fault you—"

Hannah burst into sobs and buried her face in her hands. Naomi gingerly lifted her good arm, finding any movement hurt, and rested it across Hannah's back. "Hannah, Hannah. Please don't do this to yourself. I'm alive and I'm fine. Stitches heal. Scars fade. The cougar could have killed me."

Her sister shook her head back and forth several times, fighting for control. Finally, she managed to get her voice back. "You don't understand. You lost the baby."

———

CHAPTER 3

*C*harles sat down in the chair next to Naomi's bed and took her hand, delighted she was awake. The stitches in her cheek and arms, the enormous bandage on her shoulder, the dozens of bloody scratches—they made his stomach roll. She could have died. Yet, she radiated love for him. Green eyes that glittered like an emerald, long, golden hair cascading down around her shoulders. Her little pug nose that he could tweak if not for her injuries. He had become a complete and unutterable fool for love. The woman had ruined him in the best way possible.

"You're awake. How do you feel?"

"Right as rain."

What Naomi could *not* do was lie to him. Never had been able to. Her little tale-tale signs of a tense brow, a mist of sweat on her upper lip, the unusually stiff set to her mouth warned him something was amiss, beyond her injuries.

He squeezed her hand, a wiggle of concern returning. "What's wrong?"

She looked away. "Isn't this enough?"

"You know you can't lie to me, princess. There's something else. I can see it on your face."

"I'm just sore."

"Naomi." He turned her face to him and he searched it, looking for answers, his concern blossoming into trepidation. What could she be hiding? "Tell me what's wrong." Tears pooled in her eyes and her chin quivered. There were few things that frightened Naomi, most especially to the point of tears. Really concerned now, he said firmly, "Tell me."

His gentle command seemed to strengthen her and she nodded. "I'm sorry, Charles. I didn't know. If I had, I would have been more careful. I would have been using the buggy or—" Her voice broke and she stopped.

"Naomi, whatever you're trying not to tell me, I'm sure it's not nearly as bad as you think."

She hid her face in her hands, took a deep breath and said, "I lost the baby, Charles."

"What ba—" He bit off the question as clarity dawned. *Dear God, we had a child?* Everything in him sagged as he tried to absorb the news, its implications. His and Naomi's—

His thoughts hurtled back to an evening, one night last year, when she'd confessed she wasn't sure if she could have children. Would he still love her, want her? One of the few fears he knew she harbored. Of course, he'd told her he loved her no matter what, and he'd meant it.

Which enabled him to see the light in this heartbreak, and not just the darkness. He tugged on his red, silk vest and straightened up. "Naomi…" Moved by her pain and her fear, he slid onto one knee in front of her and clutched her hands, pulling them from her face. "I'm sorry. For us both. But we will be all right." He tucked a stray strand of gold behind her ear, wondering if he should say something cavalier like, 'we can keep trying.' He decided to say as little as possible until he had a better handle on his emotions.

16

She offered him a tremulous smile. "You're so understanding. It's hard for me, though. I want to give you a child. I don't want to fail you as a wife."

"Oh, good Lord, woman. Don't speak nonsense. I told you once before the West is a hard place to live. Bad things happen. We move on. Relying on grit and perseverance."

"You said those were my strengths."

He took that to mean he could at least broach the question. "Perseverance. Can we keep trying or…?" *Or?* "Will it endanger your health? I would not lose you, Naomi. Not even for a child—"

She raised her hand to stop him. "Hannah thinks the attack was simply too much for my body. She sees no reason we can't keep trying. As far as she can tell, everything seems normal."

Charles pulled back, drifting his hand down Naomi's injured shoulder and arm. The potential *personal* danger of not having a doctor in Defiance had not hit him with any tangible impact until Naomi had spoken those words: *as far as she can tell.*

"Hannah is no doctor. She is not even a schooled nurse."

What if Naomi had some condition that would put her life at risk with every pregnancy? Hannah could sew up wounds, remove bullets, treat fevers. But she was no doc—

"This just wasn't the right time, Charles. We have to try to accept it and move on." She shrugged. "So I keep telling myself."

What if next time the pregnancy claimed the baby *and* Naomi, Charles wondered. Horrified at the thought, he surged to his feet and strode to the window to look out, at the town, at anything but his wife—the most precious gift in his life. Ever. And he'd failed her.

"Charles, what's the matter?"

Anger rose up in him. This situation simply wouldn't do. He wanted to kick himself for having not addressed it sooner. He'd been too busy wallowing in grief and guilt over the mine explosion. So many men dead and buried beneath their feet. He'd tried to hide from the remorse with a stream of cattle and lumber deals, with projects for building up the town. He'd blinded himself to this potential for a medical disaster. Adding insult to injury, Naomi had been out in those woods with his son. Mothering his mistake.

Disgusted, he swiped a hand over his mustache and sighed. "I'm sorry, Naomi, but I will make this right. I will find you the finest doctor money can buy." He turned back to her, shaking his head. "*I* failed *you*. Defiance should never have been without a doctor."

"You didn't fail me." She shifted, flinched with the movement, tried to sit up straighter. "Anyone in this town could have attempted to find a replacement for Doc. The responsibility didn't fall solely on you."

He begged to differ. Having built this town, run it, literally killed for it, he had claimed Defiance as his kingdom years ago. Monarchs had responsibilities, his personal faith in God not withstanding. *Lord, keep her healthy and I will find us a doctor.*

"No, it falls squarely on my shoulders, Naomi, and I will rectify the deficiency immediately."

CHAPTER 4

*C*harles sat at his desk, tapping a ledger with a pencil, not seeing a thing in front of him. He had drafted an ad for a doctor and wired it to several larger newspapers. A high salary, free living accommodations, an open tab at the hotel's restaurant. A hardscrabble mining town wasn't any medical professional's first choice, no matter the compensation, but Charles had faith the right man would answer the ad.

Brannagh, the brawny, fifty-something Irishman who had gone from working as Charles' bartender to more of a personal assistant, knocked on his half-open door but didn't come in. "The men from the railroad."

"Ah. Yes." He dropped the pencil and came back to the matters at hand. "Thank you. Show them in."

A moment later Brannagh held the door for two rotund, heavily whiskered men in black suits, both cradling their hats. Charles rose to greet them and they shook hands across his desk. "Bob, Henry. Good to see you." Exchanging pleasantries, the men settled in the waiting chairs. "Can I get you anything. Coffee, a drink?"

Both men declined and he nodded for Brannagh to depart.

When the door shut, he sat and Bob dove in. "Let's get to it, McIntyre. We don't want you to build your own spur line. Let us buy into it and share some of the other risks."

Charles leaned back and plucked a cheroot from his pocket, and a match from a box on his desk. Lighting the smoke, he said, "And some of the reward as well."

"Naturally. That's only good business."

"But I told you in my letter, I have no interest in reopening the mine."

"Then sell it," Henry said. "Let a mining conglomerate run it. The mine needs to be open to truly make the spur line a viable investment."

"I don't need your money to build the line."

The two men exchanged irritated glances. "We're business-men, McIntyre. A spur line and a mine make Defiance an excel-lent investment and we want in. We can provide the capital to transform the town into a real prize. Jobs bring in men. Schools and churches and dress shops will bring in families. Defiance will blossom. Lumber and ranching alone won't do it."

"It has barely been a month. Twelve men died in that explo-sion, Bob. There's still too much healing that needs to be done." In the town, and in his own heart. McIntyre, taking a puff of the cigar, watched the smoke curl in front of him and tried to imagine watching men go back down into that pit. He certainly would never send them. Ever.

"You need to think this over," Henry said, leaning forward. "What Defiance needs to heal is prosperity. Families coming in and putting down roots. We want to help you build a vibrant, healthy community. With a doctor."

Charles didn't try to hide his surprise.

"We saw the ad in the Denver Post."

He did want all that for Defiance, especially the physician. But the mine…it hung around his neck like an albatross. "And I welcome your help," he said, warring with his uncertainties, "but I won't be opening the mine." He had to suffer for a while first. His penance. Bob and Henry couldn't understand that, however.

"We've made a good, solid offer to you for the future of Defiance, for your railroad. You should think about it before closing the door."

"I am not closing the door, but I am not reopening the mine."

"Then you will sell it?" Bob said with too much confidence.

"Perhaps. Eventually." He crushed out the cheroot. "When we've healed."

"You Southerners," Henry spat. "You're too emotional."

"You Yankees are too detached. People matter."

Bob scratched his muttonchops, lifting a quizzical brow at Charles. "You've changed, McIntyre. I don't think I like it."

Charles chuckled. "Well, your opinion of me will most certainly disturb my sleep tonight."

---

*M*atthew Miller tore the fine into little pieces, placed them in the palm of his hand and blew them right back into the face of Sheriff Pender Beckwith. Piercing hazel eyes, a gaunt face like a skeleton, the tough-as-rawhide peace officer could stare a hole through most men and follow it up with a bullet.

As the pieces of paper drifted to the saloon floor, the man's edgy expression darkened to something that almost scared Matthew…almost. "Miller, I could consider that assaulting an officer."

Matthew was a big man with a wide chest and arms the size of oaks. He liked using his size to intimidate people but he knew Beckwith wasn't cowed by such. Miffed, he leaned against his mahogany bar. "Sheriff, I'm a busy man and I'm sick of these fines." He grabbed a bottle and slid it between him and the lawman. "Why don't you have a drink—on the house—and we'll let this slide."

"And I could consider that a bribe."

Matthew clenched his teeth, pondered the man a moment, then raised is hands in surrender. "Fine. I'll go by the Iron Hor —er, I mean, the *town hall* in the morning and pay this one, too." He could barely call the old saloon that without sneering.

Beckwith rested his hand on the butt of his .44. Not a threat, Matthew knew, just a lawman's way. "I'm sick of wasting my time serving you with fines for running prostitutes. I'm gonna push for arresting the girls and confiscating your tents."

"You wouldn't throw a gal in jail who's just trying to make a living. You that cold-hearted?"

"It'd be doing 'em a favor. The living conditions are better in my jail."

"You try to confiscate anything and I'll sic my attorney on this town."

Beckwith's eyes narrowed. "You'd best send him a telegram then. Have him at the ready." The old lawman glanced at the pieces of paper on the floor, dusted one off his shoulder with disdain, turned, and marched out of the Crystal Chandelier.

The nearly *empty* Crystal Chandelier.

Only two customers watched the sheriff's exit with bland curiosity. Mathew flexed and clenched his fingers over and over for the next few minutes while he tried to cool down. Pondering Beckwith's threat, he acknowledged he couldn't keep doing business this way. He not only had to do something to get some warm bodies visiting the girls, he needed to get some warm bodies into the Crystal Chandelier. His lumber mill wasn't making enough money to keep all this afloat.

He cursed Delilah one more time for dumping this mess in his lap. He'd come to Defiance expecting to find a wide-open, rip-roarin', Godless den of debauchery. Instead, a mine explo- sion and the deaths of twelve men had sucked the life out of the town, and, apparently, the infamous madam. She'd dropped the keys to the place in his hand and climbed aboard a stage headed who knew where.

She had, at least, left behind Otis. The former slave from Haiti—practically the size of an island—the black man was working over in the corner, staining chairs. He was helpful, quiet, obedient, and a lot of muscle should the need arise. He had told Matthew he did not wish to leave the position which he'd held for Delilah. He was a sort of jack-of-all-trades, good and bad. Matthew had suspected—still did, in fact—that the mountain of a man would be well worth his meager pay.

Two well-dressed—and clearly well-fed—businessmen sauntered in, pulling his thoughts back to the room. They broke off their conversation as they surveyed the quiet saloon. A familiar sense of desperation clawed at Matthew. "Gentlemen," he called, moving behind his bar. "What can I get you?"

The two men exchanged puzzled glances, but one shrugged as they approached the bar. "Business looks a little slow," he said, scratching an impressive beard. "Lumber and ranching not bringing in the customers?"

"Just a little slow at the moment." Annoyed at the observation, Matthew poured two whiskeys. "On the house." He slid the shots over to them. "I'm Matthew Miller, the owner. I also own the lumberyard."

"I'm Bob Tillman."

"Henry Hathaway."

"Gentlemen, good to meet you."

Bob, the one with the impressive muttonchops, again surveyed the saloon. "McIntyre says the lumber and cattle operations should make up for the loss of the mine, but we disagree. What say you, sir?"

Matthew tilted his head, curious who these two were. Henry's gold tie pin with *Union Pacific* stamped on it answered the question. "You're with the railroad?"

"Yes. And we'd like to invest in McIntyre's spur line down to Gunnison, but it's just not viable without the mine. Would you beg to differ?"

"I hear he's gonna build that spur line with you or without you."

"We'd prefer with. We see innumerable opportunities for more investment in Defiance—if the mine is running. He doesn't agree."

"Sounds like you want a piece of it all." The two men did not voice any disagreement. Ideas dancing in his brain, Matthew picked up a towel and began wiping down his bar. "A couple hundred miners are a small town all on their own. More so than just a big handful of cowboys and lumberjacks."

Bob nodded. "Our point exactly."

"But McIntyre sees lumber and ranching expanding." Which would be fine, if Matthew could hold out.

"Or open the mine," Henry said, teasing in his voice, "and have a town full of miners practically overnight. A much faster payout."

What Matthew would call a lifeline. "He's hell-bent on not reopening."

"We got that sense, yes. However, the ad for a physician in Defiance with very generous compensation leads us to believe he has a weakness. The town. He wants to see it grow and be taken care of. The mine would spur more growth. A doctor would assure quality care for the citizens."

The weakness wasn't the town as much as it was Naomi and her recent tangle with the cat. These yahoos didn't necessarily need that information, though, Matthew thought.

"We believe he will come around to selling," Bob said. "If the right investors with a generous package of their own show up." Bob and Henry exchanged glances again, this time knowing ones.

"You two gonna round up those generous investors?"

"I think we're going to try. You want in?"

Matthew could tell the question was asked in jest. After all, a saloon-owner wasn't loaded with enough money to buy into a million-dollar mine. Once upon a time, before sinking nearly everything he had into this place and the lumberyard, he had been. "Ah, maybe someday. Once this place starts paying off."

The gentlemen chuckled and motioned to the bottle for another shot. As he poured, though, Matthew decided maybe buying into the mine was something he should consider. Just not with these two chee chuckers.

$\mathcal{B}$illy Page let himself into Doc Cook's office, fully expecting to see his betrothed Hannah tending to a patient or at the very least organizing medical supplies. To his consternation, the office was empty and quiet as Christ's tomb.

"Hannah?" He listened but heard nothing. Assuming he'd missed her somewhere between the mercantile and the hotel, he turned to go, but then did catch a slight tap or thump in the back of the building. Maybe she went to the privy. He waited another moment, but still she did not appear.

Curious, a touch concerned, he let himself out the back door. He breathed a little sigh of relief when he found her sitting on the back stoop, face turned to the sky, the late afternoon rays of the September sun gleaming off her long, golden braid. Fall was nearly upon them. It was tempting to enjoy the fading warmth while they could.

"May I join you?"

She didn't open her eyes, but nodded and smiled. "Of course."

He dropped beside her and copied her pose. "Feels good. But a touch drier than it has been."

"It'll change. Ian said rain is coming. His joints are bothering him."

Billy nodded. Her brother-in-law's arthritis was a fairly accurate weather predictor.

They sat in comfortable silence for a spell, but he'd come determined to ask her something. "Hannah, ever since Naomi got jumped by the cougar, you've been different."

"Different how?"

He shrugged a shoulder. "A little distracted, or sad. I'm not sure. And, of course, being a man, I have to assume I might be the problem." He hoped the jest might work a smile from her.

He heard one in her voice when she answered, "No, it's not you."

"Then what?"

She took a moment to respond. "Naomi is going to be pretty scarred up from the cat."

"That's not your fault. I saw the stitches you did. Best you could have done."

She huffed in what sounded like frustration. "It's not just that. Naomi...Naomi had a miscarriage."

Billy opened his eyes and looked at her. "Surely you don't think you could have done anything to prevent it?"

She huffed again then met his gaze. "I just wish I knew more. Could have done more. I don't know...I—I know just enough to know how much I *don't* know. It's frustrating."

Billy rested his elbows on his knees and tapped his fingertips together, wondering what she was getting at. "Do you want to call off the wedding? Go to nursing school?"

What was another delay? The circuit preacher had been rerouted weeks back due to a flood that had caused several deaths over in Animas Forks. A four-week window had expanded to eight. He was once more scheduled to come to Defiance in a month. Short of another disaster. Was it a sign?

His meandering thoughts gave Hannah long minutes to

respond. Finally, she said, "Sometimes I don't know what I want, but I do know I don't want to call off the wedding."

"I don't want you giving up anything to marry me."

"I don't think I am."

"I want you to be happy, Hannah. If you're serious about nursing school, we could move back East together. I've got the money to open a business there. Go to nursing school and we'll hire a nanny for Little Billy."

Her brow twitched at the suggestion. "A nanny? I don't know...but you'd do that for me?"

He reached out and took her braid lightly in his hand. The play of sunlight in her blonde locks never ceased to amaze him. Or how her stunning eyes could change from lighthearted, cornflower blue to somber sapphire, depending on her mood. Now they were leaning toward sapphire.

"I'd do anything for you. You and little Billy are my life." He'd not meant to sound so serious, but the truth carried its own weight.

She touched his hand and smiled tenderly. "I love you, Billy Page. Now, you squirmed out of marrying me once. In four weeks, a preacher is tying the knot."

She kissed him, but her lips didn't distract him from the meat of their conversation. She'd pretty much ignored his suggestion about all of them moving for nursing school.

Which, to him, meant she was thinking about it.

---

*I*cy rain drops spit and spattered across Emilio's and Bones' path. The little sorrel shook, casting off the thin layer of water that was trying to blanket him. Emilio followed the horse's lead and shook off his coat and brushed off his legs. Which were getting cold. Good thing town wasn't much further. Thinking about Mollie warmed him right up, though.

It had taken some time for his affections to move away from Hannah, but the more time he spent with Mollie, the more their rough backgrounds had created a bond. A former Flower, she'd done some things just to survive. Orphaned at five and raised by a wolverine for a sister, Emilio had done no better. He and Mollie knew each other's sordid past and it had removed all the pretense between them. He was comfortable with her in a way he'd never been with anyone else.

And because he believed that, she scared him.

Suddenly aggravated by the cold drops biting him in the face, he steered Bones off the road and took a shortcut through a forest of white-trunked Aspens. The golden leaves offered some protection and he patted his horse. "Better, boy, sí?"

He removed the Stetson and shook his black hair. Maybe he should cut it. None of the other ranch hands wore their hair this long. Emilio's was long enough to make a short ponytail.

Without the black cowboy hat, he looked every bit the Mexican he was. None of the men said that to his face, of course. He was the second-in-command at the ranch, under Lane, but folks whispered about how partial Mr. McIntyre was to him. They couldn't know the things Mr. McIntyre and Emilio had been through. Fights, Indian attacks, explosions, to name a few.

They had forged a friendship that Emilio valued. He almost considered the man to be like a father. Closest thing he'd ever had, anyway. And he had suggested pursuing Mollie.

Emilio straightened up in the saddle and replaced the hat, cutting free with a big smile. Mr. McIntyre had never given him bad advice.

. . .

A half-hour later, Emilio and Bones merged onto a jostling, muddy Main Street and made their way to the Trinity Inn for dinner. Mollie would wait on him, finish her shift, and then the two of them had planned a walk down by the river, weather permitting. He enjoyed her company and one reason he was so comfortable with her: he could just be himself.

Buoyed by the anticipation of the meal and the company, he tied up in front of the inn and slipped inside. The dining room was still packed, but his little table over by the kitchen door was waiting on him.

He nodded to a few of the boys from the ranch who had come into town as well, and claimed his seat. A minute later a delicate, fair hand set a glass of water in front of him and he looked up into her beautiful, welcoming face.

Mollie's blue eyes glowed with warmth and tenderness. "Good evening, sir."

He grinned at her formal tone. "Good evening, señorita. What is on the menu tonight?"

"Elk steaks. Mashed potatoes. Peas. Beets. Apple pie for dessert." Emilio's stomach grumbled. They ate well at the ranch, just not that well. Mollie laughed richly, hugging the tray in her arms. "You poor thing. I'll rush your meal so you don't fall out right here in the restaurant."

"Would you still like to go for a walk this evening, when your shift is done?"

Some color rushed to Mollie's cheeks. A tantalizing smile teased her lips. "I would love to."

She started to walk away and Emilio surprised himself by taking her hand, halting her retreat. "It-it is good to see you, Mollie. I miss you when I'm at the ranch."

She squeezed his hand and said flirtatiously, "Then you'll just have to come in more than once a week."

CHAPTER 5

*H*ope could have been indignant about her plan, the subterfuge being wholly beneath her. Yet, if she wanted to serve as a doctor, well, lying about her credentials might be necessary. At least at first. Until she saw some patients and gained the trust of the community. Then her fair gender wouldn't be an issue. She had to believe that.

For the hundredth time, as weak, gray light flashed through the pines and into the stuffy stagecoach, she took the newspaper from her medical case. Folded open to the advertisement, she read again the request for a doctor in Defiance. A fine salary, living accommodations, array of patients. She was taking a huge chance coming to Defiance rather than writing, but she believed she could convince this Charles McIntyre Hope Clark was the answer to his ad.

When the stage stopped, she asked that her trunk be sent to the hotel and for directions. The driver, jumping down from his seat, pointed west and said, "The Trinity Inn is open now and they have a fine restaurant, too."

At the mention of food, Hope's stomach grumbled and she touched the reticule hanging from her wrist. Yes, a bite to eat and then she'd search out Mr. McIntyre. She thanked the driver and headed down the busy street. Tugging her coat closer against a weak smattering of rain, she took the time to assess the town.

She'd heard that Defiance was a clamoring mecca of mining opportunities. It didn't strike her as such today. Yes, there were miners with heavily laden mules moving up and down the muddy street, but also cowboys riding through town, and lumberjacks loading supplies into wagons at the mercantile. There was also plenty of elbow room between them all. On her way out west, Hope's trip had taken her to Deadwood and the pace in that mining town had been downright frenetic.

Not so here. Defiance was bustling, but at a measured pace. The reported Gold Fever, if she didn't miss her guess, had broken. The patient's temperature had returned to something akin to normal. She didn't know yet if she should be disappointed or grateful.

Up ahead she saw a sign for The Trinity Inn sitting high on a new, golden-hued, two story building. White rocking chairs lined both the front porch and the balcony above. She hoped the weather would clear as she could see herself resting her weary bones in one of those chairs and watching the sunset.

Hope found a break in the traffic and scurried across the street to the hotel. Once inside, the scent of fresh pine and steaks struck her instantly. The hotel was new, indeed, as evidenced by the bright rugs and polished floor and the bright velveteen of the lobby furniture.

Off to her left she heard the clink of silverware and rumbling chatter and double-doors opened to the dining room. Directly in front of her, a wide staircase led to second floor. Two well-dressed, middle-aged women descending them gave Hope a blandly curious glance and continued on into the restaurant. She nodded politely and crossed the lobby to the desk.

A pudgy young girl, maybe twenty, with a round, cherubic face greeted her. "Good evening. Welcome to the Trinity Inn. Will you be needing a room or are you here to dine?"

"Yes, a room. I'll need it for at least two days. Hopefully that'll be all it takes," she muttered underneath her breath.

The girl spun the register to her. "Just passing through then?" she asked, handing Hope a fountain pen.

"No, actually I'm hoping to meet with Mr. Charles McIntyre regarding a position—" She stopped to admire the writing instrument, an unusual item in a rustic town. She hadn't seen any outside of New York City.

The clerk chuckled. "It's called a fountain pen. The ink is in the chamber."

"Yes, I am familiar with them. I just didn't expect to see one in Defiance. They're quite the talk in the East."

"We've got lots of surprises here. There's a saying in mining towns: with money, men, and mules, you can get anything you want." She pointed over her shoulder. "Our new kitchen stove come direct fr—"

"Señora Betsy," a terrified voice called from the dining room. "Get Miss Hannah." A Hispanic woman skidded to a stop in the doorway to the dining room, waving her arms frenetically. "A man is choking. I do not know what to do."

Still holding the pen in one hand and her medical bag in the other, Hope rushed to the woman. "Show me."

The commanding tone in her voice spurred the woman to react. Without questioning, she turned and raced back into the dining room. A crowd of people half-surrounded a man on the floor. Another waitress held his head as he thrashed about with fading strength, his face turning bluer by the second. His motions slowed and then ceased at the same instant Hope dropped to her knees to examine him.

"He was eating a steak and then started choking," a man above her said.

She could tell immediately the patient had an extreme blockage. He would not survive till she could be ready for surgery. The pen in her hand screamed her next step.

She noted absently some motion in the crowd and she reached out, grabbing the closest hand. She thrust the pen into it as she turned to her bag. "Break that open. Make it a straw."

With practiced speed, she slid a scalpel from its velvet pocket and pulled the person with the pen to the floor. She met the wide, sapphire eyes of a girl barely more than a teenager who held up the broken pen for Hope's approval.

"Good. Now, are you squeamish?"

The girl shook her head.

"Hold his wrist and feel for his pulse. Can you do that?"

This time the young lady moved immediately to do Hope's bidding.

Hope looked up at the wide-eyed waitress still cradling the man's head. "Use your cleaning cloth to dab at the blood when I tell you to."

"Bl—blood?" the girl stammered.

Ignoring her, Hope felt along the man's throat for the cricoid cartilage, tested the flesh with her index finger and then sliced a half-inch incision to his windpipe. Immediately the blood flowed. "Your cloth, girl," she ordered impatiently. With shaking hands the waitress dabbed at the blood pouring from the wound.

Hope put the scalpel in her teeth, grabbed the broken pen from the girl checking the man's pulse, pinched the wound to open it, and inserted the instrument.

Not getting an immediate reaction, she tossed the scalpel into her bag and pressed her lips to the broken pen. She blew into the man's lungs, paused, and then repeated the action. Again and again she blew life into him.

"Come on," she whispered, her desperation growing. He couldn't die. She'd made it to him in time. She blew more air into his lungs and the girl holding his wrist gasped. Hope looked at her.

"There's a pulse." She tilted her head, *listening* to her fingers, and nodded. "A definite pulse," she said with an air of expertise that surprised Hope. "Thready, weak, but there," the girl added as if for emphasis.

Hope nodded at the surprising impromptu nurse. "We're not done yet. I have to do surgery to remove the blockage. We need to get him to the doctor's office."

The girl picked out men in the crowd. "Bob, Wade, Emilio. Let's get him over to Doc's."

"Yes, Miss Hannah," said a tall, lean man with a badge, immediately stepping forward to help.

CHAPTER 6

*W*ith every stitch, with every order the woman barked, Hannah's estimation of her own skills as a nurse diminished like melting ice. Hannah had seen Doc perform surgeries and assisted on a few, but this stranger in Defiance was clearly a trained and very skilled nurse.

The two of them had bypassed any pleasantries and small talk and tackled the issue of the blocked windpipe forthwith. Hannah had followed orders to the best of her ability and quickly found everything requested for the surgery, standing at the ready with scalpels, needles, sutures, bandages, and alcohol.

Finally, with the procedure done and the last stitch in place, Hannah whispered across the sleeping patient to the mysterious nurse, "Why don't you go sit down for a moment and I'll get you some water."

The woman, auburn hair twisted up in the new French style, was pretty, and young, maybe in her mid-twenties. She tilted her head at Hannah, azure eyes friendly, and smiled. "You knew your way around the surgery. Around this office. You were a godsend, so to speak."

She sounded almost amazed and Hannah's sagging spirits

rose again. "I helped Doc Cook out when I could. He taught me a lot. But just watching you work, I can see that there's so much more to nursing than I ever thought."

A shadow crossed the woman's face, but it passed almost instantly. She touched the patient's forehead with the back of her hand. "I don't even know your name. Mine is Do—Hope. Hope Clark."

Hannah noted the strange correction. "I'm Hannah Frink. You sound like you're from back east. Which nursing school did you go to? Have you been a nurse long? How did you wind up in Defiance?"

Hope chuckled at the onslaught of questions, but then her shoulders sagged. "I am very tired. I think I'll sit on the porch for a moment and get some cool air. Would you mind bringing me that glass of water?"

"Not at all."

Hannah delivered the drink and for the moment they sat in companionable silence, listening to the few remaining crickets sing a welcome to fall, catching notes now and again from a singer at the Crystal Chandelier and the raised voices of men, mostly laughing. A far cry from the wild-and-wooly free-for-all the town was, up until the mine had collapsed.

Charles had said at least a third of the town's population had moved on. Hannah liked the quiet, but she sensed something in it. The town seemed to be fighting for its life.

"What happened to Doctor Cook?" Hope asked and took a sip of the water. "My, it's cold. How nice."

"Doc has a springhouse out back." Hannah sighed, seeing her friend and mentor splayed out on the bed, face pale, lips blue. The glaring bruises on his face and neck. "We're not sure. He was beat up some, but we don't know if that killed him or his heart gave out."

"He was attacked?" Hope sounded alarmed at the potential for violence in the town.

"The town went through—" Hell. She almost described Delilah and her horrendous saloon and acts of retribution with that one word. "A tough time. There was a bad element here trying to take over. They caused the mine explosion. That seemed to take the wind out of them, and they left."

And a lot of folks in town still weren't happy with Beckwith for not arresting Delilah, but Hannah understood how painful a trial would have been. Maybe the sheriff had been concerned about mob violence and lynchings.

"I came here, Hannah, because I want to take up Doctor Cook's mantle. I didn't answer the ad formally. I just showed up. I want to work in a town where there is a real need."

"Well, Lord knows you're a far sight more skilled than I am —tonight proved that—but I also know Charles wants to hire a full-fledged doctor."

"No chance he'd hire a nurse now, even a very skilled one like I am?"

Hannah shrugged. "I don't know. Maybe he'd keep you on until a doctor is hired. Or even after. I don't want to speak for him." Though she suspected the man wouldn't turn away any skilled medical help.

"Hannah," Hope leaned over the arm of the rocking chair, "what kind of man is this Charles McIntyre? Is he open-minded? Does he judge people before he knows them?"

"No, he's a good man. Fair."

"How do you think he'll react to me just showing up here?"

"After what you did for Bob Ledford in there, surely he'll be glad, but there's more to this." Hannah looked out at the midnight sky, twinkling with diamonds, but saw the ugly scars marring Naomi's back, the sadness on her face when she'd told her about the baby. "Where were you two weeks ago?"

"I'm sorry?"

A chill creeping over her, Hannah rubbed her arms, rose, and went to the porch rail. The buildings up on Main Street were dark shadows, silhouetted in a weak quarter moon. "My sister Naomi was attacked by a mountain lion."

"Oh. Is she all right?"

"Yes…and no. I took care of her, did the best I could, tried extra hard with the stitches to keep them small and neat. But Naomi's wounds won't be the scars on her body. She lost the baby she was carrying, and Charles can't seem to…"

"Accept it? He thinks if there'd been a doctor here, the baby would have lived?"

"Yes. I feel so useless. Just a lowly, half-trained nurse. I can't tell him why Naomi miscarried, and I can't tell him if it will happen again, if she has some condition. So you see," she turned back to Hope, "he doesn't want a nurse. He needs a doctor. For Naomi."

"I do see."

Hope withdrew into herself for a long while and Hannah didn't bother her. Finally, the woman said softly, "Would you vouch for me when I go speak with Mr. McIntyre tomorrow? Help me to get him to let me work here…until a doctor is found?"

"Absolutely. He won't turn you away. He just may not promise you something long-term." Hannah smiled, realizing what conclusion Charles would ultimately come to and lightened her tone. "Of course, once he realizes what a blessing you would be for the doctor, you could be a circus chimpanzee and he'd keep you."

---

*A*s always, Charles was delighted to see his sister-in-law Hannah. Her golden ponytail streaming over her shoulder, stunning blue eyes and similar pug nose reminded him of Naomi and he enjoyed the girl's company. She was as bubbly as a mountain stream and injected a room with cheer.

When she knocked on his office door, however, holding her son, something in him deflated a little. Ever since Naomi had lost their baby, he'd been spending too much time thinking about a son. And, admittedly, overlooking Two Spears. *Lord, help me look past my own hurts to the boy...*

"Hannah, what a pleasant surprise." He rose and nodded at Little Billy. "And how is the young prince today?"

"Getting into everything now that he's walking." As if to prove her point, she let her son slide to the floor. Holding on to his mother's finger, the towheaded little fella ambled precariously toward Charles.

"My, look at you, young man." Charles stepped out from behind his desk and squatted to make himself an easier target for the toddler. Grinning from ear to ear, the boy let go of his mother and waddled like a drunk into Charles' arms. "Well, I'll be." He scooped up Little Billy and rose to his feet. "You'll be dancing with all the pretty gals at the parties this fall, won't you?"

"Yes, he'll be a ladies' man."

"Too handsome not to be."

Hannah giggled, shook her head. "But I know you're busy and I have to get on to the mercantile. I wanted to tell you, though, a young lady came into town yesterday."

Any statement about women coming to Defiance always made his heart stop for a moment and he set Little Billy back on the ground. "And?"

The boy toddled back to his mother. "Oh, no, it isn't bad. I think it's wonderful. She's wonderful. Bob Ledford would have died last night at the restaurant if she hadn't been there."

"Bob? What happened?"

"He nearly choked to death. Hope did a tracheotomy right there on the floor and then did the surgery on him at Doc's. She's a highly skilled nurse."

This was much better news than what it could have been and Charles breathed a sigh of relief. "You saw?"

"All of it. She came here because she knows you're looking for a doctor. She wants to stay in Defiance. Work here, assist the doctor when you hire one."

Charles returned to his seat and motioned for Hannah to claim the one in front of his desk. She shook her head and picked up her son. "I really don't have time. I just wanted to smooth the way for her. She's afraid you might turn her away, showing up without writing first and all."

"You say she's skilled?"

"The word is an understatement. I saw how fast she did that tracheotomy and I was truly impressed. I talked with her some more this morning. She graduated top of her class from Pennsylvania Women's Medical College."

"She has references, I assume."

"Yes, and she'll bring them when you meet with her."

He tapped a pencil on his ledger as his thoughts raced. "Top of her class? What of you? I know you want to nurse. What if I keep her on when the doctor is hired? What will you do?"

"I want what's best for Naomi, for Defiance. I'll help all I can and then, when you find a doctor, if there's room for me, I'll keep training. If not, I'm sure the Lord will lead me to something else."

Charles wished he could be so sure, so trusting of the Lord's will. He was working on it, of course, but it didn't seem so easy to find right now. Not when Naomi was healing from both a brutal animal attack and the loss of their child. Leaning on his own understanding seemed much easier for the moment. "It certainly couldn't hurt to have her around, then."

Hannah beamed. "Can I tell her?"

He chuckled, rose, and plucked his hat from the hook beside his desk. "I've got to get back out to the ranch. Unfortunately, it could be a month or so before I choose a doctor. So tell your nurse friend to go ahead and move into Doc's. I'll stop by in the next day or so to introduce myself and see if she needs anything."

"This afternoon," Hannah said firmly. "Naomi has an appointment this afternoon. Three o'clock."

Charles stopped. "Had my answer all figured out, did you?"

"I knew what you'd say because you want the best for Naomi. And Hope certainly has far more training than I do."

Yes, that was not a fact to be denied. "Top of her class? Well," he dropped his hat in place, "sounds as if Defiance will be fortunate to have her."

CHAPTER 7

*N*aomi sat down on the front porch step, took a deep breath, and closed her eyes. The sun on her face, the buzz of a nearby bee, and the sounds of cattle mooing, cowboys shouting, and a rooster crowing off in the distance made her smile. She needed to smile. To find something to smile about.

The wounds from the cat ached and pulled uncomfortably when she moved. They seemed to make her whole body sore, but her heart hurt worse than anything. She was trying to be brave for Charles but she'd lost a baby—their child—and sometimes the grief threatened to swamp her.

In time, she told herself, *in time we'll be past this. I'll be my normal, foolishly stubborn self, right, Lord?* But she felt as if so much of the fight had gone out of her. *A baby. Our baby. A little girl? A rough and tumble boy? Oh, Lord, it's so hard to trust Your plan sometimes.*

A knot formed in her throat and she stood up with relief at the sound of the approaching wagon. It buoyed her spirits to see Charles and Two Spears riding together. He had promised he would renew his efforts to spend more time with the boy and was keeping his word.

He needs to love him like he's his only son. He may be.

She turned away from the implication and trudged stiffly out to the wagon. Charles was wearing his favorite blue suit with a gray silk vest. Two Spears was dressed in dungarees and a plaid shirt, his black, shoulder-length hair tucked behind his ears. Both of them so different, yet so similar. Every day, Naomi could see Charles more and more in the boy's face, though the child was undeniably Ute. She prayed the lineage wouldn't be a curse.

Charles handed the reins to Two Spears and climbed down for Naomi. "Your conveyance to town, your ladyship."

Smirking at his pet name, she clutched his shoulders and allowed him to lift her up to the seat. With care, she settled in, but even the gentlest movements set the stitches to talking. She winced and Charles saw it. "You're all right?"

Naomi exhaled, willing the pain away. "I will be. I just need some time."

She hadn't meant to sound so melancholy, but Charles settled beside her and dropped a reassuring arm around her waist. "Yes. Time solves everything." He looked at Two Spears. "All right, let's practice those driving skills."

The young boy practically grimaced with intense concentration as he drove the horses. He was much more comfortable in the saddle, Naomi knew, but she also had faith he'd get a handle on this new task easily.

"Now, Naomi," Charles began, "you keep in mind you are seeing a nurse today. Not a doctor. You must weigh anything she says carefully."

"I will, but a medical-school trained nurse is still quite the boon for Defiance. And I'm sure she'll be able to teach Hannah a few things. I'm excited to meet her."

The day was warm and perfect. Beneath a cloudless, blue sky

Charles chatted about the herd's increased production, a couple of new hands from Texas joining the King M, and the lumber camp up on Screech Owl Ridge shooting a wolf. Mundane but comforting to hear him share his work with her. It didn't take long for her, however, to notice Two Spears' silence.

At first she had excused it as his attempt to master driving the team, but after a few miles the same grim look of determination still kept every muscle in his face frozen. She glanced at Charles and back to the boy. "Two Spears, is everything all right?" Come to think of it, he'd been unusually quiet since…her mind struggled to follow a timeline backward.

To the attack.

He shrugged an evasive answer and kept his focus on the horses. Naomi chewed on her lip. Fear in an Indian boy was probably not looked on well. But he *was* only a boy. And the attack was still delivering nightmares to her. How was it affecting him?

"You know, I'm feeling much better. These stitches will be out today and I'll be back to my old self again in no time." She decided to wade in and determine his level of fear. She leaned across Charles to speak more directly to him. "I'm ready to go and pick some more berries. I'm not afraid of the cat. In case you were wondering."

"You cannot go back," the stoic child said without looking at her. "At least not until the cat is dead."

"He is dead. It was a good shot, Two Spears," Charles reconfirmed. "He didn't get far before he dropped."

"You hit him. You did not kill him."

Both Naomi and Charles froze at the statement, made with what sounded like absolute confidence. He turned to Two Spears. "I told you to stay away from that ridge. If you've been up there alone I'll turn you over my knee—"

"Charles," Naomi squeezed his knee and cut him off. "Two Spears, you are a courageous warrior. Charles told me you were ready to fight the cat with nothing but a rock. Just like David and Goliath. You remember that story?"

The boy seemed to relax a touch. "He killed the giant with a rock."

"Yes, he did, but you need to grow up a little more in the Lord before you go fighting lions and bears and giants, all right? Promise me you'll stay away from up there." When he didn't answer immediately, she pushed. "Give me your good word you'll stay away from the ridge. Promise me."

Grudgingly, he nodded. "I promise."

---

*R*ebecca Donoghue yawned with afternoon boredom as she stepped off the boardwalk and headed down the alley that would take her to Doc Cook's office. Only Doc Cook wasn't around anymore, and she missed the old codger. He'd been so sweet, training Hannah to be a nurse.

Rebecca emerged from the alley and scanned the quiet road left to right. Running parallel to Main Street, Parker's Path had been the main route to the Sunnyside Mine. Now...

A dust devil swirled down the empty lane in the dry fall afternoon. The few log cabins that dotted the field across from her rose above the brittle weeds like grave markers. The eerily idle Sunnyside Mine compound, the tomb for twelve men buried in the rock, sat several hundred yards up the slope.

Lord, it's just depressing back here. Will the town ever recover? Be a place to raise a family? Can it even survive without the mine?

Can our newspaper?

Rebecca pushed the nagging worries away. *One step at a time, one day at a time,* she told herself.

Doc's small office, a little, yellow clapboard box with a long front porch, sat alone and forlorn, the last visible building on the thoroughfare. Doc's house was a hundred feet up the path but hidden by a stand of pines. Movement behind a window caught Rebecca's eye and she touched the pencil at her ear to make sure it was still there. She strode with purpose up to the door, tossed her long, dark braid over her shoulder and knocked.

A curtain fluttered. Aware she was being assessed by the new occupant, Rebecca waited patiently. A moment later, a pretty young lady with auburn hair piled into a loose bun opened the door. A crisp, white apron covered her dress. Rebecca offered her hand as the woman smiled hesitantly.

Friendly, but curious caramel eyes assessed Rebecca. "Yes?"

"Hello. I'm Hannah's sister Rebecca. You're Hope, I presume?"

The two shook and Hope stepped back to let her enter. "I am. Please come in."

She'd been cleaning. The office smelled of witch hazel, turpentine, and some odors Rebecca couldn't place.

"My, if you hadn't told me you were sisters, I wouldn't have put the two of you together," the woman said, closing the door.

Rebecca fished a notepad from her pocket. "Yes, we hear that all the time. Hannah and Naomi are the petite, fair-haired beauties. I apparently was left on the doorstep by a passing Indian tribe."

Hope laughed at the old joke which Rebecca loved whipping out when she could. "I certainly don't think it was a tribe of ugly Indians," Hope assured her. "You and your sister Hannah are beautiful. Speaking of sisters, Naomi is going to be my first patient this very afternoon."

"Hannah said she was coming to see you."

"Oh, my, Hannah has worked very hard to get things rolling here for me. I'm truly appreciative of her assistance."

"The whole town is talking about how you saved Bob. Everything Hannah has done—well, let's say you made the work of touting you easy. I don't suppose you could have had a better announcement of your arrival than saving a man's life in the middle of a crowded restaurant. I'm sure our readers are eager to learn all about you."

Hope's face tightened and her hand went to her throat. Rebecca reigned in her enthusiasm. Interviewing people had taught her to watch for tell-tale signs of discomfort.

She patted the air gently. "Please don't be nervous. You don't have to answer any questions you're not comfortable with. And I'm not looking to do an exposé. Just get enough information to help the citizens of Defiance find common ground with you. Help them feel comfortable in coming to see you."

"Yes, I nee—uh, *want* that, too."

Rebecca heard the quick correction and filed it away. "Could we sit for a moment?"

"Certainly, but I have to give you fair warning. Your sister will be here soon for a 3:30 appointment. I can't guarantee how much time we'll have to chat."

"Oh, well," Rebecca plucked the pencil from her ear, "then let's get started."

"Please, sit down." Hope motioned to the rocking chair by the stove. She grabbed a ladderback from the edge of the sitting area and dragged it closer to Rebecca, making their chat more intimate.

"Perhaps some quick basics. Your full name, where you're from, do you have any family, are you married, will your husband be joining you if you are?"

"Hope Melinda Clark. I'm from Scranton, Pennsylvania. I have two brothers younger than myself, Josh and Caleb. Twins. My father is a doctor. I am not married. I was engaged..." She trailed off, seemed to ponder what more to say on the subject. "He was not supportive of my career choice."

Rebecca's pencil slowed. "That would be his loss. Hannah said you graduated at the top of your class."

"Yes, and I think I did that just to show him he hadn't completely broken my heart."

Rebecca nodded, appreciating the woman's spunk. "Good for you. And where did you go to school?"

"Pennsylvania Women's College of Medicine."

"And you graduated in...?"

"Oh, that was 1874."

"Four years. Where have you been employed prior to coming to Defiance?"

"I prac—I mean, nursed in my father's practice for two years before I came west. I have a bit of an adventurous spirit, as Father described my wanderlust," she added with a smirk.

"I see," Rebecca, said scribbling madly. "What's your father's name. And between there and here you worked—?"

"For a doctor in Denver." She paused, again planning her words, Rebecca assumed. "He practiced in an affluent area," Hope said slowly. "I found the patients more difficult to deal with than their ailments. I didn't feel useful there."

"And, I'm sorry, your father's name was...?"

Rebecca didn't miss the slight hesitation, but Hope answered, "Dr. James Clark."

"I see. Well, I dare say you'll have more than hangnails and bunions in Defiance."

"Yes." She smiled shyly. "It's a terrible thing to look forward to...to sickness and injury. But come they will, and I plan to do my best at caring for the citizens of Defiance."

The rattle and jangle of a buggy pulling up outside took their gazes out the window. "Oh, there's Charles and Naomi now. So, quickly, one last question, if I may."

"Of course."

"Have you delivered many babies?"

Hope smiled, as if understanding the basis of concern for the question. "Yes. At last count, fifty-one."

Rebecca closed her notebook and the two rose. "Thank you

for speaking with me. I trust, if I have any follow-up questions, you won't mind if I bother you again."

Hope waved her hand. "No bother at all. Anything I can do to make the citizens of Defiance aware of me and trust me, please just ask."

---

*H*ope's palms went clammy as she opened the door to welcome the McIntyres. Rebecca thanked her again and then slipped out to greet her sister.

No, Hope thought, *they certainly don't look related.* Rebecca, tall, ebony hair, noble features, was at least in her early forties. Naomi was her opposite in every way and probably in her late twenties, though she moved like an eighty-year-old woman, apparently due to her recent injuries.

The man with Naomi was a real Adonis, as a friend from college would have described him. Charles McIntyre had a devilishly handsome face framed by wavy, black hair and a beard, and an athletic physique wrapped in a tailored blue suit. He moved with a confidence that Hope had seen only among men who were movers and shakers. Men who could take on the world and everything in it.

Only...

She blinked in surprise. The man repositioned his cowboy hat, took Naomi's hand, and, gazing at her as if she were the goddess Venus, assisted her down from the wagon with a firm but caring touch, intensely aware of her injuries.

He handles her as if she is more precious to him than rubies.

The snippet of the Scripture whispered in her mind, catching her off guard. She hadn't thought of the Bible, or her mother—or God for that matter—in years.

"How are you feeling today, honey?" Rebecca asked,

approaching the wagon and snapping Hope back to the moment.

Mr. McIntyre eased Naomi to the ground and she gave Rebecca a pained smile. "I'm all right. Some days are better than others, but I'm all right."

"You'll start having more good days than bad, once you get those stitches out." Rebecca smirked at Mr. McIntyre. "I see you're taking good care of her."

"I am afraid of what Hannah might do to me if I don't," he answered in a thick Southern drawl that, Hope thought, gave his words an almost hypnotic lilt.

They all laughed and Rebecca switched to the passenger still in the wagon. A boy of about ten with dark skin, long straight hair, fiercely dark eyes. An Indian, though dressed in western clothing. "Two Spears," Rebecca said, "would you like to walk to the mercantile with me while Naomi sees the nurse? They're all stocked up on licorice and I have a nickel with your name on it."

The boy gazed at the McIntyres with unveiled, unabashed pleading in his expression. Naomi and Mr. McIntyre nodded, laughing, and he jumped to the ground. Rebecca turned back to Hope and waved. "Thank you again, Hope."

"My pleasure."

"You can come get Two Spears at the town hall," she said to her sister as she and the boy walked away.

The couple gave their approval and then headed for Hope and her front porch. "Mr. McIntyre. Mrs. McIntyre. It's my pleasure to meet you. I'm Hope Clark."

They shook hands and she ushered them inside, Mr. McIntyre removing his cowboy hat as they entered. Walking to the center of the room, where an examination table sat surrounded by cabinets, shelves of supplies, and counters for working space, Hope turned. "I don't mean to be presumptuous, but I found the lack of privacy for this particular area unsettling. I've strung a curtain to separate it from the waiting area."

Both Naomi and Mr. McIntyre seemed to regard her with surprised admiration, each lifting an eyebrow at her statement. They surveyed the wire dissecting the main room, a curtain hanging on it but bunched tightly against the wall.

"I think that's a wonderful idea," Naomi said. "I don't know why Doc Cook never did it."

"Because it will make the waiting area the size of a broom closet," Mr. McIntyre said resting his hat on the hook by the door , making Hope wonder if she'd made a mistake.

"Men," she said, hoping to sound jovial, "tend to overlook such simple things but simple things can provide so much comfort to a patient. And I do wish to put the patient first."

"As you should," Naomi said, giving Mr. McIntyre a sideways glance.

"Yes, well," he said, tucking a thumb into the gun belt at his waist, "Doc was a good man and a good doctor, but he was also pretty cut-and-dried. To the point. No frills."

"I don't mind a few frills," Hope said, smiling at Naomi who beamed back at her and her spirits soared. If she could win this *precious jewel* over, Mr. McIntyre was sure to follow. "So, Mrs. McIntyre, if you'd like to step into examination room one," Hope stepped back and motioned toward the little room, "I can answer any questions you might have, Mr. McIntyre, about my credentials while she undresses. My references are on the window ledge there behind you."

As he moved toward the window, Hope slipped into the room with Naomi. "Hannah said you were attacked by a mountain lion and she put thirty-five stitches in your shoulders and side?"

"Yes. And a few other places."

"I can't imagine how terrifying that must have been."

Naomi started undoing the buttons on her blouse. "I kept praying for the strength to fight."

"Fight?" Hope repeated as she helped the woman slip out of

her shirt. "It has been my experience most people in a similar situation pray for help."

"Naomi, you'll discover," Mr. McIntyre said through the door, "is not a woman to run from a fight, even when she should."

Hope half-smiled at Naomi. "We might have something in common."

"Lovely," Mr. McIntyre dead-panned.

Both women giggled and Hope's confidence grew. "Well, let's start by taking a look at your stitches."

Hope was quite impressed with Hannah's work and said so aloud as her gaze drifted intently over the wounds. Neat, precise sutures followed the tracks of claw marks down Naomi's shoulder and side. Some of the stitches on smaller wounds had been removed and they looked as if Hannah had done a fine job there as well. Naomi was healing in fine order.

"Miss Clark," Mr. McIntyre called, "these references are from your father and a few of his patients. Where have you been since," he paused, "since '77?"

"A doctor in Denver. As I told Hannah, I did not care for his wealthy patients. They were tedious to deal with." Hope lifted off a bandage at the top of Naomi's shoulder and examined several unstitched puncture wounds—bite marks. A raging pink, they were deep but clean. Still, the cat had done a lot of damage. "Can you raise your left arm for me?"

"He would not give you a reference?" Mr. McIntyre asked.

"Frankly, Mr. McIntyre, I didn't leave Denver on the best terms." Not a lie exactly. Naomi raised her arm and Hope saw her flinch when the elbow was about shoulder level. "I'm sorry, that's painful for you?"

Naomi hesitated an instant, then nodded. "The bite hurts. Down deep."

Trying to mask her concerns for her patient's injury and Mr. McIntyre's curiosity, Hope kept her face blank as she pressed lightly on Naomi's deltoid and trapezius. Naomi winced and tensed her muscles.

"I'm sorry. I know this is uncomfortable," Hope apologized. Outside, Mr. McIntyre grunted and Hope tried to offer a truthful explanation. "My bedside manner when it comes to foolish complaints"—She had Mrs. Chalmers squarely in mind as she spoke—"Well, perhaps I could learn to be a bit more diplomatic."

"Perhaps," he said flatly.

Hope turned her full attention to Naomi, resolving to deal with Mr. McIntyre later. "The cat may have torn a tendon." She couldn't know for sure and only time would tell. "Such injuries are difficult to heal, so use your arm as little as possible over the next two weeks and then I'll examine you again. Is the pain manageable, or do you feel you need laudanum?"

"No."

Hope nodded, encouraged by the woman's grit. "All right. Now, we'll get the rest of these stitches out today, and then," Hope paused, sensitive to the situation. "Hannah said you lost the baby you were carrying. And that you didn't know you were pregnant. Is that correct?"

"I had missed a monthly. Was late on the next one. I was beginning to suspect when...when the cat attacked." Naomi turned pleading green eyes to Hope. "Hannah said the loss of the blood could have caused the miscarriage and that I might not have anything to worry about. As far as getting pregnant again."

The shuffling of papers and pacing footsteps on the other side of the door stopped. Hope nodded. "Entirely possible. Blood loss, shock. Early in a pregnancy is the most dangerous time for a fetus. But we'll get to all that. Let's take out these stitches first."

A little while later, Hope performed Naomi's ladies' exam

and made an unexpected discovery. She paused her movements and Naomi seemed to sense something.

"Is anything wrong?"

Hope removed the speculum and stood up. "You can get dressed now. Let me wash up and I'll join you and Mr. McIntyre shortly."

CHAPTER 8

*N*aomi dressed and joined Charles in the sitting area. He rose, pulled her into an embrace, and she melted against him, enjoying the scents of lilac soap and apple-tinged tobacco. "That didn't take very long. Stitches all out?"

She nodded, breathing him in—scents so uniquely, wonderfully him.

"How do you feel?"

At the moment? "Peaceful." She snuggled into him and he kissed the top of her head. "I'm stiff," she said, recognizing the seriousness of his question. "And it's going slow, but I'll mend."

She was carefully rolling her left arm in a circle as Hope dried her hands on a towel and joined them. The young woman met their gazes with a little too much confidence, rocking on her heels. Naomi couldn't decide if the new nurse was forcing cheer or using it to hide something. Charles intertwined his fingers with Naomi's, as if wondering the same thing.

Hope drummed her fingers on her thighs and pursed her lips. "I want to preface what I'm about to tell you with a dose of grace, if you will. Hannah is a fine nursing assistant. If she chose to pursue a career in nursing, I have no doubt she would be a welcome addition to the medical field."

Charles lifted his chin and dropped a hand on his gun, his eyes narrowing with suspicion. "But?"

Hope took a deep breath. "Judging by your wounds, Naomi, you must have been covered head to toe in blood when they brought you to Hannah. To the untrained eye, blood and tissue, well," she shrugged, "it could be an easy assumption to make."

Naomi tilted her head. Hope was trying to protect Hannah from something. "Whatever you're dancing around, just say it. Hannah didn't sew my arm to my chest or anything, so whatever you don't want to say can't be that bad."

"You're still pregnant."

A pristine silence settled in the room, thicker and more perfect than any Naomi had ever experienced. Neither she nor Charles moved, breathed, spoke. Her mind froze.

"A little bleeding early in a pregnancy is not unusual. That, mixed with the wounds inflicted by the cat...this was an easy mistake to make." Hope smiled. "I hope it's good news to you and I hope Hannah won't be too hard on herself for the mistake. Please don't hold it against her."

Naomi needed to sit down. "And you're sure?"

"Very."

She staggered back and Charles helped her find the chair. "I'm pregnant." *I'm pregnant.* She couldn't seem to get the impact of the words. *I'm going to have a baby.* She looked up at Charles who knelt before her, still holding her hand. His dark, mischievous eyes shined, white teeth gleamed, such a contrast to his black beard and mustache. She leaned closer to him and tested the words. "I'm going to have a baby."

"A baby." He kissed her, kissed her again, and she sensed he was holding back giddy laughter. He pulled her to her feet and turned to Hope. "Thank you, Miss Clark. Please feel free to settle in as you see fit—with the understanding I am still intent on finding a doctor for Defiance. Especially now."

A soft knock on the door ended the appointment. "My next appointment."

Naomi smiled at Hope, the meager movement of muscle not expressing a fraction of her joy. "Thank you. Thank you for coming to Defiance."

---

*T*he cat sunk his fangs into Naomi's neck and she screamed in agony. Claws that felt like bolts of lightning ripped open her back. He tried to pull her away from Charles—she reached for her husband and gasped at the sight of her bloody hand, flesh ripped away from her fingers.

A fog drifted between them and Charles faded from her sight, yet she knew he was still there. The cat bit down again, torturing, tormenting, the pain slicing her afresh. She was on the ground now, fighting. He growled demonically as he tore flesh from her forearms. Screaming for Charles, Naomi fought back, pounding the cougar in the face, trying to avoid his fangs, smearing her blood across his snout.

Suddenly, it wasn't the cat on top of her but Matthew and she froze, more afraid of him than the animal. He leered at her as he pinned her arms over her head. "You'll watch him die, too."

Her fear turned to rage. "No," she bellowed, "I won't let you hurt him. I won't—"

"Naomi, good God, wake up." Her heart hammering in her chest like a thundering herd of buffalo, gasping for breath, Naomi opened her eyes. Charles had an arm around her and grasped her face with his other hand. "It's all right. It was a dream." In the moonlight, she could see his eyes, wide with concern.

But he was all right. She touched his face, felt the prickle of his beard beneath her fingers. It had been a dream. Just a dream. Naomi melted into his chest and he wrapped her in a warm, safe hug. She forced her breathing and her heart to slow down. Just another nightmare.

"Were you dreaming about the cat again?"

"Yes—" and no. She could still feel Matthew on top of her and pressed closer into Charles. "These nightmares need to stop. They can't be good for the baby."

Charles chuckled softly. "She hung on through the attack. She may be tougher than you think."

"She?"

"I have no doubt, Naomi, you will give me a daughter." His gentle tone rang with light-hearted sarcasm.

She nuzzled his chest, everything right again in her world. "You might be surprised."

Yes, merely dreams. And they would pass in time.

———

CHAPTER 9

The idea to buy the Sunnyside Mine wouldn't leave Matthew, even though a large Saturday night crowd in the saloon gave him hope for the town's fortunes. He surveyed the smoky room from the first landing on the staircase and reminded himself a healthy number of customers wasn't as good as outright-busting-at-the-seams. Like the Chandelier was used to.

He'd told the girls to stop entertaining customers for a week in an attempt to get that prig of a mayor Ian Donoghue off his back. Closing down one pastime had funneled a few more bodies here, but it was only a temporary solution. A poor one at that. Things needed to change in Defiance.

The town needed men.

Men wallowed in sin. Bred it. Demanded it. Thank God, couldn't live without it. Enough of the right men showing up in Defiance would swing the pendulum toward prosperity with the unstoppable force of an avalanche. Best of all, there wouldn't be a darn thing the sheriff, the mayor, or even Charles McIntyre could do about it.

And wouldn't it just frost Naomi for the town to turn back

to the den of iniquity she'd wanted so desperately to get away from? So desperately, in fact, she'd asked Matthew to come rescue her and her sisters.

Only, he'd been a day late and a dollar short. Again. Losing her to a less-than-equal rival.

He shook his head, reminding himself to stop picking at an old wound and get back to the matter at hand.

The mine. It had to reopen.

McIntyre needed some kind of nudge. Something to move him, convince him to divest himself of the Sunnyside. Sell it and walk away, not merely sit on it. Matthew needed a plan to create the nudge.

He knew people back in California. People with money. A few of them so rich they could light their stoves with stacks of hundred dollar bills or stuff their mattresses with the cash.

Yes, that was a way to proceed. The idea blossomed in his brain like an ink spill. He'd send out some telegrams, see if maybe—

"Yeah, she's gonna have a baby. The little sister made a mistake."

Matthew's attention immediately shot to two men having a drink at the end of the bar, a few feet below him.

"Mighty big mistake," one observed.

"Mebbe so, but my wife heard the whole thing."

"Imagine *Charles McIntyre* with a baby," the flushed miner whispered too loudly. "Didn't think I'd ever see that."

"Might give him a better disposition."

"Might. I hear tell he's already going soft. A kid just might turn him sweet and all." The man took a swig of his beer and wiped away the foamy mustache. "I don't reckon it was meant for my wife's ears, though, so don't repeat it."

"She sure is a busybody." The other man lifted his beer toward his lips. "Anybody see her with her ear to the key hole?"

"Not this time." The two men had a hearty laugh and moved

on to discussing the paltry amount of gold coming out of the creek.

Matthew's grip tightened so hard on the rail, he could feel the wood giving beneath his fingers. His jaw clenched with a herculean force.

A baby. The bastard stole Naomi from me and now they're going to start a family. That should be my baby...

Jealousy, dark, wretched, foul, writhed in his heart. *He's gotten everything he ever wanted. He's gotten everything I've ever wanted. But I came so close...once.*

Matthew had met Naomi on the street a few weeks back, right before the mountain lion had got hold of her. He'd attempted to chat. She'd merely smiled, said she was in a hurry, and pushed that half-breed son right past him. Matthew thought Christians were supposed to forgive.

And now she and McIntyre had a brat of their own coming into this world.

Matthew rubbed his temples, trying to massage out the darkness. But something in his brain writhed, strained, snapped.

No. No. NO!

He was done.

He'd had enough of losing. Losing to someone like his brother had been one thing. John had been a good man. Deserving of a woman like Naomi. But to lose her to Charles McIntyre—an infamous pimp—had been a nearly incapacitating blow. Now, they had a baby on the way?

Matthew'd had all he was going to take.

At that moment, he decided no matter what it cost him, no matter what steps he had to take, if he had to sell his soul to the very devil himself, he was going to break Charles McIntyre. Break him financially, spiritually, any way he could think of.

And make sure Naomi watched it all come undone.

*H*annah dropped down hard in the chair near the stove. Hope clutched her shoulder, gave her a reassuring squeeze. "Please don't take this too hard, Hannah. You saved your sister's life. Therefore, you saved the baby's as well."

"But I told her—I said—my diagnosis—the blood—I was wrong. I was wrong." Hannah felt like she might be sick, so deep was her regret and humiliation.

"Calm down." Hope came round to face her. "The circumstances were quite stressful. And you had no one to turn to. No teacher. But you'll learn. I—and experience—will teach you. Eventually perhaps nursing school. You will learn." She nudged Hannah's chin up. "Focus on the two lives you *saved* and move forward. Can you do that?"

Hannah swallowed against the nausea rising in her stomach. Hope was right. Naomi was alive, and now, so, too, was the baby. *Oh, Lord, did I save their lives?* That would make the humiliation worth it.

"We have to move past this. There are patients coming in today."

Hannah rose slowly to her feet and smoothed her apron. "Then let's get ready for them."

*A*nd the patients came. Several a day. Hannah thought she was happier about it than Hope, as Hope was teaching her so much. Just today Hannah had learned some basic anatomy, pre-clinical procedures, and recognizing early signs of heart failure. Hope's methods were new, modern, her knowledge arguably as wide as Doc's. Perhaps even a little beyond.

Taking a whistling kettle off the stove, Hannah poured

scalding water over a sink full of instruments. The last bit of washing before they closed the office for the evening. She returned the kettle to the stove as the door to examination room two opened.

"Take those twice a day," Hope was saying to a young man as she walked him to the door. Pale as a gravestone, he nodded slowly but attentively as she talked. "Don't miss a day. Two every day for five days, then come back and see me." She stopped at the threshold as he stepped out on to the porch. "And, from now on, cook your venison till the juices run clear."

"Yes, ma'am." He raised the bottle of stomach pills. "And thank you. Oh, how much do I owe you?"

"Um, let's say a dollar." The man fished some coins from his pants pocket, gave them to Hope and nodded his good-bye. She watched him for a moment, then shut the door. "My, this was a long day. I'm ready to put my feet up—"

A knock on the door stopped Hannah from answering. Hope puttered her lips in exhaustion, but opened the door again. "Yes, can I help you?"

"I need to see the doctor." A slender woman with sickly gray shadows under her eyes pushed past Hope and marched into the office. Her faded, low-cut dress and tinted red hair announced her vocation with certainty. "I'm not leaving till I do." She spotted Hannah in the corner at the sink and narrowed her eyes at her. "You're too young to be the doctor. Where's the doctor?"

Hope cleared her throat and shut the door. "I'm the—I mean, I am—you see, um, there is no doctor here, but I am a very competent nurse. I'm sure I can help you."

The woman appraised her with a suspicious stare and pursed lips. Pushing frizzy hair off her forehead, she raised her chin. "I need rid of the baby I'm carrying. I can pay. I've got cash."

Hannah gasped and Hope's mouth fell open. "By 'rid of,'"

Hope spoke carefully, "do you mean you want to abort your pregnancy?"

"My money's good. Here." She raised her arm to display a worn, beaded reticule hanging from her wrist. "I always try to go to either a real doctor or a real nurse. No shysters."

"Always..." Hope faded off. "How many times—?" She bit that off and started again. "I'm a doc—I mean, a nurse. I can't take a life. I took a vow to only save lives."

The woman sniffed and appraised Hope with a curled lip. "What's your price?"

"I said I don't perform abortions. The money has nothing to do with it, I'm sorry. I can help you deliver the baby."

Hannah stepped forward quickly. "Have it and you can give it up for adoption."

The woman cut narrowed, storming eyes at her. "Oh, yeah, I know you. You knocked on my tent once. You and Mollie. Invited me to church. Well, the only thing I'm interested in saving is my waistline and my income."

The callousness of the woman's words hit Hannah like a slap. How lost and blind was a person to believe a baby could be discarded like dirty bathwater? *A baby... Oh, God, open this woman's eyes. Soften her heart. Don't let her kill a child.*

"I'd be happy to examine you," Hope said, "give you some prenatal care, but abortion is out of the question."

"Pre-na—what?"

"Monitor you. Keep you healthy for the pregnancy. Deliver the baby when the time comes. Help you through the entire process."

The woman snorted in disgust. "That sounds like a racket, for sure. No, I ain't having this baby. If you won't rid me of it, I'll find someone who will."

"There is no other trained nurse in town," Hannah added in a rush, hoping the argument might give the woman pause.

"Oh, there's somebody. There's always somebody."

She turned to go but Hope clutched her elbow. "Please don't do this. It could be dangerous for you."

For a moment, Hannah saw a softening in the woman's hard features. A sad expression tugged at the corners of her mouth. "I can't bring a child into my world. If I die, maybe that's the best outcome."

Speechless, heartbroken, Hannah prayed for the woman as she slipped out the door.

"If I don't help her, she could die," Hope whispered, staring down at her hands twisting in her apron.

"If you do help her, a child *will* die. Could you live with that?"

Hope didn't answer her.

CHAPTER 10

*S*everal days later, a young black woman came pounding on Hope's door in the middle of the night. Someone in Tent Town needed help. Now, she scurried ahead on the dark path, illuminated here and there by the amber glow of tents, as Hope scrambled to keep up, holding her medical bag in a death grip.

Shortly, the girl stopped at a tent and jerked her chin toward it. "She's in there. Been a mess since yesterday morning. I'm two tents down if you need me."

"Actually, yes, I need you to go fetch Hannah Frink. She lives at the hotel."

"I don't want—"

"Or you can stay and assist."

The girl made an offended huffing noise but headed off toward main street.

Hope ducked into the tent and found the woman from the other day—the one who had practically demanded an abortion —lying on her cot, groaning, drenched in sweat. Hope lifted the covers and grimaced at the blood-soaked nightgown.

Suspecting the reason for a call from a soiled dove at this

hour, she had come prepared with various tinctures and menstrual cloths. After an examination, Hope suspected a tear in the cervix, possibly one in the uterus as well. She administered asphenamine and quinine, pressed in bandages, and waited for Hannah to help her move the patient.

The woman moaned softly. Sweat glistened on her forehead and drenched her ruby hair. Her pulse was weak and thready. Whoever she'd found to perform the abortion had been nothing short of a butcher and Hope was seriously concerned.

"I'm here." Hannah said, rushing into the tent. She grimaced at the pale, sweaty woman, but recovered quickly. "I brought our wagon. In case."

Guilt and fear squeezed in on Hope. "Good. The bleeding is too heavy. If her uterus has been punctured, surgery may be the only way to save her."

"Surgery?"

"But in these primitive conditions it could kill her. She's already lost too much blood. She is in a weakened state. The fever is evidence of infection."

"It sounds like she is dying," Hannah said softly, shock in her tone.

"Yes."

"If you don't do surgery, what else can you do?"

"Wait." Which was the same as saying *nothing*. Her stomach twisted. If only the bleeding would stop on its own. *If only she'd sent for me sooner...* "I have to move her to the office," she muttered, thinking out loud but aware of Hannah. "Help me get her in the wagon."

———

A change came over Hope that Hannah had seen once before—in the restaurant when she'd saved Mr. Ledford. Here in the office, with the patient resting on the table and ready for surgery, Hope stood straighter, her voice became more authoritative, her hands moved with skill and confidence as she wielded the scalpel.

In spite of the dire situation, Hannah was fascinated by the peek at the inside of the female reproductive organs. Hope narrated under her breath, explaining anatomical references like the anterior superior iliac spines, the subcutaneous fat and rectus sheath, entry into the peritoneal cavity, on and on.

Hannah had assisted Doc with enough minor surgeries to know one thing: something about this patient wasn't right. Her flesh was too pale. Her heartbeat too slow. The loss of blood was possibly too much to overcome, never mind the trauma of the surgery.

But Hope worked calmly with focus and determination. Hannah dabbed the woman's forehead with a towel—the sweat there the only indication Hope was under pressure.

"There it is, there's the puncture. Get me the iron."

Hannah rushed over to the stove and plucked a small cauterizing iron with a rosewood handle from the fire. The wood was warm, but manageable. She rushed it back over to Hope who pressed the tip to the wound. The scent of burning flesh filled Hannah's nostrils and she had to force down the urge to vomit. "All right." Hope laid the instrument on the counter. "Let's close her."

Hannah swung around to the tray of medical implements beside the iron and picked up the threaded, crescent-shaped needle. As Hope sutured the wound, Hannah deflated a little, overwhelmed with all there would be to learn in a real nursing school.

"I can see why you were top of your class. I had no idea nursing schools taught this—taught surgery."

Hope swallowed, paused for an instant, then kept going. "Yes, nursing school. You'd be surprised what they teach you now."

"It was very demanding, I suppose?"

"Very."

"Did you think Defiance would present such a challenge?"

Hope extended a waiting hand. "Scissors." Hannah responded and Hope cut the thread. "Honestly, I didn't know what to expect."

"You've truly been called to nursing. I can see God's hand in everything you do." Again Hannah caught a pause, a stutter, as if Hope was debating what to say and in the end said nothing. "I think you might be more gifted with a scalpel than Doc—" An idea, a crazy, irrational thought struck Hannah and she peered intently at Hope.

Hope leaned in to inspect her finished stitches one by one, but seemed to sense Hannah's gaze. "What?"

No. That was a crazy idea. Why would she lie? She had the references, and clearly a medical background. But what kind of medical background exactly? "You're so skilled. Almost like a doctor."

"Yes," Hope said, standing up. "Almost like. Now, let's get everything cleaned up."

"I don't know, Billy. I can't put my finger on it." Hannah toddled along the aisle of the mercantile, helping their son practice walking. Little Billy gripped her index fingers and swaggered drunkenly between the canned tomatoes on one side and barrels of flour on the other.

"Try," he said, without looking up from the ledger he was working on at the counter. "Fumbling for words might help you figure out what bothers you about her."

"It doesn't bother me. That's not the right word. I just get this sense she's holding back or…"

"Hiding something?"

"Maybe, but that makes it sound bad. I don't think it is. She's just a very private person."

"Could she be running from something or someone?"

"She mentioned a man. He didn't stick with her. He didn't want her to be a nurse."

Billy's eyes did come up at that. "Then he was a fool and she's better off without him."

Hannah's heart swelled. Billy believed in her. He made her think she could be a nurse—one as well trained as Hope. And he was even willing to uproot their lives. "Maybe she's trying to get over the heartbreak by coming to Defiance—someplace remote and adventurous."

Billy chuckled. "If she wanted adventurous, she should have come when Delilah was at the height of her chaos."

Her back beginning to ache from stooping over, she set her son down on his rear end and straightened for a good stretch. Yes, only a few months ago Defiance had been a den of wild debauchery and shamelessness. Delilah and her Crystal Chandelier had risen from the ground like a hungry demon singing a siren's song. Then that awful man had sabotaged the mine, blowing it sky high, burying twelve men beneath tons of rock.

Maybe the town with them.

"Charles thinks Defiance is bouncing back," she said, lacing her words with optimism she didn't quite feel.

"He and I have talked about it. The town can grow, but the pace will be slower without the mine."

"Not the most attractive place for a world-class doctor to come, but Charles is convinced he'll find one. In the meantime, Hope is the most skilled nurse I've ever seen. You wouldn't believe the surgery she performed this morning. Did I tell you—?"

"Twice. You told me twice."

She laughed and swept Little Billy up into her arms. "Well,

I'm out of stories then, little man. How about you and me go back to the hotel and get us some lunch? Are you hungry?"

"Howy," Little Billy said, grinning. "Howy."

"Oh, listen to you talking!" She slathered his little cherubic face with excited kisses. "I'm so proud of you, little man."

"Howy," the toddler said again, grinning.

Billy shook his head and came out from behind the counter. "He's growing so fast." He ruffled his son's downy blond hair, but the joyous smile faded and he narrowed his eyes at Hannah. "You're still sure?"

"I wish you'd quit asking me. I don't want anything more than for us to be a family."

"What about nursing school?"

She wanted to go more than ever because she'd made such a colossal mistake with Naomi's diagnosis. Her confidence hung in tatters, yet formal training would prevent future blunders. "I'm still not sure. I need to wait."

"On what?"

"Something in my spirit says sit tight. I can't tell you any more than that." She could hardly believe she still wanted to be a nurse but the dream wouldn't die. Could she—could Hannah— become a nurse like Hope?

Or dare she dream of something even bigger?

"Maybe working with Hope will help you find your focus."

Hannah blinked. No, this was not the time to share such a crazy thought. She had to pray about it. Wait for clear direction. Sit tight. "I've already learned it'll be far more work than I suspected. I don't know why she didn't go on to medical schoo—"

And the other crazy notion returned.

"What?" Billy asked.

"I wonder if she did try to go medical school. If she was rejected or failed? Or maybe that was the plan the young man didn't agree with. Maybe he thought nursing school should have been sufficient."

"Hannah." Billy laid a hand on her shoulder, she knew, to calm her racing mind. "This is all conjecture. Simply ask the woman."

———————

CHAPTER 11

"It's more than fair, I will say." Charles could not dismiss an offer on the mine out of hand, not without sharing it with his partner, Ian. He slid it across the desk to the Scotsman with the grudging compliment.

"Let's have a look then." Ian pulled his spectacles from his sweater's collar and worked into them.

As he read over the business proposition, Charles smiled at his friend's belly which had become more noticeable as of late. The argyle sweater he wore did not hide it, and Ian's beard had turned completely gray. He was aging comfortably, as he had hoped to do, surrounded by Rebecca and her sisters.

To Charles, Ian was more than a friend and a business partner. He was also his brother-in-law, a label that epitomized the myriad changes he, Ian, and the town had gone through in the last few years. Some made him smile, some made him sick.

"'Tis a fair offer," Ian said. "I find that almost surprising. Have you ever heard of this..." he carefully read the company name aloud, "MP&G Western Mining Conglomerate? And what of the members listed here?"

"The Board of Directors. Charles Crocker and Allan Ladd

are quite wealthy. Crocker is a railroad man. Ladd made his fortune in the gold rush and invested wisely. I am not familiar with the other two gentlemen."

Ian returned the paper and settled back, crossing a leg over one knee. "As I've said, I think we should sell it. This is a good offer. It would rid ye of the albatross the mine has become to ye. Ye'd be flush with capital. Ye could focus on the spur line."

Charles sighed heavily. "What if the mine is reopened and another accident happens? More men die?"

Ian laced his fingers over his paunch and pursed his lips. "I understand yer concern for the men who work the mines. It is admirable. Ye tried to make the mine as safe as ye could. But what happened could not have been foreseen. The catastrophe perpetrated by Delilah was more the fault of a broken, vengeful heart than a lapse in safety standards."

"Yes, I guess that's fair. She and Logan seemed destined for tragedy."

"Aye. Ye know, Scripture says every man shall bear his own burden. Yers is enough for ye. Ye need to quit trying to bear everyone else's as well."

"Perhaps." He shook his head, putting the offer aside for the moment. "Regarding the spur line and getting the lumber milled. I've no desire to send our wood to Matthew's sawmill. I think I will buy it."

"What if he won't sell it to ye?"

"Then I will build my own."

Ian nodded. "Ye've got several men working for ye with experience enough to manage one. Either way, it would be unwise to allow him to become a bottleneck for ye."

"Exactly my thinking. I don't trust him. We need to insure ourselves against any dependency on his lumberyard."

"Anything else?" Ian patted his stomach. "Rebecca is meeting me at the hotel for lunch."

"It does my heart good to see you so happy. There is nothing more important than family."

Ian's face fell. A pinch between his gray brows expressed his sympathy. "Again, I'm sorry for yer loss. If ye need anything, ye know Rebecca and I are here for ye."

"We may be calling upon you for nanny services." Charles tried and failed to keep a foolish grin from betraying his news.

Ian regarded him with a mix of confusion and amusement. "Lad, ye're trying to tell me something but I'm not tracking."

"A moment ago I was thinking you are a friend, a mentor, a business partner, a brother-in-law. There is one more label we can hang on you, though."

"Aye, what's that?"

"Uncle."

A cup of coffee pressed to her lips, Rebecca watched Hannah drizzle molasses over a steaming biscuit, tear off tiny pieces and feed them to Little Billy. Her glassy stare, however, said her mind was elsewhere. Around them, the Trinity Inn's restaurant reverberated with chatting customers, tinkling silverware, and the clank of dishes.

"Billy thinks I should just ask her outright."

Rebecca set the cup down. "Why don't you?"

"Oh, I suppose, eventually I will. I just thought by now she would have revealed a little more of her story to me."

"You said she's a private person. Those kind don't open up easily."

"I guess. It's just that sometimes when she talks, it's like she's saying one thing but thinking another. I don't know." She picked up a napkin and dabbed at her son's face. "I can't explain it."

"Awkward pauses? Sentences that seem to redirect abruptly?"

Hannah looked up. "Yes."

Rebecca nodded. "When I interviewed her, I had that same sense. As if she almost says one thing, but then quickly corrects and says something else."

"So, what do you think? Do you agree with me that something's amiss? But not necessarily something terrible," Hannah was quick to add.

"Possibly."

"I think it has something to do with her fiancé."

"This is all conjecture." Rebecca took another sip then grasped the cup in both hands. "Pointless speculation until…"

"Until what?"

"Until I actually do a little digging."

"Well, good morning, ladies."

Rebecca and Hannah looked up into Mollie's face. Her blue eyes twinkled and her cheeks were a healthy shade of rose. She was wearing her hair differently now, as well. Piled on her head in a French twist with several long, golden curls trailing down her back. The style made her look more mature.

"There's my favorite man." The girl bent down and smacked a wet raspberry on Little Billy's cheeks. The child rolled with hysterical giggles.

She's glowing, Rebecca thought, and grinned. She knew the look. She'd seen it on Hannah and Naomi. Even herself. Love painted hearts with an unmistakable hue. "Good morning, Mollie. You look beautiful."

"Oh," Hannah snapped her fingers, "I forgot to tell you, Rebecca." She reached across the table and tagged her sister's arm. "Billy just promoted Mollie to dining room manager."

Mollie straightened up and the glow coming from her brightened exponentially. "Yes. Yes, he did."

77

"Oh, that's wonderful." Rebecca was truly happy for the girl. "You'll be running the whole hotel before we know it."

Mollie winked. "That's the plan."

Hannah chuckled. "And I'll see a little more of the man I'm supposed to be marrying. What did Emilio say?"

"Oh, I haven't seen him yet to tell him. Probably see him tonight."

Hannah clutched Mollie's hand and squeezed excitedly. "I'm sure he'll be thrilled for you. For you both, if there's any kind of future planning going on."

The pink in Mollie's cheeks spread up her face and down into her white, cotton shirt. "No, no. We're just both, um," she cast about as if looking for a chore, "Well, I've got some inventory to check. Have a nice day, girls."

She strode off in a hurry, leaving Rebecca and Hannah laughing, but the humor seemed to die suddenly in Hannah. Rebecca didn't miss the abrupt fade. "Honey, are you jealous?"

Hannah's eye bugged. "No. Heavens no. I just had a moment of...missing Emilio's company. Or, really, missing the way things were. We were all so close when we lived in the hotel."

Rebecca smiled, a little sadly. "Those were good days, but they weren't meant to last forever. Life moves on. Naomi's happy out on her great, big, rolling ranch. I love Ian and we both enjoy running the newspaper. You and Billy, Emilio, Mollie, you'll all find your path."

"You're right, I know. I just hope we all don't drift too far apart."

"Well, we can keep working on one reason to gather together." Rebecca bit her lip and winked. "Let's finish the details for your wedding."

At first Hannah looked a touched perplexed, then her expression softened. "He loves me and he wants me to be happy."

Rebecca was gratified to agree. "Yes. Turns out, Billy Page is a good man. I would have never put money on it, but your love brought out the best in him."

———

CHAPTER 12

The rattle of a buggy pulled Naomi's and Emilio's attention from the horse he was saddling in the barn and they both peered up the road. "It's Hannah," she said, stepping outside to see better. Her sister was riding with Billy, holding Little Billy between them.

A sense of relief washed over Naomi. She was eager to see her little sister and had been trying to get to town. Gathering here at the ranch was much better. She could only assume the misdiagnosis of the baby was hanging over Hannah and Naomi was desperate to share her joy—not any blame.

Emilio tested the cinch on Buttercup's saddle then flipped the stirrup in place. "You're all set, Señora Naomi. Can I help you into the saddle?"

"I don't suppose I should turn down the help. I'm still pretty stiff."

Determined not to let her wounds hold her back, Naomi climbed into the saddle, with a little boost from Emilio. Moving like an old woman, holding her left arm pressed to her side, she managed to get her seat.

The brim of Emilio's cowboy hat did not hide the deep

crease in his brow. He looked decidedly uncertain about this ride. "Are you sure—?"

"I will not be bedridden. And now it looks like I won't be going far anyway. Thank you for your help." She winked at him. "I won't breathe a word to Charles if you don't."

Biting his bottom lip, he nodded and stepped back from the horse. "Sí."

Naomi took a deep breath, squeezed her thighs against Buttercup's sides and *tsked*. The horse moved and quickly they worked up from a jog that tweaked every former stitch with pain to a lope as smooth as a rocking chair.

It came to an end too quickly. "Well, what a nice surprise." She reined in her horse alongside Hannah, the transition jarring every wound. "What brings y'all out this way?"

"Should you be riding?" her sister asked, disapproval evident in her scowl.

Ever the nurse, Naomi thought. "I'm not going jumping. I'm careful."

"Charles sent for me, Naomi." Billy pulled back on the reins, slowing the team. "He around?"

"No, he hasn't come back from the lumber camp yet."

"Well, we're a little early. We can wait."

"Mollie's watching the store for us so we decided to make an afternoon of the visit." Hannah shifted Little Billy on to her lap so the boy could see better. "Can you blow Aunt Naomi a kiss?" Obediently he performed his new trick with pudgy fingers and Naomi's heart melted.

She nudged her horse closer and leaned over to ruffle the little man's hair. The exertion caused every wound to smart in protest, but she grit her teeth against the pain. "Oh, I love your kisses. You've made me so happy!" Her heart full of joy, she straightened up and simply endured the pain. "Billy, why don't you go fetch Charles? You can take Buttercup here. Hannah, we can talk over some coffee."

Billy set the brake. "Sounds like a fine idea. Girl talk while I go find the King rancher."

O n the way into the house, Naomi paused on the porch and looked out at the ranch. Spread out around them, a valley of grass turning amber for fall accommodated two thousand head of cattle. Cowboys whooped and hollered, their every move stalked by a dust cloud. Down by the river, a forest of Aspens quivered in the breeze, golden leaves fluttering to earth. Above it all, the snow-capped San Juan Mountains watched over them in majestic silence. Ever since the cougar attack, she'd found herself stopping to appreciate this view over and over. And it was even better from the back porch.

"You'll never get tired of this will you?"

Puzzled, Naomi looked over at her sister. "Tired of what?"

"The wide open spaces, the freedom, the fresh air. Charles. It's all over your face."

Naomi let an embarrassed grin break. "I am pretty happy. And I won't take any of it for granted now. Not even a single breath."

Hannah shuddered. "The bite on your shoulder was meant for your neck. He could have—"

"But he didn't," Naomi interrupted. "I'm looking at the good, not the bad. God was with me. Watching over me, strengthening me."

"Are you still having the nightmares?"

"No, at least, not every night now, but…"

"But what?"

Naomi let her gaze drift back out over the wide, sweeping valley she called home. "I dreamed about our son." She patted her stomach protectively. "He was tall, dark like Charles. A teenager in the dream." She smiled in spite of the knot forming in her throat. "And he was riding Bullet at a wide-open gallop across the field there. He dipped down between the hills...I lost sight of him." She paused, remembering what about this dream disturbed her. "Then he reappeared, only it wasn't him. It was Matthew. And I was terrified of him."

"Just because it was a scary dream, it doesn't mean—"

"Anything? I suppose, but it's happened before, my dreams turning into him. I guess in my mind he represents evil." She tugged on Hannah's sleeve. "Let's go brew a pot."

A few minutes later they were seated by the fire, holding cups of coffee and watching Little Billy scoot around on the rug, pushing a toy train and making train noises.

"Chug, chug, chug—Chooo-chooo."

Hannah smiled and turned her attention to Naomi. "I will say, Uncle Matthew sure has turned into something I don't recognize."

Naomi wrapped all ten fingers around her warm mug, dispelling a sudden chill, in spite of the fire. "I will not worry about him today. I am blessed beyond measure and there's certainly nothing he can do to change that."

"Yes," Hannah's face fell. "Speaking of blessings—"

"Hannah, I know you want to apologize, but don't bother." Naomi reached out and clutched her sister's free hand. "I'm going to have a baby. You probably saved him because you saved me—"

"But what if I'd administered the wr—"

"There are no what-ifs. Can't you see that? God used you with the knowledge you had. You saved us. Nothing else matters, Hannah. Nothing."

Hannah pulled away, taking a sip of coffee to hide blinking back tears. "We have a patient in town. A woman who nearly died from a botched abortion. She actually came and asked Hope to perform it."

Naomi had to bite back a knee-jerk and very unkind

response about the woman. But she did manage, "A prostitute?" The question itself was loaded with judgment.

Hannah nodded. "And she talked like this wasn't her first. She was so callous and so, I don't know, detached. The baby was a problem, an inconvenience. Not a human." She shook her head and exhaled a long, slow breath. "Chilling. It's just chilling someone could be that blind to the truth."

"I assume the baby died?"

Hannah nodded and Naomi again had to work to tame her tongue.

"I look at her and then us," Hannah continued. "The difference in the way we view life is astonishing. She would throw away a baby. You would do anything to have one. I would do anything to save one, especially yours."

"I know." Naomi set her coffee on the table beside her chair, the drink upsetting her stomach. A common occurrence lately. "I know, too, you'll take good care of me and your new nephew when he arrives."

"I will. And Hope will. I swanny, she's as good as a doctor. I don't think Charles knows how blessed we are to have her."

"I think he appreciates her, he's simply adamant about getting a doctor to Defiance. And I do mean adamant. He's placed ads in newspapers across the country."

"She's so skilled, I—I, well, I find her very inspiring."

Naomi tilted her head, waiting for the explanation of what Hannah *wasn't* saying.

Her little sister twisted in obvious discomfort. "Billy thinks I'm being so *patient* about the wedding because I might really want to go to nursing school."

"Don't you?"

"On the one hand, I don't think I'm worthy. On the other..." Hannah narrowed her eyes at Naomi and leaned forward a little. "What if I wanted more? How would you feel about that?"

"More than nursing school?"

"What if I wanted to be a doctor?"

"A doctor?" Naomi had not meant to scoff, but a hint of it raced out with her shock, and Hannah's face fell. Naomi berated herself for the slip up, but still... "You're serious? You want to be a doctor?"

Hannah rose and wandered a few feet away, her back to Naomi. "I'm so amazed by Hope's skills and it's obvious she could do more, be more. She makes it seem possible and there *are* a few female doctors in the country."

Naomi took a deep breath and laced her fingers together in her lap. "Well..." *That's a lot to think about.* She decided to say so. "Have you considered what you'd have to give up, how hard it would be, the amount of studying you'd have to do?"

Hannah didn't answer right away. After a long silence, she finally said, "I could do it."

"I have no doubt." Naomi rose and stood closer to the fire, her back to Hannah. "But the sacrifice. Women have to give up so much to pursue careers."

"But if you got hurt again, or if anyone I love got hurt again, think what a difference that training could make."

"Well, I think you've done a wonderful job saving lives with what little training you've had." An idea dawned on Naomi and she turned to Hannah. "You're not responsible for saving the world. You know that, right?"

Hannah shrugged a shoulder then frowned. "You don't think a woman should be a doctor?"

"What? I didn't say that."

"The sacrifices. The choices. Wife. Mother. Doctor. Either. Or."

"I don't think it's necessarily either-or, but God did make us different from men. We have different concerns and needs. Different abilities suited better to certain tasks. Generally speaking, we tend to be more emotional. Doctors need to have a certain amount of stoicism—"

"We're not as stable as men." Hannah rose as well. Anger had crept into her voice. "You don't think a woman should be a doctor."

"Stop putting words in my mouth. I never said that."

"Then what are you saying?"

Naomi took a breath to clamp down on her own irritation before speaking again. "We just have to make choices that men don't. How to raise our children if we have careers, for one. I just think you sh—" She bit that off. Hannah was not in the mood to be bossed. "I hope you ponder carefully what you might have to give up and what you really want out of life. I mean, think hard."

CHAPTER 13

*N*aomi almost failed to stifle a bored yawn. Leo LeBeaux was a fine lay preacher but the little Frenchman didn't preach with as much fire as Logan had. She missed the former gunfighter's passion in the pulpit. She also found it difficult not to be distracted by LeBeaux's ears. Large and always pink, as if the man was flushed, they stuck out more than the average set.

Frustrated with her mental rabbit trails, she shifted slightly on the hard pew and lamented the fact that LeBeaux also preached much longer than Logan had. How odd he took more time to say less.

Oh, she was just being petulant. Logan had been able to stir her soul with his heartfelt sermons. LeBeaux had a heart to preach and was learning the skill of oration. They could be patient.

However, a glance to her left at Charles and to her right at Two Spears, confirmed her suspicions. The blank, bored expressions on their faces said they missed Logan, too.

Mercifully, a few moments later, LeBeaux wrapped up his sermon on pride. Amid friendly banter, handshakes, and smiles, the congregation spilled out onto the porch. A cool day, the sky spit intermittent drops of rain at them.

Pulling her cape tighter, Naomi paused to consider Tent Town. It had changed, but only in the number of sinners. The traffic was lighter on Sundays, but clearly some of the men passing by were intoxicated, as denoted by their staggering gaits. A few women with clothes baskets on their hips tossed haughty glances at the church as they headed for the creek. Somewhere on the other side of a row of tents, the rising volume of two men arguing peppered the air with profane insults.

As Naomi and Charles stood discussing supper plans with Rebecca, Ian, Hannah, and Billy, a frail woman wearing a baleful glare, pushed between Mollie and Emilio, working surprised expression from them, and climbed the three steps to the porch. Her bloodshot eyes bored into Charles as she strode straight up to him and summarily slapped him across the face. The sound echoed down the street like a rifle shot. Naomi gasped as the group surged forward as if to protect Charles. Charles didn't move. Didn't raise a hand to his cheek. His expression didn't even change.

"My husband is dead because of you. He died in that hellhole you called a mine."

"How dare you?" Naomi took a step forward, but Charles subtly waved her off.

"Let her say what's on her mind. Maybe it will give her some peace."

"The only thing that will ever give me peace is to see you hang for the deaths of all those men." The woman's bony chin quivered with her pain. "You and Delilah."

Charles' jaw clenched. Naomi saw his throat move but still he didn't respond to the ugly accusation. His family and friends gawked at the grieving wife, but kept their silence.

"I'll take your money," she continued, "only because of my boys. But it don't buy my forgiveness."

LeBeaux slowly pushed through the congregants and faced the woman, positioning himself between her and Charles. "I am sorry for your loss, but this man is not responsible for your husband's death. And no anger, no vengeance, will return your beloved to you. You must offer forgiveness so that your wounds over this loss will heal."

The woman's eyes widened as if she couldn't believe the suggestion. "Forgive him?" She cut her eyes at Charles, and Naomi's soul recoiled at the hate she saw burning in them. "I don't have a husband. My children don't have a father. I have to leave my home because I can't afford to keep it. Forgive you? I'd like to cut out your heart."

No one said anything. The silence laid on them like a cold winter fog. Her eyes spilling tears, the woman spun and raced back down the street.

Naomi, hurting for her husband, slipped her hand into his. Every line, every muscle in his face looked brittle, like ice—a thin veneer barely hiding his pain. He had paled, the contrast between his white skin and the dark beard and eyes jarring.

"She didn't mean any of that, Charles. She's just grieving."

"The mine was as safe as a mine can be," Ian said firmly. "It was never meant to handle an explosion of dynamite. The collapse was no one's fault but Delilah's and Smith's."

Charles sighed, but didn't say anything. His gaze stayed riveted on the woman.

Assuming the last thing her husband wanted now was a large family gathering, Naomi turned to Rebecca. "I think we'll excuse ourselves from Sunday supper."

· · ·

*T*hey were halfway home before Naomi finally decided to speak, prompted by the perplexed expression on Two Spear's face in the back of the buggy. She laid a hand on Charles' thigh and said softly, "You can't keep blaming yourself. You shouldn't blame yourself at all."

"I own the mine."

"Exactly. You own it. You didn't dig the tunnels yourself. You didn't hire every single miner yourself. You certainly didn't tell Delilah to blow it up. People make their own decisions, Charles."

"The fund I set up for the widows and orphans—she took the money. All of them did. Still, there is so much hate."

"They're grieving. They need time. The money you gave them at least takes a few worries off their minds. One day, I think they'll be able to see that...and your heart. One day, we'll all be past this."

He leaned forward, resting his elbows on his knees, the reins loose in his hands, his shoulders riding high with tension. "One day."

Naomi tried to squelch her irritation but her husband wasn't acting like himself. "What's the matter with you? The old Charles McIntyre wouldn't have given a nickle about those men and their families. The new Charles McIntyre has turned himself into a whipping boy."

Charles sat up abruptly, opened his mouth to argue, she presumed, but his eyes darted back to Two Spears and he bit back whatever he was about to say.

Naomi softened her voice. "The deaths of those men are not on your head."

"Someone has to suffer for what happened."

She let out a long, exasperated breath. "Someone already did. On a cross."

*M*onday after lunch, Hannah left Little Billy with his father and headed to the doctor's office, planning to spend the afternoon with Hope. With two patients in recovery, she wondered if she should offer to work some kind of regular schedule for the next few days, something Hope could plan on.

She let herself into the office, found the sitting area empty, but heard a bed squeak in examination room one. Where they had put the soiled dove. Hannah peeked through the crack in the door and was disturbed to find Hope sitting on the patient's bed, fingers pressed to her forehead, eyes closed.

"Hope?"

Slowly, she lifted her gaze to Hannah. Puzzled when she didn't say anything, Hannah looked past her to the patient. For a moment Hannah thought she had passed, but then her chest moved—a small motion. She was barely alive.

She sighed sadly and stepped into the room. "Is she going to make it?"

"I don't know."

"The surgery was flawless. If she doesn't make it, it's not your fault." Hannah stepped over to the woman and touched her hand lightly, whispering a prayer for healing.

"I don't even know her name."

"I'll try to find out."

"If she'd just given me a chance sooner." Hope stood up and moved as if she were carrying the world on her shoulders. "How is this going to look if she dies? The new doctor losing a patient?"

Hannah searched her friend's drawn face. "Doctor?" And she knew, with inexplicable certainty, she knew. "Doctor," she said firmly.

Yet, Hope tried to deny it. "Did I say doctor? I meant nurse, of course." She turned sideways as if to slide past Hannah, but Hannah blocked her.

"You *are* a doctor, aren't you? Why lie? Why pretend to be a nurse? Did you do something wrong? Did someone else die?"

Hope stepped back. "I assure you I am a very capable nurse."

"Then tell me the truth."

Hope hung her head. Debating, Hannah assumed, and therefore didn't rush her. The woman glanced back at the sleeping—dying?—patient. "In Denver, the women's group ran me out. Said a female doctor upset the balance, so to speak. That I would have their husbands expecting them to bear children *and* become lawyers and bankers as well. An unacceptable disruption to the status quo."

"That's awful."

"Yes, and foolish and ignorant. I have a gift. I can heal people. They should have left me alone." She sniffed and lifted her chin. "Please don't tell anyone. Especially Mr. McIntyre. Not yet. I need a chance to prove myself."

"He wouldn't run you out because you're a woman."

"How would Naomi react? I believe she thinks I am a competent nurse. Would she consider me to be as competent a doctor?"

Hannah thought back to her own conversation with Naomi.

Hope snorted. "I see it on your face."

"No, no, you don't understand. And I know my sister. If she knew you were a doctor, she'd think you're every bit as capable doing either. Every bit as capable as a man."

"You think so, do you?"

"Yes. Yes, I do. She's been very encouraging about my aspirations." If not a little shocked. And maybe a touch hesitant, truth be told.

"Because nursing is primarily a woman's field. Tell her you want to be a doctor and see if her attitude changes."

"I'm sure it wouldn't." Her voice lacked conviction. Naomi

had expressed doubts, but only about Hannah and her goals, not about her potential skill or giftedness. Hope, on the other hand, had already achieved her medical license. "You have a gift from God. My sisters would expect you to use it."

"God." It seemed it took some effort for Hope not to sneer. "I don't know what God expects, but people have very definite expectations of what women can and should do. Often the expectations seem to clash."

Hannah wanted to ask Hope about her distance from God, but decided this wasn't the time. "You want me to hold my peace?"

Hope looked down and fidgeted with her own fingernails. "Yes. If you would. I will tell Mr. McIntyre and Naomi. I just need a little more time." She glanced back over her shoulder at the patient in the bed.

———

*A*rms loaded with a box of canned tomatoes, Billy emerged from the back room of the mercantile and drew to an abrupt halt. Hannah was leaning on the counter, twirling a lock of her pony tail around her finger, studying a medical book Hope had loaned her. Beside it lay the Montgomery Ward catalog opened to wedding dresses.

The juxtaposition of the choices was glaring and made Billy uneasy. He would move wherever Hannah needed to, to go to nursing school. He had meant that when he said it. He believed Hannah could have both—a nursing career and a family. If he believed it, surely she did.

Didn't she? Did she think she had to choose between family and career? He walked up and gently set the box on the counter. "Are you pondering Chantilly lace or setting broken bones?"

Startled, she stood up. "Oh, well, at the moment, compression fractures to the spine, but," she swiped up the catalog as if to convince him the gowns were important as well, "I've already ordered a gown. You can't see it." She pressed the catalog to her chest.

Billy pondered the news. "I'm glad to hear it. And I know you'll be beautiful in whichever one you get." He decided to test a theory. "What have you learned about compression fractures? What are they?"

Her face lit up and her enthusiasm bubbled over as she explained the injury. "They're fractures that occur when a break collapses one or more vertebrae of the spine. They are linked to osteoporosis or thinning of the bone tissue. It is most often seen in the elderly and the infirm."

Billy's heart sank. Taken aback by the sudden change, he turned to the case of tomatoes. Tomatoes. He was happy here in this small town among friends and family, running a hotel and a mercantile.

Would that life be a prison for Hannah? Would small town life be enough if she came back here as a nurse?

"Billy, what's the matter?"

He hadn't meant to show anything, but they were only weeks away from the wedding. Married. A life commitment. "You have to search your heart, Hannah. You have to make some choices." He turned to her. "I want to be a part of your life, but I won't be an anchor, something that holds you back, drags you down. What do you want out of life? Is it here? With me?"

Hannah deflated as if she'd been called an ugly name. "Why are you even asking me these questions?"

"The change in you from talking about the dress to talking about compression fractures was like night and day. Maybe we should postpone the wedding again."

Her mouth fell open. Billy couldn't believe he'd offered up the idea, but maybe they both needed a little time to figure out their future plans and goals. *God, what would I do if I lost her?*

He took her hand, to reassure her and himself. "I love you

more than the air I breathe, and I believe you love me." He touched her cheek. "Which is why I can say with everything in me, I want you to be happy. I also thought we had things figured out, but maybe we don't." Hannah started to argue, he knew, but he raised a hand to her lips. "Think about what you want, Hannah. We'll talk about it at dinner tonight."

---

*C*harles laid his hand on the plaque imbedded on the mountain near the mine entrance and closed his eyes. He could recite every name on it by memory. Some good men, some bad men, were buried beneath his feet.

What's the matter with you? Naomi's words brought his head up. *The old Charles McIntyre wouldn't have given a nickle about those men and their families. The new Charles McIntyre has turned himself into a whipping boy.*

Someone has to suffer for what happened.

Someone already did.

On a cross.

Charles removed his hat and fanned his face with it, thinking, ruminating. His sins were forgiven. And, as Naomi had so eloquently pointed out, he couldn't pay for the sins of the men who'd died.

He had tried to protect them. He had tried to mitigate the risks, run as safe an operation as possible. But there was always the unforeseen. A man should be ready to meet his maker at any moment.

The catastrophe perpetrated by Delilah was more the fault of a broken, vengeful heart than a lapse in safety standards.

Delilah.

She'd walked away, slithered off into the darkness. Did she have nightmares? Did she feel the loss of these men? The deaths had affected her, but Charles believed Logan's death had rattled her more. A loss from which he doubted she would ever recover.

Part of him hoped she was miserable. Wracked with guilt. Sitting alone in the corner of a dusty saloon fading away.

Suffering as Charles had suffered.

The spiteful thought brought him up short. He had no right to feel this way about her. Jesus had suffered for all this. The sins of murder, pride, selfishness, greed, bitterness. Everything that led to the explosion. Continuing to carry the burden or wish it on Delilah made the cross pointless.

Help me, Lord. I'll do the best I can to let it go. Of all of it.

Charles let his hand fall and straightened up. The offer from MP&G Western Mining Conglomerate rustled in his breast pocket. Decided, he dropped his hat back in place.

The town can be saved, Lord. I don't know about Delilah.

I'm going to be a father. It's time to move past this.

CHAPTER 14

*H*ope dished a tiny amount of broth to her weak but conscious patient. The woman, whom they had discovered was named Mary Ann, was pale as a cadaver but alive and kicking—well, alive anyway. She could barely hold her eyes open, but after three days of murky consciousness, Hope had to try to get something in her. Fear, however, wiggled in her gut at the unspoken but dire prognosis.

The warm liquid poured into the woman's mouth. Mary Ann closed her eyes and swallowed. Hope breathed a little easier and offered more. Each time she had to touch the patient's lips to get her to take the sip, but soon the small cup was empty.

"That's a start." Hope set the dishware down on the night stand. "Can you tell me how you feel?"

"Like dog vomit," the woman answered unexpectedly in a weak, raspy voice.

"Whoever performed your abortion punctured your uterus. You nearly bled to death."

The woman's eyes fluttered open, a startling green against

the pallor of her skin and bold red hair. "I knew something was wrong. Too much blood."

"You should have come to me straightaway."

"You shoulda done it."

Hope knew what she meant, and the comment was like an ice pick to her heart, pricking her conscience, confusing her moral compass. "I told you, I save lives. I don't take them."

"Lucky for me." She tried to moisten her lips. Hope poured her a glass of water and helped her drink. "Thanks. I don't know what you're so worked up about," she said between sips, her voice growing a little stronger. "I saw it once. It weren't nothing but clumps of blood."

Hope, too, had seen both aborted and miscarried fetuses. Different stages of development. "Though I do not believe in God, Mary Ann, I do think it presumptuous of humans to arbitrarily declare when a clump of blood crosses over to life."

Mary Ann waved a weak hand at her in disgust and pulled away the water. "You don't believe in God but you won't end a pregnancy. You don't make no sense." The woman's body relaxed and Hope could tell she was on the verge of sleeping.

"Mary Ann, can you tell me who performed your procedure?"

"Why?"

Hope thought a noble lie was called for. "Training. I could train her so this doesn't happen again."

"Amanda. How long...how long have I b...?"

"How long have you been here?" The woman nodded. "Three days. You'll be several more recuperating. And I'd suggest you take a few months away from your vocation, if you don't retire altogether."

Mary Ann snorted sleepily. "Too long." She drifted off. "Too long to be away."

*A*manda swaggered into the Crystal Chandelier, rewarding the hungry stares of patrons with her own inviting glances. A pretty negro girl, Matthew thought, but her vocation was showing on her. Wearing a low-cut gown, Amanda didn't exactly glow; her caramel skin was, in fact, a little dull; her eyes didn't glitter with life, only reflected a weary soul. Weariness that she masked with anger or bravado, whichever suited the occasion.

She spotted him at the bar and made her way toward him with a determined stride. Curious, he laid aside the latest fine from Ian—this one for violating the town's gambling laws. So far, he'd paid one thousand dollars in fines. If the MP&G deal didn't come through or business didn't pick up fast—well, there were no *ifs*. Something had to happen.

He wasn't going to pay this town another red cent.

Amanda was one of the few soiled doves he had working who hadn't been caught yet. Beckwith was a bloodhound, though. Probably wouldn't take him much longer. Maybe such was the reason for her visit.

"Afternoon, Amanda," he said as she approached. "What brings you around before sundown?"

"I ain't your madam, so you could say I'm here as a favor. Thought you might like to know about Mary Ann."

It took him a moment. The older, prickly redhead? "What about Mary Ann?"

"She nearly died. I would have bet against her living, but the new nurse in town got to her. So, she ain't dead. Yet. I hear the jury is still out."

Matthew didn't quite follow this disjointed tale. "What happened to her? Where is she?"

"She tried to get rid of her baby and it didn't go well. She nearly bled to death, but this nurse has her now and is watching over her. Mary Ann might make it."

Matthew considered the news. Mary Ann was popular because she was greedy. She rarely turned away a man because it was late, she was tired, or even had her monthly. He wondered how long she would be down.

"You don't mind me sayin' so, Mr. Miller, you either need to manage your girls more closely or get yourself a madam."

"I don't need any help managing women."

"A good madam knows things. How to keep the girls in line, get 'em turning more money, where to go to get rid of a baby. What to do after. You know any of that?"

Matthew scratched his neck. "Maybe not as much as I should. I made my money in lumber. Whores were recreation."

"You should get a madam then. And I'll tell you something else."

"Well, you're just full of advice today."

The girl glanced at the fine laying on the bar. "I worked for a house over in Omaha. The town fathers tried to shut us down, too. Hit us with fines and violations. Made up vice laws just to confound us. You know what the owner did?"

"No, but I bet you're going to tell me."

"She moved. The whole operation. Outside the city limits. Five feet over the line."

Matthew raised his head, intrigued by the suggestion. "That isn't practical for me. I can't move the Crystal Chandelier. I've got too much in this building."

"Tents are cheap. Besides, what have you paid in fines so far?" She held Matthews' stare for a moment, then shrugged. "Happy to help if I can."

With that, she drifted off through the slim crowd of attentive men, nodding, smiling, swinging her hips, stirring up business for the night. At the bat wings, she glanced back at Matthew—a smug grin on her lips—and pushed out into the sunlight, the fall breeze swirling a handful of leaves into the saloon.

Well, the gal had given Matthew a few things to think about.

Did he really have time for wrangling soiled doves anyway? He did have more important fish to fry and the bigger plan was beginning to absorb more and more of his time. Just getting Sally to slap ol' Charles across the snout at church had taken a day of conversation and two double eagles. But the word was she had pulled off the attack with gut-wrenching perfection.

The thought lifted his spirits and he pondered having one of his girls come by for a visit. After all, a benefit of this setup was a little *personal recreation* any time he felt like it. Only, ever since he'd heard about Naomi being with child he had not been availing himself.

He felt differently now. Focused. Determined. Like things were on the verge of changing—in his favor. Amanda and her big ideas were inspiring.

He grinned.

In more ways than one.

$\mathcal{T}$wo days later Matthew finally admitted Amanda was on to something. When he found himself hunched over in a sagging, dirty tent, two screaming, cursing, writhing soiled doves snared in the crook of each arm, he decided he'd had enough. He was no nanny. He had better things to do than settle petty squabbles.

"I know you went through my drawers," one girl snarled.

"I ain't been in your tent," the other snapped back.

"I smelled your cheap perfume!"

"Stop it right now," Mathew's voice boomed.

The girls ignored him and continued squirming, twisting, striking out, intent on sinking their nails into each other. They were tiny compared to his massive girth and holding them was easy but tedious.

Fine. His patience gone, he squeezed until the fight went out of both of them and they clawed helplessly at his arms. Then he held on a little longer till they lost consciousness. Reflecting on how golden the silence was, he dropped them to the dirt floor like rag dolls.

He sliced the air with his hands, divorcing himself of the mess and swore, *I am not doing this again.* He flung the tent flap back and stormed onto the dusty, rutted path that wound through Tent Town.

"Amanda!" He bellowed. Hers was the last tent in the row of six and he stomped toward her abode, a few passing miners watching with curious stares. "Amanda!"

Before he reached her threshold, she stepped out to meet him, followed by a blue-gray cloud of smoke and the sweet smell of opium. That brought him up short. "I thought you quit that."

"Oh, I did." A sound came from the tent and a moment later Will Boggess appeared beside her, his dull brown eyes droopy, dreamy. Amanda shoved him back into her tent. "Sleep it off, Will." She grabbed Matthew's arm and pulled him away from her home. "Let's you and me take a walk."

Matthew was not averse to the idea and let the girl lead him. She was half-dressed, wearing only a low-cut shift, corset, and petticoat. He saw the goose flesh rise on her arms and peeled off his blanket coat. "Here."

She slipped into it, all but disappearing inside the huge girth of it. "You here about my idea?"

"Yep."

She pulled the coat tighter. "Then here's my offer. Move all these tents outside the town limits. Promise to build me a cabin, and I'll manage your girls for twenty-five percent."

"Twenty-five percent?" She was crazy. "I'm not giving you that much of a cut."

"Whatever these girls are bringing in now, I can double it.

That'd be worth your while. You wouldn't fuss over twenty-five percent then."

Matthew's irritation was simmering. He began to suspect Amanda was still smoking opium. "How do you propose to double what these girls are doing? Sounds pretty pie-in-the-sky to me."

"How often you come down here to check on them?"

"Once a week. Sometimes twice."

"Exactly. You don't stay on top of 'em. They sleep till three or four in the afternoon. Don't start taking customers till dark. Don't take customers after one or two in the morning, if the notion strikes. They need a task master."

"And you've got experience with that?"

The subtle lines in her face hardened. "Oh, yes."

Matthew rubbed his neck, thinking things over. "Move the tents, huh?"

"You had any sense, you'd open another saloon outside the city limits, too."

She'd pointed out that tents were cheap. He'd been pondering her wise but arrogantly delivered advice ever since they'd talked. "All right." He stopped walking. "I'll move the tents. You manage the girls. But first I've got to find a place."

A sly, all-knowing grin twitched on her dark pink lips. "Kentucky Jack is letting his three claims go. Says they're played out. They're side-by-side and plenty big enough for everything we want to do."

Matthew almost chuckled but bit it back. Amanda was hungry. A hungry madam was apt to bite the hand that fed her. Screams like banshees at war erupted from the tent where he'd left the gals on the floor and he made up his mind. "Well, I'll get by there and talk to him. In the meantime…" He gestured grandly, bowing and sweeping his arm in the direction of the feuding women. "They're all yours…"

. . .

*M*atthew left Amanda to deal with the squabbling hens and nearly jogged back to the Chandelier, his mood now was so light. Something told him he'd made the right choice hiring Amanda and he felt like a kid who'd managed to steal candy from the dry goods store. Moving the girls and maybe opening a rowdier saloon just outside the town limits would toss a monkey wrench into McIntyre's and Donoghue's plan to close him down. Child's play, however, compared to what he'd like to do McIntyre...and Naomi.

As he approached the Chandelier, a freckle-faced boy in a Western Union cap saw him coming and ran up to him. "Got this for you, Mr. Miller."

Matthew backed up a step and glanced at the yellow envelope. A telegram. He fished some change out of his pocket and exchanged it with the boy for the notice.

Well, this could be the door to a fortune or one slamming in my face. He swiped a hand over his lips. "Here goes nothing..." Heart pounding, he snatched the telegram out, tossing the envelope to the wind.

Two words greeted him: OFFER ACCEPTED.

He smacked the note against his palm in victory and slid his gaze up the busy path that led to Defiance's Main Street. Laughing, he nearly kicked his heels together on his way into the Crystal Chandelier. Oh, the things he had to plan. The people he had to hire.

The lives he had to destroy.

If idle hands are the devil's playground, Naomi, just wait till you see what he does with willing hands...

CHAPTER 15

s Charles strode down Water Street, the main thoroughfare in Tent Town, he was taken aback by the decline in the area. There were fewer people on the road; the tents had weathered noticeably since his last trip here. More weeds than he remembered grew along some of the less traveled paths. The denizens stirring about were bleary-eyed and slow moving. The strong scents of opium, bacon, and wood fires hung in the chilly air.

The mine closing and the creek playing out was killing Defiance and the rot had started in this quarter. Very little gold, less work. No urgent reason to get out of bed.

Well, Lord, mining might kill them, but so will opium and hopelessness. We'll get this town moving again.

The goal was the only thing giving him the humility to seek out Matthew and offer the man a deal. The idea turned his stomach, but it could rid Defiance of a pestilence and put a lumberyard in Charles' hand. If Matthew was hard up enough for money, he might say yes.

And leave Defiance.

Convinced this course of action was the right one, he strode on toward Matthew's home, the Crystal Chandelier.

Without its raunchy shows and rowdy crowds, the saloon and theater was a ghost of itself. Thumbs tucked in his vest pockets, Charles stood at the doors, peering over them at a meager noon rush. The piano rested silently in the corner, the muttering voices of men enjoying liquid lunches the only sound in the smoky air. He pushed in and scanned the room but did not see Matthew.

"Something I can help you with, McIntyre?" A velvety, baritone voice asked.

Charles cut his eyes to the left. Otis looked up at him from a grouping of chairs he was in the process of painting. Charles liked the mountain of a man much better engaged in such peaceable pursuits. He hoped it stayed that way.

Letting the doors swing shut behind him, he said, "I've come to see Matthew. Is he around?"

Otis laid his brush down across a bucket of paint and rose like a behemoth stirring to life. "He's upstairs." His wide, ebony face hardened with disdain. "I'll see if he's available."

In other words, would he deign to meet with his rival? Charles tried not to take offense. He was in the enemy camp now. Matthew had tried to steal Naomi, and then let an Indian take a clear shot at Charles' back. There was no love lost between the two men, to say the least.

Matthew had hung on in Defiance longer than Charles had expected, but he knew the man was struggling financially. Perhaps today he could drive the final nail in the coffin.

He sensed a glare and looked up. Mathew watched him from the top of the stairs, the heat of his gaze almost a physical slap. Taller even than Otis, wider in the shoulders, but light in every way the Haitian was dark, Matthew leaned into his employee and whispered something. Otis nodded, sauntered down the steps and slipped behind the bar.

Matthew ambled down after a moment and waved McIntyre over. They met at the mahogany as Otis slipped a bottle and two glasses between them. "What brings you to my humble establishment, McIntyre?"

Tension sizzled between them as their eyes, at about the same height, locked, though Matthew was almost as wide in the shoulders as Charles was tall. The two men had not spoken since Matthew's arrival in town, when Charles had warned him about the newly passed Red Light Abatement Laws.

Thus far, the fines had not chased Matthew out of town. Maybe money would nudge him. "I've come to make you an offer for your lumberyard and saloon. I'll buy them both."

Matthew's icy, hazel eyes widened and he turned to the bar. "Well, now." He poured himself a shot, offered the bottle to Charles who waved it away. Matthew capped it, picked up his own drink, swirled the liquor. Charles clamped his jaw, intent on not showing any impatience over this game.

Finally, Matthew tossed back the drink and set down the glass with a loud clink. "They're not for sale."

"You haven't heard my offer."

"Wouldn't change anything."

Charles shifted, resting his back and elbows on the bar so he could survey the crowd. *Crowd* being a generous description. "How much longer can you hold on? Beckwith wants to raid your cribs, arrest your girls. We can keep coming at you. Pass more public nuisance laws."

Matthew poured himself another shot. A slow grin lifted his lips and Charles knew something was going on here he didn't comprehend. "I hear you're selling the mine."

He couldn't even begin to imagine how Matthew had come by that bit of information, but he held his best poker face. *How* didn't matter. The *what* did. What did Matthew think he was going to get out of holding this information? Charles would argue nothing of value.

"What I do with the Sunnyside won't affect you. We're going to legislate you out of Defiance. Go with some money in your pocket or not. It's up to you. But you will go."

"But why would you want to buy my lumberyard?" Matthew mused, ignoring the threat. "Oh," he snapped his fingers. "You need a sawmill for all that lumber you're bringing off the mountain for your spur line."

Charles scratched his bearded jaw to hide his shock. Matthew had entirely too much information about his business. The intelligence could have only come from a few sources. Namely, his railroad contacts. He would find and plug the leak. Later. Right now, he had to reestablish the upper hand with Matthew.

"It would have made things easier for me to buy your lumberyard and go from there. A little faster, but no matter." He lifted a brow in victory. "I'll build my own. Which will further impact your bottom line. Remember, I did offer."

The troubling smirk did not leave Matthew's face. "Yes, yes you did."

*W*ould the bad news ever stop coming when it came to Amanda?

Depressed, Hannah set down the fresh sheets at the foot of Mary Ann's bed and nearly sighed aloud.

Hope, about to examine their patient, looked up. "I can see by your face you recognize the name." She pulled the stethoscope from around her neck and straightened. "You know the woman who did this to her?"

Hannah nodded. So much potential. Such a shame. "She used to be one of Charles' Flowers back when the Iron Horse was open. She left for a while, came back, and when she did, he offered to send her to school rather than see her go back into that work."

"My, that was magnanimous of him. What did she want to do?"

"Be a teacher. She said. Charles was going to set up a scholarship for her, pay her way. She walked away from it." Hope didn't say anything and Hannah figured, like all of them, Amanda's actions left her speechless. "She had an opium addiction," she continued. "Emilio and Mollie tried to help her through it, but she won't leave her current vocation."

Hope gripped the stethoscope, her knuckles turning white. With a sigh, she dragged a hand over her hair, poked absently at her bun. "Apparently she's attempting to add new skills to her bag."

"Abortion?"

"Yes. Her ignorance and lack of experience is clear. It's a wonder Mary Ann is still with us."

"Because you have the skills." A troubling thought bubbled up in Hannah. "Do you think Amanda is going to keep providing this service?"

"You know her better than I, what do you think?"

Hannah couldn't tell if the question was rhetorical. Nonetheless, she pondered her few run-ins with Amanda, mulled over the comments Mollie had made about her. "I think she will, yes. She strikes me as greedy. As someone who wants money and power now, anyway she can round it up."

"Then I will go see the marshal about her. If a woman dies from another botched abortion, I won't be able to live with myself. She has to be stopped."

"I know Marshal Beckwith well. I'll go with you, if you'd like."

"That's probably wise. The both of us voicing our concerns may spur him to action."

"*N*ot a thing I can do." The marshal reached for a cold cigar sitting in the ash tray on his desk. His bony face, usually hard, intimidating, softened as he lit the stogie. "Dang shame."

"Nothing?" Hope said, taking an incredulous step back from his desk.

He blew smoke heavenward for a moment, and the ladies gave him time to answer, but Hannah was antsy. She sat down on the edge of the seat in front of his desk. "I don't believe that."

"The town has been incorporated. Ian is the acting mayor. I'm duly sworn. Inside those lines," he pointed lazily to a map of Defiance hanging on his wall behind him, "I'm the law. Outside of them, I don't have any jurisdiction."

"Well...well," Hannah sputtered. "We can pass more laws. We can—"

"Won't change anything. Miller has pulled a fast one on us."

"What do you mean?" Hannah asked.

Marshal Beckwith leaned back and rested a foot across his knee. "He moved his operation. Outside Defiance's limits by about thirty feet."

"What?" Hope folded her arms over her chest angrily.

"Yep, he told me straight up he wasn't going to close his saloon or stop running girls. But he would leave town. Now I know he was laughing at me when he said it."

"Move them. He just moved them?" Hannah couldn't believe the man she used to call *uncle* had turned into such a lying, deceitful, manipulative monster. What had happened to his soul?

"Marshal—" Hope started, worked her lips silently for a moment and finally managed, "can you give us any encouragement? Any advice?"

"Yeah, get her to break the law inside the limits."

Hannah hung her head. There had to be something they could—

"What if Mary Ann pressed charges?" Hope asked softly.

"Who's Mary Ann?"

"My patient. The reason we're here. The one this Amanda nearly killed."

"If the crime happened inside the town limits and if she'll press charges, I'll arrest Amanda and get her bail set high as I can. Sounds to me like this is a couple of big ifs."

Hope sighed. "Yes, it is. But I'll try. Amanda is a butcher. One of these girls is going to die if we don't stop her. So, I have to do something."

Hannah agreed with all that, but couldn't shake the feeling Hope was warring with just what the *something* should be.

———

CHAPTER 16

*C*harles had a million and one things to do. He did not have time to take a jaunt off the trail. He needed to get to the lumber camp. Yet, when he passed the rugged path that led down to his ranch—by way of the ridge—something tugged at him. The October breeze and skittering aspen leaves seemed to beckon to him to follow them.

He drummed his fingers on the saddle horn pondering, debating. *Is this a whim, or Your Spirit leading me, Lord?*

He decided the insistent nudge to go look for the cat was not based solely on his own nagging worry. He gently pressed his knee into Traveller and tugged the reins. The horse obeyed and down the path they went, at a slow, meticulous pace.

Charles didn't know what he was looking for. Bones? The cat had to be dead. Still...

He scanned the rocks, the pebble-strewn path, a bare and dying blueberry patch—where Naomi had been attacked. The memory of her screams and her body in the jaws of the animal made him flinch and whisper a prayer of gratitude for her survival.

He pushed on. The elevation rose quickly and he emerged

on the barren, rocky ridge, Traveller's hooves echoing dully on the granite. The noon day sun heated the rocks, raising the temperature here to a level that had a few lizards skittering about. Yet, the place felt...haunted.

Puzzled at this unease in his soul, Charles shrugged away a chill then dismounted. He walked around, surveying the rocks and the myriad crevices. Nothing. Of course, the cat could have crawled beneath a rock or even into the pines to die. He glanced skyward. And if the buzzards had found him, they would have finished their work long before now.

Yet he hadn't seen any circling in the sky on his trips to the lumber camp.

He sucked in his cheek and tried to picture the cat. Where it would have been before attacking. Where it would have run after getting shot.

Charles turned and noticed the outcropping of rocks several yards up that overlooked the blueberries. Dropping Traveller's reins, he plucked his rifle from the scabbard and started climbing.

A good ten, sweaty minutes later, he crested a ledge and discovered the opening to his den. Hands on the rifle, he quickly surveyed the low, shallow cave. No cat. He breathed a little easier, but chided himself for stumbling on to the lair. The hair on the back of his neck stood up as he realized the animal could be watching him from anywhere.

He glanced down at Traveller. Calm and steady, the grey Saddlebred swished his tail every now and then as if imagining flies on the cool day. Charles took a deep breath and moved closer to the cave. Just a foot or so in he leaned over and studied the space.

Dried blood, now the color of rust covered the floor of rock, leaves, and small branches. Dried yes, but the floor had been disturbed. Repeatedly. And the remains of a rabbit sat in the corner. Flesh still clung to the bones. A fresh kill.

The realization snaked its way into his consciousness.

He'd survived.

The cat was still alive.

Stunned by the inarguable fact, he squatted down for a closer look. Then he saw them: two, small footprints in the dust.

Moccasins.

"*I* don't know. It's bad enough he's got a half-breed son I gotta pussy-foot around. Having a Mexican Indian for a boss turns my stomach."

Emilio jerked to a halt just before coming around the corner of the bunkhouse. There couldn't be any doubt who Buck, the new hand, was referring to.

"Listen, hoss," Lane's easy Texas drawl drifted on the breeze, "you just do the work and keep your mouth shut. You cross either one of those Indians and McIntyre will fall on you so hard you'll think the hand of God hath struck you. Trust me. I've seen what he can do."

"Ah," the man spat, "I ain't afraid of Mr. Fancy Pants."

"Well," wood squeaked as if Lane was rising off the porch railing, "I can fix a lot of things but stupid ain't one of 'em. Ask around. You don't come to the truth on your own, I'm sure McIntyre will enlighten you."

Lane stepped off the porch, rounded the corner and nearly walked into Emilio. Both men stared at each other for a moment, then Lane raised his dusty cowboy hat in greeting and walked on by. Emilio understood. He did not need a nanny. He didn't need Lane or Señor McIntyre to fight his battles. Neither did he want to look for trouble, but Emilio had already seen what prejudice simmering in the ranch hands could do. One man a while back had tried to hurt Two Spears.

To his eternal regret.

Well, Emilio would handle his own problems, keep Señor McIntyre out of them, and make sure no one tried to hurt the boy again.

He sucked in a deep breath and stepped around the corner into the last rays of the setting sun—and Buck's line of sight. Sitting on the porch, rolling a cigarette, the man brought the paper to his lips and paused. He was a greasy mongrel with thin, drab-gray hair and a long scar down his left cheek. Trouble waiting to happen. Not the best hire Lane had ever made.

Buck's dry lips curled into a sneer. "Something I can help you with?" His voice was raspy and deep.

"The foreman was giving you good advice, señor. Charles McIntyre is no one to make an enemy of, but then," he paused for effect, "neither am I. Lane can't fix stupid. I believe I can."

Buck's sneer faded and he looked a little uncertain. Quickly, though, he brought his head up a touch. "Some day I might take you up on the offer." He ran his tongue over his teeth, as if evaluating the situation. "Yeah, I reckon today's not the day, though."

His bland tone sounded as if he was taking other things into consideration and decided to heed them. Regardless, he did not take Emilio's offer for a fight and Emilio couldn't push it. At least not honorably. "Any time you change your mind, let me know." Puzzled as to why the man had backed off, Emilio started to walk on by, but thought a clarification of something might be in order. This man was trouble, regardless of the words coming out of his mouth. "Two Spears is like a little brother to me. You understand this?"

Buck's eyebrow twitched and he nodded. "Sure."

———

CHAPTER 17

*C*harles could appreciate the difficult path of becoming a man. A good man. His own father had certainly been a less-than-stellar example of wise and noble parenting.

And this was why it took Charles several days to determine how best to deal with Two Spears. The boy had been in the cat's den. Alone. The animal could have killed him, eaten him, and they might never have found him. His stomach fluttered at the horror of the idea, made all too real by the images of the cat jumping Naomi.

But then Charles looked down at the squirming, panting, black-and-white ball of fluff in his arms and smiled. *Thank you, Lord, for protecting Two Spears. Now I'll do my part.*

He rounded the corner of the barn and his grin widened. Foreman and old war buddy Lane Chandler was showing Two Spears a roping trick. The lariat floated over their heads in a huge circle, Lane controlling its spin with great skill.

"Now, when I say jump, boy, jump."

Two Spears nodded at the foreman and readied himself.

In perfect Texas cowboy form, Lane turned the rope and it spun vertically beside them like a whirling door. "Now." Lane snatched the rope and instantly he and Two Spears jumped through it. "One more time." Again, Lane snatched the rope and in a blink of an eye, he and the boy leaped through.

Two Spears was laughing uncontrollably holding his sides, as Lane slowed the lariat, dropped it to the ground and reeled it in.

The laughter and the smiles were infectious. Perhaps the man was letting go of some his bigotry toward Indians. "Lane, it's good to see you haven't lost your touch."

Two Spears's laughter faltered, but returned, and then his eyes landed on the creature in Charles's arms. "What is that?" He hurried over, the rope trick all but forgotten. "I have never seen a dog with so much hair."

He reached for the puppy and Charles let him go. The animal licked and barked and carried on happily in the arms of his new owner. Behind him, Lane pretended to grumble as he reeled in his rope. "Sure. One-up me with a puppy. And he's right. That's a hairy critter. What is it?"

Charles straightened up and shoved his hands in his pockets. "That is a Laika. A sled dog from Russia. I got him off Stanislav Kuznetsov. He assures me he will be a loyal companion and fearless watchdog."

"Can I keep him? Look at his eyes," Two Spears whispered, taken with the dog. "As blue as Deer Lake."

"I got him for you, Two Spears. Every boy needs a dog." *To keep him out of trouble.* Pleased his plan seemed to be going so well, Charles knelt down to get eye level with the boy and the squirming pup. "But you must listen to me. He is small and young. Watch him closely. Everything out here will try to carry him off. Keep him close to the ranch until he is much older and much bigger."

A hint of suspicion percolated in the boy's expression. "How long will that be?"

"Oh, not long. He'll grow fast. But right now, everything

from eagles, to coyotes, to cougars," he emphasized the last one, "will want him for supper."

The boy stuck out his chest and raised his chin. "I will watch over him and, then, together we will kill that cat."

Charles tried not to let his concern over the ill-advised plan show, so he smiled and changed the subject. "What will you call your new friend?"

Two Spears thought only for a moment. "Hestoxena'hane."

"Hest...ox..." Charles faded off. "That is a mouthful. What does it mean?"

The boy's dark eyes hardened into agates. "Cat Killer."

---

*N*aomi had her hand on the Doctor's office doorknob when it opened suddenly and she found herself staring into Hannah's wide, China blue eyes. "Oh," Naomi pressed a hand to her chest, startled. "I was coming to see you. Join me for lunch?"

"Ah, praise the Lord, you're a godsend." Hannah grabbed Naomi and dragged her inside the doctor's office. "I thought I was going to have to run all the way there and back. I need to send a telegram and Mary Ann is sleeping. I would feel so much better if there was someone here to watch over her. Would you mind staying for a few minutes while I step out?"

"Of course not."

"Thank you. I won't be gone long at all, but I'd feel better if you were here. She's feverish. If she wakes up, tell her I'll be right back."

"Where's Hope?"

"Tent Town. They found a man unconscious in his tent this morning and sent for her."

Hannah seemed flustered as she hugged Naomi and barreled

out the door. Naomi stood on the threshold for a moment, tapping her fingers nervously on her thighs.

She wanted to take a peek at this Mary Ann. The arrogant phrase tweaked her conscience. *This Mary Ann.* As if the woman was a monster to be ogled.

Oh, I'm sorry, Lord. While she makes me angry, I know you love her. Help me see her with your eyes.

But the baby...

Her hands went to the small bulge barely showing at her abdomen. A child she didn't know but already loved with a frightening ferociousness. And, yet, there were people who would discard a child like a piece of trash and that angered her.

I'm sorry, Lord, she apologized again. *I'm not being very kind with this matter.*

Determined to give her judgmental attitude to the Lord, Naomi slipped quietly into the woman's room and sat down in the chair beside the bed. Naomi marveled over the patient's astonishingly bright red hair, but her skin was ghostly pale, which made the feverish flush to her cheeks brighter as well. Beads of sweat peppered her forehead and upper lip. Her breathing was shallow, a touch ragged.

Any other patient would have provoked a little sympathy from Naomi. She would have perhaps taken the towel from the water bowl and laid it across her brow. She could do so now, but the action would be born of duty and not love.

Struggling with her feelings about a woman who could so coldly cast away a baby, she forced herself to dig for some compassion. She wrung the towel to dampness, folded it, and gently laid it across Mary Ann's forehead.

At first Naomi thought she had managed the action without waking the patient, but then Mary Ann's eyes opened. Cold, glittering jade, they stormed with suspicion when she discovered Naomi.

"Who are you?"

"Hannah's sister. She ran to the telegraph office. She'll be back shortly."

The woman grunted, closed her eyes again. Naomi looked around the spartan little room, wondering if she should say something else, but—to her shame—had no desire at all to engage Mary Ann in conversation.

Maybe she'll just keep her eyes shut and go back to sleep—

"You ain't like her." The woman's voice barely topped a whisper.

"Pardon?"

"Hannah. You ain't like her. You're judgy."

Naomi frowned. She assumed she knew what the word meant, but why would Mary Ann use it? "I'm not sure I understand."

"I can tell just by the way you were looking at me. The set of your jaw."

Naomi inhaled deeply at the cut, but let out the breath quietly. "You're right. Hannah told me why you're here. It's hard —no, impossible—for me to understand how someone can do what you did to something so innocent."

Mary Ann swallowed, opened her eyes and looked hard at Naomi. "And somebody like you will never understand."

"Somebody like me?"

"Holier than thou. All full of yourself. Probably married. Got a husband who takes care of you. Ever had to work a day in your life?" She snatched her gaze away. "Besides, it ain't even a baby that early."

"Who I am or what I have or haven't done doesn't change one simple thing. What you did ended a life." Anger had crept into her voice and Naomi prayed for kindness or possibly to be struck mute. She closed her eyes and managed, "I'm sorry. I understand your life is hard," she said, trying to sound gentle, "but taking life is wrong."

After a moment, Mary Ann nodded and looked as if she was

trying to keep her chin from quivering. "Yeah, maybe the wrong one of us died."

"That's not what I meant to imply."

"Don't matter." Mary Ann sighed heavily. "Layin' here sure has given me time to think. A lot of mistakes to tally." She shook her head as if disgusted by what the cataloging had revealed. "A lot of mistakes."

Naomi opened her mouth, desperate to say something deep, about God's love, about redemption, but nothing came out. She heard the front door and thanked God Hannah was back.

She couldn't shake the feeling, however, that she'd lost an important battle. Missed an opportunity. The guilt weighed heavily on her.

Next time, she promised God as she stood. *Next time, Lord, I'll be gentler. I'll try not to be so sanctimonious. Soften my heart.*

CHAPTER 18

*R*ebecca bounced her gaze back and forth between Hannah and Naomi. A rare treat, all three of them had managed to gather for breakfast at the inn. The room was filled with the rumble of muttering guests and the heavenly scents of blueberry pancakes, coffee, and bacon. As Rebecca buttered a slice of sourdough bread, Hannah and Naomi were looking at the Montgomery Ward catalog, opened to the gown she'd ordered. Their conversation struck Rebecca, though, as a bit listless.

She had the sense both of them were distracted and trying to hide it. Naomi had let her coffee get cold. Hannah hadn't touched her pancakes. None of them had laughed yet.

"So, you went ahead and got it?" Rebecca asked, puzzled by the odd mood at the table.

"Yes. I'm very happy with it."

I didn't say you weren't, Rebecca thought, puzzled by her sister's distraction. "You've set the date and we can move ahead with the planning?"

Hannah pulled away from the catalog and picked up her

fork. "We're trying to find out when Rev. Potter will be coming to town."

"You must be getting excited."

A tiny crease appeared in Hannah's forehead and she brushed it away as she tucked a golden strand of hair behind her ear. "Yes, but we still have some decisions to settle."

Rebecca didn't hear an invitation to press the subject and decided to focus on the other moody sister at the table. "Naomi, how are you feeling? Your injuries are healing well? Are you having any morning sickness or...?" She trailed off as Naomi shook her head.

"I'm feeling fine so far." She rotated her left arm. "And this is coming along. I'll be good as new soon."

"That's wonderful. You know," Rebecca snapped her fingers. "We need to plan an engagement party so Hannah and Billy can announce their date officially."

"Yes, we should," Hannah agreed but with only about half of her usual effervescence.

Rebecca wanted to slam her forehead into the table. "What's the matter with you two?" Her tone snapped their heads up.

"Nothing, why?" Naomi asked, reaching for her coffee.

Hannah started poking at the pancake. Rebecca reached over and picked up the unattended catalog. Left open to the page of frilly, dainty wedding gowns, and one was circled. A lovely thing, it featured a wide neck, a flower at the waist, a beige overskirt hinting at the white underskirt, a bustle covered in a trail of white silk bows, and a long train.

"It's beautiful. And I'm glad we're starting a new tradition with you."

"Hannah—" Naomi grimaced over her cold coffee and set it back down. "I'm glad you had the courage to tell me you didn't want to wear my gown. Rebecca's gown. Our gown." Finally, a sincere chuckle rose from the group.

"No," Hannah swallowed her only bite of pancake. "Three weddings in one dress was enough. I *would* like to start a new tradition. Besides, Rebecca's only going to be able to reconstruct the dress so many times. What if your daughter wants to wear it?"

"I suppose that's a possibility." Naomi glanced down quickly at her barely protruding stomach.

The conversation died off and Naomi and Hannah concentrated studiously on their meals. Rebecca decided she wasn't ready to give up on getting to the source of their dour moods. "How is working with Hope going, Hannah? Have you learned anything else about her?"

"Fine. She's a very skilled…" Hannah looked pointedly over at Naomi, "nurse. I'm learning a lot from her. And you don't need to look into her background, Rebecca. She, um, is just trying to put her fiancé behind her?"

"That's the reason for her secrecy?"

"Yes." Hannah dove quickly into another bite of pancake. Too quickly. Rebecca bit her lip, wondering about Hope and why Hannah seemed intent on squashing any further investigation.

Beside her, Naomi sighed. "Hannah, I'm sorry if I hurt your feelings about women and careers. I want you to be happy. It would be a huge step, but if Billy is supportive—"

"Are we still talking about nursing school?" Rebecca asked.

"I think our little sister here is toying with the idea of medical school."

Rebecca gasped. "Is that true, Hannah?"

Hannah took a deep breath and straightened in her chair. Rebecca could tell by the tilt of her little sister's chin she was ready for a fight. "Do you think women can be as good as men at being doctors?"

"I don't see why not. Midwives have been doctoring for centuries."

Naomi shot Rebecca a disapproving frown.

"Naomi doesn't agree," Hannah pointed out.

Her expression tensing, Naomi laid down her fork. "I didn't say that. At least I didn't mean to. I just told Hannah to consider the cost of medical school—commitment-wise. The time away from Billy and Little Billy. And the responsibility of the position. The stress. I simply suggested she consider all that."

Naomi's calm, almost sad-sounding, comments left Rebecca puzzled. Where was her sister's fire? "Those are wise words." Rebecca nodded her agreement at Hannah, but then shifted back to Naomi. "But that's not what is bothering you. It's something else."

Naomi twitched her lips, gave the coffee another try but put it down in disgust. "I left something undone yesterday and it's nagging at me. I had a chance to share the Gospel with someone and didn't take it."

"Who?" Hannah asked.

"Mary Ann."

Hannah nodded. "For some reason I sort of figured you had something to do with her agitated state. She was…a little restless after you left."

"She called me judgy."

Hannah snorted but snuffed it quickly. "I tried to talk to her, but she was, I don't know, moody. Withdrawn. Her fever has spiked again. But maybe you could go back by and see her."

Naomi nodded. "I did this morning but she was sleeping. Hope suggested I try again in a day or so. I have to get back to the ranch now." She stood up rather abruptly and laid her napkin on the table. She seemed chagrined at her own sudden movement and spoke with a softer voice, "Let me know about dates for the wedding and the party."

Hannah and Rebecca nodded and Naomi excused herself with a weak smile. Rebecca needed to leave as well, but she just wasn't satisfied with the way the conversation was ending. She decided to say so. "She's always been so hard on herself. This will eat her up until she talks to Mary Ann. But I want to talk about you. Medical school. That's a huge step."

"Don't you think I could do it?"

"Yes," Rebecca said firmly. "But you'd have to be sure. Naomi's right. The commitment is weighty, to say the least. For much of it, you'll be losing time with your family."

Hannah drummed her fingers on the red gingham tablecloth. "Sometimes I just feel so, I don't know, out of control. Like a whirling dervish. I could have done so many things wrong since Doc's death. I just don't want to make any more mistakes."

Rebecca tried to hear the real meaning behind Hannah's words. Was she afraid? Afraid of more mistaken diagnoses? Afraid she might hurt someone instead of help them? "What you've learned from Doc has laid a great responsibility on you, Hannah." She reached out and clutched her little sister's hand. "But is it your *calling*? Could it be a season? The answer is between you and God. Listen carefully for His voice. And we will support you, whatever you choose to do."

"We meaning Naomi, too?"

"Yes, even Naomi. You know she'd come around. She loves you."

"*I* dunno, Johnny Reb. It's bad." Lane poured a ladle of ice-encrusted water from the rain barrel over his head and dirt-smeared neck and stood up. A cold night had barely turned into a warm day. Shaking the water out of his collar-length, golden locks, he dropped his hat back on his head and sighed. "Hate to be the one to tell ya. Plague."

The word made Charles' blood run cold.

Swallowing, he stepped away a few feet to where he could scan the herd out on the west section. Half of the herd, anyway.

The other half was up near Screaming Woman Canyon. Maybe that was a good thing. He shook his head in disbelief. "In both herds?"

"Nah, just this one. So far. Joey came down this morning with the update." Lane sucked on his teeth for a second, pondering. "The herd up at Screaming Woman has been separated from this one for over two weeks. I feel good about them. But this herd..." He exhaled wearily and turned to the same view Charles had. "Yeah, this herd I think is gonna get hit pretty hard." He rested his hands on his hips, fingers draped over the .44 on his hip. "We need to keep 'em isolated. If it keeps spreading—"

"Quarantine and slaughter. The only ways to stop it. Don't risk letting it spread outside this group." He cut his eyes to Lane. "Do you understand? Don't hesitate."

"Yes, sir."

Charles had seen ranchers lose their entire herds by reacting slowly to an outbreak of plague. He would not be one of them. The epidemic in England in '67 had decimated the country's ranching industry. "The men who are with the other herd, keep them there. At least twenty-one days. They don't come down. No one goes up. Send one man with supplies, someone who hasn't been around this herd."

Lane sucked in a breath and flinched. "Twenty-one days. They ain't gonna like that."

"I'll pay them a bonus, but you get them to stay put."

"And if they start seeing signs of the plague?"

Charles turned back to the herd. *God forbid.* "We'll do what we have to do."

*M*atthew hooked his beefy finger in the handle of his coffee cup and leaned back in his chair, dragging his drink across his desk. Meetings about mine operations bored him. He would prefer to focus on spending the generous funds MP&G had provided for building up the town, and the town's goodwill. But he had to take the bad with the good. "Proceed."

"I think we can accomplish two things with a new shaft." Weston Powell, the company's new geologist and mine expert, shoved his spectacles up on his nose and spread the blueprints of the Sunnyside before them. A young man, but he knew rocks like Matthew knew liquor. He tapped a spot on the drawing. "Core samples suggest going in from here."

Matthew leaned in, held flat a rebellious corner of the paper, and watched the young geologist drag his finger across the drawing. "Because?"

"Because this may give us shallower—meaning faster— access to the vein. I think we'd cross it about here, but I also think we can excavate the bodies safely."

Matthew froze. "You're saying we could get those men out?" *Parade a dozen coffins right down Main Street? Rip open all those old wounds? Fill the valley with wailing and weeping?*

Could he be so lucky?

Weston straightened and nodded. "Yes, I think so."

Matthew shook his head. "You better *know* so before we send any more men down that particular tunnel."

"Yes, sir, I understand your concern perfectly. The explosion destabilized a portion of it, as you know. My plan is to come in from the backside of the collapse," he was tapping the map again as he spoke, "plant a few smaller charges and see what else shakes loose. Once that's done, I suspect we may be able retrieve at least some of the bodies."

Matthew studied the black-and-white diagram of the mine. "So, some of the men may have been trapped, not crushed."

"Always a possibility."

Dying slow, terrifying deaths in pitch darkness. A shiver ran through him.

"I'm sure the families would appreciate anyone we could find," Powell said.

The families. Matthew blinked. "Yes, of course. This is for the families. Christian burials for their loved ones."

CHAPTER 19

$\mathcal{H}$ ope had experienced many odd smells emanating from patients over the years, but Mr. Lane Chandler smelled the oddest. And the best.

The man sat quietly on her examination table, holding his hand, wrapped in a red checked tablecloth, pressed to his chest. She rolled her tray of basic first aid supplies over and smiled up at him. He returned it with a grin of his own and she noticed the weathered lines around his hazel eyes, the deeply tanned but handsome face framed with rather shaggy blond hair, and the pale skin of his forehead. The place protected by his hat.

"Now, let's have a look at that hand."

He dutifully extended the limb and she began to remove the covering.

"I don't normally come to see a doctor—er, I mean, a nurse, or well, any medical person for something so slight, but Johnny Re—I mean, Mr. McIntyre insisted."

Hope drifted her fingers softly along the edge of the deep cut gouging its way across the man's palm and frowned. "I'd say this is more than slight, Mr. Chandler. You're going to need several stitches. Otherwise, this will never heal properly."

"Dang," he whispered. "It's my ropin' hand."

"Precisely why we need to stitch it. Without closing it up, a wound this long and deep will scar terribly, reducing your mobility. You want your hand back in working order don't you?"

"Yes, ma'am." He grinned sheepishly. "I reckon I do."

"I'll numb it. The stitches won't hurt."

"Ah, pshaw," he waved away her concern. "I dug a Comanche arrow outta my own shoulder once. After that kind of pain, I can tolerate an itty bitty sewing needle."

Hope tilted her head, admittedly a little too intrigued by the man. She found the way he told the story of a Comanche arrow in his shoulder and then used the word *itty bitty* in the next breath...charming. And, my, but wasn't he handsome?

She frowned at the repetitive thought and forced herself to focus on the tools of her trade. "This will hurt. I'm sorry." She clutched his hand and poured alcohol in the wound. Mr. Chandler winced but that was the extent of his reaction. "All right, let's get the stitches in. You're ready?"

"As I ever will be."

Amused by his bravado, she smirked slightly and laced a needle with the catgut. "Did your shoulder heal all right?" she asked conversationally.

"Yes, ma'am. Just an occasional soreness. Mostly on cold mornings."

"You're very fortunate to have survived such an ordeal." She guided his hand to the table, resting it palm up, and cautiously put in the first suture; he seemed to barely notice.

"Yes, ma'am. Texas was a wild and wooly place ten-fifteen years ago. It's only a little better now. We whooped the Indians but the rougher elements have been flocking there since the war ended."

"Why is that, do you suppose?"

"I reckon 'cause the law ain't too intrusive there. A man can pretty much do what he wants, long as he doesn't cause too much of a ruckus."

"Will you be going back any time soon?"

He took a moment to answer and Hope for some reason felt certain he was studying her. "I had planned to give McIntyre a year. Help him build his herd and his ranch. I might give it a little longer. Especially now."

"What's going on now?"

"We found plague in the herd. It'll be a small miracle if we separated them in time."

Hope knew instantly that was the odd smell. "You're destroying the carcasses." Purification by fire.

"Yes, ma'am. We've been burning cattle for two days."

"Will his herd survive?"

"Some of it. Maybe. I've seen a few ranchers make it after something like this. Most throw down their hat and curse heaven, though."

"Mr. McIntyre doesn't seem the kind to give up."

"Nah, he ain't. He'll make it. If he has to start over with a half-blind bull and a lame cow, either way, he'll make it."

"It's good of you to commit to helping him."

"He's an old friend and Texas ain't going anywhere."

"That's true." She placed the fourth stitch, now truly amazed at Mr. Chandler's tolerance for pain. She'd had patients for whom a procedure like this would have put them on the floor, sobbing. "I've always heard Texans are tough. You seem to epitomize the myth, Mr. Chandler. I know this can't be enjoyable."

"You might be surprised." Puzzled, she glanced up. He was grinning like the proverbial cat who ate the canary. "You know, your hair is the color of honey dripping out of the hive on a summer morning. You should wear it down."

The verbose but poetic compliment both shocked and amused Hope. She blinked and went back to her sewing, commanding the unprofessional smile to retreat from her lips.

"Know what else they say about Texans?" he asked.

"No."

"We're determined past the point of being smart. You engaged or anything of the such?"

The sudden, unexpected question caused her hands to pause, but she recovered quickly and continued with her sewing. "Not anymore." Conversing with Mr. Chandler was much like chasing a rabbit—you never knew which way it was going to turn.

"Oh. Mind if I ask what happened?"

Hope decided Texans also had no boundaries about conversational propriety. Yet, she wanted to answer the question. "He didn't approve of my choice of vocation."

"You mean he didn't want you to help people?"

Well, it boiled down to that, didn't it? But Mr. Chandler was likely no different than Edward, she reminded herself. If he came to know the truth about her. "He thought the medical profession was reserved for men."

"Heck, you're better off without him then. Pardon me for saying so, but he was surely a special kind of stupid if he thought like that."

Again, Hope's hands paused and before she could help herself, a giggle escaped. "Yes, I think so, too." With effort, she bit down more laughter and continued with her stitching.

"My momma was one of the first women to settle in Texas. Our spread was pretty far out from town. My pappy was a Texas Ranger so he was gone a lot. Momma ran the farm and raised me and my three brothers."

Hope assumed he was rambling to occupy his mind, so she nodded and kept on with her task.

"I've seen that woman fight brush fires, crazed steers, and rabid coyotes. She's faced twisters, Comanche raiding parties, and Mexican cattle thieves. Only time I ever saw her cry was when my brother Joey got bit by a rattler."

"I'm sorry."

"Oh, no. He didn't die. Through her tears, she sucked out the poison, bandaged him, then went and found the snake, shot him, and we ate him for supper."

Once more Hope's hands paused. She looked up at Mr. Chandler. The mischief in his gaze raised her suspicions. "I've also heard Texans have a penchant for tall tales."

His face fell. "Miss Clark, I have been known to spin a yarn now and again. But never about my momma."

*T*hroughout the rest of the day, Hope found herself revisiting her time with Mr. Chandler. Not well educated, as evidenced by his poor grammar, he was none-theless disarming. He made Hope feel as though he might be the one man who did believe a woman could be a doctor. If his *yarn* was to be believed, his mother had had quite the effect on him.

Killed the rattlesnake who bit his brother and they ate it.

Hope had to fight the smile tickling her lips.

"What did I miss?"

Hannah's voice shattered Hope's silly ruminations. Busy cutting bandages at the counter, she stilled and wondered how to answer the question. "Miss?"

Hannah sashayed over to the counter, a knowing smirk on her face. "The only time a woman looks that lost, she's thinking about a man. Just who came in here today?"

Hope shrugged as if she couldn't quite recall. "Mr. Ledford stopped by for his check-up."

"Aaaaaand…"

"Oh, there was, uh," Hope rolled up the remaining bandages. "A cowboy, I think. Yes, a Lane Chandler. I believe he works for—"

"Charles and Naomi. He's their foreman."

"Oh." Hope started folding the bandages into neat, little

squares. "Yes, I believe he mentioned that. He cut his hand badly on some barbed wire. Seven stitches."

Hannah giggled but her amusement burst into full-fledged laughter. Certain she was the butt of some joke, Hope turned to face her tormentor. "Do you have something to say, Hannah?"

"You're smitten."

"I beg your pardon?"

"Oh, please. You know every person who comes in here after two seconds. *A Lane Chandler*," she mocked. "As if you could confuse him with some other cowboy."

Hannah practically snorted with her scorn and Hope felt her cheeks begin to burn. "Well, yes, he is handsome but he's also just…well, he's just…"

Hannah's expression flipped from amused to annoyed. "Just a cowboy? Not good enough for you?"

Hope averted her gaze, embarrassed by Hannah's interpretation. "No, that's not what I meant. I only meant to imply we wouldn't have much in common."

"Maybe Lane talks like he's from Backwater, Texas, but he manages a herd of 3000 head—or somewhere in the vicinity. With the outbreak, I'm not sure. He keeps up with the range, the men, the ranch's expenses. He's actually very good at what he does. Or so Charles says."

Hope sighed, unwilling to admit any attraction to Lane. "He is a patient, Hannah. It's unprofessional to think of him any other way. And that's where this conversation ends, if you don't mind."

"Hmmm." Hannah shrugged. "You're right. So, if he happens to show back up here in a few days, I'll do the tending."

CHAPTER 20

$\mathcal{H}$ope stood over Mary Ann, contemplating desperate measures to get her fever down when the woman convulsed violently. Blood suddenly spewed from her lips. Coughing, gurgling, she reached for Hope with fear in her eyes. Hope clutched her shoulders, tried to lay her back down in the bed as blood spattered them both. Mary Ann convulsed once more then went limp in Hope's arms.

Dead.

Hope knew it before she checked the woman's vitals, but she went through the motions nonetheless. Meticulously.

But there was no pulse. No breathe. In a heartbeat, she had passed from life to death.

The silence in the office at three in the morning was haunting, somber. Final. Hope pulled the stethoscope from her neck and sat down in the chair next to Mary Ann's bed. Embolism? Most likely. Somewhat common after surgery.

Was this her fault or Amanda's?

Hope tilted her head and studied Mary Ann. Even though crimson smears led from her lips to her chin and down her throat, the pinched v on her brow was gone and those tight, tiny wrinkles that had plagued her mouth had smoothed. Her green eyes stared vacantly, but there was no fear in them. She looked at peace.

"I hope you are, Mary Ann. I hope you are." Hope reached out and closed the woman's eyes.

At a loss to describe how she felt emotionally, Hope pulled a rag from her pocket and absently wiped the blood from her own face. *Well, at least you're out of the battle now, Mary Ann. Maybe things are better on the other side. Maybe you can actually rest there. My father says there is nothing after death. The other side is simply sleep.*

On this side, however, Hope had her hands full. The situation began to dawn on her. A patient was dead. Most likely from the abortion, but surgery was dangerous under the best of conditions. It couldn't be ruled out as the cause, either.

Perhaps fate had simply determined the timing of the blood clot. Regardless, she had to tell the marshal, and soon the town would know.

Moving as if she were going to her own funeral, Hope dragged off her blood-spattered apron, slipped into her coat, and set off for the marshal's office, oblivious to the hour. Each step, however, grew stronger, more determined as she thought about Amanda. Ultimately, Mary Ann's death was due to her own choices but...

But Amanda was pedaling a trade she had no business practicing. And Hope was going to make sure her potential clients knew that and about Mary Ann's death.

At Main Street, instead of crossing the quiet intersection lit with weak lamps and heading to the sheriff's, she turned left and marched straight across to Water Street. Some street. After she passed the rear of the assayer's store, the avenue turned into a narrow, rutted, shadowy path. Tents, nearly all dark, lined both sides. The wee hours of the morning, even in Tent Town, were deader than a cemetery.

Fear tried to speak some sense into her and her steps slowed.

No, I will not be cowed by shadows. Amanda can't hurt anyone else.

Hope's anger burned brighter and pushed back the fear. She marched on and came to another intersection. A few of the tents here glowed amber from lamps within. A woman smoking a cigar stood out in front of one wearing nothing but a petticoat and camisole, somehow ignoring the cold air. Leaning back on the tent pole in her entrance, she seemed to be waiting, scanning the muddy, rutted street with a dreamy gaze.

The young girl, not more than twenty-five, pale, blonde, and probably a touch anemic, addressed Hope. "Aren't you on the wrong side of town, honey?"

"Maybe." Hope approached. "Do you know a woman named Mary Ann who worked down here?" Hope caught a whiff of alcohol.

The girl's brow furrowed, she blinked, seemed to process the question a little slowly. "I dunno. Maybe. Why you looking for her?"

"She's dead. I was hoping to let any friends she might have had know about her."

The woman chewed on her bottom lip. "That's too bad. She baked apple turnovers every now and again."

Hope waited for more, but when it didn't come, she pressed. "Friends. Anyone I should talk to?"

The girl took a drag on the cigar and shrugged a shoulder. Smoke whirled out in front of her as she exhaled. "We work for Matthew, but he handed us girls over to Amanda."

Hope flinched. "Does that mean she's in charge of you? And Mary Ann?"

"Yeah."

"Where can I find her?"

She pointed across the intersection down a dark path.

"Cross the creek. You'll see the tents. They're calling it Hell's Half-Acre."

"Thank you. Um," Hope started to leave, but swung back around. "If you get in a bad way, need medical attention, my name is Hope. I'm the do—nurse in town. Come see me. Don't go to Amanda."

"Sure."

"No," Hope said firmly. "Don't go to Amanda."

"All right."

"And tell…tell your friends."

*T*he night closed in around Hope as she strode down the trail. If not for the half-moon above, she would have been lost, out here without a lantern. She didn't want to think about the wisdom of this plan. She just wanted to tell Amanda to stop practicing medicine. But the trivial fact Mary Ann was remembered for making apple turnovers egged her on. In the midst of her grim existence, the woman had baked treats for her friends. It made her human. Doctors had to keep a distance from their patients, her father had said. It protected your mental state.

Well, Hope could see the wisdom of this view now. Her mental state was quite disturbed. In fact, deny it all she like, she was angry. Amanda had to be stopped. Mary Ann deserved some justice.

Her lace-up boots thumped across a wooden bridge that traversed a wide, shallow creek and ended in a compound consisting of a dozen or so tents, one small log cabin and one larger, well-lit, canvas-and-wood building. Voices, laughter, and clinking glasses filtered out from the bigger structure—obviously the saloon. The smell of beer and smoke tainted the night air.

Of the smaller tents, a red lantern burned in front of each

one, boldly announcing the owner's vocation. Hope noted the small log cabin on the end did not have the *subtle* sign for entertainment hanging outside.

The madam's residence? Amanda's?

A man exited one of the tents, still adjusting his suspenders, and strode toward the saloon. Hope waited for him to pass and then hurried over to the cabin. A warm, amber glow emanated from its papered windows. She paused, listening, and heard the rustle of movement.

She waited a moment longer, then said simply, "Amanda?"

Somehow she sensed the person inside coming to a standstill, but offered no reply.

"Amanda?" Hope tried again.

"Who's there?"

"My name is Hope. I'm here about Mary Ann."

Amanda took so long to step out in the dark, Hope thought she wasn't coming at all. Much longer and she would have barged into the woman's cabin.

Instead, the black girl surveyed Hope with suspicion, a hand on her hip and a challenging tilt to her head. "What about her?"

"I'm sorry to inform you, she passed away a little while ago."

The girl drummed her fingers on her hip for a moment, then simply shrugged. "Well, that's life in the cribs."

She started to turn but Hope snaked out an arm to stop to her. "How can you be so callous?"

Amanda scowled at the fingers on her arm, lifted a burning gaze to Hope. Not cowed, Hope didn't move for another second, then slowly released the girl's arm—without apology.

"Missy, you'd best be careful comin' around me, acting all high and mighty. That's a good way to get hurt."

"Like Mary Ann?"

"I don't know what you're talking about."

"You punctured her uterus when you performed the abortion."

Amanda flung a hand up, dismissing Hope and turned. "I don't know what you're ta—"

Hope grabbed her shoulder and spun her gruffly back to face her. "How dare you. Don't turn away from me when I'm speaking to you."

Amanda's eyes rounded. "Oh, yes, mazzuh," she said, perfecting a Southern slave accent. "I'm so sorry, mazzuh." She glared at Hope. "What was I thinking, turning my back on a white girl?"

"The color of our skin has nothing to do with this. Your procedure all but killed Mary Ann. She would have bled to death had I not intervened."

"Then why is she dead now?"

"I suspect a pulmonary embolism due to the surgery, but I can't be sure."

Amanda narrowed her eyes, an attempt Hope thought to hide her confusion over the medical term. "So you had a hand in this, too."

Hope raised her chin. "Yes, I did. I'll be telling Marshal Beckwith what happened. The whole truth. He can decide who's at fault."

Even in the shadowy opening, Hope could see Amanda's face pinch, her jaw tighten. "You don't want to be doing that, missy. You'll be calling down more trouble than you want."

Hope conceded the point. Though it didn't matter. "Maybe. But I still have to do the right thing and that is stopping you." Done bandying words with the girl, Hope spun and headed back toward town. Just before the rippling of the creek drowned out any noise behind her, she heard the distinct sound of footsteps running to the saloon.

CHAPTER 21

*T*apping a deck of cards in his palm, Matthew grinned at the bustling crowd in his tent saloon. Not near as big as the Crystal Chandelier, but busy. He made his way through the crowd to the plank bar packed with rowdy, muddy miners and dusty cowboys. Cigar smoke choked the air, chips jangled and clattered at the poker tables as men whined or laughed over the direction of the game. A rough place, but the customers were happy and Matthew had more money rolling in from it than he had in two months at the Chandelier.

Not that he needed it now, but this place was a burr under the High-and-Mighty-Town Fathers' saddle and that tickled Matthew to no end. At four in the morning, the men and girls in their cribs were all still going strong. He hated to admit it, but Amanda had known what she was talking about. Turned out, she was a fine saloon manager, too.

As if on cue, the door on the tent flung open and Amanda burst in, headed straight for him. Pushing through customers, ricocheting off drunks, skirting tables, she marched toward Matthew like Sherman headed to Atlanta.

Hmmm, he wondered. *What's put a knot in her corset?*

"I just had a visitor." Heaving bosom and ebony fists planted on her hips communicated the message it was an unwanted visitor.

"And."

"Mary Ann died and that new nurse in town is blaming me and going to the marshal. She's gonna try to pin it on me."

"When?"

"Right now."

Matthew didn't want Beckwith poking around his affairs. He didn't want him anywhere around, period. And this troublesome new nurse—an idea struck him and he grinned. The new nurse who would be taking care of Naomi and the little McIntyre bun in the oven.

Well, all that money rolling in from the MP&G Conglomerate had to be good for something. He surveyed the crowd, found the new man from Texas, and waved him over. Buck Chambers laid down his cards, picked up his hat, and weaved his way to Matthew.

"Yes, sir." The man tucked a stringy lock of brown hair behind his ear, the scar on his cheek twitching as he nodded. "What can I do for ya?"

"Got a little job. A hundred dollars if you do it tonight. Now."

The man immediately dropped his hat in place. His hawkish features tightened with eagerness. "Consider it done."

Matthew cut his eyes to Amanda. "Show him which way she went." He watched them snake back through the crowd, quite sure Chambers would do the job with relish. He'd performed admirably out at the King M. Sneaking in sick cows had been no small feat, and then working at the ranch to keep it spreading. Best of all, no one suspected a thing.

Matthew's lip curled in a satisfied smirk. *And now McIntyre and Naomi are going to lose the new nurse. Tsk, tsk. The only professional medical help in town is dead.*

What a terrible loss.

---

*A*ssuming Amanda was going for help, Hope rushed across the bridge and darted headlong into the shadowy path that led to Tent Town. At the first intersection, she paused. She'd been so mad the first time she'd marched through here, she hadn't paid attention to her surroundings. All these tents looked alike in the dim moonlight.

Hadn't she turned left at a tent with laundry hanging out in front of it? Or had that been a right? A noise from behind her jolted her heart and she whirled around.

Laundry swayed eerily in the light breeze, but Hope didn't see anything else. Leaves rustled in the trees. All the tents near her were dark and silent. Surely, if someone assaulted her, she could yell for help.

Oh, she was being ridiculous and made an attempt to calm her racing pulse. She exhaled and tried to think through her rising panic.

Deciding that moving was better than standing frozen to the spot, she arbitrarily took the right. Unfortunately, the path ended abruptly several yards down in the midst of a grouping of tents. Hope swallowed. She had no choice but to go back— again, a subtle noise from behind, like the soft padding of foot-steps, tweaked her ears. Skulking, sneaking footsteps.

She wanted to call for help, but what if she was imagining things? She couldn't risk looking like a nervous fool. No one in town would trust her. No, she had to *know* if she was being followed.

Her heart racing now with real fear, Hope looked around and saw a narrow trail between two tents. Probably a dead end, but it led into the trees. She could hide in there, covered in darkness, see if anyone was following. She rushed down the path, slowed when she entered the trees. Briars tugged at her skirt, moonlight filtered weakly between the lodge pole pines. Young evergreens, many of them only five or six feet tall, growing amidst the tall trees, looked like men standing still. Waiting for her.

Hope slapped a hand over her mouth to muffle her breathing and scolded herself for being a scared rabbit. Hide somewhere. She picked out a grouping of three shorter, thicker cedars and circled around behind them. Quietly, she eased her way in among the branches and watched the trail from whence she'd come.

Snoring, soft and rhythmic, emanated from the tent closest to her. Somewhere, several yards away, someone strummed the gentle, haunting notes of Annie Laurie. The song was one of her favorites. Surely no one would attack—

A twig snapped behind her. Before she could turn, a sharp, burning pain sliced deep into her side and she screamed.

"Mind your own business, woman." A man's voice, harsh, and gravelly, warned.

The knife twisted and Hope screamed again.

CHAPTER 22

*H*ope opened her eyes, registered two fuzzy figures standing at the end of the bed, then closed them again. Why was she so tired? She felt as if she was buried beneath a mound of mud.

"Hope, can you hear me?"

Hannah's voice. Why was she—? What was Hope—?

The darkness and the memory of the attack rushed back at her. Her eyes fluttered open once more and she fought to keep them open. A short, squat man of about thirty or so held on to the foot rail and stared at her, his wide, brown eyes brimming with concern. Hope twisted a little to the right and Hannah sat down on the bed.

"You're going to be all right. Thanks to Corky, here."

"Aw, I didn't do anything," he said, backing away from the bed.

"Corky was an ambulance driver in the war. He had enough sense to shove his shirt into your wound and get you here."

"What hap—?" Hope's voice cracked. She swallowed and tried again. "What happened?"

"You don't remember?" Hannah asked, concern creasing her brow.

"I remember someone came up behind me. Before I could turn...pain. In my back. Maybe near my kidney."

"I think that's what they were aiming for but missed, or you turned too quick."

"I heard you scream and launched right outta my tent." Corky stepped up to the bed again and grabbed the rail. "I saw a man push you down and run hell-bent for leather into the woods."

"And you came to help me?" she said slowly. "Thank you. Did you see the man...?" She struggled for the words. "To get a description?"

"No, ma'am, I'm sorry, I didn't. I sure wish I had. I didn't know it was you 'til I picked ya up off the ground. I recognized you from the restaurant, when you saved Ledford."

A wave of exhaustion washed over Hope and she closed her eyes. "Thank you," she managed again.

"Yes, ma'am." She heard footsteps, fading away, and a moment later a door closed. The bed moved and she sensed Hannah rise to her feet.

"Your rescue is a true miracle, Hope. Corky's only been in town a few days. He left Defiance a while back and wasn't ever supposed to show up here again." She paused. "He heard Delilah had disappeared and supposed it was safe. A godsend for you."

"Yes," Hope murmured. But no. Not God. She didn't have the strength, however, to debate destiny, fate, and a Higher Power. "Maybe later," she mumbled.

"Um," Hannah hesitated. "Well, praise God you're alive. The marshal will be by around noon to get the details. And..." She trailed off, then whispered, "and find out what the heck you were doing in Tent Town."

*M*atthew figured there was no better way to inform McIntyre of the cliff in front of him than run an ad in the paper. Twisting the knife, as it were, in him and Naomi.

Feeling like the cock of the walk, Matthew let himself into the town hall that also housed the newspaper office—and drew up.

Very few things remained to remind him of the Iron Horse's sordid glory, but the silence here...it was almost awe-inspiring. Heavy. Serious. Like a library.

The bar remained, covered now in stacks of paper. Shelves that had once held liquor supported rows of books. To his left, a knee wall and a counter cut the former sitting area in half. Behind them, a press the size of a grizzly dominated the office area of the *Defiance Dispatch*. Rebecca sat at a desk off to the right, placing type on a composing stick, completely engrossed in her work.

Matthew softly shut the door behind him and sauntered up to the counter. "Good afternoon, Rebecca."

Her head came up and he thought he heard her gasp. She took a moment, he supposed to plan her response, then rose and turned to face him. "Matthew." Her dark eyes smoldered with suspicion as she approached the counter. Her regal features barely veiled her disdain, and she offered a perfunctory smile. "How have you been?"

Such a cold, formal tone from a woman he'd once considered family. "Just fine. And you?"

"Fine. Thank you." To relieve them, he assumed, of some of this awkwardness, she picked up a pencil and pad. "What can I do for you? Or, uh, is this a social call?"

"No, no. Business. Just business." *I wouldn't dare intrude on your perfect family, Rebecca.* "I'd like to buy an ad."

"Oh, all right. Happy to help." She poised the pencil to write. "What would you like it to say?"

"First of all, it's a full page."

"A full—" Her eyes bugged and she smiled. "All right. Yes. And…?"

"It should say the following. The MP and—" He snapped his fingers. "You know, as a matter of fact, I have it all written out." He started pilfering through his pockets until he pulled a folded sheet of paper from his breast pocket. "It should say this exactly."

He unfolded it, smoothed it out on the counter and slid it over to her.

A tense little dip in her brow, Rebecca pulled a pair of spectacles from her collar, slipped them on and began to read. Enjoying the emotions crossing her face—polite, perplexed, stunned—Matthew rested an elbow on the counter and waited.

After a moment, Rebecca pursed her lips and shook her head. "The mine is re-opening? I knew Charles had sold it, but I thought it would be a while—I don't think the town is ready, Matthew. There's still too much heal—"

"The town'll get over it. We're opening November first. The word is already on the streets in Frisco and Denver. Miners will be filtering in any day now. The best way for the town to heal is to move forward."

"The widows aren't ev—"

He stood up to his full, towering height. "The widows need husbands. The children need fathers. Get some men in this town and Defiance will start growing again and so will the families."

Rebecca dropped her gaze back to the advertisement. "And these businesses that are coming in. All owned by this MP&G Western Mining Conglomerate?"

"Some. Some I own. We want the people to know the mine means industry, creating a bustling, prosperous town. We don't have to wait for ranching and lumber to take off. We'll all build Defiance together."

"I see you're on the board of directors."

"Newest member." Matthew freed a slow, easy grin and tapped the paper. "Make sure," he winked, "that's at the top. In big letters."

***

*M*atthew strutted down the boardwalk, ignoring the chilly breeze, and chuckled over his last words to Rebecca. *Make sure that's at the top in big letters.*

Oh, he wished he could see McIntyre's face when everything that was rolling downhill started rolling right over him. Matthew strode on, men instinctively moving out of his way. Today, it wasn't just his size making them step aside or shift their path. No, today, he knew it was the grin on his face. Like a wolf that had its pick of the sheep.

"You look awful pleased with yourself."

Matthew's grin evaporated immediately. Buck. Buck had failed to kill the little nurse. If they weren't right here on the boardwalk passing in front of the bakery, he might kill the man for lousing up such a simple assignment.

"I am pleased with myself. You, however, I could hang up and skin." He cut his eyes at the man, thinking how he'd like to give him a matching scar down the other side of his face. He looked away quickly, though, as if not talking to him. "How hard is it to kill a woman? In the dark? Alone?"

Buck stuck a finger in his ear, flicked away a piece of wax. "Yeah, about that. You don't owe me nothing. I didn't finish the job."

Matthew spit a curse at the man. "You bet I don't owe you."

"I don't know the area. I should have waited a little longer. I did, however, fix things at McIntyre's lumber camp."

Matthew glanced around. Men on the street noticed him. Big, handsome, clean clothes. Buck, on the other hand, blended in the with the rough and dirty crowd of miners, carpenters, cowboys, and lumberjacks. Still, he couldn't afford to be seen talking to an employee of the King M. "I'll expect to hear something soon then."

With that, he abruptly turned and crossed the street, leaving Buck in his wake.

CHAPTER 23

*A*fter Matthew left, Rebecca pressed a hand to her mouth and studied the ad he wanted to run.

Announcing the return of the Sunnyside Mine. Under New Management

*The Board of Directors of the MP&G Western Mining Conglomerate—*Charles Crocker, Allan Ladd, Jeffrey Huntington, Mordecai Sands, William Terrell, and Matthew Miller—*are pleased to announce acquisition and operations of the Sunnyside Mine, opening November 1.*

We believe the town of Defiance does not have to die a slow, painful death when so much wealth still exists beneath our feet and in the valley's creeks.

We are so committed to the success and survival of this fair town, we are also bringing many new businesses with us. For too long, one man has controlled Defiance. It's time Defiance controlled its own destiny.

Restaurants, a mercantile, a new bank, a wheelwright, a blacksmith, a butcher, and a dress shop.

The future of Defiance is brighter than it has ever been.

Rebecca jiggled the pencil in her hand, unhappy with this

news. To her way of thinking, none of this bode well for the town, Charles, or her family. Matthew had the audacity to imply Defiance was under a dictatorship, which was absurd. Charles had a lot of power, but he no longer abused it. She was certainly more comfortable with him guiding the town than someone as vindictive as Matthew.

And what of these businesses? Several of them would compete directly with Charles's holdings—the mercantile, the hotel's restaurant—

"Lass, ye look as if ye've seen a puppy dying in the street."

Rebecca didn't look up at her husband's voice. She waited for him to come alongside her at the counter then she showed him the note. "Matthew just brought this in."

Ian read it, the somber expression on his face growing darker and darker. "This is meant to stir up trouble."

"Should I run it?"

He thought it over, but nodded after a moment. "Aye. The folks in town have the right to know what's going on."

"How much of this does Charles know?"

"Therein lies the crux of the matter. He did not know *this*." He pressed his finger to the paper, pointing at Matthew's name. "And I dinna think it will go over well."

As Rebecca was attempting to fathom the impact all of this was going to have on Defiance, Micah Lyons, one of the first gold miners here, burst in. Rebecca flipped the paper over as she and Ian straightened to greet the man.

"Morning, Micah." Rebecca picked up her pad again. "How can we help you?"

A young man, dark hair, dark eyes, whispered to be a little *off*, strode to the counter. He smelled like dirt and sweat. His brown hair hung in unwashed tangles from beneath his tattered hat. "I got me a letter to the editor I want to run."

"All right. Fine. You want it in the next issue?"

He handed her the folded note. "Yes, ma'am. You run that soon as you can."

The moment she took possession of the letter, the man nodded sharply at them and charged out of the office. Rebecca looked at Ian. He shrugged. "He's an odd duck. Let's see what he's written."

A few sentences in, Rebecca was wondering about the timing of the letter. And the author. "This doesn't sound like Micah."

"Agreed. 'Tis too eloquent."

Rebecca went back to the top and started reading aloud. "We can't be bought. We can't be bribed. We will not be quiet any longer. We want justice and we shall have it.

"Once the mountain quit falling and the death toll from the Sunnyside Mine disaster was finalized, we, the surviving family and friends of those lost men, realized we were casualties too. Casualties of injustice.

"It is common knowledge Delilah Goodnight paid Randall Smith to sabotage the mine. Yet, she left town freely, with no one in pursuit. No charges. Her whereabouts now are unknown or protected.

"Charles McIntyre then had the audacity to pay widows and orphans blood money in an effort to whitewash his sins and quell their grief.

"Twelve good men buried beneath our feet cry out from their dark grave demanding to know who else has Charles McIntyre paid. Obviously, our illustrious Marshal Pender Beck-with played a key role in spiriting Delilah Goodnight out of the grasp of justice. Why did he protect her this way? Or should we ask, for whom?

"We, the family and friends of the deceased, are also citizens of Defiance and we demand the law be involved. Legitimate law. For a legitimate investigation. Delilah Goodnight needs to hang for what she did. Marshal Beckwith should lay down his badge and retire in disgrace." Rebecca halted, then whispered, "Charles McIntyre should go to prison. Signed..." She scanned the list quickly, "at least thirty names. Oh, Ian, we can't print this." She slapped the letter down on the counter and spun her back to it.

He picked it up and sighed. "'Tis no doubt inflammatory. And we've no obligation to run it."

"But...?"

"But I dunna think that will stop the snake that seems to be stirring."

"Do you think most of the town feels this way or it's all coming from the families?"

"What is more interesting to me is who wrote this letter. And why now?"

A week later, the *Defiance Dispatch* was published without the scathing letter but with the unfortunate ad from MP&G. To Rebeccca's dismay, the next morning she found a copy of Micah's inflammatory letter tucked between the town hall's front doors. By the afternoon, she learned dozens, maybe hundreds, of copies had been slipped quietly under front doors, weighted with rocks and left in front of tents, tacked up on barn doors, dropped into saddle bags, even impaled with a knife and stuck on an outhouse door. Simply put, they were everywhere.

But who had printed them?

M atthew, reaching for his towel to wipe the remnants of soap from his face, paused at the knock on his door. "Yeah?"

"It's me, Mr. Miller."

Mathew finished his face and tossed the towel down next to the ceramic bowl. "Sam. Come on in."

The short, blubbery attorney slipped into the room and softly shut the door behind him. "You asked to be notified when all the handbills were distributed. They have been."

"Good, good." Matthew checked his shave one last time in the mirror then pulled his suspenders over his broad shoulders, the cloth straining at his biceps. "We'll be putting that printing press to lots of good use. Those were just the beginning."

"I definitely think it's wise to be able to counter the voice of the only paper in town. You and MP&G need to be heard."

"McIntyre has a chokehold on Defiance. We are going to break it."

"And to that end, the other, uh, measures we've discussed are in motion."

Matthew smirked, but didn't speak. Sam had no idea what was in motion. And wasn't 'measures' a polite way to put it?

"A pity we couldn't get the spur line from him," Sam mused.

"It ain't over yet."

"I would caution you against over-reaching. We have several plates in the air now. Just take him down a notch. Humble him so we can deal with him."

Matthew studied the portly man. Piggish, overweight, but sharp as a tack in his tailored, houndstooth suit. "Is it your job to keep a tight rein on me?"

"The other members of the board have given you a significant amount of leeway—not to mention cash—to get the mine open, build up the town, and create goodwill toward MP&G. Your personal feelings for McIntyre concern them."

"Tell them not to worry. He won't be riding me off the rails."

Miller laced sweaty, sausage fingers together at his gut. "Then moving on. I wanted to clarify for the next handbill. You think pushing the town's potential prosperity over the safety measures we're introducing will sway them to our side?"

"Mention the safety precautions, but ultimately folks are

gonna care more about the money going in their pockets. Two hundred miners are gonna need places to spend their pay."

"Appeal to their greed rather than address their fears?"

Matthew plucked his hat from the bed post. "Greed's an ugly word, Sam." He pressed his hat to his chest, and affected a sappy tone. "Prosperity, my friend. A growing town provides opportunities for success. We're not just opening a mine. We're providing a lifeline to this community. Jobs, money, bright futures for enterprising folks." He rolled his Stetson down his arm, popped it from his elbow, sent it spiraling into the air and caught it on his head. Oh, it was the harbinger of great things coming when he could perform the trick perfectly. "We're gonna bring Defiance back from the dead."

And create a few corpses in the process...

CHAPTER 24

*P*erhaps a mother's intuition awoke Naomi. She liked
to think so, as she sat up and looked around the
bedroom, painted in deep shadows. Instinctively her hand went
to the growing bulge at her belly but there was no pain, no
nausea. Beside her, Charles rested uneasily, troubled no doubt
by the sickness in the herd. Besides his hitched breathing, no
other noises came from the house. Faintly, in the distance, cows
mooed intermittently. What was wrong?

Lord, what is it?

A sound from the porch sharpened her senses. Then a
familiar *thump, thump, thump* eased her nerves. She knew the
sound of a puppy wagging his tail. Relieved, she pulled her robe
from the bed post, eased into it, her arm reminding her how it
liked to stiffen up overnight, and slipped outside. Silhouetted in
dim moonlight, Two Spears and Cat Killer sat on the end of the
long, front porch together, the boy swinging his legs over the
edge, the puppy beside him, playfully chewing on a sock toy.

"Two Spears, what are you doing up?" She rubbed her arms
against the chill. "Is Cat Killer all right?" They had built a pen
for the pup and he slept fine there. On occasion, Two Spears

had asked if he could sleep in the little shed with the dog. An idea Naomi had vetoed forthwith.

She joined them at the edge of the porch. "Two Spears?" The puppy promptly rolled over and began tugging on the hem of Naomi's robe. The little boy sighed deeply but she didn't think it was related to the pet. "Talk to me." She redirected the puppy to the sock toy and sat down beside her son, pulling her robe closer. "Please."

"Will you want me to stay when the baby comes?"

"What? Of course. Why would you think I wouldn't? Charles and I have enough love for you and a baby." She ruffled his hair. "With love left over." He didn't laugh at her joke. Biting her lip, she decided not to make any more. He was clearly troubled. "I love you to the moon and back. So does your father. A baby won't change that."

"How can you love me? I did not fight for you. You told me to run and I ran. Like a squaw."

"Oh, Two Spears, you have to let this go." She hugged him to her with a fierce grip, his pain breaking her heart. "I told you to run because I would have rather died than see you dead. You are too valuable, too precious to me. I couldn't have stood losing you."

"A man would not have run," he said into her shoulder, his voice strangled.

She kissed the top of his head, his black hair glimmering in the silver light. "Two Spears, you are still a boy. I know you don't want to hear that, but the time for you to be a warrior has not yet come. You must grow in stature and wisdom."

He sniffed and pulled away from her. "One-Who-Cries said a man must always fight for his family."

One-Who-Cries. Lord, will that man's influence ever fade from Two Spears mind? "Yes, a man should fight for his family. But he should choose his battles, Two Spears. When you are a man, you will be wiser about doing so. Do you understand?"

His little jaw worked back and forth but finally he nodded. "I understand."

But Naomi was smart enough to know this boy wanted to be counted a man more than anything—wisely or not. She feared the burning desire might well make him dangerously foolish.

---

*T*he King M ranch had a fine cook but, in Emilio's opinion, Willy couldn't hold a candle to the cook at The Trinity Inn. When Mollie set the steaming plate of meatloaf and mashed potatoes in front of him, he nearly clapped his hands with delight. She delivered his meal—double-portions, he noted—and smiled warmly at him.

"Hope you're hungry."

"Sí." He noted she was wearing her hair differently, twisted up with little golden curls trailing down her neck. "Your hair is pretty that way."

She blushed and shrugged modestly. "Thank you. Can I get you anything else?"

"Just some coffee when you have a minute. Take your break and sit with me?"

She nodded. "I will. In a few minutes."

She slipped away to wait on other customers. He watched her for a minute, checking on folks, filling water glasses. The first bite of the meatloaf, however, was a fine distraction. He could have sighed at the savory flavor. He was lost in the meal when a conversation at a nearby table snatched his attention back to the world around him.

"It brings up a good point, that handbill," a man was saying. "Delilah just snuck out of town like a weasel in the dark."

"She didn't face justice," another said, his tone muffled by food. "Beckwith watched her go. Let her go. And McIntyre's still king of the hill."

Silverware clinked at the table. "And good men lay dead at the bottom of that mine," another man said, anger in his voice. "It ain't right. Ain't right at all."

"Maggie Burleson and some of the other women, they took his money," the first man said. "But it ain't nothin' but blood money. McIntyre payin' 'em to keep quiet."

"Someday, he'll get his," the second man said, still filling his mouth with food. "Someday, somebody is gonna drop a rope around his and Beckwith's necks."

"Whoever tries it," the first man said, "he'd best have an army with him."

The meatloaf lost some of its flavor and Emilio put his fork down. He remembered talk that had sounded much like this. A long time ago, when he and his sister Rose were still with the bandits. One man had challenged the leader. Factions had developed, splitting the gang. Rather than fight like men, one group had lynched the leaders of the other group and then took over.

A lynching was an ugly thing to behold. He flinched at the snippets of memories: men weeping in terror, feet suspended in the air and kicking wildly—so hard in fact, boots went flying. Strangled, gurgling noises, then a somber stillness.

Emilio took the napkin from his lap, laid it on the table and rose. On his way out, he glanced over at the men he'd heard running their mouths. All complaining about the injustices in the aftermath of the mine explosion, as if they'd been here. But Emilio didn't know any of them.

---

*C*harles was on his way to the logging camp when he heard the rifle shot. It echoed through the pines and golden aspens in a foreboding wave. Aware it could be either trouble or an emergency signal, he spurred Traveller and the appaloosa surged to a gallop. They raced through the rugged, rocky forest, emerging onto an open hillside—and a scene of devastation.

The chains on a logging wagon had broken and a massive Douglas fir with the girth of a Percheron had ripped down the mountain like a marauding grizzly, gouging the ground and flattening trees. Logs littered the ground in wild confusion over a path fifty yards long. At the bottom, the horse limped about, dragging its broken tack. Near the animal, a wagon lay shattered in a dozen pieces. Men were scrambling pell-mell toward a body lying a few feet beyond it.

Charles shouted, "Yah," and urged Traveller down the steep slope at a breakneck pace, skidding to a stop at the group of men. "What happened?" Jumping from the saddle, he dropped to one knee on the ground beside his foreman Bart Zimmerman, who was kneeling next to the injured man. Blood gushed from the lumberjack's nose and mouth.

"Chain broke," Bart said in a heavy Russian accent. "Log roll right over him."

"Well, quick, let's get him in a wagon and down the mountain—"

"Sir—" Bart reached out and stopped Charles from moving. "He will not make it."

Anger surged through Charles. "Are you a doctor?"

As if settling the argument, the man lying on the ground convulsed, coughed, and exhaled his final breath in a frothy, red mist. The world fell silent. Even the breeze in the forest died, respecting the moment.

Charles swallowed and stood up. "Tell me why the chain broke." He didn't even know the man's name. Where he was from. How long he'd worked here in the lumber camp. Guilt tried to tweak Charles' conscience, deriding him for not knowing the answers to these questions. "I want to know what happened."

"Well," Bart solemnly closed the logger's glassy eyes and rose as well. But he didn't say anything else. A tall, spindly man with a bushy beard, he hung his head and squeezed his own eyes closed. The men standing around followed suit. Properly reminded of the solemnity of the moment, Charles kicked himself for his insensitive reaction. These men had just lost a comrade, possibly a friend. Not to mention, the accident could have killed anyone of them.

He waited a moment then said, "I'm sorry for my callous reaction. I didn't mean to seem cold, but I want to know what happened here."

With a heavy sigh, Bart surveyed the field of wreckage, his gaze darting everywhere. Something arrested his appraisal and he stepped quickly away from the group and over to a mass of logs and chains. "I saw it bust free. Looked like chain snap but not at hitching point." He picked up a length of chain, studied it, discarded it. Continuing his survey, he picked up another handful of the iron links.

Charles pinched the bridge of his nose, turned to the crew behind him. "Wrap up..." he paused for a name.

"Haggerty," a grimacing lumberjack offered. "Dan Haggerty."

"Let's get Dan to town for a proper burial."

Haggard, weary lumberjacks stirred, moving slowly, like ghosts. Charles got out of their way and joined Bart. "Anything?"

Holding a stretch of chain in his hands, Bart brought it closer to his face for a better inspection and narrowed his eyes. A troubled crease furrowed his brow.

"What is it?"

"No accident." Shock laced Bart's voice; his eyes locked with Charles. "It has been—how you say?—filed." The man passed the broken length of chain to Charles.

He grabbed it and peered closely at the iron. Truly, one link looked to have a perfect cut that went about three-quarters of the way through it before ending in a violent twist. Cut just enough to guarantee it would break at some point in the near future.

"Bastard," Bart whispered.

Charles ran his thumb over the link. Sick cattle. An accident here in the lumber camp. Could they be related? No, he pushed the thought away. Coincidence. But someone had sawed into this link. There could only be one intention behind such a deed. "Has there been anyone hanging around the camp? These men. How long have they been with you?"

Bart shrugged. "I see no one other than crew. All these men have been here since the first. Since," he struggled for the right word, "original. All original crew. And all of us, we barely get out of way."

Charles watched them for a moment, tenderly wrapping the dead man in a ragged quilt. Would one of them have done something like this to his own crew? Seemed a rather unpredictable plan to hurt someone if you couldn't guarantee you'd be out of harm's way.

Charles chewed on his lip, pondering the mystery. "Keep a man on guard duty tonight. I'll send up some extra men in the morning. Check all the chains, all the axes, all the saws for any damage. You understand?"

Bart nodded, wide-eyed with concern. "In Russia, rival loggers do these things often."

Only, Charles had no rivals in Defiance.

Matthew flashed in his mind.

I stand corrected, Lord.

CHAPTER 25

The late September breeze carried the scent of campfires, seared flesh, and warm dung to Charles as he tied Traveller to the corral fence. Two auxiliary corrals had been built, over a mile out from the ranch, upstream and away from the infected herd. Here, healthy cows bellowed, men whooped and waved their hats, directing new stock through the gates of one pen or the other. He'd purchased an additional hundred head from ranchers over in Gunnison. Half of the beeves were yearling heifers prime for breeding. After branding, they would head on their way to the north and join the healthy herd on four thousand acres.

He took a deep breath and grimaced. Contrary to what one might think, a burning cow did not smell like a steak. Death had its own scent. It smelled the same here as it had up at the lumber camp—an odor of something fearful, primeval.

Lane saw him and tipped his hat. "Boss." He sauntered over and rested an elbow on the top rail. "So far, the other herd is still—"

"Lane, listen," Charles interrupted. His friend's face tightened with concern. "There's been an accident at the lumber camp." Charles lowered his voice. "I want you to send a couple of boys up there to sort of be extra eyes. I'm on my way into town to see Beckwith."

"How long you want 'em up there?"

Charles appreciated the fact Lane never questioned an order. And not because he didn't have a backbone. He simply trusted Charles. "Just a day or so. I've got more lumberjacks coming in. They may already be in town."

"An accident, you say?"

"Yes." Charles raised his chin. "A link on a chain was filed nearly all the way through. Cost a man his life."

Lane whistled. "Oh, that kind of accident. Know who did it?"

"I may have an inkling who is behind it."

"Should we be worried here?"

Should they? "Worried, I wouldn't think so. But vigilance cannot hurt."

"All right. I'll tell a few men to go up there and keep their eyes peeled for trouble."

"You were saying about the herd?"

"The other half is still healthy."

"And the sick half?"

"We'll burn the last of the bodies today."

"Don't bring the others back down for at least a month. Keep them isolated."

"Yes, sir."

A shift in the breeze made Charles look past the corrals and back toward the ranch. He experienced a moment of déja vu as Emilio and his new palomino suddenly appeared from behind a hill, cantering at a good clip toward them. His mind jumped back to the day the young man had delivered two telegrams, one setting the arrival time of a preacher and the other warning of a murderous Indian on the rampage.

And even from this distance, something in Emilio's tense shoulders said he was delivering equally sobering news.

Charles pushed off the corral fence, ignoring Lane's puzzled look, and hurried to meet Emilio before he got too close to the men and aroused curiosity. Emilio and his mount crossed the last hundred yards at a slower, but determined, pace, trotting up to him. The boy seemed to sense Charles' desire for discretion and tried not to draw undue attention.

"Señor McIntyre."

McIntyre raised his hand and laid it on the horse's nose to stop his prancing. "What's wrong, Emilio?"

His top hand glanced about and leaned into his employer. "I rode up to the surveyor's camp with the supply wagon like you asked, but there is no one there."

"What do you mean there's no one there?"

The boy shook his head, at a loss to explain adequately. "The tents are set up, a fire was burning, but the coffee was burned. There was personal gear and equipment sitting around, and the horses were tied to a picket line, but no men. We waited for a time, then I went looking for them. Nothing."

"Signs of a struggle?"

"No, sir, but…"

Charles lifted his brow, waiting.

"Tracks. At least three men on horseback. Headed east, but I lost them in the shale. I thought you needed to know."

Charles checked the position of the late afternoon sun, resting atop the distant mountains. Only a few hours till dark. They could get there before nightfall, but not back. And he needed to see Beckwith. Still, something nagged at him that this couldn't wait. The lumberjacks would most likely tell Beckwith what happened. Charles could discuss it with him tomorrow. "Supply wagon still there, you say?"

"Yes, sir. I told him to wait."

"I'll get Traveller and ride back with you."

Logic argued Ruble and Barnes, the surveyor's he'd hired out of Denver, were most likely off doing just that—surveying. His gut, however, argued a more sinister scenario. He walked down the fence to where Traveller was waiting and unwound the reins.

"Another accident?" Lane asked softly.

"We'll see." He spun his horse away from the corral. "Please tell Naomi not to wait up."

---

*T*wilight throwing the world into lengthening shadows, Charles surveyed the clearing in the pines occupied by two tents, surveying gear, bed rolls, and horses still tied to a picket line.

But no surveyors.

He kneed Traveller and the horse ambled over to the supply wagon, their breath swirling in the cold air. Wilt Baxter sat in the driver's seat, his shoulders hunched, but he didn't look cold. His faded blue eyes glittered with fear.

"Wilt, you all right? You look like you've seen a ghost," Charles said.

"I wandered around a bit, didn't see nothin' but there's something here. I'll tell ya, men don't just disappear. If they're dead, we'll see their ghosts at midnight."

Superstitious old coot. Charles had to fight a sneer. He was in no mood for the old sailor's legends and myths born of a life at sea. "I think the quiet is getting to you."

"Yeah. It ain't natural. It's too quiet."

For an instant, Charles entertained the notion the woods did seem a touch somber, but at dusk most animals settled down. Besides, it was getting on into fall. Regardless of his logic, an uneasy chill ran up his spine. "Why don't you cook us a hot meal, Wilt? We'll spend the night here in case Barnes and Rubles show up. Emilio, before we lose the light, let's nose around some more."

The old man grumbled but nodded. "I'm gonna build a big fire tonight, too."

"You do that," Charles said absently, spinning his horse to face Emilio. "Show me which way they went."

They followed a deer trail out of the camp, through a forest of aspens, finally emerging onto a mountainside covered in shale. Loose and dangerous at any time, deadly at night. Worse, the slide disappeared over a cliff.

A fat, full, harvest moon rose on the horizon, casting bright, but eery light on the area. Charles gave his eyes a minute to adjust and the details came into focus. On the opposite side of the slide area, there appeared to be two trails, one heading up the mountain and over the ridge, the other down into the darkness of thick evergreens. "You know where those trails go?" he asked Emilio.

"No. Maybe old Indian paths. They don't look too used."

"Any chance they doubled back?"

"I am rusty, but I do not think so."

Charles dismounted, handed his reins to Emilio, and walked slowly down the shifting, sliding path. As he eased his way along, looking for signs of a disturbance, a hint of anything human, he hoped the two surveyors had been kidnapped. For a ransom, perhaps? To take a bite out of Charles? Ransom gave someone a reason to keep them alive.

He thought something glinted in the shale and he swung his head back to the left. There, yes. A glint of gold. He did not, however, relish the idea of moving toward it. Toward the cliff. Shale was notoriously fickle and as apt to slide as snow.

"Emilio, toss me one end of the rope off my saddle." The young man complied and Charles tied his end around his waist. "I see something. I doubt it's something worth dying for." Emilio secured the other end to the saddle horn.

Charles stepped off the slender trail, astonished how easily and willingly the shale slipped, drifted, slid. A cautious step at a time, he made his way toward the object that lay about halfway between the trail and the cliff. A few more feet and he knelt down and retrieved a pocket watch. He flipped it open and it chimed a soft, tinny version of *Blue Danube* chorus. Not weathered, not scratched, it was obvious the watch had not been here long.

He rose and turned to Emilio who had wrapped the rope around Traveller's saddle horn. "They were her—"

The shale cut loose and Charles' feet went out from under him. Emilio grabbed the rope and Traveller's halter as Charles went down on his bum. He rolled over on his stomach, scratching and clawing for purchase as he rocketed toward the cliff.

Dear God, let that rope hold—

"Mr. McIntyre!"

Charles' feet, then his legs launched over the edge before the rope snatched him to a violent stop. His movement arrested, he let out a breath he didn't know he'd been holding.

"I've got you, Mr. McIntyre. I've got you."

The rope started pulling Charles back as he glanced over the edge. Another ledge. Only a dozen or so feet below—

"Wait!" Something. He'd seen something. He needed to be sure. The motion stopped. "Lower me again, about a foot."

An instant later, he was sliding down again in another shower of shale. Grasping the rope with a fierce grip, he peered over his shoulder, over the edge of the cliff. The moonlight revealed two broken, twisted bodies fifty feet below him on another ledge.

The men stared up at Charles, the moonlight hiding their eyes in black, soulless shadows. It did not, however, hide the bullet holes in their foreheads.

———

a gray sky hung low, promising a cool, gloomy day ahead. Naomi pressed in close to Charles' for warmth, while trying not to restrict his ability to drive the wagon. He patted her knee absently but kept his eyes forward. His mind, she knew, was not on the bustling ranch around them, the dreary sky overhead, or their trip into Defiance.

Oh, Lord, she prayed, lightly hooking her fingers on his arm, *how can I help him? What can I say?*

"Someone is playing a dangerous game with me, Naomi. It has to be Matthew."

"I would have thought he'd learned his lesson dealing with you."

"Men like him don't learn anything. They follow the same, vengeful path their whole lives, heedless of the destruction in their wake."

"Yes, I guess that about sums him up."

"But, without proof, I don't know what Beckwith will be able to do."

"Let's take it one step at a time, Charles." She reached into her pockets and pulled out her gloves. "Tell him everything that's happened and see where it goes from there." She started working cold fingers into the gloves. "Maybe things aren't as related as you think."

"Maybe..." His expression hardened and she wondered what was happening to his heart. "But I will find out."

"*O* ut of my jurisdiction, but I'll ride up there and look around. Get Wade and bring the bodies back." Beckwith rose from his desk, snuffed his cigar, plucked his hat from the hook on the wall. "Go weeks with no real trouble, now I've got a dead lumberjack, two dead surveyors, and a nurse who's been stabbed."

"Stabbed?" Naomi stepped forward. "Surely you don't mean Hannah?"

"Nah. The new gal. Hope. Said she went over to see Amanda about Mary Ann's death and—"

"Mary Ann's dead?" Naomi felt as if the floor fell out from under her feet.

Charles clutched her elbow. "Are you all right? Who is Mary Ann?"

Sick with regret, Naomi shook her head. "The prostitute Hope saved. Hannah said Amanda performed the abortion and it was butchery." Needing to sit, she eased into the chair in front of Beckwith's desk. "I missed my chance." *Oh, God, forgive me, I missed the chance to tell her about You.*

"Well, uh," Beckwith pressed his hat to his chest, clearly knocked off-balance by Naomi's reaction.

"What happened to Miss Clark?" Charles asked him.

"Is she all right?" Naomi added.

"Think so. She was over at what folks have taken to calling Hell's Half-Acre. The little compound Matthew's running outside the town limits. Gambling, drinking, prostitution. But, again, I've got no jurisdiction." Beckwith sounded thoroughly disgusted. "Anyway, she spoke to Amanda, accused her of causing Mary Ann's death, and said she was coming to see me. She'd just crossed the creek when she was attacked. That, at least, did happen in my jurisdiction."

There was so much information in the lengthy statement, Charles seemed to stumble over it. "I—I don't understand. He closed the Chandelier? Moved it?"

Beckwith nailed Charles with a baleful glare. "Never shoulda officially accepted the job as town marshal. You've tied my hands. He's outside the town limits by about thirty feet."

"Thirty feet? How clever of him."

Naomi cared less about where Matthew conducted business

and more about Hope. "Were there any witnesses to Hope's attack?"

"Corky heard her scream. Ran to help, saw a man hightailing it through the woods. No description. Maybe he was tall." Again, Beckwith sounded disgusted.

Naomi looked up at her husband and flinched at the flint in his eyes. Brow creased, hands behind his back, he paced like an agitated lion as Beckwith finished.

"The nurse can't give me a description, either. The way I figure it, Amanda put somebody on the woman's trail. To hush her up is my guess, but, until I can prove that, not much I can do. Maybe I *should* retire."

Charles stopped. "Where'd that notion come from?"

"You ain't been in town for several days." Beckwith strode to the door and dropped his hat in place. "Go see your sister-in-law."

CHAPTER 26

*C*harles and Naomi crossed the busy street in silence. He knew she was upset about Mary Ann. He was preoccupied with the certainty that his sick cattle, the murders of the surveyors, the sabotage at the lumber camp, and the fact that Matthew had moved his operations to outside the town limits all tied together in a larger plan.

Truth be told, Charles believed the old rivalry was raising its ugly head again. He and Ian had tried fining Matthew out of existence. Instead, they'd only managed to fine him out of town —literally. And, Charles believed, pushed him to more dangerous acts.

He and Naomi stepped up on the boardwalk and into a surprisingly immovable wall of miners. At first, the men regarded Charles with open disdain, as evidenced by the cold stares and slightly curled lips. The man directly in front of Charles, bone-thin and rangy like a buzzard, locked gazes with him.

For an instant, Charles was surprised but the gambler in him rose to the occasion and he regarded the miner with a long-practiced air of hauteur. "Something I can do for you and your friends here?" Eyes ricocheted off the gun on his hip. He saw their fear and pushed the advantage. "Please don't let my sidearm dissuade you if you have something you'd like to say."

The men shifted, their posture deflated as they seemed to lose their nerve. The man standing before him dropped his gaze.

Charles sneered at their cowardice. "As I thought. I'm sure you all have some place to be."

Grumbling, they shoved their hands into their pockets, looked anywhere but at him, and sidled on by like whipped dogs.

Once they were out of earshot, Naomi exhaled a long breath. "What was all that about? I've never seen the men in this town act like that to you. Ever."

"Yes," Charles muttered, disturbed by it as well. Their respect —their fear of him—was it beginning to waver? Emilio had told Charles of a conversation he'd overheard—disgruntled miners. Charles had glossed over Emilio's concerns as paranoia. Now he was second-guessing the dismissive attitude. Was his grip on the town slipping?

Charles wondered—not for the first time—if he wasn't the murderous monster he used to be, could he really expect to hang on to Defiance?

He glanced over his shoulder at the retreating group of men. He'd put them on the run, backed them down. He did still wield power…and he still liked it.

Would the desire for it always be his weakness?

Help me keep my eyes on You, Lord, and I'll fight this your way. At least I'll try…

*C*harles made a valiant attempt to convince himself the war for the soul of Defiance would be fought by good Christian warriors on their knees. The handbill of Micah's letter and the advertisement from MP&G rattled his belief. They both reeked of hatred, violence, and vengeance. In short: Matthew.

"Micah didn't write this," he said, handing the handbill and the newspaper back to her. Thunderclouds formed in his soul. "I have no doubt Matthew either wrote that letter or hired the one who did. It explains the men we met on the street. And Matthew's on the board of MP&G." That was particularly interesting. "Which implies he is well funded enough to pay for some mischief and mayhem."

Charles walked away from the women to stare out the town hall's window. "What are you up to, Matthew?" he whispered to the passing traffic.

Paper rustled behind him and a moment later Naomi gasped at the handbill. "What is he thinking? This—this letter will tear the town apart. He's just reopening old wounds. Why did you print this, Rebecca?"

Good question and Charles rounded on his sister-in-law. Rebecca crumpled the paper. "We didn't." She tossed it into the trash can where it belonged. "We wouldn't. Ever. We printed the ad in the newspaper, not the letter."

Charles scratched his beard thoughtfully. "Then he has his own printing press." Wasn't hard to see what the plan was for it, either. "He's going to wage war on my holdings. And apparently, try to turn the town against me." Did his battle strategy include sabotaging a lumber wagon? Shooting surveyors? Spreading disease to cattle? Attacking women?

Was he after vengeance or power?

He glanced at Naomi, her cheeks red, but adorable with anger. Oddly, something about her appearance brought a memory back to him with a jolt. Charles recalled the look in Matthew's eyes when he'd spotted the savage Indian One-Who-Cries aiming his rifle at Charles' back. Matthew had kept silent

—because a dead Charles McIntyre meant a clear path to Naomi.

Was this all about her?

---

*M*atthew did not enjoy Sam's company, but knew since the little troll was reporting on him back to MP&G, tolerance was called for. He poured the lawyer a drink and slid it across the table. "Ching Lee is in the back, cooking up steaks."

The Chandelier was empty at the moment, except for them. The Number Two, however, over in Hell's Half-Acre was doing a booming business. He'd go over in a little while, but for the moment, despite the company, he was enjoying the quiet.

Sam picked up the drink and swirled it around. "Steak, steak, steak. My wife does a wonderful baked chicken. I miss her chicken." Gloom settled on his face and he set the drink back down.

"Well, go home then. Have the board send a different attorney out to watch me."

"I'm not *just* an attorney," he said, sounding offended. "I was a journalist first. One of the things I'm supposed to do is help you swing the people of Defiance over to our side. The handbills seem to be working nicely."

Matthew chuckled. "Yeah, a few more of them and half this town is going to lynch McIntyre."

Sam frowned. "No, I don't think we'll push them that far. That would be unconsci—"

The front doors squeaked and both men looked over. Davis Ferrell peeked in, then stepped inside. "Look, Sam, it's Ichabod Crane."

The gangly lawyer, who moved with the nervous grace of a cockroach, frowned at the comment and strode toward them.

"Your creative language is getting you in trouble, Mr. Miller." He looked at Sam. "And you are?"

Sam stood up to shake the man's hand, just as Matthew leaned back in the chair, draping his arm over the back of it. "My attorney."

"Sam Bullock."

The two shook and then Davis reached inside his coat. "Perhaps I should be presenting this to you. Mr. McIntyre is suing your client for libel, slander, and defamation of character."

Sam took the legal papers, scowling at them. "That is tedious, time-consuming case work."

Ferrell cut his eyes to Matthew. "Exactly. *Very* expensive. *Very* time-consuming. We have named the members of MP&G's board in the suit as well. Good day, gentlemen."

Ruminating on this new development, Matthew sat in silence for several minutes after Ferrell left, while Sam read the suit. Finally, the man set the paperwork aside and went back to his steak.

"Well," Matthew said, "What's he up to?"

"Exactly what Mr. Ferrell said. This is an attempt to tie you and the board up in court and make you spend money. No one wins here except the attorneys." He wiped his mouth. "Which is fine by me, but I doubt the board will be thrilled."

Matthew pushed his steak away, his appetite gone. He was almost surprised at McIntyre for employing a such a civilized, but pure paper-tiger attack. Not usually his style. Yep, maybe the king of Defiance really had gone soft. Maybe fatherhood had quenched the man's fire, made him cautious.

In which case, taking Defiance was going to be that much easier, if not as much fun.

His gaze drifted back to Sam. Easy, but only if he kept interference from MP&G to a minimum.

CHAPTER 27

*E*milio settled into his corner table at The Trinity Inn and waited for Mollie to notice him. Tonight, she didn't even bother taking his order. Within five minutes, she was at his table setting down a bowl of beef stew and coffee.

His joy must have shown on his face. Mollie clutched his shoulder and laughed. "I'm starting to wonder if your extra visits into town are to see me or just to sample Lucy's cooking."

Emilio's face froze. He honestly considered her joke for a moment and realized the pause implied all the wrong things. "It's not the cooking," he said, consciously trying to keep his foot from his mouth.

Mollie's face softened, practically shone, and Emilio breathed a little easier.

"I wasn't sure," she said hesitantly, pulling her braid around to fidget with it. "The way you took off out of here last week."

"Oh," he waved away her concern. "I remembered I had something I had to tell Mr. McIntyre. Something important. I'm sorry." And he was. Turned out, Mr. McIntyre had been almost dismissive of Emilio's concerns. "It won't happen again."

After a moment, she brightened, like a candle glowing to life.

He felt his apology had been accepted, especially when she said, "I'll go ahead and get seconds in the works." Biting her lip, she smiled shyly and headed back to the kitchen.

Emilio picked up his spoon, but his hunger for the stew had tempered. It was awfully easy to say the wrong thing to a female. Of course he came for the food. But he also came to see Mollie. He came *mostly* to see Mollie. He couldn't see any reason not to enjoy the good food while he was waiting for her shift to end. Seemed a perfectly reasonable way to spend his time—

A squeal pulled his attention across the room. *Not again*, he thought, until he realized Mollie was the one in trouble this time. She was snatching her hand free of someone's grasp and her expression roared disapproval. Emilio launched to his feet and raced over to her.

That fool Buck was reaching for Mollie again, pawing at her hand. "I'm not asking you to marry me, little sister. Just have a drink with me."

"I said no, thank you."

Before she had finished rebuking Buck's advance, Emilio was standing beside her, glaring at Buck. The man's eyes widened a hair, then his jaw tightened. "What's the matter, compadre? Am I cuttin' in on your dance?"

Emilio was so angry he could barely speak. "Sí." Buck had laid hands on Mollie and something furious and explosive had risen up in Emilio's heart. He took a breath now to think this through, get his self-control back, because this sudden loss of rational thinking surprised him. "But even if you weren't, you don't act like that in here. Behave or I'll get the marshal."

"Oooooh," Buck shivered melodramatically inside his grimy jacket. "Not the marshal. Guess I'd better behave." He looked down at his half-eaten steak, shook his head as if lamenting it, then swung his gaze back up to Emilio, the scar on his cheek turning bright pink. "Or not." In a blur of movement, Buck shot up from his chair, drove his right shoulder into Emilio's gut, and the two went flying into a nearby table with a thunderous crash. Guests screamed and scattered, silverware and china clattered, gravy, mashed potatoes, and peas spilled everywhere.

Buck scrambled clumsily to his feet, slipping on the potatoes. Emilio clung to the man's collar, rose with him and threw a sloppy, off-balance punch that barely connected. Not fazed by it, Buck took a jab at Emilio's chin. He dodged it, and followed it with a right hook. Good and sound, it snapped Buck's head back. He staggered, slipping free of Emilio's grasp.

While Buck shook out the cobwebs, Emilio planted his feet and raised his fists. Before the fight could go on, deputy Wade Davis' long, lanky frame appeared out of thin air and he stepped between the two warring parties, his face under his cowboy hat as red as his hair. "That'll be enough, boys." He glared at Buck, raised his eyebrows at Emilio. "I'm surprised at you. What goes on here?"

Mollie stepped out of the crowd of displaced diners. "Emilio didn't start this. This one," she jerked her chin toward Buck, "didn't want to take no for an answer. Get a whiff and that'll explain everything."

Buck moved forward suddenly and Wade raised a hand. "You stay put. Move again and I'll arrest you." He sniffed. Whiskey wafted off Buck like smoke from a fire. "Probably will anyway."

The man backed down. Billy pushed through the crowd and surveyed the mess with a scowl. "You all right, Emilio?"

"Sí. Sorry for the damage."

Billy waved him off and looked at Buck. "You can pay for it now and leave, and we'll call it a night. Or you can let Wade here escort you to jail and we'll go from there."

"You ain't even going to question him?" Buck looked fit to be tied that no one was blaming Emilio.

Billy narrowed his eyes at the new man in town. "Mister, if Emilio had to fight you, I know there was good reason."

Buck sputtered, cursed, swiped his hat from the table. "Ain't the first place I've busted up." He reached into his front pants pocket and pulled out some coins. Glancing at the two double eagles, he held out his hand. "Forty dollars should cover it." Billy took the money without saying a word. Buck shifted his attention back to Emilio. "Am I fired?"

Was he? Emilio had the authority. But Buck was an acceptable ranch hand. In fact, he was hard-working and showed up every day on time, sober. This fracas hadn't been work-related.

Truthfully, Emilio didn't want to be accused of firing the man out of jealousy over Mollie. "Improve your manners and I'm willing to give you a second chance, but it's up to Mollie. Apologize to her first. "

Buck looked neither contrite nor cocky. "Well, I'd like to keep the job, so…sorry, ma'am."

Mollie took a deep breath. "Fine. Apology accepted. Just leave."

Emilio nodded, willing to move forward. Buck plopped his hat in place and shouldered his way out of the restaurant.

Across from him, Mollie gazed up at Emilio with a look even he couldn't misread—adoration.

The stitches in Hope's back looked good and clean. Hannah exhaled with relief and dropped the woman's shirt. "No sign of infection. I'd say you are healing up well."

Hope turned and gingerly laid back down in the bed. "I am fortunate and I know it."

"I wouldn't say it was fortune that kept the blade from dicing your kidney."

Hope closed her eyes. "Providence then?"

"You make Him sound so distant, so impersonal."

"To me, He is."

"I'm sorry." *For you.*

Hope flinched as if she'd heard the thought. "Hannah, I was raised by a highly esteemed doctor who believes solely in science. He had great aspirations for a son to follow in his footsteps. He got a daughter instead and made do. Match that with Edward, who wanted to make me over in the mythical, iconic image of womanhood. They were in a friendly tug-of-war and I was the rope. Can you blame me for seeing God as a controlling, distant, selfish know-it-all?"

"It sounds like your whole life other people have been telling you how to think."

Hope stiffened. "How dare you."

"I'm sorry, I don't meant to offend, but you need to know not all men are like that, and especially not Jesus. He is good and He loves you."

Hope sagged, as if she could barely manage any patience with this conversation, but Hannah wouldn't be deterred. "You're not here in Defiance by accident. Charles was like you. He didn't have time for God either. And his reputation—" Hannah whistled in awe, "it would curl your hair. Now look what love has done to him."

"That's all well and good, Hannah. I'm glad Mr. McIntyre found something he can believe in. As I said, I believe in science. With science, only facts matter. What's provable. No moral dilemmas. Should I or shouldn't I perform abortions? There was no reason not to have helped Mary Ann."

Silence fell between them as Hannah realized Hope was still blaming herself for Mary Ann's death. Surely, she wouldn't—

No, Lord, don't let her dismiss innocent life like that. Mary Ann made her choices...

"Men make up the rules, Hannah," Hope continued. "Women are forced to play by them. If we break them, we're penalized. Treated like pariahs. Mary Ann was merely trying to stay in the

game, as it were. Take charge of her choices *and* her consequences."

A sick feeling washed over Hannah. "Would you consider
killing a baby?"

Hope squirmed. "To save a woman from Amanda? Science
would tell me yes."

Hannah's heart felt so heavy. Hope needed real *hope*, not
science. She needed to see sin had consequences. People made
their own choices, but the innocent shouldn't pay for them.

"When is Mary Ann's funeral?"

"The funeral is today," Hannah said hesitantly. "Did you want
to—?"

"Yes." Hope pressed her hand to her back and slowly sat up
again. "I very much would like to go. If you'll help me."

"Of course."

Though Hannah wasn't convinced it was the place for them.
*Please, Lord, open Hope's eyes. Help her to see how lost and adrift
those girls are. How lost SHE is without You.*

---

*H*er back throbbing mightily from the wound,
Hope leaned on Hannah, and they, along with
Mollie, inched their way up the hillside. Hope gathered from the
scant conversation between the two girls that Mary Ann had
been an acquaintance of Mollie's.

"These girls. You know many of them?" she asked Mollie
carefully.

A gust of cold wind drew them closer together as aspen and
maple leaves swirled in the air over their heads. Mollie nodded.
"I used to be one of them. I was on the verge of suicide when the
Lord pulled me back from the edge."

Hope forced the sneer back from her lips. More talk of Jesus.

It made her so uncomfortable, but, like Hannah, Mollie would not be stopped.

"I was in a terrible place and the sisters showed up. They told me about Jesus, about the hope I had in Him." She stopped and looked at Hope, light shining in her eyes. "If that was my name, I'd never be able to say it without a smile. Knowing what Jesus has done for me, it would be like a prayer on my lips."

Hope offered a polite, but awkward smile, and nodded. "That's lovely."

"I know I sound crazy. But if you'd known me before, how miserable I was…" she shook her head and shivered. "If something saved my life, you could understand why I would want to talk about it, right?"

"Of course." The fact that Mollie had apparently left the sordid lifestyle tweaked something in Hope's belief about soiled doves and their potential to change, to seek out different, better career choices. Perhaps, if someone showed them compassion— through actions as well as words—then maybe these women could find the courage to believe in themselves.

But Hope was a doctor, not a spiritual savior.

Thankfully, the girls reached the hill-top cemetery and conversation about Jesus faded. A small gathering of six or seven women and one very large, handsome, blond man stood round the grave.

"Who is that?" Hope asked Hannah. The delay in the girl's response declared her discontent with him.

"He was my uncle. I guess he still is, I don't know. Naomi's first husband John died. Matthew came to take us back to California with him and he's been a thorn in *our* side ever since."

Her own wound throbbing, Hope grimaced and gave Hannah a small nod of understanding. They joined the group of mourners at the grave and were immediately met by baleful glares. Except from Amanda. The woman looked about to speak when Matthew inched forward. "You've got some nerve coming to this funeral." His glance flicked over all three of them but rested on Hope. "Especially you."

"Uncle Matt—"

"Matthew," he corrected sternly. "Just Matthew now. And your friend here is the reason Mary Ann is six feet under. You all should leave."

Hannah started to protest, but Hope jumped in first. "Mary Ann died because Amanda is a butcher."

"You've got your story wrong, missy," Amanda snarled. "Don't go blaming your butchery on me. Mary Ann was fine. She panicked over a little bleeding and you opened her up like a can of oysters." Amanda turned to the other girls present. "She's just trying to save her skin by making me look bad. Well, I didn't kill Mary Ann. She did."

"That is not true," Hope protested stepping in close to Amanda.

Amanda leaned toward her as well, dropping her hands to her hips. "If you're so skilled, why didn't she come to you first?"

"She did."

A stunned silence settled on the group. "Then why didn't you do it?" One of the girls beside Amanda asked.

"Because I don't d-do that...abortions," Hope stuttered.

Amanda and Matthew grinned and Hope realized she had stepped into a trap.

The black girl nodded to the group. "She can't do anything else, either, sounds like. You know who to come see if the occasion arises."

"Stop it," Mollie yelled, stepping in between Hope and Amanda and pushing them apart. "This is awful." She scanned the other girls. "This is no way to remember Mary Ann. The best thing you can do for her and yourselves is leave this life." She speared Matthew with a heated glare. "You're no different than their customers." She swung back to the girls in attendance. "I used to be just like you, you know that. You don't have to live like this. Come to the inn any time."

"We'll help you," Hannah interjected eagerly. "Like we helped Mollie."

"You need to leave," Matthew suggested softly, menacingly.

Obvious hurt crossed Hannah's face and Hope felt a twinge of embarrassment for her. Mollie held firmly onto her angry expression for the man.

"Come on, Hannah." Hope took her hand. "He's right. Obviously, we shouldn't be here." Hannah clenched her jaw and took Hope's elbow. As the group parted to let them pass, however, Hope stopped and met their gazes with her chin raised. "But know this, ladies. I'm not the liar here."

At least, I'm not lying about who killed Mary Ann.

———

CHAPTER 28

*B*illy wiped his mouth and laid his napkin down on the table. "Let me take him so you can finish." He pushed his ash blond hair off his forehead and reached across the table. Though the hotel dining room was bustling and noisy, their boy was nearly falling asleep in Hannah's plate. Eyes drooping, he went willingly to his father and curled up against his shoulder. Billy leaned back with him and watched a sullen Hannah poke at her food. "I'm surprised you thought the funeral was a good idea."

She stabbed a pea. "They're so lost. They need to hear—I thought they'd at least be polite. Tolerant. It was a funeral, after all."

"I get the distinct impression Matthew is interested in building a lot of things in Defiance, but harmony isn't one of them."

"What makes you say that?"

"I've noticed men in Defiance who aren't here for the gold. At least, they aren't miners."

"Well, I heard Matthew's opening a new saddle shop, a blacksmith shop, a furniture store, even a pharmacy."

"To compete with Charles' businesses. But that's not even what I'm referring to. Some of these men are trouble, Hannah. I've seen their kind before." Could, in fact, still feel a few punches from an incident in Dodge City. "They're here to stir up trouble. One of them could have attacked Hope. And that handbill about stringing up Charles—this could all get very dangerous very fast."

"Emilio said he heard some bad talk like that in the restaurant." She bounced her fork in her hand. "But I can't believe the whole town would turn against him."

"It wouldn't take the whole town. Just a few loudmouths and a handful of men with guns."

"You should go see Charles then and tell him what you think."

"I was planning on it. But, listen," he delicately shifted Little Billy a touch higher on his shoulder and reached out for Hannah's hand. "I want you and Hope to be very careful. I'd like to tell you to quit nursing—" Hannah's eyes widened and he nodded. "Yeah, I know. So I won't say that. But Emilio and I talked about it. We're going to make an effort to keep an eye on you two. Mollie as well."

Unexpectedly, Billy saw a softness start to glimmer in Hannah's beautiful, azure eyes. She smiled at him, but the warmth in the expression baffled him. It seemed to be saying something he couldn't hear.

"Can you believe you ever ran out on me?"

Billy's spirits plunged. He hugged his sleeping son and swallowed against the tightening in his throat. He'd nearly lost Hannah and Billy. Once, by abandoning her and then, when he'd finally made it to Defiance, she'd been building a relationship with Emilio.

Still smiling, she squeezed his hand. "I know you love me. I know you love Little Billy."

He brought her hand to his mouth for a kiss. "And I'll never leave you again. Not unless you want me to."

Her eyes saucered. "Want you to? Nothing could make me want you to leave us. I want to spend the rest of my life with you."

"What about nursing?"

She sighed, but it sounded more like exasperation than sadness. "Nursing is a career, one I want. But I know what I want more." The smile shifted to one of mischief. "I got a package today."

He raised his eyebrows waiting for her explanation.

"My gown. My wedding gown. And I can't wait to wear it."

---

*H*ope sat down at the window of the waiting room and stared out at the evening settling in. Long shadows reached across the forlorn path that led to Main Street. Time for dinner and she should head to the hotel, but she didn't feel like eating. Or, more precisely, after the cold reception at Mary Ann's funeral, she didn't feel like eating alone.

Oh, she always saw someone in the hotel she could chat with but...sometimes those polite conversations left her feeling so empty. And right now, she was more empty than usual. Worse, since the attack, she was nervous about walking home alone and had prevailed upon the marshal and the deputy to escort her these last several nights. Yet somehow their company had left her more unsettled than ever.

Sighing, she faced up to the fact that she was lonely. Lonely and longing for a real friend. Perhaps something more than a friend.

The Regulator clock's *tick tick tick* hammered away at the silence in the office and Hope let her gaze drift down to her hands, folded in her lap. She'd had a busy day with several patients, and she was gratified to be making inroads with at least some of the town's residents—a reminder why she should go to the hotel for dinner. She often saw people there she'd tended. Met their families. Made a few new patients.

Unbidden, her mind drifted to Mr. Chandler. Again. He had come in today to have his stitches removed. He'd worked smiles and chuckles from her and scowls for a smirking Hannah. The girl's teasing was merciless. Thinking about the two of them both lifted Hope's spirits and made her sad.

A knock on her door jerked her head up. Assuming a patient was calling, she rose quickly, ignoring the slight twinge in her side. Relieved at having the maudlin thoughts chased away, she opened the door with a smile. "Good eve—"

Her heart did an unexpected flutter when she discovered Mr. Chandler standing on her threshold. Twirling his hat in his hands, he'd obviously bathed and his hair, blond as corn silk, had been trimmed recently. He wore a red cotton shirt under his sheepskin coat, and a black string tie. He'd shaved, as evidenced by tight, smooth skin and the smell of lilac water. His hair, the color of sunshine, gleamed in the office's light. Quite the change from the dusty, dirty cowboy she'd treated.

"Mr. Chandler."

A bashful smile tweaked his lips. "Ma'am."

"What can I do for you? Is your hand all right?"

"Yes, ma'am." He held it up and wiggled his fingers. "Fit as a fiddle. You did a fine job taking out the stitches today. Heck, you did a good job putting them in. I'm barely gonna have a scar."

"That's lovely to hear. What can I do for you? No other accidents, I hope."

The man opened his mouth, but no sound came out. He grinned sheepishly and tried again. "I don't know what's the matter with me." He cleared his throat and squared his shoulders. "Miss Hope, I was wondering if you'd like to join me for dinner?"

A *yes* rose immediately to her lips, but she caught it before it escaped. She wasn't sure this was wise. His keen, hazel eyes bid her to think otherwise. "Um, well, I was just on my way to the hotel for supper. I suppose it would be all right if we dined together. But I'll pay for my own."

He screwed his handsome face up into a pensive frown, but after a moment relaxed it. "I reckon that'll have to do for starters."

"Well, if you're sure."

Mr. Chandler extended his elbow. "I am, ma'am. I am."

Once at the hotel, Hope began to regret the decision. Mollie seated them, handed them the menus, and promised to return, but not before Hope caught sight of an amused smile twitching on the girl's lips. *Well*, she thought, *when we ask for two checks, that should alleviate any gossip.*

Across from her, Mr. Chandler jiggled the menu, which would indicate he was not actually reading it. He seemed nervous and after a moment laid it down. Hope did not meet his gaze as she tried to concentrate on the food choices, but she could feel his stare.

"The pot roast is pretty good," he said.

"Yes, and I see baked chicken on the menu tonight. It has not disappointed me."

"The steak's the best, though. Comes fresh from the King M."

"Oh."

"Not much of a beef-eater?"

"No, I'm just not sure what I'm in the mood for." Considering she had three choices... "I think I'll get the baked chicken."

"Yeah. That's good, too. Me, I'm leaning toward the steak."

"You don't get tired of it?"

"Not yet." He chuckled and she offered a little smile, puzzling over how she'd come to be dining with him.

"So, that fella who didn't want you to become a nurse—"

"Edward, yes?"

"Yeah, uh, you sure don't say his name with any affection."

Their conversation was interrupted by a young Hispanic girl who poured their water and took their order. When she left, Hope tried to refocus on Mr. Chandler's question, except he hadn't actually asked one. "I'm sorry. We were speaking of Edward."

"There it is again. An edge in your voice. You're still pretty sore at him?"

The observation took Hope back. Edge? Sore? Meaning angry? Hurt? "I can honestly say, Mr. Chandler, time has allowed me to realize we both made the right choice. He couldn't live with my desire to, uh, nurse, and I couldn't live without it."

"So, you've got no regrets he got away?"

"Mr. Chandler, forgive me, but these are very personal questions. Still…" She smoothed the napkin in her lap. "I am glad to be where I am." She looked up. "I mean, I'm glad to be in Defiance."

Surprise and amusement rolled across the man's face almost instantly, ending with what Hope would have described as something amorous. "I'm glad you're in Defiance, too."

"Mr. Chandler, please, I'd—"

"Lane. Please call me Lane."

She hesitated, then nodded. "Lane. I'd like to emphasize that I'm here to work. Serve the community. Make Defiance a better, healthier place to live. Do you understand what I'm getting at?"

"Sure. Sounds like you don't want any romantic entanglements." He pronounced the words carefully, as if he had read them on a sign somewhere.

"Precisely. I very much do not want to mislead you."

"So I shouldn't get the wrong idea?"

"Yes."

"You're just here 'cause I was walking this way?"

"More or less."

"But my company isn't repulsive?"

"Repulsive, no."

Mischief danced in his eyes. "You know why *I'm* here?"

"Not exactly."

"I got to thinking about you being stabbed and already back to tending folks. But Hannah said you walk to dinner alone. Every night. I can't come in to Defiance every night, but I'm gonna do what I can to help keep you safe."

"Oh." Hope was both pleased and oddly a little disappointed. "You're merely trying to act as a bodyguard? Like the marshal and his deputy. They do walk me home."

He narrowed his gaze and studied her intensely for a moment, to the point Hope felt she was revealing unintentional truths. As if agreeing, his pleased grin reappeared, bigger this time. "Bodyguard? Not exactly. I'm gonna prove out that other Texas myth. The one about being determined past the point of smart. Only thing is, determination usually works out for me."

CHAPTER 29

From the top of a hill, Charles and Traveller stared down at the idle railroad camp. The horse grumbled, sounding as disgusted as he felt. Frost glimmered on the edges of the seven sturdy wall tents, the housing for lengthy stays, as smoke billowed out their chimneys. Work on the winter cabins had not started yet, as evidenced by a wagon still loaded with logs. Stacks of iron rails and timbers for the rail bed sat off to the side, untouched.

No progress. Of any kind. In three days.

A group of a dozen men, some holding their morning coffee, stood around a roaring campfire, yelling over each other and gesticulating wildly. The still, cold morning carried their words up to Charles clear as a church bell.

"Mighty steep inclines. That usually raises the pay."

"I'm not working for a penny less than $12 a month. This is harder work than he said."

"Twice as steep as we thought."

"Mountains are always hard. He shoulda knowed that meant more pay."

"Plus we gotta get across the Animas."

That last voice, high-pitched, nasally, like a Texas twang, Charles realized had risen to the surface more than the others. And always with a complaint.

Like now.

"That trestle's gonna have to be a hundred feet high. We ain't got enough men for that."

"And I ain't doing the work of two men if I don't get paid for it."

So, this was the strike about which Emilio had heard whispers. These men hadn't even settled in and something—or someone—had set them to complaining about wages and work.

So be it, he thought, nudging Traveller forward. "Let's dive right in and deal with it."

Horse and rider sashayed into the midst of the melee. One by one the voices fell silent and eventually a pristine quiet reigned. Charles looked the men over one by one, and settled on one gentleman with greasy hair and a craggy, weathered face. "You Jack Tempe?"

"Yeah, that's right."

"Texan?"

"Third generation."

Charles nodded. "Maybe you should go back there. In fact, I know you should. You're not working here anymore."

"All I did was talk to these boys about—"

"All you did was sow discord. And throw us over a week behind schedule." Charles leveled a stern glare on the other men. "I did not misrepresent any portion of this project. You were told there were mountains. You were told you would be building a trestle, at which point I would be bringing in more men. If you are not happy with your agreed upon wages of ten dollars a month, you can leave with Tempe here."

"You can fire me," Tempe said, stepping forward, "and all these men. But you got to replace them. That'll take days." A tiny fraction of the man's lip twitched with smugness. "You'd be better off to negotiate."

A valid point, but Charles' pride rose up in him. He wouldn't be pushed into…

Into thinking with his pride instead of his good sense?

One man, Jim Turner, tossed a hammer down at the edge of the fire. "While you think about it, Mr. McIntyre, I'm going to go into town to get some supplies and have a drink. You take your time."

"You boys write down your demands and I'll consider them."

The expressions of the men staring at him turned slightly triumphant. Charles held onto his grim expression but knew he'd lost ground with the offer. Compromise from Charles McIntyre was a sign of weakness to these men. Turner lifted his chin in arrogance, thereby choosing the path Charles had to take.

Lord, forgive me…

"But, for now, Jim, you'll pick up that hammer and get back to work or you'll deal with me personally." The man didn't move. "I'll be happy to give you a nudge," Charles added.

Tension singed the air. The man's eyes darted to the hammer, to his co-workers, back to Charles. And Charles merely waited. An undervalued skill—the art of the quiet, patient bluff. Only, this was no bluff. If the man pushed, Charles would have to push back.

Apparently, Turner came to the same conclusion. He snatched the hammer up from the edge of the fire, paused for a moment to glare at everyone, then squared his shoulders and stomped off to finish his shift.

Satisfaction over the power he wielded surged through Charles. He looked at Tempe and tapped the brim of his hat. "Give my regards to Texas."

*S*atan *goes about like a roaring lion, seeking whom he may devour.*

The Scripture wouldn't leave Charles' head. It had haunted him for two days now.

He drifted a few steps over and sat down on his favorite rock beside the Animas River glimmering brilliantly beneath a full moon. He looked out across his land, across the remaining, smaller herd dotting the hills a mile away. His gaze traveled beyond them to the distant mountains, washed in the mystical moonlight.

He loved this land. His ranch. If all the cattle died, he would start over. If the lumber mill and sawmill ground to a halt, he would invest again to reopen them. If all the men on the railroad quit, he would be patient and replace them. If he went broke, he would start over and rebuild his fortune.

He could survive losing all of it except Naomi, Two Spears, and the child he hadn't met yet. Eventually Matthew would figure that out. And come for them. And Charles could not—would not—allow it to go that far.

Ultimately, Father, I believe he wants to hurt her. And I will stop him.

YOU will stop him?

God tried to speak to Charles' heart, but he stood up, purposely closing his ears to the still, small voice. "This is my fight. I'll draw him out. He'll make a mistake and Beckwith can bring in the U.S. Marshal." It would be neat, clean, legal.

Or else.

———

CHAPTER 30

"*I* tell you, Ian, I believe Matthew is behind it all." Charles dropped his pencil, rose from his desk, and stormed to his window overlooking Main Street. Traffic was increasing. Miners willing to work at the Sunnyside were drifting in every day. Businesses were going up at an impressive rate over in Tent Town, intent on beating winter. The faint thunder of hammers in a flurry of construction mingled ominously with the clatter of men and horses on the street.

Was history repeating itself? Only, instead of Delilah trying to corrupt the town, was Mathew going to do the dirty work himself this time? But why, exactly? "There is a larger plan here than I'm seeing."

Behind him, Ian sighed. "Perhaps ye're right, but I'm willing to entertain another idea."

Charles rubbed his leg. The battle wound had been bothering him more as of late. Stress-related, he assumed. It always flared up when his mind wasn't right. When he was leaning toward dark thoughts. As in, the pleasure he would get from shutting Matthew down. Permanently. He turned to his friend as a way of physically backing away from the image. "Another idea. Such as?"

Ian shrugged. "I was thinking we should study the possibility things aren't as related as ye think. For example," he pulled a pipe from his breast pocket and began to prepare for a smoke, "The incidents we are looking at are yer sickened cattle, the sabotage at the lumber camp, the murder of the surveyors. Aye?"

"Aye." What was he getting at? "The labor strike, too, don't forget."

"What if the cattle are sick because of natural causes and the surveyors crossed the wrong land owner? They do tend to make enemies when they're cutting out slabs of land on which to lay track. And men will strike for more money. 'Tis historical fact."

Charles decided to give some weight to the counsel. A wise man would. "True. Cattle get sick. Surveyors can enmesh themselves in the politics of power. There's still the death at the lumber camp—clearly due to sabotage."

"True. Though nothing here connects it directly or obviously to Matthew."

"I offered to buy his lumberyard and sawmill. He would have figured that, if he did not sell, I would simply build my own. He has reason to stop me. But there's more here." Charles waved his hand back and forth, erasing a mental chalkboard, and tried to find the bigger plan behind all this. "He's on the board of this MP&G, a position which suggests he is either well-funded or well-connected and will be even more so when the mine re-opens. And twice men have considered standing up to me." Ian's brow rose. "I trace that directly back to the inflammatory rhetoric Matthew is paying that spineless attorney to print."

Ian took a few thoughtful puffs on the pipe, let the smoke swirl around his head. After a moment of silence, he nodded. "A battle for yer kingdom?"

"Suggesting this is about the town?" Ian shrugged a shoulder but Charles shook his head. "Yes and no. It's more personal than that."

"He wants to ruin ye then? Ye ran him out of town once. He'd like to return the favor?"

Was that the reason? Bruised pride? Revenge? His gut told him something different. "I went by Davis Ferrell's office today. Did you know he has left our fair town? Cleared out yesterday, Timmons at the bank said."

"Left? What prompted that, do ye think?"

"Timmons said he saw Otis coming out of Farrell's office a few hours before Ferrell left."

Ian grunted. "The man was as jumpy as a rabbit. Probably didn't take much to scare him away. What do ye think Matthew is after then, if he is behind all this? And scaring Farrell out of town implies something."

"He wants to be lord and master of Defiance. But it's for Naomi."

Ian's brow pinching, he rose from his chair, his skepticism written all over his face. "That's a bit unlikely, don't ye think?"

"Why?"

"Well, based on everything ye've said, the planning, the plotting it's all—I dinnae ken, do ye not think it's a bit elaborate if he's just trying to win back a woman?"

Charles sucked on his cheek and tried to reason all this out. And perhaps that was the problem. There was no reason. No rational thought. It made more sense if Matthew was simply insane.

"What if he's not trying to win her back?" Charles looked at Ian. "What if he just wants us to suffer. Or her, specifically? I need to flush him out. See what he's really after."

"If it is aboot her, this could start a war."

Pondering the idea, Charles drifted over to the edge of his desk, tapped his fingers on it in absent rhythm. This constant struggle to be either a man of God or the man who ruled Defiance was maddening at times. But maintaining control over the town was the only way he could guarantee Naomi and the baby's safety. "Then I'll finish it."

"Pray before ye do anything."

"Of course. My first thought." The lie burned on his tongue. *I will pray, Lord. Duly reminded...*

"*W*hat if he's not trying to win her back?" Charles said softly, thoughtfully.

Naomi lowered her hand, just shy of knocking on the office door.

"What if he just wants us to suffer. Or her, specifically? I need to flush him out. See what he's really after."

"If it is aboot her, this could start a war?"

They had to be talking about Matthew. What was he up to now? Eavesdropping was a terrible practice, but if he was trying to ruin Charles, Naomi should know. And she wouldn't put it past Matthew. He'd always been one for holding grudges.

She could hear tapping and imagined Charles drumming his fingers on his desk. "Then I'll finish it."

"Pray before ye do anything."

"Of course. My first thought."

Naomi turned away and slipped quietly outside before the fury bubbling up in her exploded to the surface. Matthew had been nothing but trouble since coming to Defiance. Naomi was sick of him. Sick of him endangering her family, her town, her husband. Something had to be done with the man. *Oh, Lord, what is it going to take to stop Matthew?*

The old Charles, a voice whispered.

No. Naomi clenched her hands into tight fists. *No.*

CHAPTER 31

Then I'll finish it.

Naomi couldn't get Charles' threat out of her head. It had a chilling effect on her. Like a funeral bell. And the terrifying nightmares of Matthew only added to her edginess.

Finally, she knew she had to go see her brother-in-law.

Maybe...maybe he could be reasoned with. Naomi looked heavenward. *Maybe, if this is about me, Lord, I can play on his feelings. Maybe he'll see this*—she patted her stomach—*and give up, have compassion, wish me well...*She sighed. *It's worth a try.*

Or so she argued as she strode toward the old Crystal Chandelier, one hand resting on her obviously expanding abdomen. Tent Town was busy again, bustling with men settling in, preparing for the mine opening, or working on various buildings that were under construction. So many, in fact, she had to stop at an intersection and get her bearings. She only recognized it because the laundry was still there. On each side of it, new businesses were springing up. Their signs said a leather shop and a blacksmith shop would be opening soon.

She turned right and worked her way down Water Street, surprised by the bold stares of men who clearly were new in town if they didn't know who she was. She ignored them and hurried on, each step causing her doubts to grow.

What if Matthew isn't there? What if he's across the creek, outside the town limits? Lord, if he's here, I mean to talk to him. But if he's over there, I won't go. I won't put one foot in Hell's Half-Acre or Popcorn Alley.

She hated that name. She'd heard it a while back in Billy's mercantile. The doors to the cribs swung open and slammed shut so fast in the new red light district, men had taken to calling it that.

Well, I hope Amanda is happy.

Naomi stepped up on the boardwalk and crossed to the Chandelier's doors. Carefully, she peered over the batwings, standing on her tiptoes. A meager crowd filled a few seats here and there, fogging the air with a thin layer of cigar smoke. She spotted Matthew standing at the end of the bar, reading something.

Suddenly her heart went wild but she'd come too far to turn back. If she could do or say anything to get him to let go of this vindictiveness, or this thirst for power—or simple revenge—whatever was driving him, she had to try.

She trudged toward him, her feet heavy as lead bricks on the sawdust. Finally, she stood behind him, once again surprised by the width of his shoulders, his stance so similar to John's. Her heart never failed to leap a little at the sight of him—only because he was the mirror image of her beloved dead husband. She would always love him. But time and life had moved on, bringing her to Charles.

"Matthew?"

He stiffened, didn't move for a moment, then slowly turned to her. The brief flutter of tenderness softened his features, his hazel eyes warmed, but almost immediately a mask of stone replaced it all. His gaze turned hard as flint. "Well, what brings you to this side of town, your royal highness?"

A very bad idea, an inner voice told her. All of a sudden she was sure this was a mistake. Nonetheless, she was committed. He towered over her like a behemoth, his broad, plaid-covered chest filling her view. She felt tiny and fragile next to him, like a brittle cornstalk. "I want to talk to you." She tried to keep her voice calm, gentle, and steady.

He motioned toward the bar. "Can I get you something to drink?" He dropped his gaze quickly over her stomach. "Coffee, maybe."

She shook her head. "No, I…" She decided to lay her cards on the table. "Matthew, do you want to rebuild Defiance or do you just want to hurt me?"

"What? What kind of a question is that?"

"I remember how you used to be. You always took things too far, too personally. You got angry, held grudges. Hurt people," she added solemnly. "You lied to us about ever receiving my second letter. You knew we were happy here yet you came anyway. So sure we'd leave with you."

His lips thinned in irritation and he turned away from her, lacing his fingers together and resting them on the bar. "I won't deny I lied about the letter. I just thought you'd taken leave of your senses. My intentions were good."

"And I believed that. But then you bankrolled that awful woman to open this place in an attempt to swing Defiance back to its former, sordid glory."

He chuckled and the sound made her blood run cold. "That was a good plan till Delilah got too ambitious. Blowing up the mine was stupid."

"Matthew, please," she touched his arm and he jolted, pulling away from her. Naomi pleaded with her eyes. "There's always been some good in you. Please don't do this."

A cold smile too reminiscent of a serpent's slithered across his lips. "Just what is it you think I'm doing?"

"I know you've brought men into town to cause trouble.

We've had a suspicious death at our lumber camp. The surveyors the railroad sent out were murdered. Charles is having labor issues. Our herd has plague—"

"Hold on, hold on," he straightened up, waving his hand. "Do you hear yourself? What next? You gonna blame me for locusts? Frogs? Killing the firstborn?"

Yes, it was a lot to accuse him of, but somehow, like Charles, she knew he was involved. "You're building businesses to compete directly with ours. And I saw the handbill. The miners weren't that angry with Charles before you came. You're stirring them up. Why can't you just live here in peace?"

He snorted in disgust and massaged his neck as if her allegations made him tense. "You're crazy, Naomi. You're so in love with that tin horn god, you'll believe anything bad he says about me."

"Yes, I am in love with him. Madly, deeply, truly." Every word seemed to rub salt in the wound and she regretted causing him any pain but he had to be made to understand. Matthew's jaw tightened, his lips fought a sneer, his eyes burned hot, but Naomi resolved to get some things said. Maybe if he knew for sure all of her belonged to Charles— "Turns out he's a good, honorable, decent man who loves me the same way—"

Matthew's big paws struck out and latched onto Naomi's shoulders like vices, gouging into her flesh. "*I* am a good man, Naomi!" He bellowed into her face, shaking her violently, hurting her neck, making the cougar's wounds twinge. "I am a decent, honorable man and I could have loved you!"

"Let me go, you're hurting me," she screamed back shrilly.

"I could have given you children, carried on John's name." He shook her harder, digging his fingers deeper, obviously intent on causing her pain. "Now you're carrying his brat? Why didn't you ever give me a chance?"

*S*eemingly overnight Tent Town had transformed not into a reflection of its former self, but a newer, younger, more vibrant self. In the late afternoon sun, Charles noted most tents had given way to wood structures, some finished, some still rising from the ground, casting long shadows. Not even dark, yet men hustled to and fro with renewed vigor in their steps. The air was heavy with the scent of fresh-cut pine and the sweat of industry.

He strode through the traffic on the street, not quite sure he was doing the right thing, but he was doing the only thing. Baiting Matthew into making a foolish mistake was dicey but the alternative was brutal and not one Charles wanted to exercise. It would open too many doors to a dark past.

He couldn't lose himself to that man again. He had to set Matthew up for a fall the law could handle. His former Flower, Rose, was behind bars. They could get Matthew there as well.

He passed by the laundry and turned on Water Street, for a moment having to double-check his sense of direction. He could clearly hear the tittering female laughter and the raised voices of men vying for more cards, more chips, more liquor. More sin.

He followed the sound of debauchery across the stream to Matthew's newest establishment, The Crystal Chandelier Number Two. On the way, he passed a row of tents, men coming and going from them at a noticeable clip; a few loitered about. Waiting their turn. The sound of the screen doors opening and slamming shut like corn popping followed him, taunted him. He'd been a purveyor of such vice. Who was he to think he should be the one to stop Matthew?

Shame rose up in him and he swore he would fight for the soul of the town, not just his family. He marched through the doors of the newer, smaller Crystal Chandelier and surveyed the robust crowd, searching for Matthew. Otis was behind the bar lighting a cigar and they spotted each other.

"He's at the Number One." The man exhaled gray smoke and picked up a glass. "Unless you're here for a beer."

Charles didn't waste time answering. He turned and headed back. Naomi was back at the hotel, waiting for him and he'd told her he wouldn't be long. Truly, he didn't think what he had to say to Matthew would take long. It was the reaction he was having trouble predicting. She was out of harm's way. Two Spears was with Emilio. However this finished off, at least they were safe.

He didn't want to kill Matthew, but wouldn't hesitate to pull the trigger should the need arise. Therefore, he would not describe himself as eager to incite violence with the man, but he was willing to end it.

He bounded up on the porch of the Crystal Chandelier and shoved through the batwings.

For an instant, he couldn't believe he saw the flash of blonde hair and the petite figure through the smoky haze. There was, however, no mistaking his wife.

CHAPTER 32

*E*very word out of Naomi's mouth was like a spike driving into Matthew's brain.

Madly, deeply, truly.

Pound, pound, pound.

Good, honorable, decent—

The last word snapped his fraying patience like a chain holding a demon. He grabbed her, dug his fingers into her flesh, wanted to rip the skin and muscles from her bones, so blinding was his fury. She had betrayed his brother. She had used Matthew. Lied to him. Hidden her relationship with the West's most notorious pimp.

Naomi cried out and still he dug his fingers in deeper. And now a baby with the bastard— "Why didn't you ever give me a chance?"

Cold steel touched the back of Matthew's head, accompanied by the silky cocking of a revolver. He froze and Naomi gasped. Staring over his shoulder, the fear in her eyes changed to something more like desperation or concern. "Charles, don't," she managed to choke out. "Don't."

Matthew heard the soft breathing of his enemy but wasn't

fooled by it. It masked a fury that strung his life up on a thread as precarious as a spider's silk. Tempe rose from a table a few feet over, but Matthew jerked his chin, signaling him to stand down.

McIntyre swallowed. An effort, a *herculean* effort, Matthew suspected, to control his rage. All too aware of who was on the other end of the gun pressed to his skull prompted Matthew to seriously ask himself did he want to die? Slowly, he released Naomi and raised his hands. No, not yet anyway. Not like this, not with his brains scattered all over her. But he wasn't sure if anything could stop Charles McIntyre—

"Step away from him, Naomi." The deadly chill in Charles' tone sent a shiver up Matthew's spine. He was taking his last breaths unless he did something. Fast. This turn of events galled him. It wasn't part of his plan. Not at all. He should be afraid but he was merely disgusted.

Naomi's chest rose and fell at a breakneck pace as she slipped away from him and McIntyre—out of the line of fire. Matthew raised his hands higher. "I'm sorry, McIntyre. You got every right to kill me for touching her. I wouldn't have hurt her. I'd never hurt her. I just—" he licked his lips. Only one way out of this. "Tears me up, is all. I've always loved her."

"And you're always coming in second."

Matthew's jaw felt like it turned to hot metal over the jab. Acid burned in his mouth. Curses of the darkest sort leaped to his tongue, but he bit them back. *One day, I won't, McIntyre. One day...* But he said aloud, "Yeah, I know. Second-best."

McIntyre pressed the barrel harder against Matthew's head. "Say it again."

He could tell the man was speaking through clenched teeth. Matthew frowned, looked around at the room of spellbound drunks and whores, their gazes alight with fear. "W-What?"

"Say it again," he said slowly, quietly.

"Se-second best." He could barely spit out the galling words.

"Again. Louder. With conviction."

Matthew crushed his jaws together. He debated if the bullet was the better choice, but swallowed the bile rising in his throat and hissed out the words. "Second-best. I am second-best." *But, unless you pull that trigger, I will also be the last man standing...if it takes everything I have.*

"This is my town, Matthew. Naomi is my wife. Say it back to me and make me believe you understand."

Matthew glared at a wide-eyed, horrified Naomi, arms wrapped protectively over her stomach. Whatever he'd believed was love burned up in a funeral pyre in that instant, leaving only smoldering hate behind. "This is his town" he spoke to her. *But I'm gonna take it from him, Naomi.* "You are his wife." *And I'm gonna make you his widow.* He looked over his shoulder. "Satisfied?"

The pressure of the barrel left his head. "Turn around."

Mindfully unclenching his jaws, Matthew pivoted, lowering his hands at the same time. McIntyre, similar in height, but lighter, of a slenderer, but just as deadly, build, glared at him. His gun still in his hand, hung at his side. Dark eyes burned bright with hate…a bottomless pit of cold, dark, animosity.

Oddly, Matthew felt as if he'd won something here, besides his life. A battle of a different kind.

"I came here today with one objective." McIntyre spoke slowly, quietly. "I leave with another. So hear me, Matthew. Unless this ends now, next time…I won't utter a sound. Do you understand?"

Matthew raised his chin but held his peace.

Apparently, that wasn't good enough for McIntyre. "Say it."

Matthew gave thought to lunging for the gun, but prudence got the better of him. Was he staring at the old Charles McIntyre? He wondered. Had he pushed him that far? Matthew thought maybe he had and was glad. "No more chances."

Watch it all burn down now, Naomi. He's not so Good, honorable, or decent, and I'll prove it.

---

*N*aomi felt like she couldn't even touch her husband as they exited Matthew's saloon and made their way to Main Street. The heat of the fury and hate coming off him hurt her, physically. She'd only been this worried about her husband's state of mind one other time—when Tom Hawthorn had practically strangled her. Matthew had a longer history. She could understand if Charles was at the end of his restraint, but he couldn't give in now. His faith might not recover.

"What were you doing there, Naomi?"

His question made her stumble. After what they'd just been through— "That's your first question?"

Charles spun to her, reached for her shoulders, but pulled back at the last moment. Hands clenched tightly, lips pursed into a razor thin line, he backed away from her. He glared at her, but a mix of emotions warred on his face. His thinly trimmed beard and mustache accentuated the devil in him— only now it wasn't so handsome. He was livid with her.

And she knew it. "I'm sorry," she whispered meekly, aware passers-by were staring.

He pinched his brow and exhaled, taking a long spell of silence. She didn't dare rush him. "I'll ask again. What were you doing with Matthew?"

What had seemed initially like a good idea, then veered off to questionable, had wound up going straight over a cliff. "I—I thought I could talk to him. Reason with him. Get him to stop coming at you." She shook her head, realizing now how incredibly foolish the idea was. "He's—he's—" *Could have loved you. Could have?*

"What?" he practically growled.

Was it anything? The anger she'd seen in Matthew's eyes, the ice she'd heard in his voice. *Carrying his brat...*

"He used to love me. I thought I could appeal to his heart, but," she locked gazes with Charles, "I think he hates me now."

"And he knows about the baby. How could he know?"

"I don't know. Hannah and Rebecca wouldn't tell anyone. Neither would Ian. No one else knows."

"Except our new nurse."

"Surely she wouldn't tell."

Charles pivoted away from Naomi and dropped his hands on his hips, fingers drumming on the cylinder of his .44. She could hear the gears turning in his head. When several seconds passed, however, and he still hadn't said anything, she risked touching his shoulder. "What are you thinking?"

He turned his head. In profile, his features were hard as flint. "Go back to the ranch."

She peeled her fingers off. "I know you're angry with me, Charles, but I was—"

"Naomi," he snapped. "I need time to think."

A little of her own anger tried to flare. He was mad at her, but closing her out as well. She sensed this was a pivotal moment. The urgency to pray for her husband slammed into her. He was in a battle, and was teetering. "I think we should pray—"

"I'm going for a walk." He spun and stormed away from her. "Ask Rebecca to give you a ride home."

Offended, Naomi huffed but held her peace as he disappeared between two tents, smacking laundry out of his way.

CHAPTER 33

*C*harles wanted to release a primal scream of pure rage, but would keep it bottled up until he was out of town. He was striding with grim determination back toward Traveller at the livery when Ian fell into step beside him.

"I know that look, lad. Who's aboot to die?"

Charles held his peace, took a few more steps then stopped abruptly. Ian was two steps ahead on the boardwalk before he realized he'd lost his friend. Expression questioning, he pivoted on Charles.

"Naomi. And then Matthew. Or maybe Matthew first, I'm not sure." Charles dragged a hand over his mouth, disgusted with the words that had slipped past his self-control. He didn't mean them but this venting was exactly why he'd parted company with Naomi. To avoid her being the recipient of the steam.

Ian shoved his hands in his pockets and rocked on his heels, waited for a miner with his pack to pass by. "Well, that dusna sound good."

"She injected herself into a situation, Ian, and made things much, much worse. She actually went to see the man to ask him to back off."

Ian grunted and shrugged a shoulder. "Perhaps that wusna wise, but why specifically was it a mistake?"

"I walked in the saloon and he was shaking her, screaming in her face. I think he was actually going to hurt her."

Ian whistled in shock.

"I made a mistake. I did not kill him."

"It's best that ye didn't."

Charles shook his head. "I lost my temper, but I didn't kill him. What I did, Ian, was worse. I humiliated him. Matthew isn't like Tom Hawthorn. Tom crawled out of town with his tail between his legs. He'll never be back after the humiliation I inflicted."

"Ye think Matthew is different?"

Again, the moment when One-Who-Cries drew a bead on Charles' back leaped to his mind...and Matthew had just stood there, waiting for the shot. "Yes"

"Come, lad," Ian reached out to him. "Let's walk off some steam."

Not a bad suggestion, Charles acquiesced. The two wandered aimlessly down the mostly-empty boardwalk. Long shadows stretched across the street. The scent of dinners on the stove— cabbage, elk, and onion—mingled with the familiar stench of horse manure and the few unwashed miners making their way along. Charles didn't miss their expressions as they passed—he saw more disdain and less fear. Two more handbills accusing him of basically murder had hit the streets of Defiance. Eventually, Charles was going to have to deal with the propaganda.

He stopped again. "I have miscalculated." *In more ways than one, I think.*

Ian caught on quicker this time and halted as well. Over in Tent Town, someone plucked a cringe-worthy version of *Buffalo*

Gals on a banjo. It twanged in the evening air, along with the drunken, screechy wail of a woman trying to accompany it. Down near the livery, one of Matthew's building crews was still pounding away at a project. The *thwack, thwack, thwack* of their hammers was almost in time with the music.

A cold breeze kicked up, fully hinting at the winter days not far off. Charles sighed. "I thought at the very least Naomi was safe from him. Now I'm not so sure." He swallowed and turned to his friend. "And he knows about our baby. I think the news may have unhinged him."

Ian's eyes bulged. "How in the worl—we must go to Beckwith straightaway. He can arrest Matthew for laying hands on Naomi."

Charles shook his head. "Simple assault will not hold him long enough." He narrowed his eyes at Ian. "I will not let him hurt her."

"You canna kill him, Charles. Ye canna take the law into yer own hands. The man ye were—he's dead. Ye've a new lease on life through Christ—"

"I don't want to kill him," he snapped. The flare of temper came from the fact that killing Matthew was *exactly* what he wanted to do. But Ian was right. The old Charles McIntyre must not under any circumstances climb from the grave.

But he was stirring…

"Beckwith used to be a Pinkerton," Ian pointed out. "Maybe that's the way to solve this. Get MP&G to pressure Matthew to leave Defiance using something more damaging than a mere libel suit. I would bet the board of directors have some skeletons in their closets."

"You're assuming Matthew wants money and power more than he wants to see me humbled. Or dead. As I said once before, I don't think I believe that."

What does this mad man want? Me out of the way? To punish Naomi? Both?

"I've a suggestion," Ian said carefully. "As I've listened to yer conversation, I've heard *I, I, I*. Lean not to yer own understanding. Seek the One who has all wisdom. He'll give ye direction."

Charles was humbled but at the same time annoyed with his friend. Ian found it so easy to preach. His life, his businesses, weren't coming undone. His worst enemy had not laid hands on his wife. "I *have* gotten caught up in handling this myself." Merely to end the conversation, he conceded, "Yes, I'll make time to pray before I do anything."

---

*E*milio laid a new pair of leather gloves down on the counter and grinned sheepishly at Billy. "Things are going all right with her, I think."

Billy draped an arm over the cash register and leaned toward him. "Listen, brother, I'm not supposed to say anything," he glanced around as if to make sure he wouldn't be overheard, but they were alone in the store. "If Mollie finds out I said anything, she'll kill me. You understand that, right?"

"Sí." But Emilio shook his head.

"Well, it's just that she implied to Hannah you were moving a little slow. After fighting for her honor and all, I think she was expecting something." He scratched his nose. "Might be time to put a few cards on the table, Emilio. You know, fish or cut bait."

Oh.

"You two have sort of been dancing around the flame since you got hurt in the mine explosion."

Emilio sighed and fished some coins from his pocket. "I am no good at this, Billy. I do not understand the way women think. I think Mollie likes me but I'm not really sure how or in what way. What if, like Hannah, she wants to be friends—?"

"Aah." Billy nodded, as if a fuzzy picture had come into focus. "You don't understand what Mollie's telling you."

"She hasn't told me anything."

"Oh, yes she has, my friend." Billy chuckled and opened the cash drawer, its little bell ringing crisply throughout the store. "Just, um, well, ask yourself a few questions."

"Like?"

"Like, when you're with her, does she touch you on the arm or shoulder? Does she laugh at all your jokes? Does she give you little openings to compliment her or flirt with her?" He took Emilio's money and made his change. "Believe me, brother, if you answered yes to any of those questions, she's speaking loud and clear."

The doorbell rang and both men looked over at it. Speak of the devil. Mollie drifted in, saw them, and an immediate, glowing smile lit her face as if she were beneath a stage light. Emilio thought she looked particularly pretty this morning in a snowy white shawl, a pale blue dress the color of her eyes, and her hair down around her shoulders.

"Mollie. Good morning." Billy shoved the drawer shut, amusement gallivanting freely in his voice. "Listen, would you two do me a favor? I need to go see Charles. Watch the store for me for a couple of hours?"

Mollie, her gaze glued to Emilio, nodded. "You're the boss."

Billy skedaddled, grinning all the way out the door, leaving them alone in the store. Emilio leaned his hip on the counter as Mollie sidled back behind it, peeling out of her shawl and gloves. Sighing a little sigh, she rested her hands on the wood. "My, he seemed in a hurry."

Emilio chuckled and looked down at his new gloves. Unexpectedly, he remembered things here in town before the sisters had shown up. He had lived in a little storage closet at the Iron Horse Saloon, worn ragged clothes, and emptied spittoons and chamber pots. Mollie had been a Flower in the saloon and never smiled, back then. Things had improved for them both. That old life seemed a hundred years in the past.

"Where'd you go?"

Mollie's question intruded on his thoughts and he came back to her. And saw her. Really saw her. Pretty golden hair cascaded down her shoulder in a waterfall of sunshine. Eyes the blue of an alpine pond shimmered in a way that warmed Emilio's soul. Slight and petite, she made him feel strong, protective. And he'd shown he would protect her after backing Buck down. In fact, Emilio had been surprised at the fury that the man had evoked, touching Mollie the way he had.

"You're looking at me...but you're not seeing me."

Emilio blinked at her deadpan tone, but her lips were twitching like she was trying to avoid laughing at a joke. "Sorry. I was thinking about our old lives and how much better things are now."

Her smile faded. But she didn't look sad. More like she was remembering a close call that had ended well. Relief, was it? "Things surely worked out. I know I'm grateful to the sisters and for knowing Jesus. He changed everything for me, Emilio."

He bit his lip, pondering. Emilio himself had sort of slipped into a friendly relationship with Jesus. But, as with Mollie, he hadn't made a full commitment there, either. She surprised him by reaching across the counter and tucking a strand of hair behind his ear. "That one's always hanging in your face."

"Should I cut it? Should I try to look more like the white cowboys on the ranch?"

"No," she said firmly. "You are you. I love you just—" she gasped and moved back an inch. "I mean, I love the you I've gotten to know. I mean—" She frowned and shook her head as her cheeks flared a pretty shade of pink.

Emilio reasoned if she'd spoken these words in a friendly way, why did she look so mortified? Maybe it *was* time for a commitment of some kind. A step to try to figure out what Mollie meant to him. Emilio raised his hand and cupped Mollie's cheek.

"Mollie, I would like there to be an agreement between us. Would that be all right?"

"You mean like I should *expect* to see you every Saturday night?"

He leaned down to her and brushed her lips. "And every Wednesday night and Friday night." He kissed her lightly, his spirits soaring with delight that he'd taken a step toward something exciting. Even better, she kissed him back and his pulse went wild. He hadn't kissed the girl since coming-to in Doc's office and he'd blamed the interaction on a fuzzy head. Now, he was kicking himself for waiting so long to do it again.

"An agreement it is," she whispered against his lips.

For a moment the softness of her lips, the sweetness of her breath scrambled his wits. Yes, indeed, he was very sorry he'd waited...

———

CHAPTER 34

"The board will be highly disturbed by this turn of events, Matthew." Short, portly Sam stormed over to the bar in Matthew's office and poured himself a whiskey. Sweat glistened on his brow.

"What makes you think I had anything to do with it?" Matthew asked, annoyed the lawyer had stormed in here like he owned the place, slinging accusations. "Surveyors get killed or go missing all the time."

"What of the attack on the nurse?" Sam slammed back the drink and poured another. "What of the death at McIntyre's lumber camp?"

Matthew scratched his chin. "Cutting timber is dangerous business. Accidents happen all the time. As far as the other, she had no business walking alone in Tent Town. In case you haven't noticed, Defiance isn't where the choir practices."

Sam huffed and fumed for a moment, then finally, said, "I'll be no party to murder. The members of the board won't, either. Poisoning cattle. Hiring agitators to cause labor strikes. These things are acceptable, but you go too far." He swallowed the second drink as if he was throwing water on a fire. "They were already very unhappy about the ridiculous, frivolous libel suit—"

"Calm yourself, Sam, before you have an apoplectic fit." Matthew pushed back from his desk and rose to join him at the bar. He poured himself a shot and raised it in front of him. "Give the board a message for me." He swallowed the whiskey, savoring the burn. Pain gave meaning, toughened souls, strengthened resolve. "I strongly suspect the libel lawsuit will go away. Strongly. Furthermore, you tell them nothing injurious will be linked to them in any way, shape, or form that stems from my activities. Nothing."

"Can you guarantee it?"

"I can guarantee what I commission. The agitator you hired to work on McIntyre's spur line, he's your business. I'll take responsibility for the others."

"How can you be so sure they'll keep their mouths shut?"

"Any one of them crosses me, they know I'll kill 'em."

"But the libel—"

"McIntyre's attorney skedaddled out of town. After his chat with Otis," Matthew let his gaze bore into Sam, "he couldn't leave fast enough."

The lawyer gulped, seemed to ponder the statement, then quickly poured himself another drink. Matthew had never seen him imbibe so zealously. The stress was getting to the man. It could make him unreliable.

"I'm not cut out for this." Sam wiped his lips. "I can handle the politics, the propaganda, the agitators who push for unions, higher wages. I am an expert in liable law. But anything else—"

"You just keep to yours, Sam," Matthew said calmly. "Do what you do. I'll do the rest."

CHAPTER 35

*H*ope looked up at the clock. Five minutes to four. Through with scheduled appointments for the day, she sat down to start compiling patient files. Apparently, Doctor Cook had not bothered to keep records on any of his patients. Consequently, he hadn't even maintained a desk here in the office.

To create a necessary workspace, Hope had moved both guest chairs to one side of the stove and purchased a small desk and chair at the mercantile for the other side. She'd placed them right in front of the window. The position provided a perfect view of the street out front. Like now. The thoroughfare was empty, except for a scrawny, red dog sniffing out the trail of something interesting.

"He'll be here," Hannah sang, too much amusement in her voice. "It's Friday." She reached into the cupboard for fresh sheets, her smirk in plain view.

Irritation flared in Hope. "I don't know what you're talking about."

Hannah laughed richly and hugged the sheets to her chest. "I know. I think that's what I find funniest of all."

"Please either explain yourself or finish changing the bed." Hope picked up her pencil and began to study the patient file in earnest.

Hannah paused, as if thinking about a reply, but simply shook her head. "I'll let you figure it out." She lifted her chin. "There he is now."

The two women watched as Lane emerged from the alley, riding a black stallion. Leading a little, golden palomino, the trio trotted lazily toward the office. A picnic basket hung from the saddle horn on Lane's horse.

"Looks like he has different dinner plans for you."

"A picnic in this weather?" she muttered.

Again, Hannah smirked. "I'm sure he's got a plan for keeping you warm."

Heat rushed Hope's cheeks. She truly did not like having her personal life on display like this. There was no way around it, however, in a town this size. Perhaps it was time to once again explain to Lane he was wasting his time.

Only Hope didn't want to send him away.

Oh, what have I gotten myself into?

The cowboy's knock on the office door jolted her heart. Hannah chuckled. "I'll just go finish that bed."

She slipped out of the room as Lane peeked around the door. "Miss Clark." He stepped in and pulled his tan Stetson from his head. His sheepskin coat added twice the girth to the man, making the room, and Hope, feel small. She noticed he'd again made an effort to clean up a bit. "I thought I might interest you in dinner and a show this evening."

She wanted to say no, she wanted to ask him to leave and not come back. She didn't want to give her heart to Lane Chandler, even if he might believe she could be a doctor. There'd be something else, some other desire of Hope's that went against expectations for a woman. Something to make him try to control her.

On the other hand, she supposed she could make an effort to find out how egalitarian he actually was.

"Got fried chicken from the hotel," he added. "Fresh baked biscuits. Rosemary mashed potatoes—"

Hope's stomach gurgled and Lane grinned. She gave in, betrayed by her hunger. "That does sound inviting. And what's this about dinner and a show?"

"I have to take you somewhere. We kind of have to hurry. Don't forget your coat. It's chilly."

*A*n hour later, beneath a spectacular blue sky, Lane had spread a blanket in the middle of a wide, grassy pasture on the side of a mountain. At the bottom of the clearing, quivering in the breeze, a forest of brilliant gold aspens cascaded down the hill and disappeared below the slope. Beyond them, in a magnificent vista, the valley opened wide, rolling up to the feet of the snow-capped San Juans. She shielded her eyes against the low-hanging sun that cast long, stark shadows across the stunning scenery. The view went on for miles and Hope could even see Defiance, a few miles in the distance, sprawling along both sides of the Animas.

"It's beautiful." Blowing a warm breath on her cold fingers, she turned back to Lane. He had tied the horses several yards away to the branches of a lone cedar and was retrieving the picnic basket. Near the animals, an outcropping of granite jutted heavenward a good thirty or forty feet high. "A lovely sight for a picnic." If a bit chilly.

"Struck me that way, too," he said, joining her again. "If you'll do the honors," he raised the basket to her, "I'll build us a fire."

When Hope had the meal all spread out on the blanket, she realized they had quite the feast. Besides the chicken and potatoes, Lane had brought a tin of green beans, a crock of butter for the biscuits, two mason jars of lemonade to sip on, and a half-dozen sugar cookies.

She settled on her knees on the edge of the blanket, near the fire that was burning well. Still, she had not shed her coat. "My, Lane, this is very generous of you."

"Generous?" His brow pinched as he stretched out, resting on one elbow, the food between them. "Generosity ain't what I was going for. Makes you sound like some sort of charity case."

Hope chuckled and moved from her knees to resting on one hip. "Um, is *thoughtful* better?"

"Some closer. Still ain't right, though."

His gaze changed, warmed, and again heat flooded Hope's cheeks. She quickly moved back to her knees and started filling a plate for him. He made her nervous when he looked at her like that. Staying busy kept her from meeting those haunting hazel eyes and losing her train of thought.

She pulled a biscuit apart for him and dragged a thin layer of butter over it. Some got on her finger and she stuck the digit in her mouth, and discovered he was still watching her. She removed it slowly. "That wasn't very ladylike of me, was it?" She reached for a napkin instead to clean her hand.

"Kind of cute, I thought. One last guess. What was I shootin' for with all this?"

She finished piling food on to the plate and held it out to him. "I'm sure I don't know."

He sat up, scooted a little closer, resting an arm on one knee. "Romantic." He took the plate. "I wanted to give you a romantic dinner, Miss Clark. Do you object?"

Lord knew she should. "Do you think a woman can be a doctor?"

He blinked and pulled back at the strange question blurted out so suddenly. After a moment, however, he relaxed and took the plate from her. "I don't know what that's got to do with the price of tea in China, but I would think a woman could be a fine —" He stopped.

Hope held her breath. His next words would seal his fate with her.

"Is that what you wanna be? Really?"

"Yes."

"And ol' Edward said it was a terrible idea."

"Forbid me."

"Well, for my part, I wasn't just joshin' when I told you about my momma. She could have been a doctor if she'd had the opportunity. Or a lawyer. Heck, even a politician. She was tough and sharp as any man I ever knew."

Hope breathed a little easier, but he still hadn't answered her question.

"I think you should go to school and become a doctor. Be the best one you can be and then write Edward a letter and tell him all about it."

Hope literally felt something melt in her heart, just melt and drain away. All her fear and mistrust of Lane vanished.

The horses nickered and the sound of crunching gravel drew their attention back to the animals.

"Oh, here, look," Lane whispered. He set down the plate, jumped to his feet and pulled Hope with him. Before she knew it, he was standing behind her, holding her close, and pointing at the horses. "Be real still and watch the rocks."

Unnerved by his nearness, his warmth, his arm around her midsection, she struggled to get her brain going. She moistened her lips and did as he told her. "What am I looking for?"

"You'll know."

Motion caught her eye. Her mouth fell open as a small cat, golden in color, covered in dark spots, appeared out of nowhere carrying a small rodent in its mouth. Using its unusually large paws, it leaped and scrambled up the rocks with the grace of a ballerina.

"Bet she's got a den up there. Watch." A moment later the cat stopped near the top, trotted over a few feet and then disappeared from view. "Bobcats. We've got something like them in Texas. Smaller, less fur."

"She was beautiful."

"But that's not what I brought you out here to see." Lane turned her to face the valley, now deep in shadows from the setting sun. Again, Hope put her hand above her eyes as a shield. Still holding her, pulling her into him a little closer, Lane pointed down at the aspens. "Watch."

Hope couldn't think. She could feel Lane's chest pressed against her back, the rhythm of his breathing. His arm across her waist was strong, possessive, comforting. His breath caressed her ear as he whispered, "It'll take a minute. Just wait."

Goosebumps rose on her flesh and she closed her eyes against the feelings raging in her, but darkness only made it worse. The power of his presence doubled around her. It was as if she was standing in the path of an electrical storm. The air tingled, the hair on the back of her neck stood up. His fingers pressed in, almost a caress she could feel through her coat, and the blood seemed to rush from her head. Involuntarily, she leaned against him.

"There," he whispered.

And she saw it. The setting sun struck the forest of aspens perfectly and fire seemed to emanate from every leaf. She gasped at the beauty. A magical, shimmering effect, it took her breath away. The trees danced and glowed with leaves of fire. Fire, but not burning. To her surprise, she remembered the story of Moses and the burning bush. She half-expected to hear God's voice.

"Indians call it something like Creator's Fire. I don't know the Ute word. Only happens a few times a year, they say."

"It's beautiful." Her heart racing, she took a deep breath and added, "It's romantic."

Lane chuckled softly and wrapped his other arm around Hope. His lips touched her ear and lightning shot through her.

"Now, that's what I was shooting for," he whispered.

But Lane did not take the embrace any further. Instead, he chuckled softly and released her. Hope was arguably...disappointed.

"Reckon we should be getting back," he said, walking away. "Dark's coming on fast."

CHAPTER 36

*E*milio shoved his glove in his back pocket and took Mollie's hand in his. Still in his chaps and coat because he didn't have long in town today, the pair sauntered down the hotel's porch toward the mercantile. He liked holding her hand. It was a little thing to notice, he supposed, but she fit. Holding her hand felt as natural and comfortable as the reins in his. He wouldn't phrase it to her that way, of course.

They stepped out into the sunshine and the light glinted off her blonde hair as she pulled her shawl tighter. Little, golden strands danced around her face in the breeze. Everything about Mollie was light and airy and delicate, but she had a strength about her that he liked best of all. She was the kind of woman who would load your gun while you were shooting at Bandidos. If you had her love, you had it—*her*—for life.

"What?"

He didn't realize he'd been walking and staring at her. Embarrassed, he lowered his head and, on a bold whim, pulled off his hat and kissed her. She didn't pull back but did break the kiss first and looked around, giggling.

"Was that too bold?" he asked, wondering if he'd swung too

far away from the slow mover she'd complained about. He dumped his hat back in place chiding himself for the foolish notion.

"It was unexpected." His shoulders slumped. "But nice," she added quickly. "Very nice."

Both of them smiling, his confidence buoyed, they commenced to walking again. "Only coming into town a couple of times a week doesn't seem enough. I get to missing you more and more."

She blushed but didn't say anything. Emilio was all right with her silence. The color in her cheeks spoke volumes.

"Miss Mollie, glad I saw you walk by!"

Emilio and Mollie spun on the boardwalk. Asa Hatchette hurried toward them, his game leg dragging a bit, as he waved a telegram in his hand.

"This came in a couple of hours ago. Here ya go."

"Oh," she took it from him and reached toward the reticule on her wrist. "Do I owe you anything?"

"Nope. Paid for on the other end." Bushy gray eyebrows wiggled up and down, mirth danced on his face. "Even if it wasn't, this one would be my treat."

"Oh, well, thank you."

"My pleasure. You just come on by the office whenever you're ready to send a response." He winked at her, acknowledged Emilio with a friendly nod, and limped back the way he had come.

Mollie put a hand to her stomach. "My, I've got butterflies. Who could be sending me a telegram?"

"Here, I'll give you a little privacy. Why don't you take a seat on the bench and read it. Sí?"

"Yes, yes, all right," she said absently, drifting over to the seat in front of the leather shop. Emilio took a few steps down the boardwalk to window shop at the bakery.

Trying to pretend disinterest, he couldn't help sneaking

glances. She opened the telegram, read it with keen interest, then her hand covered her mouth and she—

She looks like she's going to—

Cry. She's crying.

Emilio raced back to her. "Mollie, what is it? Are you all right?"

Tears streaming down her face, she turned those disarming blue eyes on him and shook her head. "My mother is alive, Emilio. She got my letter. Emilio, she forgives me and wants me to come home."

---

*E*milio drew an emotional Mollie to her feet and led her quietly away from Main Street, down to a sunny spot along the Animas. Strewn with boulders the size of wagons, the stream gurgled calmly and flowed on down toward Silverton. He leaned against one of the waist-high rocks and waited while Mollie gathered her wits about her. Back here at least she had some privacy to recover.

"Thank you for taking me off the street," she said, using the corner of her sleeves to dab at her eyes. "I was just so taken aback. I can't believe it. I hope I didn't embarrass you."

He waved the notion away. Emilio knew Mollie had made several attempts to find her mother. As far as he knew, nothing had come of them. This was sure some news. "Your mother, then. She is well, yes?"

Mollie sniffled one last time and straightened her shoulders. "Yes. She sold the farm and has moved twice, but the sheriff in Atchison mentioned I was looking for her to another sheriff and, lo and behold, he knew her. He got me the address and I decided to write a letter, Emilio." She fixed her gaze on him, raised her chin. "Tell her everything. All of it. The good and the bad." She stepped over to him and slumped beside him on the rock. "If she wasn't going to forgive me, I wanted to know before I wasted a trip back to Kansas."

Back to Kansas? Emilio folded his arms over his chest. He should have seen this coming. "You're going to leave."

Mollie turned and moved closer to him, hung her fingers on his arm. "Yes, I want to see her. I miss her very much. It would only be a visit."

He heard the hesitancy in her voice, as if she wasn't sure that was the truth. Disappointed by her planned departure, unsure of how this might play out for them, he understood his concerns didn't matter. He laid his hand on top of hers and smiled. "I am very happy for you, Mollie. My mama and papa have been dead since I was five. You are blessed to have her. Go and stay as long as you need to."

She squeezed his arm. "You could come with me."

He had to ponder the suggestion a moment. Sí, he supposed he could, but it didn't seem the best way to hold on to his job at the King M. He liked his job. He liked Mollie.

Would he miss her?

Yes.

A lot?

Maybe so. But enough to uproot the life he'd been building in Defiance, out at the ranch? He wasn't sure.

"Will you at least think about it?" she asked, as if reading his doubts.

"Sí." He patted her fingers, knowing he wouldn't think about anything else. "Sí."

"It spread," Charles said blandly. He wasn't surprised. He'd hoped, of course, but he was not caught off guard by the news. He turned away from the corral and looked at Lane. "The whole herd then?"

233

Lane snatched off his cowboy hat and tossed it with disgust into the dirt. A dust cloud rose from it. "Dang it. There's no reason. We kept 'em separated long enough."

"Unless someone purposely spread it." Lane looked up and Charles dropped a hand to the butt of his gun. "That's possible, isn't it?"

"Yeah, sure. Mighty rotten thing to do."

Charles ground his teeth, wishing he had his hands around Matthew's neck. "Evil you might say."

"Charles." Naomi appeared like an angel in a vision, golden hair loose and flowing, a ready smile softening already beautiful features. An adorable bump at her stomach that reminded him she was carrying his child.

She slipped her gloved hand into his. "Let's take a walk." Her warm, jade eyes compelled him, and he nodded. She was trying to calm him down, he realized, and Naomi was, truly, a sanctuary for him. Now that he'd gotten over wanting to kill her for her visit to Matthew...

"Lane, I'll be back. I already know what I want to do."

The foreman swiped his hat off the ground and nodded dismally. "Yeah. All right. I'll be here."

"Pardon me if I was abrupt." Naomi clutched Charles' arm with one hand and raised the collar on her coat with the other. They meandered past the barn and down to stroll along the bubbling Animas. "I thought you might need a moment to focus."

"You heard then?" he asked, his voice husky with seething anger.

"Yes. What will you do?"

Pray before ye do anything.

He sighed, unable to ignore Ian's advice. "First, I'm going to pray, but I'm fairly certain I am sending Lane and half the men to Texas for a whole new herd." He watched her face carefully. The news seemed to relax her. The tension between her eyes, the little lines around her mouth smoothed out. "You look, dare I say, pleased, princess?"

"I believe I am. I don't want you to give up."

"Did you think I would?" The possibility surprised him.

"No. I was afraid you might still be so angry with Matthew you wouldn't think straight and you'd let him drag your focus away from God."

"Well, I *am* angry. Very angry." He wouldn't lie, but neither would he tell her just where his thoughts were, either.

She stopped abruptly and turned him to her. "Do you think he's behind your sick cattle?"

"Yes."

She shook her head, her remorse obvious. "He's baiting you. I know I tried to put daisies on the situation, but you're right. This underhanded nonsense—the stirring up trouble—is just like something he'd do. He's awful. And he's dangerous."

"I used to be dangerous, too." He caressed the little scar on her cheek and gave her a half-smile. "Or have you forgotten?"

She didn't return the humor. "I know how you struggle, Charles. I know how the old Charles would handle this. Don't let Matthew push you into doing something...something you'll regret."

"If he pushes me that far, Naomi, God help him."

She clutched his lapels. "Let God help you, please."

Charles slipped his arms around his beautiful, precious, pregnant wife. A ferocious sense of protection again reared its head as he thought about Matthew shaking her like a rag doll. "You've nothing to worry about, Naomi. Nothing at all."

But Matthew should be very worried indeed...

CHAPTER 37

"I've never seen him so angry, Rebecca. At least, not with me." Disturbed at the recollection, Naomi sat down on the knee wall separating the press from the office area of the *Defiance Dispatch* and clutched her sore arm. Matthew's shaking had done her no harm, really, but her arm had flared up with an unexpected ache. "We're past it. I've promised I won't meddle. But Matthew—he's changed. I don't know how, but he's different."

Rebecca took her hand off the Devil's tail and walked away from the press to take a seat at her desk. "That day he marched in here, wanting to buy an ad, I sensed something. He was strutting. I think he'd like to ruin us all, not just Charles."

"Maybe." Naomi couldn't shake the look in his eyes when he'd grabbed hold of her. "Charles isn't upset with me anymore but...I don't know. Whatever this is between him and Matthew..." She faded off, struggling to articulate what she sensed. "You know, after John and I were married, Matthew struck me as angry and desperate. Now he's just angry. Period."

Rebecca picked up a pencil and tapped it on a yellow pad. "Desperation, you could argue, smacks of hope."

"Exactly. I think he's finally given up hope of us ever being together." She shook her head. "And I don't think I like what's replaced it. Maybe that's what Charles is reacting to. I don't know, and I can't get what I feel is an honest insight from him."

"You think Charles is lying to you?"

"Lying, no. Just not…letting me in. That's the thing. I can't explain how I feel, or what I'm worried about."

Rebecca absently walked the pencil back and forth in her fingers. "And you say Matthew knows about the baby?"

"Yes. You and Hannah wouldn't tell anyone. How could he have found out?"

Rebecca lifted an eyebrow. "Our new nurse?"

"That's what Charles said, but surely she wouldn't be so unprofessional as to blab something like—"

"She is lying about her credentials."

"What?"

Rebecca sighed and pulled an envelope from her desk drawer. "I wrote some letters. It was a whim, really. I didn't expect to discover anything amiss, but Hannah suggested Hope was hiding something, so…she's no nurse. Or at least, she didn't graduate from Pennsylvania Women's College of Medicine."

"She must have some kind of medical training. She's very skilled."

Rebecca chewed on her bottom lip. "She performed a tracheotomy in the restaurant, followed by emergency surgery which saved Mr. Ledford. On the other hand, she performed surgery on Mary Ann and lost her."

"Hannah said she was already in a bad way from Amanda's butchery."

"True. And I may not be fairly assessing her skills."

"But you have a theory about Hope, I can tell."

"Doc Cook told me one time he came to Defiance because he lost a patient back in Nebraska. Took him a long time to get over it. If he ever did."

"But he was hiding here, that what you're getting at?"

"Yes. Maybe Hope is doing the same thing. Running from her own mistakes."

"Well, Hannah said it had to do with Edward, the fiancé, not something medical."

"No." Rebecca frowned. "I mean, I don't know. Something feels off about that story. I've sent out at least a dozen telegrams and letters. I'm going to keep digging—especially since we might be relying on her to deliver your baby."

"I just can't believe she'd tell Matthew such a private detail. That would imply she has some kind of relationship with him."

"I'll get to the bottom of it."

---

*R*ebecca drummed her fingers on her desk as she stared intently at the telegram. In the silence of the town hall, the tap of her fingernails was too loud, and she quit.

"You asked me here, remember?" Marshal Beckwith's gruff voice cut into her thoughts.

She looked up at him as he freed the buttons on his corduroy coat. "Yes, I'm sorry." The words, all in capital letters on the yellow sheet of Western Union stationery screamed at her. DR. CLARK IS A FINE PHYSICIAN FOR A WOMAN. I RECOMMEND HER FOR TREATING ALL FEMININE AILMENTS. DR. J. CLARK, PHILADELPHIA

For a woman? Just who does he think he is?

Rebecca noticed the increased, agitated pace of her fingers and stopped them. "I have a mystery on my hands, Marshal. You used to be a Pinkerton. I thought perhaps you could help me."

To his credit, the old man tried to hide his disdain as he stroked his bony jaw. "Let's hear it."

She picked up the telegram and passed it to him. "Our new nurse is much more than that—she's an actual doctor."

Beckwith straightened up and read the note. "That's interesting. She's lying about her credentials, down-playing them. Why?"

"I don't know. One patient under her care has passed away, but Hannah—a source I trust—is convinced the death was not Dr. Clark's fault. Furthermore, Dr. Clark did, according to witnesses, perform a skillful tracheotomy with the calm, steady demeanor of a seasoned physician."

"She drink?"

"Hannah is certain she doesn't. There is one thing, though. Dr. Clark has mentioned that she had a fiancé who did not approve of her career choice. Turns out he is a doctor as well."

"Hmmm. Could be hiding from him. Maybe there was some abuse." He glanced down at the telegram again, then slid it back across the desk. "Who's Dr. J. Clark? Father, brother?"

"Her father."

"He's quick to recommend her but points out she should limit herself to female patients. Doesn't sound like he knows about her dropping the M.D. after her name either."

"Uninformed and biased," she muttered.

Beckwith frowned. "You sound like you think a woman doctor should work on anybody?"

"I think that exactly. Anyone in *need* of a physician isn't going to be, I imagine, too particular about the physician's gender."

He grunted. "Maybe not in a pinch. So why do you care about this, as long as she's competent?"

"She's lying. Isn't that reason enough to care?"

Beckwith rose slowly to his feet and swiped up his Stetson from the edge of the desk, his demeanor suggesting he was bored and ready to move on to more exciting mysteries. "Then my suggestion would be to ask the father outright what he knows and then maybe find the fiancé. I reckon that could give you the whole picture." He started to turn but stopped. "Any reason you haven't just come out and asked Dr. Clark about all this?"

Rebecca was chagrinned. "Hannah asked me to quit investigating Dr. Clark. She said we had nothing to worry about."

"Hmmm."

Oh, that maddening grunt again. Rebecca wanted to throw something at the man.

"Well," he dumped his hat on his head. "Sounds like you've got a moral dilemma on your hands, Mrs. Donoghue." He flipped up the collar on his coat. "Good day."

The marshal sauntered out of the town hall, leaving Rebecca with the distinct impression he was laughing at her.

In his stoic, silent way.

CHAPTER 38

*H*annah drew up for an instant when she saw Mrs. Tunstall standing on the porch of the doctor's office. A pale, homely-looking woman with a large nose and hardly any chin at all, her desire to be liked by everyone in town grated on Hannah's nerves. But there was no going around her.

"Mrs. Tunstall, you have an appointment today? Is everything all right?"

The woman spun away from the door, eyes wide, her face a mask of guilt. "No, no, I was just, um, thinking I was feeling faint, thought I might slip in to see Miss Hope." She rushed down the steps, tugging her coat tighter around her. "But I'm feeling right as rain now. I'll be going. Good to see you, Hannah."

She scurried off, leaving Hannah to wonder about her odd behavior. Shaking her head, Hannah climbed the steps to the office when she heard voices. Clearly. Hannah stopped and looked over her shoulder. Watching Mrs. Tunstall hurry away toward Main Street, Hannah could hear Hope discussing a treatment with a patient. In detail.

The door opened and Hannah stepped out of the way, not

quite ready to go inside. Hope bid the patient, a scruffy miner, goodbye, then saw Hannah standing off to the side. "What are you doing out here?"

"Hope, I have to ask you something and you must tell me the truth."

"Of course."

"How is it possible someone outside of my family could know about Naomi's baby?"

"I couldn't begin to guess."

"Have you had any dealings with my uncle Matthew?"

"Besides the funeral, no."

"You'd not seen him before that or since?"

"Perhaps you should be a lawyer instead of a nurse. No, I'd never seen him before that. I have not seen him since."

"Do you know Mrs. Tunstall?"

"Somewhat. She comes quite often and sits on the porch for a while and then leaves. I've asked her several times if there was something she needed help with, but she says no. I'd come to the conclusion she's, well, a little touched."

"A little gossip is more like it. She's the nosiest—" Hannah bit off the unkind words. But Mrs. Tunstall was nosy and always eager to *share* her gossip. Charles had mentioned Matthew had information about his ranch and business dealings no one should be privy to. Hannah saw a pattern. "I'll be right back. And you need to stop giving patients advice near the front door."

Hannah raced down the porch and practically ran back to Main Street. Emerging from the alley, she caught sight of Mrs. Tunstall coming out of the bakery. Feeling a bit foolish, she almost gave up the idea of following the woman—until she saw Otis, across the street, waiting in the eaves of the assayer's office. Mrs. Tunstall saw him as well. She glanced furtively up and down the boardwalk and then crossed the street to him.

Hannah shifted to hide behind a post in front of the bakery

and peered around it. Otis and Mrs. Tunstall had a brief conversation, Otis handed her something that the woman stuffed in the reticule at her wrist, and then marched off. Otis turned and headed back in the direction of Tent Town.

---

*H*ope waved goodnight to Hannah and Billy as she closed the door and turned back to the empty office. On the nights Lane was not able to come into town, Hope had finally taken to cooking small meals in her home. Tonight, however, she was so tired, she doubted she had even the energy for that.

She leaned back against the door and took a deep breath, trying to exhale her fatigue. One broken arm, a badly twisted knee, a debilitating back spasm, a deep laceration that had barely missed the femoral artery, a child with a foreign object up his nose—the day had been long, varied, challenging. Hannah was a godsend, but Hope wished the girl knew more. She was learning, however.

A knock on the door startled Hope and she jumped away from it. "Yes?" She opened up to a young woman of about twenty-five, overly slender, pale red hair, a ragged shawl pulled tightly around her shoulders.

Fear glimmered in her hazel eyes. "You don't remember me."

Hope searched her memories. Something about the girl—yes. "You were at Mary Ann's funeral."

The girl nodded. "Can I come in? I know you're closed, but I waited until everyone was gone."

Hope dreaded what this might portend, but motioned for her to come in. "I'm—" She always stuttered over the introduction—"Hope. Please just call me Hope."

The girl drifted over to the stove, growing cold now. "My name is Adrianna and I'm in trouble. I need you—" She swallowed and turned back to Hope. "I need you to get rid of this baby."

Hope's spirits sank. Would these girls never stop this insanity? "I don't do abortions."

"You don't understand. You don't help me, Matthew will throw me out once I start showing." Her voice rose in panic with each word. "I've got no place to go. There's nothing else I can do in this town. And I'm scared. I'm scared to go to Amanda."

Hope rushed to her and clutched the girl's shoulders. "Shhhh. Calm down. It's all right. I won't abort the baby but I can help you through this. You can stay here. We'll help when the baby comes. Do you have any family—?"

Adrianna recoiled as if Hope had suggested she drink poison. "I've got nobody. I can barely feed myself. I've got no business with a baby."

"You could give it up for adoption."

Adrianna's mouth fell open. "I've got to work." She stepped back, slipping out of Hope's hands. "You people in your church-going-God-fearing world. What am I supposed to do? Take in customers with the baby in the cradle right beside my bed?"

"I don't mean to suggest I can snap my fingers and fix your life. I am saying, however, if you want out, I'll help you." Her father's voice echoed through her head, warning her against getting involved with the personal disasters so many patients created for themselves. Humanity, however, was more than the Hippocratic oath. "I will help you."

Adrianna sighed heavily, shook her head. "You know, I've had six abortions. Men did 'em all. The women—the nurses and the midwives I tried—always turned me down. The way you pleaded with us at the funeral, the way you talked to me that night, I thought you might be different. Might care about us more than the baby. The baby ain't here," she slapped her chest, "I am. I'm here. I gotta try to survive this life."

. . .

*H*ours after Adrianna left, Hope sat quietly in the dark office, watching the moon rise over the buildings. The girl had left in tears, convinced Amanda was her only chance to—to what? Keep heading down this path of misery and disease?

Hope wiped sudden tears from her own eyes, surprised they had escaped her neat little box labeled *moral decisions*. An emptiness that went deeper than mere loneliness washed over her, flooded her soul. She had no one she could talk to about the decisions she was facing. No one would understand.

Hannah would be horrified at the very idea of working with a soulless person who would kill a baby. Lane, she was sure, would think less of her for being so callous about life. Hope's father had thought abortions beneath him, unless the patient was a senator's indiscreet mistress. And while she'd never discussed *performing* the procedure specifically with Edward, he had said once he was a believer in actions and their corresponding consequences. Being denied an abortion might teach the girl a lesson.

Only these girls weren't learning. Nor were they trying to improve their lot in life. So they would go to Amanda.

And someone would die. Maybe two someones.

CHAPTER 39

$\mathcal{M}$atthew stood quietly on the balcony of the Crystal Chandelier and inhaled deeply as evening settled over Tent Town. He breathed in not just the scent of fresh pine from the several buildings under construction, but the aroma of power.

Grinning, he surveyed the hustle and bustle below him. Defiance and Tent Town were coming back to life. All this business was keeping his sawmill humming. The restaurant had opened and was doing a brisk business. The blacksmith over by the laundry already needed to move to a permanent structure so he could store more iron and corral some horses. The mercantile had undercut Page's place and swung a substantial number of miners away from Billy.

Downstairs, the crowd was growing steadily for the legal trades of drinking and gambling. Vice was still across the creek, out of the town limits. But Matthew wasn't sticking to his side of the tracks. Oh, no. He'd quietly invested in the leather shop over on Main Street, along with the livery and the laundry. Mrs. Lee had driven a hard bargain, but, in the end, she'd seen the wisdom of taking Matthew on as a partner.

And he knew, beyond the shadow of a doubt, it was all grating on McIntyre's nerves. The power in this town was shifting and, unless he missed his guess, that wasn't sitting well with the former king of Defiance. Matthew was inflicting death by a thousand cuts, prodding the man to shed his goodness, his decency. Eventually, McIntyre would snap and fight back—

"King of all you survey?"

Sam. Speaking of grating on nerves… "As a matter of fact, I believe so."

The lawyer joined him at the rail and studied the street flowing with miners, prostitutes, women carrying their wash, gold panners intent on finding the last nugget in Bear Creek, and the miners waiting on the mine to open soon. Their breath mingled and swirled in the frosty, evening air. "This is where you should stop, if you know what's good for you."

"Stop what?"

Sam sucked on his teeth and shoved his hands in his pockets. "You've done well. The mine is ready to open and should be running at full capacity soon. The town is coming back to life, thanks to the miners flowing in to work. The businesses you've opened look promising. And the attitude in Defiance is definitely turning away from McIntyre to MP&G as the town's benefactor."

"But."

"That Donoghue fella notified the members of the board he is going to retain the Pinkerton Agency to investigate them for malfeasance."

"Mal what?"

"Malfeasance. A vague term for wrongdoing."

Matthew understood immediately. "Dirt. He's looking for dirt on them."

"Exactly. He warned them. He won't follow through if they remove you from the board."

Matthew clenched his teeth. The play was good. Not brilliant, but good. At least better than that libel nonsense. "Pressure them to remove me." Attack from the rear.

"And they are rethinking your involvement, as a member of the board at least. Manhandling McIntyre's wife." Sam shook his head. "That was a colossal mistake. McIntyre won't stop at anything until you're out of this town. He's made that abundantly clear to them." The man rocked nervously on his heels. "They're buckling and they don't even know about the murdered surveyors—not directly traceable to you or them, of course. I feel, however, it would cause them some concern."

Because you would imply my involvement, wouldn't you, Sam?

Then Matthew understood why Sam was here. "Sounds like they have a decision to make. Or has it already been made?"

"They asked for my assessment." Sam shrugged. "But the handwriting is on the wall. They want you out. You've become a liability. Publicly anyway."

An odd calm settled over Matthew as he continued his appraisal of the street below. He had made a decision as well. Instead of fury boiling in his veins, he felt relaxed, almost peaceful.

He draped an arm over Sam, startling the lawyer. "Let's you and me go inside and have dinner. I need a thick, bloody steak." As Matthew guided Sam away from the railing, he reached to his waistband and slid his gambler's knife from its holster.

---

*M*atthew had just about forgotten Weston Powell worked for him. The MP&G conglomerate's geologist spent his daylight hours at the mine and at night disappeared into his room. He'd caught Matthew coming out of his room and for an instant Matthew couldn't even remember the man's name.

"Uh, Mr. Miller, I have some news." The scientist stepped a

little closer, hat in his hand, his young, clean shaven face tense with sympathy.

"Powell. Yeah, what is it?"

Powell shoved his spectacles up on his nose and cleared his throat. "Three. We were only able to retrieve three bodies. The rest are buried under too much debris."

Lost miners. Found.

He had to forcibly stop himself from doing a little jig.

Matthew didn't care if they could only get one body. A funeral procession was a funeral procession. "I want those men in coffins by this afternoon. We'll have a procession right down main street and up to the cemetery. Make it happen."

Powell's pale green eyes widened. "I don't do—"

"You do now." Matthew locked the door to his room then turned back to his geologist, raising an eyebrow at him, leaning his impressive bulk toward the smaller man.

Powell stammered foolishly, indignantly, for a moment, then bit off his complaints. "I'll see to it."

"And I'll make sure Otis gets the word out to every soul in Tent Town."

CHAPTER 40

*H*annah had so often thought her actual marriage would never happen. The dress made the dream tangible. She turned and shifted, lifting the ivory, lacy skirt, and spun around, studying her reflection in the mirror.

Rebecca stood by the window, clutching her hands together and grinning like a weepy-eyed fool. "That is a beautiful dress. And it requires so little tailoring."

"I know." Hannah stopped and assessed the gown's detailing. It was simply beautiful and showed off her little waist to perfection. The bustle and draped skirt were the latest fashion. "Do you think Billy will like it?"

"Honey, that's about the dumbest question I think you've ever asked. That boy has killed himself trying to win your hand." Rebecca meandered up behind Hannah, pushed her sister's braid out of the way and finished buttoning the dress. "He's been beat up, shot at, and ridden hard miles to rescue you from bandits." She rested her chin on Hannah's shoulder and met her gaze in the mirror. "When he sees you in this, I know he'll think it was worth it. More than worth it."

Hannah drifted her hands over the bodice and then the skirt.

"I have made him wait a long time. We could have had Marshal Beckwith marry us."

"Yes, but everyone understands."

Hannah tilted her head. Once they were married, Hannah and Little Billy would move out of the hotel and into Billy's apartment over the mercantile. And once the store had a reliable manager, they had talked about building a house on one of the several lots he owned on the edge of town. And then more children. She wanted children. She wanted to build a life with Billy.

And she wanted to become a nurse.

He'd told her she could nurse as much or as little as she wanted. He would move them to wherever she wanted to go to nursing school. Billy had done everything he could to prove he loved her, would never abandon her again, and that she could trust him.

"Rebecca?"

Her sister looked at her in the mirror. "Yes."

"Nursing school is two years."

"Yes."

"And I'm eighteen."

"Yes."

"I have time, don't I?"

"Time for what?"

Hannah shook her head. What was she thinking? Why couldn't they start right now? Billy had waited so long. Kept his word since coming to Defiance. Honored her. And she'd taken it all for granted. His sacrifices. His perseverance. His patience. And what had they done?

He'd said it so often. Life is too short.

"I need to see Billy."

She was flying down the steps and out the door before she realized it. Rebecca was calling her name, but the closer Hannah got to Billy's store, the faster she ran. Sleepy heads turned, men just rousing to their morning work pointed and chuckled as she fluttered down the street in ivory silk. Their laughter grew louder and heartier. They could laugh all they liked. She didn't care.

Nursing school wasn't going anywhere. She wanted her man.

---

*B*illy closed his ledger and stretched. The books were in good shape. He had his father's head for business. That was about all he wanted to inherit from the man. If he was as driven as his father, he'd be more upset about the bite Matthew was taking out of the mercantile.

He pulled the pocket watch from his vest. Five till seven. Time to open the store.

He stepped out of his office, and strode to the middle of his mercantile and stopped abruptly. The stove popped and crackled and sent out its warmth. In the early morning quiet, he scanned the stocked shelves and full barrels, and pondered his life. This store, his partnership in the hotel, and now a few rental properties had Billy sitting pretty. He had everything ready for a family. But he could afford to move if that was what Hannah wanted.

For the millionth time, though, he wondered if she wanted nursing school more than she wanted him. In which case, he wasn't inclined to marriage. He'd been praying about trying to force an answer out of her—so he could make plans...or move on.

Raucous laughter coming from the street interrupted his musings. Curious, he strode on over to the door, unlocked it, flipped the sign to *open* and stepped out into the cool air.

He had to blink. Twice.

"Hannah?" Skirt hiked over her ankles, she was rushing

across the street at a frantic speed, her eyes locked on him as if he were about to toss her a life preserver. And was she wearing a wedding gown? "Hannah, what are you doing?" She raced up to him, stood before him, breasts heaving, cheeks flushed from her run, golden braid a mussed mess. He scanned her dress, top to bottom. "Are you wearing your wedding gown?"

"Billy," she clutched his lapel. "I'm eighteen years old. I've got time, Lord willing, to do what God calls me to do. And first, I want to marry you."

While he was pleased—abundantly so—he was still confused. He laid his hands on her shoulders. "What? Do you mean now?" His brain couldn't keep up with the words coming out of her mouth. "I don't understand. Has something happened? Why are you in your gown—"

She pressed a finger to his lips. "I just realized we can't do anything apart. Whatever our future holds, it can't happen until we're together. Husband and wife, mother and father, business owner and nurse. Wherever God is taking us, we're going together." She brushed a strand of ash-colored hair off his forehead and smiled. "And, yes, today. As soon as we can get everyone gathered."

---

*N*othing like pulling a wedding together at the last minute, Naomi thought as she held on to Charles' arm and waited for Hannah. At least this time Marshal Beckwith wasn't conducting the ceremony at the jail.

Charles, Ian, Billy, Emilio, even Lane, had pitched in and moved things around in the hotel's dining room to clear a space in front of the huge, river rock fireplace. Naomi, Rebecca, and Hope had placed some pumpkins and Indian corn on the hearth. The kitchen staff had been directed to whip up a cake and some deserts. Though Billy had closed the dining room to guests,

Hannah had declined a dinner after the ceremony. A brief reception was all she wanted. The groom did not argue. Little Billy would be spending the evening with Aunt Rebecca and Uncle Ian.

Naomi separated from Charles and took her place with Hannah, Mollie, and Hope to one side of the fireplace. Billy stood next to Beckwith, holding Little Billy, their backs to the fireplace. Charles, Emilio, Lane, and Ian, all wearing white shirts, black string ties, and black, silk vests formed their own line on the groom's right. The girls were wearing unmatched but lovely silk gowns.

The bridesmaids' gowns had never been ordered so Naomi had brought several dresses into town from which they could all choose. Gifts from Charles, she was delighted to see them get some use. They did not fit Hannah, Mollie, Rebecca, or Hope perfectly, but Naomi doubted anyone noticed whether a gown was too long, a touch short, a smidgen tight. Judging by the tender, unguarded expressions on Lane's and Emilio's faces, those two cowboys were smitten.

Wistful as she thought of her own wedding, Naomi admired her handsome husband. Tall, strong, his dark mustache and beard trimmed to perfectly trace his jaw and mouth. Wavy, black hair, broad shoulders. So devilish looking, but Naomi knew the Godly man in him and had never loved someone so much. Their eyes met and he winked subtly at her, then his expression softened, smoldered, and she blushed.

Rebecca waited at the entrance to the dining room from where she could see the stairs, fairly quivering with excitement.

"Oh, here she comes," she said, beaming. Billy sucked in a deep breath, brushed his lapel, and looked at Little Billy. "Here comes Momma."

Her heart bursting with happiness, Naomi touched elbows affectionately with Rebecca as she jumped in line with the bridesmaids. She could hear the swish of satin as Hannah descended and Naomi wished they would have had time to find someone to play the traditional wedding—

Music?

Naomi cocked her head, as did Charles. Yes, that was music —a horn of some kind—playing a song outside in the street. Growing louder. Suddenly her husband's expression darkened and everyone else reacted to the sound, tilting their heads, or looking out the window. Scowling, Charles marched past the wedding party, toward the front door.

Naomi followed, as did everyone else. Passing through the lobby, she glanced up at the stairs. Hannah stood on the landing, beautiful, glowing, her gown and hair perfect. She was watching the group, however, with a vexed expression. "What's happening?"

"Give us a moment," Naomi said, hurrying after Charles.

She came up beside him on the porch as a funeral procession trudged by. A man playing a somber dirge on his trumpet led the way, the sound piercing the stunned silence of the wedding party. Behind him, three pine coffins and pallbearers, escorted by at least fifty mourners, made their way past the hotel, the sound of their marching feet soft and haunting. The boardwalks had filled up with curious onlookers, many of whom had removed their hats in respect.

The ferocious glares from the mourners tossed at Charles as they passed shocked Naomi. She was sure, if she raised her hand, she'd feel the hate coming off the group. All of it directed at her husband.

At the very end, Matthew followed the last coffin, walking alone. He and Charles locked eyes, but Naomi couldn't describe their expressions as glares. More like two warriors preparing to square off, and dread wiggled in her gut.

She sensed the members of the wedding party gathered around her, but no one spoke, no one moved. They all merely watched without making the slightest sound. The quiet was heavy, physical, like a cloak.

When the funeral procession was out of earshot, Naomi heard a sigh. The group turned to find Hannah, standing in the doorway, her face a mask of misery and uncertainty. As Billy went to her, Naomi watched Charles put on his own mask. One of fake cheer.

"What are we doing out here?" he asked ushering the group toward the entrance. "We have a wedding to celebrate." He winked at Hannah. "And we're burning daylight."

The group filed in, but Naomi hung back purposely to see the looks Charles exchanged with Ian and Marshal Beckwith. A powder keg had been lit and they all knew it.

CHAPTER 41

he funeral had attracted fifty hardy, angry souls but the wake at the Crystal Chandelier Number Two had tripled that number. Of course, Matthew's offer of one free beer for all those mourning the men lost in the mine explosion hadn't hurt attendance.

Smiling, nodding in agreement, sometimes chiming in with the complaining voices raised in anger, he drifted through the drunken crowd. So many men had come to commiserate after the funeral, the "mourners" spilled out of the saloon into the compound. And, oh, weren't his guests angry.

"Stood there looking at us all like a king."

"In his mind, he is," Matthew muttered in passing. "Defiance is his town."

"I would have liked to knock him off that porch."

"Take an army with you if you try it," he cautioned.

"If he was still the owner, I'd blow up the mine with him in it."

"He still owns a lot of Defiance." Matthew raised his finger, "But violence won't solve anything."

"He should have paid for the funerals instead of you, Mr. Miller."

"It was my pleasure," Mathew offered oh-so-humbly.

And through the crowd he drifted like a demon, whispering in men's ears, planting thoughts, watering others, keeping the soil tilled with beer and spite.

***

*B*illy just about did a Virginia Reel coming down the steps to the mercantile. This fine November morning had dawned on a new world. He nearly clicked his heels together as he jumped from the third step to the ground and waltzed over to the stove.

He stoked the fire, adding kindling and tossing in a pine log. All the while, his thoughts were on his wife upstairs, sleeping like an angel, his littlest angel asleep in the crib beside her. It had taken a while to get here. He and Hannah had come through some dark, dangerous times. He'd even been shot for her and she had removed the bullet—few couples could claim that kind of bonding.

But they'd made it. They were finally a family. He closed the door on the stove and whispered a prayer of thanksgiving—

Glass exploded and rained down on him in a deafening, high-pitched, ear-splitting cacophony. Instinctively, he covered his head and hunkered down. A barrage of gunfire followed immediately from the street, echoing off the buildings, rolling through the air.

"It's a warning, Page," a man yelled from outside, his voice framed by the neighing and grumbling of several horses. "Tell McIntyre we'll have justice."

Billy clambered behind the stove, expecting another volley.

"Billy!" Hannah screamed from upstairs.

"Stay down!" he bellowed back, and scrambled on his hands

and knees to the shattered storefront to peer out. Dust obscured the men and horses racing from town in the pale, morning light. He raised his hands to wipe his face and saw the blood. He'd cut both hands crawling across the glass.

"Hannah, you and little Billy all right?" *Please God...*

"Yes, we're fine. What's happening?"

A war has started.

Instead of telling her that, he pulled a handkerchief from his back pocket, pressed it into his left palm, and said calmly, "Just some drunk cowboys. Stay put till I get this glass cleaned up."

CHAPTER 42

*R*ebecca was amused by the dude's look of displeasure. Stepping out of the stagecoach, he paused to survey his dusty shoes and scowled at them. *Doesn't he know he can shine them?* Wondering who this stranger was, she leaned on a post in front of the marshal's office, giving her reporter's curiosity some freedom.

The rock thrown through Billy's window had, according to her new brother-in-law, been the result of some drunk cowboys staying too long in Tent Town. She wasn't sure she believed him, but, regardless, it wasn't much of a story. This stranger might prove more interesting.

Clutching a black bag in one hand, the man brushed the dust off his suit with the other and glanced around at Defiance. A typical day in town, miners, wagons, horses, and donkeys flowed down the street like a determined river. The stranger, young and handsome, blond hair falling over his forehead in a rather elegantly haphazard way, regarded Defiance with a disdainful grimace.

"Your bag, sir."

Before the man could turn, Jim, the stagecoach driver, carelessly tossed a satchel down and it landed hard in the dirt, raising a dust cloud. The passenger clutched the black bag in his hand tighter, as if glad Jim hadn't been given control of that one. The stagecoach driver smirked and moved to the next piece of luggage, which he gently handed to the waiting passenger.

This was such curious behavior for Jim, Rebecca decided to amble a little closer, get a better look at this gentleman who looked as if he'd just stepped out of the pages of the Montgomery Ward catalog.

To his credit, he ignored Jim's gruff treatment of his belongings and brushed a curl off his forehead. "My good man, could you tell me which way is the hotel?"

"Trinity Inn. Down the street, on the right." And Jim added under his breath, "Your Lordship."

"And the doctor's office?"

Rebecca perked up. The stagecoach driver handed off the last bag and looked over the stranger's head. "One street over. Can't miss it. Only a couple of buildings back there."

The dude retrieved his other bag from the ground, nodded curtly at Jim, and started walking. Rebecca decided to follow him and see if he was more inclined toward the hotel or the doctor's office—her eyes shot to the bag in his hand.

A doctor's bag?

*T*he stranger turned down the alley and emerged on the path that led to the mine and the doctor's office. Rebecca hung back and watched as a group of men wearing threadbare clothes and carrying lunch pails passed him. They looked the well-coiffed stranger over and chuckled—no doubt at his tailored suit—and continued on their way.

As they passed by, they revealed the man staring at the old sign: Thomas Cook, M.D. Behind it stood the simple clapboard building functioning as Defiance's medical office. Rotating his shoulders, the man strode toward to the door with obvious determination. Rebecca hurried to catch up with him and fell into step beside him going up the walkway.

"Good afternoon. Headed to the doctor's office as well?" A flicker of irritation crossed his face, as if Rebecca was a gnat that should be shooed out of his presence. Intrigued rather than offended, she did at least offer an apology. "Forgive me if I'm intruding. Just making conversation. We do seem to be walking in the same direction…"

"I was walking. You were racing."

His sarcasm caught Rebecca off guard, but only for an instant. "I'm Rebecca Donoghue. My husband, Ian, and I own the *Defiance Dispatch*, the newspaper in town. And you are?"

"Minding my own business." He crossed the porch and approached the door, Rebecca on his heels. Raising his hand to knock, he said, "Forgive me. I don't mean to be rude, of course, but one wonders if all visitors in town are followed about by the editor of the newspaper?"

"I wasn't following you. I said that."

He ignored her and tapped on the door. Hannah sang out, "Come in."

The man was at least polite enough to hold the door for Rebecca. When she stepped in front of him into the office, inviting warmth hit her in the face, along with the smell of witch hazel, and, faintly, the almondy scent of laudanum. Allowing her eyes to adjust, she discovered Hannah lighting a long match at the stove.

"Are you all right?" She straightened, the match burning in her hand. "Is this an emer—oh, Rebecca." Hannah's gaze ricocheted between Rebecca and the stranger. "What's wrong?"

"Nothing, *Mrs. Page*." The sisters grinned at each other, enjoying the use of Hannah's married name. "I ran into this gentleman on the street. We were both coming here—"

The man stepped forward. "I'm looking for Hope Clark. I understand she is your new...nurse."

Rebecca heard that same, suspicious pause. At least now she knew why and suspected this man knew the truth about Hope. Hannah bit her lip and glanced at a closed door. She lit the lamp on the wall and blew out the match. "She's with a patient. Whom may I say is calling?"

"Edward Pratt. Dr. Edward Pratt."

———

CHAPTER 43

*H*ope touched Hank Jeffers throat, checking his pulse at the carotid artery. Much stronger than last night. A good sign. She touched his forehead. No fever.

Yes, it looked as if the first accident from the mine was going to prove minor—a concussion and a broken ankle. She was pleased and hoped things stayed this mundane.

The door clicked behind her and she turned. Hannah's wide-eyed expression of—what?—fear, confusion alarmed Hope. "What's the matter?"

Hannah swallowed. "There's a Dr. Edward Pratt here to see you."

Hope felt her knees try to buckle and only with great concentration managed to stop them. Her heart dropped to her stomach and her mouth fell open. Heat rushed her cheeks.

Hannah slipped in and shut the door behind her. "Do you want me to tell him to go away? Or have the marshal remove him? Or..."

"Tell him I'll be out in a moment." *As soon as I collect myself.* "A moment. Or two."

Hannah nodded and started to go, but Hope reached out to

her. "Hannah, I'm sorry. Would-would you mind leaving?" *I can't bear an audience right now.*

"Of course not. I'll take Rebecca with me."

Hope waited until the muffled voices on the other side of the door faded and she was sure Hannah and Rebecca had left. She faced the door, squared her shoulders, took a deep breath, raised her chin, and stepped outside.

Edward looked up from the stethoscope he was tapping into his hand and smiled with enthusiasm. "Hope, my, my, the mountain air has made you even more beautiful and I didn't think that was possible." He tossed the stethoscope on the counter and crossed the room to clutch her shoulders. "I have missed you." He leaned in for a kiss and Hope made sure to give him only her cheek. Grinning, Edward lingered with his lips against her skin. "Still angry?"

Hope erupted and pushed him away. "Don't patronize me." She flinched and looked over her shoulder, concerned she'd awakened her patient. "What are you doing here?"

Sighing, he quirked an eyebrow, as if the answer should be obvious to her. "I've come to take you home. You've tried to make a go of being a physician in a man's world. It hasn't worked. Come back to Philadelphia with me and be my nurse... and my wife, of course."

"I see father has kept you informed."

"Of course. He—" Edward bit off the comment and glanced around the office. "I understand Denver didn't work out. Still, I had expected more than a small, spartan office in a remote mining town. This place smacks of desperation."

Hope clenched her jaw. How could her father have done this? The last person in the world she wanted to see was Edward. She'd won a titanic battle to assert herself, chase her dreams, and get out from under all these domineering men in her life who didn't believe in her—and now she would have to re-engage in the battle? No, no, no.

"I'm not desperate. I'm working in my full capacity as a physician here and I have patients."

"Full capacity? Aside from the title. I understand you've told everyone here you are a nurse."

"How do you know that?" She hadn't even told her father the details of her current situation.

"A reporter in town contacted your father. In the course of their corresponding through telegrams, the truth came out."

Hope wilted. *Rebecca Donoghue. Intrepid reporter.*

"Now, now, don't look so sad." He tapped her chin playfully. "I'll let you be all the doctor you want to be in my office. Just don't call yourself one. It's unseemly."

Hope's ire ignited again. "You are too arrogant to be believed, Edward." Oddly, Lane Chandler leaped to her mind. If he knew the truth of the matter, would he truly believe in her? She shooed away the thought. "I'm not leaving. I'm not going anywhere with you. And I'm certainly not marrying you. I will stay here and practice medicine."

Edward gave her that look again. The raised eyebrow, a slight smirk on the lips. She hated the way it made her feel like a petulant child.

"I have always admired your determination, Hope. It's time, however, to put all this foolishness aside. I admit I may have been a bit harsh with you as you've pursued this dream. I'm sorry." He took her hand in his. "I love you and want you by my side."

"You mean under your thumb." She pulled her hand away. "No. I have to…I have to continue to chase my dream. Be true to myself. If I let you do this to me, the compromises would never stop until I was a ghost." The thought made her shiver. "I help people here in this town. Maybe I'll never tell them I'm a doctor, but I think I will. And I think they'll want me to stay."

"It's a man's world, Hope. *Medicine* is a man's world. You don't stop this daydreaming, you're going to get hurt. People here may be crueler than the ladies in Denver, once they find out you've been lying to them."

The comment was like a dagger. Edward had always known the perfect words to slice her in two, expose her biggest fears, dissect her insecurities. How could she have ever loved this man?

"I have to get ready. I have several patients coming in today."

Edward pushed a golden curl off his forehead and straightened his shoulders with a miffed sniff. "Fine. This is not the end of our discussion, but I'm tired. Stagecoach travel is for the uncivilized. I'm going to get a room and some rest. I'll take you to dinner this evening and we can continue our talk."

"You should just leave, Edward." She said it with too much pleading, but she wished so many things right now. His departure was at the top of the list, however.

"Honestly, Hope, I thought you might be inclined to leave this little burg but wouldn't be surprised if you weren't. Hence, I have a confession."

Hope wondered how much worse things could get, but knew, by that smug look on Edward's face, she was about to find out.

"The town father, a Mr. Charles McIntyre, hired me as Defiance's new doctor. You're my nurse, whether you like it or not."

*A*ll day long, Hope struggled to maintain a warm, positive bedside manner with the patients. She appreciated Hannah's understanding smiles, though. The girl had offered her ear if Hope wanted to talk, but Hope had declined. At least for today. Later, she had told her. Later, after she'd had a chance to recover from the shock.

And the knives in her back—no pun intended. *Medicine is a man's world. Mr. Charles McIntyre hired me as Defiance's new doctor.* Hope wanted to spit nails. The arrogance. The pride. Both men acted as if she were a servant to be moved about on a whim from downstairs to upstairs maid.

Oh, how she could scream, wanted to climb a mountain and rage with the frustration of it all—

Hannah surprised Hope with an unexpected hug as she prepared to leave for the night. "You're a wonderful doctor, Hope. All this is going to work out. God didn't send you to Defiance just to see you leave. I wish you knew Him. He'd show you the way."

Hope smiled indulgently. "Thank you, Hannah. You have a good evening." She walked the young nurse to the door and smiled at the sight of Billy waiting in a wagon, their son bouncing on his knee. Though, Hope thought, the man looked a little tense. Or perhaps just tired.

He nodded at Hope as Hannah settled on the bench beside him and the trio rode off together in the lengthening shadows. Hope watched them disappear in the alley. For some reason, Hannah's pleading played over and over in her head. *God didn't send you to Defiance just to see you leave. I wish you knew Him. He'd show you the way.*

He'd show you the way.

God.

Hope didn't need God or any other oppressive male to show her the way. She knew exactly the path she wanted to take. She wanted to be a doctor, help people, and the fact that she was a woman should be completely ignored. Anything a man could do as a doctor she could do. The pride, the vanity, the insecurities of men like Edward and women like Mrs. Chalmers were maddening.

About to turn and go back inside, a woman emerged from the shadows across the street. Hope studied her for a moment, trying to figure if she knew her. Shortly, the girl drew close enough and Hope placed the face.

Adrianna. She looked well enough, so Hope assumed she

hadn't had the abortion yet. Perhaps she was here to talk about a different path. The woman strode to the edge of the yard and stopped. Hope nodded. "Good evening, Adrianna."

"I just wanted to make sure."

"Sure of what?"

"That you won't help me. If you're still stuck on no, I'm going to see Amanda tonight." The woman pulled her coat tighter as if the very thought chilled her to the bone.

Hope flinched. "I will help you." She stepped off the porch and hurried up to the woman. "There are options. You don't have to—"

"I've got one option and I'm set on it. You either help me or I'm marching myself right over to Amanda's cabin."

Hope swallowed. It was a simple procedure. Over in a matter of minutes. She was quite sure she could do it and cause very little discomfort to Adrianna.

But a life would end.

One that hadn't even really gotten started.

Tissue and blood. That was all. Not a life.

No one had to know. A patient's confidence was sacrosanct.

She looked up. Adrianna's brown eyes glimmered with fear but determination as well.

Hope pinched sweat off her lip, nodded slowly. "Come inside."

CHAPTER 44

"*D*o you remember this spot?" Charles tossed a blanket out on the ground as Naomi wandered over to the edge of the cliff—but not too close; the drop made her head swim. The view from here, however, was worth it: miles of rolling hills in the golden valley below, the shimmering Animas snaking its way through it. The majestic, jagged San Juan Mountains around them, some tipped with snow, some painted in swatches of yellow from the turning aspens. For November, they were experiencing a wonderfully warm day. Hence, the inspiration for the picnic.

Once the baby came along, moments—plans—like this would be so much harder to bring about.

She smiled as she scanned the vista. Down in one of the clearings, she spotted their home. Their ranch. Originally, only a one-room log cabin that they'd spent their honeymoon in—without a roof. They had added on to it and built several additional buildings around it. They were planning a huge Thanksgiving feast with all the ranch hands and the family. It was only a few weeks away. Then Christmas would be here...and then the baby.

Oh, the time was flying by, and suddenly Naomi had a desperate desire to slow its march. She wanted more time. Wanted to make every second count. A strange chill swept over her and she hugged the baby she was carrying.

Charles came up behind her and wrapped her in a warm hug. "Surely you are daydreaming about me."

"In a way." Not sharing his good humor, she moved his hands to the baby. "I was thinking how fast the days are slipping by us. I don't want them to. I want to stop time."

He kissed the top of her head. "I agree. I wish I could have a thousand years with you. And that would not be enough."

"We'll be together in Heaven."

"Somehow I don't think it will be the same."

This time she did see the humor and chuckled. "Maybe we won't miss that. We'll be with the Lord. Imagine."

"I'm trying very hard…but…" He sighed and nibbled on her neck.

In spite of the goosebumps he raised on her, in spite of her racing heart, she laughed. "You are incorrigible."

He turned her around. "Because I have the love of my life in my arms. Jesus is…well, let's say He most likely understands my hesitation at giving up certain earthly pleasures. He made me, after all."

Naomi was laughing as Charles kissed her, but the humor quickly gave way to passion. His lips possessed her, evoked her willingness to submit to any of his desires. His hands roamed freely, and heat cascaded through her. Eyes closed, her breath coming in short, rapid bursts, she experienced the masterful, wonderful, playful touch of her husband.

"I thought we might dine first," he whispered against her throat, "but now I think I am hungry for something a little different."

Half-drunk with desire, she nodded. "The chicken can wait."

"Shall I build a fire?"

"After. I'll get the buffalo robes."

*L*ater, after they'd made love on the sunny mountainside, they dressed and enjoyed their picnic lunch. Then, pleasantly stuffed, they curled up together beneath the robes again and stared up at the whispy clouds.

"I'm so happy Billy and Hannah finally tied the knot," Naomi mused aloud.

"He certainly waited on her long enough. What do you think caused her sudden change of heart?"

Naomi considered how Hannah had explained it to her and offered her own interpretation. "She didn't say it this way, but I think ultimately she was afraid being married might squelch her desire to nurse. And while she wants domestic bliss, nursing blesses her soul."

"She won't give it up," he said, sounding very certain.

Naomi agreed. "Yes, I think you're right. She's called to it."

They fell silent for a spell, each lost in their thoughts. Eventually, though, reality came back to them.

"It's getting late," he said sounding remorseful.

"Yes, I know. Two Spears will wonder where we are."

"Yes, and, if I know Lane, he'll be worrying as well."

"Do you think we're in danger?" She rolled half-way over on him and raised up to look into those beautiful, mysterious, dark eyes of his. But she also saw the stares of the men in the funeral procession. They'd given her nightmares. "As in, I shouldn't ride into town alone or…"

He took several seconds to answer, playing with a strand of her hair while he thought. "You do not need to go anywhere alone, especially while you are carrying my child."

She smirked at his singular ownership and decided to

lighten the subject rather than focus on the darkness. "Have you thought about any names for *your* baby?"

"I am inclined toward certain Biblical names."

"Such as?"

"For a boy, I like Ezekiel. Maybe Gabriel. For a girl, perhaps Sarah or Esther."

A rumble of thunder drew their gazes across the valley. A massive, bruised thunderhead was forming, rising high, heading for them. Lightning leaped from the cloud in a magnificent display of God's power. Unusual for this time of year. It almost struck her as a harbinger.

Uneasy, Naomi didn't want to be caught in it. "We need to beat that home."

"We will." They stood up and he reached for his gun belt, slipped it around his hips. Pressing a quick kiss on Naomi as he buckled it, he said, "Thank you for a lovely afternoon, your highness. I thoroughly enjoyed myself."

She smacked his arm and heat flooded her cheeks. How he could still embarrass her with a saucy phrase and the quirk of a dark eyebrow. "Yes, well…" was all she could manage as she reached down for the other robe.

On the way back to the ranch, he drove the wagon and she tidied her appearance, re-braiding her hair, then snuggled against him for warmth. They rode for a mile or so in a companionable silence as she pondered their afternoon. A smile touched her heart and rose to her lips.

For a while today, time *had* stopped. "It was a lovely picnic. We couldn't have asked for better weather in November. God made it perfect just for us. I love you, Charles McIntyre. We should do it more often."

"Oh, I heartily agree." He winked at her as he drove the wagon out from behind two large boulders and emerged onto the main road.

She smacked him on the arm again. "You have no shame."

The sudden hard, angry set to his profile confused her, until she realized he was staring at something. She followed his gaze as he pulled the wagon to an abrupt stop.

A dozen men on horseback waited in the road, blocking it, holding rifles at the ready. One of them was swinging a hangman's noose around and around, and grinning like a demon.

CHAPTER 45

$\mathcal{T}$he instant Charles saw the men he reached for his Colt, but one of them, a dark-haired, bushy-headed mongrel, had already leveled his rifle on Naomi. "You act the fool," he warned, "and she'll die for it."

Charles let his hand hover over the revolver as he assessed the group. He was reasonably certain he could kill two, maybe three, but beyond that? No, a foolhardy strategy, especially with Naomi and their child in the line of fire.

Tamping down fear and fury with a prayer, he raised his hand, but kept it within striking distance, in case an opportunity opened up. "What do you men want?"

The one swinging the rope chuckled. "I thought that might be pretty obvious."

Charles knew men, their specific natures. There was no bluffing in this group. They'd come to kill him. But why? He studied their shadowy, hard faces. "I recognize you." A blond-haired boy of about twenty, one drifting eye. "And you." The man with the noose, fat, scruffy, missing a front tooth. Charles shook his head at the others. "I take it this has something to do with the mine?"

The boy with the drifting eye inched his sorrel forward. "My pappy died in your mine. And there ain't been no justice for him. You walking free, Beckwith bulldogging the town, Delilah living unfettered and safe somewhere—it's all dragged on too long."

Words straight out of one the handbills Matthew was peddling around town. Only with worse grammar. "Killing me or anyone else is not going to bring your father back, son. Besides, despite what you've been reading, I had nothing to do with the explosion. Nor did Beckwith. All of it is on Delilah."

"But Delilah ain't here," the fat man with the noose said.

Naomi's fingers dug into Charles' thighs. He could sense her panic. It stalked him as well, but he wouldn't give in to it. *God, You cannot let her die here. Please save her.* "If it's a fight you want, I'll gladly oblige. But I would like my wife to ride out safe. Surely you are not such low-born scoundrels you would hurt a woman."

The bushy-headed mongrel chuckled. "The noble Charles McIntyre." He grinned, revealing the dark gap in a neighborhood of yellowed, crooked teeth. "We ain't uncivilized. You climb down outta that wagon and she can go."

"No, Charles," she whispered, squeezing his leg with a death grip. "I won't leave you."

"You'll do exactly as I say." He sounded calm, though his heart was beating wildly. All he wanted was for Naomi and their child to get out of this. Nothing else mattered.

"You climb down now. Come on and the missus can go," the mongrel said. "She'll head for help, but we didn't see a thing, did we boys?"

Laughter rumbled through the group. Various men responded with, "Nope, I was napping." "I was down panning in the creek. You saw me there, Bill." "Sure did." "I was at the Number Two having a beer. With Mike here and Henry."

They would all act as each other's alibis. Their word against Naomi's. And Charles'—if he survived this.

He took Naomi's hand and smiled quickly at her. "It will be all right, Naomi."

"Come on, git down." The boy tried to intimidate Charles with a glare, but with only one eye, it fell short. "Let's get a move on."

"I love you," he whispered softly to Naomi. "And I'm sorry for—"

"Nothing. I love you," she rushed. "Do what you do and get out of this. I want you home for supper."

He understood what she was saying. And if it came to it, he would do his best to kill them all. Gut-wrenching fear for her safety roiled in his belly. He pushed past it and slowly climbed out of the wagon, looking for an opportunity to use his Colt, but with Naomi in the middle…Sighing, his boots touched the ground and he raised his hands.

"Ride out Naomi. And *don't* do anything foolish."

Eyes glimmering with tears, chin quivering, she picked up the reins, hesitated then snapped them. As the horses moved, the man with the noose pointed his rifle at Charles. "Take off that hog leg. You don't need it where you're going." He casually shifted the barrel over to Naomi as she rode away at a snail's pace.

God, why isn't she moving faster? Go, woman, go.

He had no choice. Charles lowered his hand, moving like a fly in honey. If Naomi could just get a little farther away— Suddenly, the boy with the wayward eye, still holding his rifle, leaped from his horse to the wagon. He shoved Naomi violently backward over the seat and stomped down on the brake.

"Naomi!" Charles pulled the Colt and was instantly met with the cocking of a dozen rifles—half of them pointed at her. He could drop the man assaulting his wife…and then they would both die. Knowing what these men likely had planned for her, perhaps that was the better outcome.

His finger tightened on the trigger. *So easy to drop him...*

Fear in his eyes, the kid grabbed Naomi by her braid and jerked her to her feet. Railing at him, she managed a beautiful knee to his groin and his compatriots flinched in amused empathy. He doubled-over but managed—amazingly—to hang on to the wildcat.

"That's it, Tom," someone said. "Don't let a woman best ya." The others laughed heartily. "'Specially one with a bun in the oven."

Bent in half, red-faced, clearly in pain, Tom wrestled his arm around Naomi's neck, straightened up and positioned his rifle between them, pressing it into her back. Fear like acid burned in Charles' mouth and he prayed for his wife to come to her senses.

Naomi settled down.

"Dang," a man muttered.

"I know," the man with the noose chuckled. "Quite the little spitfire you've got there, McIntyre. She that lively in the sack?"

Charles still had the boy holding his wife in his sights. But pulling the trigger would seal her doom. No one had addressed the gun in his hand because they knew who had the upper hand here. If Naomi was not in the midst of this, Charles would have tried. He simply couldn't risk her life. She could yet get free of this mess. Stranger things had happened.

Lord, we need a miracle. Save her. Save my child.

Grudgingly, he slid the .44 back into his holster, loosened the gun belt and let the hardware fall to the dirt.

"Good man." The rider with the noose moved toward Charles. "Tom, you bring the little gal back over here. I wanna keep her close to me."

Acceptance of their plan for Naomi moved Charles from

fear to cold, hard hate. Now he had nothing to lose. *God, help me...and forgive me.*

An unyielding determination to survive this and kill these men—every, single one of them—blossomed in his heart like a bloodstain on a shirt. He'd start with the fat man with the noose. "You get down off that horse. Try to put a noose around my neck."

The man's jaw wiggled, expressing a little concern. "I'll oblige ya. You try anything and we'll just shoot her."

"She's dead anyway. None of you have hid your faces." All of the men exchanged nervous glances. "You never intended to let her go. You are the kind of vile miscreants I will not regret killing."

A nervous chuckle circulated among the group. "Mighty bold talk from a man about to die." The fat man seemed to find his nerve again and snorted in disgust. "You ain't so much, McIntyre. I'll hang this rope on ya, but first I'll have a little fun." He climbed down off the horse, hooked the noose around the saddle horn, and faced Charles with his fists raised. He was not only a fat man, he was tall, and broad as a barn. "Hope you can throw a punch because I can take—"

Charles jabbed him twice in the mouth, snapping his head back and drawing blood. He managed a third strike to his sizable gut, a wasted effort. The fat absorbed the blow. Recovered, the assailant dove into Charles, knocked him back, sent him flying into the side of the wagon. Blows rained down from both of them.

Head blows, Charles told himself. *Head blows. Ring his bell. Daze him. Dive for the gun...*

Shaking his head, Charles pushed the giant off him, took an instant to breathe, and then charged back in before his opponent was ready. He threw powerful cross punches, but this time the man seemed to absorb them, even to his head, though blood trickled from his lips. Charles felt a stinging in his own ribs, sharp, throbbing pain in his jaw. Desperation seized him. He had to get his gun. Or the fat man's gun. Any gun. Naomi's life depended on it.

On him.

The fat man wiped at his mouth and sneered. "This is too much trouble."

"Charles," Naomi screamed.

Skull-cracking pain exploded in the back of Charles head, spreading out and then through his brain like a wildfire. His legs wobbled; his knees buckled. He found himself kneeling on the ground, swaying, unable to gather his thoughts. He could hear Naomi screaming, knew he should care but he was in the midst of waking from a dream. His body felt as if it had turned to pudding and he wanted to go back to sleep.

Stay awake, a voice ordered, but it was the voice of a stranger. Charles couldn't roust himself to enough to care.

"Hurry up before he gets his wits back."

Something rough, scratchy fell on Charles' shoulders, around his neck. He stared dumbly at it for a moment.

A rope. He picked it up, confused by its presence. Why was Naomi screaming? He couldn't make sense of any of this. A wave of nausea rolled over him as hands grabbed him, dragged him to his feet, sending another jolt of blinding pain through his head.

And then the light around began to dim.

"Wake him up," a gruff, fading voice ordered. "He needs to see this coming."

CHAPTER 46

"Nope, that ain't good at all."

Lane stepped away from the ledge and snatched his Sharps from his saddle. Emilio's mouth fell open. He was going to try to save Mr. McIntyre—from up here? "You can't make that shot. It's too far."

"I reckon I better try or we ain't gonna have a boss." Lane laid the rifle on a knee-high rock on the edge. After hearing Billy's report about the attack at the mercantile, Lane and Emilio had decided they'd better find Mr. McIntyre and tell him. They'd stopped at the overlook to have some water and figure where else to look when they didn't find him at the sawmill. Emilio couldn't believe his eyes when they'd discovered a group of men about to lynch his employer. Lane had not hesitated, going immediately for his Sharps.

A heck of a shot if he made it. "It must be eight hundred yards."

"Seven, give or take."

"I can't even see the rope."

Lane laid down with the Sharps, flipped up the rear sight

leaf, flexed his stiff hand and drew a bead on Mr. McIntyre, who was standing kind of limp in the back of the wagon. One fella seemed to be holding him up.

"I always have had good eyesight," Lane mumbled.

"What if you miss and hit Mr. McIntyre?"

"I won't miss."

A fat man tossed the noose over an oak branch and tied it off. Over to the right, Naomi was pitching an insane fit, writhing like a snake and screaming wildly. Some fella had her, though, in a bear hug from behind, her feet lifted off the ground, and was working intently to avoid her flailing kicks. Near them, the rest of the group watched from their mounts, still as tombstones.

"You ever make a shot like that before?"

Lane snugged the rifle up against his shoulder, shifting on the rock, moving quickly and with purpose. "Anticipate," Lane whispered so softly Emilio almost didn't hear him. "I gotta anticipate..."

Intense concentration tightened every muscle on the man's face. His eye narrowed as he stared down the barrel, past the sight. Could he see the rope? The bullet would find it, Emilio had to believe that. He imagined the cold steel of the trigger beneath his finger and let calm sink in...

Lane could do this. Father, please guide that bullet...

The fat man who'd held the rope raised his hand to slap the rear end of one of the horses hitched to the wagon. As his palm swooped down, Lane fired. The animals bolted. For an infinitesimal fraction of a second McIntyre was suspended in the air kicking mightily but then fell hard to the ground on his shoulder, head, and back.

Lane cocked and fired again at a man sitting astride a horse. He backflipped out of the saddle and the horse bolted. Men and horses scattered. The kid holding Naomi pushed her over the side out of his way and leaped into the woods. The man who'd tossed the rope over the tree limb hunkered down like a sparrow fearing death from above. Lane took the shot. The man exploded backwards and landed spread eagle on the ground. The man in the wagon who'd been holding McIntyre for the noose clawed crazily for the reins and sent the horses bolting.

Lane cocked the rifle, followed him for a breath, then fired. The driver flew forward in a spray of red, landed on the horses and disappeared with them around the bend.

Lane waited for a moment, his eyes searching for movement. Like a herd of frightened deer, though, the mob had scattered and disappeared into the trees. A few survivors had gotten away...for now.

Lane jumped to his feet. "Let's get down there."

"Holy cow," Emilio whispered, swinging up into his saddle.

"Lucky shots," Lane said, wheeling his horse around.

"No, señor." Emilio shook his head as they took off at a charge. "That was a lot of things," he yelled over the pounding hooves, "but luck was not one of them."

---

*E*milio agreed with Lane that the bodies should lie where they fell. The important thing was getting Mr. McIntyre medical attention. When they rode down to the sight of the attempted execution, they found Naomi cradling her husband, crying and praying over him.

"We'll get the wagon and be right back, Miss Naomi," Lane told her. "Come on Emilio." She didn't even look up as they rode off. Fortunately, the horses had only run a few hundred yards. The dead weight of the man tangled in the tack had confused them.

They were back with Naomi in a matter of minutes. They set

her and her husband in the back and then all of them rode hard for town. At one point, Emilio, driving the wagon, had suggested maybe Lane go on, let the doctor know they were coming.

He'd glanced around warily and shook his head. "Nope. We stick together."

CHAPTER 47

*H*ope greeted them at the door as they skidded to a gravel-flying, horse-whinnying stop in her front yard. "I heard you coming. Is everything—oh, Naomi. Lane. What—?"

"Some men lynched Mr. McIntyre." Lane launched from his saddle, didn't bother to tie his horse, and dropped the tailgate on the wagon.

Hope gasped, rushing to help. "What?"

As Emilio set the brake and ran back to help Lane, a pale, blond-haired man pushed past Hope and joined them at the tailgate. "Quickly, get him inside. Is he breathing?"

"Yep," Lane answered, looking a little puzzled at this stranger.

"You say lynched him?" The man looked at Mr. McIntyre's neck as Lane and Emilio dragged him from the wagon. "Did he hang for long?"

"Nah." Lane got a good hold on Mr. McIntyre's shoulders and he and Emilio double-timed it toward the front door. "A fraction of a second."

Hope let them pass and then reached up to assist Naomi. "Come on, let's get you inside."

"You should have seen it," Emilio said, backing through the front door. "One heck of a shot. Close to a thousand yards."

"Who are you, any how?" Lane asked, looking at the man sideways as they laid Mr. McIntyre in a bed. "I thought Hope did the doctoring 'round here."

"Pratt. I'm Doctor Pratt. Hope is sticking to nursing." Emilio saw Lane's face harden with what he would have labeled as disapproval. Pratt pulled his stethoscope from his neck and shoved the ends in his ears. "Nurse Clark," he yelled over his shoulder. "I need your assistance." Pratt eyed Emilio and Lane. "Gentlemen, if you'll excuse me. You can wait outside. I assume the lady is his wife. Please assure her that her husband is in good hands."

---

*E*milio opted to stay with Naomi while Lane made the effort to let Hannah and the others know what had happened. He would also ride out to the ranch, share the information with the men, and come back with Two Spears.

Naomi had quit crying, but her green eyes were still wide with fear and glued to her husband's face. Every once in a while, she would swallow and take a deep breath, fighting for her composure, Emilio assumed.

He'd made a few comments attempting to reassure her, but she had not responded, merely hugged her midsection and sat quietly in a chair by her husband's bed. He stared out the window, but the shot Lane had made repeated over and over in his head. The crack of the rifle, Mr. McIntyre suspended in the air for only an instant, then hitting the ground so hard his head had bounced. How small the window for error had been but Lane had threaded it like a needle.

"It was a miracle," he whispered aloud unintentionally, and Naomi looked up at him.

"That he's alive? Yes."

"That too, sí, but the shot Lane took." He turned to her. "Señora, I couldn't even see the rope. And he had to time it perfectly…"

Naomi smiled. A peace flooded her expression and Emilio found the look calmed him as well. "God is in the business of miracles, Emilio."

"Sí, señora, sí."

CHAPTER 48

The office had filled up quickly with the family of Mr. McIntyre, there to wait through the night with Naomi. He had a severe concussion and was unconscious. How severe, only time would tell. If he wasn't awake in the morning, Hope thought they might start using the word "coma" to describe his condition. But not yet. Not yet.

Naomi and her sisters and Mr. Donoghue stood in the center of the office's small waiting room, praying. Uncomfortable with the emotional superstitions, Hope slipped out the back to steal a moment of quiet. She sat down on the stoop and stared up at a sky alive with twinkling diamonds, jarringly vivid in the cold, clear night. Her soul ached within her, but she fought not to give into silly, weepy tears.

Yes, perhaps their hope was superstitious and misplaced in a fictional god…but they had hope. And each other.

Hope felt profoundly sad and the ache for something she couldn't name formed a lump in her throat.

"Oh, stop this," she whispered harshly. "You're acting like a child."

She was simply overwrought. Annoyed by Edward's presence, his take-over of her office and position, and Mr. McIntyre's complete insensitivity to hiring him and not telling her...

Yet, even as she went over this list of grievances, it was Adrianna's face that rose in her mind over and over again. No matter how much Hope wanted to, she couldn't bury a nagging...regret.

The procedure had gone perfectly. Letting her rest for twelve hours, Hope had then seen her home before Hannah came into the office. Hope had checked on her once. The woman was recovering fine and Hannah was none the wiser. Edward hadn't even bothered himself with questions.

Adrianna was back in her dark, seedy little world. Any trace of the pregnancy had been scraped from her womb. Like it never happened.

Then why did Hope feel so awful?

She hugged her knees and rested her forehead on them, eyes closed to shut out the darkness.

"Penny for your thoughts?"

Lane's voice brought her head up. "What—?"

He dropped on the steps beside her. "That him? The fella who didn't agree with your choice of vocations?"

"Yes, that's him."

"What's he doing here?"

She sighed. "That's a very good question. He wants me to go back to Philadelphia with him. I refused and that's when he told me Mr. McIntyre had hired him as the town doctor. He saw the ad in the *Philadelphia Enquirer* about the same time Rebecca contacted my father trying to get the truth about me."

"The truth?"

Hope flinched. She was tired and had slipped. Well, everything else in her life was going awry, why not wave goodbye to Lane. She didn't want to. The realization surprised her. But she was in the mood to be maudlin. Why not wallow in a little more pain. "I am a doctor, too, Lane. Not a nurse."

"I don't understand. You say it like you're telling me you're a horse thief or something."

Puzzled, she turned to look at him full-on. The moonlight glimmered in his wavy, blond hair, flattened at the temples with a perfect imprint of his hat. His shirt and vest were streaked with dark smudges of dirt. He smelled like sweat and leather. So different from Edward with his tailored clothes, delicate hands, overblown ego. "You really don't care that I'm a doctor? You don't think that it's not an appropriate vocation for a woman?"

"That's hogwash. And if you don't mind me saying so, Adonis in there might be all smart, and wears tailored suits, and acts like God because of those letters after his name…but I bet he's not half the doctor you are."

Lane's simple, ineloquent words of encouragement were like rays of sunshine on Hope's heart…until she thought of Adrianna. And her spirits crashed again.

"You really don't mind that I'm a doctor?" She was having trouble believing him.

"That's like asking me if I mind air."

Hope smiled. "Thank you. You can't imagine what that means to me."

"But?" He tilted his head, looked at her sideways. "Somethin's gnawing at you."

Hope had never been one to hide from her problems, hold things back from people. This secret she was keeping, though, was doing exactly that—gnawing at her. On the slim hope Lane might not hate her, she shared it with him.

"I helped a woman from Tent Town terminate a pregnancy the other night." He sucked in a deep breath, straightened up, but didn't say anything. Hoping he was reserving judgement, she rushed on. "I did it for all the wrong reasons and against my better judgment." She swallowed. "And I hid it from Hannah."

To Hope's horror, tears suddenly filled her eyes and rolled down her cheeks. Humiliated by the water works, ashamed of what she'd done, she put her face in her hands and wept quietly. "I'm supposed to always put the patient first. And protect life, not stop it." She could barely speak, her throat was so tight. "I did it because I was angry about Edward showing up, about Mr. McIntyre hiring him without telling me—worse, to show those squawking hens in Denver women can make their own choices."

She shook her head, her misery complete. "I never once thought about the patient. What was best for her. Whether the procedure was wrong—" Not exactly true. "No, I...I pushed those thoughts away."

When the silence stretched on, and her hope he might still think kindly of her was fading, she begged him, "Say something, please. Even if it's unkind."

"My ma did the same thing."

"What?"

"My ma did the same thing. When she was young. Before she met pa. My saintly mother was not always so. But she told me one day what she'd done and that she regretted it. She said—" his voice warbled strangely, and he paused to clear his throat. "She said she was looking down at me and my brothers one day, all of us playing at her feet, and she wondered. Wondered about the one who wasn't there. What would he have done with his life if she'd given him the chance—"

"Oh, Lane, please stop," Hope sobbed. "I know what I did was awful—"

"Shhh." Lane gathered her up in his arms, held her, whispering, "I ain't condemning you. That ain't my point."

Hope writhed in her misery. She'd failed her profession. She'd failed herself. And, yes, she had to accept that she'd snuffed out a life. How would she ever get past this?

"My point," he continued, "is that we all do things we regret. We all make mistakes. Some mistakes cast long shadows, but you can't let them ruin you. Learn from them. Move past them."

Hope sniffed, wiped her face, and sat up. "Did your ma—I mean, your mother—did she move past it? Was she happy?"

"Well," he tugged on his ear. "At the risk of sounding like a preacher, Ma became a God-fearing woman. She said many times Jesus had washed her white as snow. Her sins had been forgiven. And yes, I believe she was happy. Honestly, though, I never understood what she was trying to say until—" his voice dropped to a somber tone, "until I saw the misery you're in. I hope you...I hope you find peace. I truly do."

---

*L*eaning on a porch post, Emilio rubbed his eyes and stared over the backside of the businesses lining Main Street. The sun was just turning the morning sky from slate gray to soft pink. Behind him in the doctor's office, Naomi, Hannah, and Rebecca were holding their vigil over the unconscious Mr. McIntyre. A few feet over, Ian tapped his pipe clean on the rail and grunted. Neither he nor Emilio cared for Lane's suggestion.

Lane paced a few feet down the porch, spoke with his back to them, his breath swirling around him in the cold morning air. "I understand your silence, but for me, it's the Texas way. I'm not calling for our own lynch mob, but we need to take some of the hands from the King M and throw a little fear of God into the right people." He turned to them slowly, his hat pressed contritely to his chest. "Charles told me Matthew is the one putting all this into motion. So he needs to know the King M boys will ride for the brand. All fifty of us."

"Ye could start a war, lad."

"No, sir, but we will finish it before they decide to string up Emilio here or maybe catch Naomi, Rebecca, or Hannah alone." Emilio and Ian both straightened to attention. "Sticking a knife into Hope shows they ain't got no compunctions about harming a woman. That mob was intent on making Miss Naomi watch. I doubt it woulda stopped there."

"Sí." Emilio flexed his fingers, thinking how such attacks could just as easily been aimed at Hannah or even Mollie. "Maybe he is right. Matthew, his mob. They fear nothing. Not God. Not the law."

"Ye don't know who participated in the lynching. Beckwith is investigating—"

"I don't have to have the right men in my sights. That fella Miller and his circle of buzzards need a little cold water thrown on 'em. Besides, this is out of Beckwith's jurisdiction," Lane reminded them.

"Aye, but I wired the territorial governor a few weeks back, requesting our marshal be deputized as a U.S. Marshal. That will change things dramatically."

"How long's it gonna take?"

"Unfortunately, I don't think the governor was in any hurry. Now, though, this attack on McIntyre will change things, I'm quite sure. Beckwith is going to wire and request U.S. Marshals be sent to Defiance immediately. One way or another, we're getting more law."

"Still gonna take too long," Lane muttered, staring at the ground.

Emilio took a deep breath and rubbed his chin. Mr. McIntyre had saved his life countless times, given him a job, never treated him like a Mexican, often treated him like a son. If it hadn't been for Lane, Emilio would have watched a group of lawless beasts hang his mentor—his friend—in front of his wife.

Emilio locked his gaze on Lane. "Compadre, you're right. Let's ride to the ranch."

Ian seemed to catch the meaning and started to protest. "Boys, ye need to let the law—" Hard looks cut him off. He studied them for a moment then nodded. "Aye, all right then.

Legal games havena scared him. If ye can promise me there'll be no bloodshed, I'll give my support."

Lane dropped his hat on his head. "We're just gonna give 'em a little clarity on their situation, Mr. Donoghue. I reckon it'll be all they need."

"And if ye're wrong?"

"Then they're rabid cur. And I'll do what needs doing."

CHAPTER 49

*M*atthew was feeling mighty full of himself this morning. Though he wasn't pleased a group of eager beavers had nearly lynched McIntyre, he was inordinately gratified by the terror the incident had inflicted. Better than he'd planned.

He leaned over his vanity and splashed water on his face, part of his morning routine to awaken, but this morning he was just about dancing on air. The reports from the boys involved told of a courageous McIntyre, but Matthew knew the event had scared the liver out of the man—if for no other reason than Naomi had been threatened.

That drew him up for a moment, reminded him he needed to be careful with the mob mentality. He didn't want McIntyre dead yet and some of these boys were a little too anxious. He wouldn't take them for granted again.

He grinned at himself in the mirror. *The snake charmer needs to keep playing the right tune, but maybe a touch softer.*

Humming, he dressed, decided to skip his morning coffee and head straight on over to the Crystal Chandelier Number Two. He had begun to like that location better than this gloomy, empty saloon in the mornings. Sometimes he thought he heard ol' Sam's voice now and again, lamenting the fact he'd never taste his wife's baked chicken again.

Shaking off the thought of the lawyer's ghost, Matthew jogged down the steps and nodded a greeting to Otis, who was building a fire in the stove. "I'm gonna head to the Number Two. Bring my breakfast over there."

Otis tossed a final piece of wood into the Franklin. "Yes, sir."

An explosion of gun fire froze them both. Then louder booms rocked the air, vibrated over the floor. "What the—?" Something was happening—where? Hell's Half-Acre? Matthew started to lunge for the door, paused for an instant. He'd left his gun upstairs. No time. He decided instead to see what hell was breaking loose over near the Number Two.

Otis was on his heels as they bolted through the motley collection of tents in Tent Town, thundered across the bridge and skidded to a stop in a melee of yelping cowboys on horses, guns blazing. Around them, tents were burning and miners and prostitutes were running for cover. Matthew surveyed the attackers and locked eyes with Lane Chandler. He felt his lip curl involuntarily into a sneer.

Chandler whipped his mount with the reins and raced up to Matthew. He held an unlit stick of dynamite in his hand. "Just the man we were looking for."

"Yeah?" Matthew took in the smoking ruins of the Number Two and had to purposefully remind himself to think through the rage rising in him. "What's this all about?"

"It's a message, Miller. You take on Charles McIntyre and you take on his whole ranch. We ride for the brand. We ride for him. Any harm comes to him or his family," Lane leaned forward in the saddle, attempting, Matthew supposed, to intimidate, "or anyone in his circle, any of his businesses, and we'll be back. Your boys aren't the only one who know how to swing a rope."

"I don't know what you're talking about, but if you think this is going to go unanswered—"

"You'd best proceed carefully, Miller." Lane dropped the dynamite into his shirt pocket and lowered his hand to hover over his Colt. "You've hurt women. In my book, that makes you a rabid coyote. Only one thing to do with one of them."

Matthew saw in Chandler's cold, hazel eyes a man who meant what he said. And if he was as good with a .45 as he was with the Sharps, Matthew had best heed the advice.

For the time being.

The noise and chaos died down as at least fifteen men reigned in behind Lane. All King M men, including the Mexican kid Emilio. Except for one, sitting astride his gray gelding. Buck was either brilliant...or very, very stupid.

Matthew would find out later.

For now...he shrugged a shoulder. "All right. Your message has been delivered." He scanned the crew of cowboys in the background. "Don't worry. We'll be open again by dark. Y'all come on back for a beer."

The comment was met with flinty stares.

Lane's gaze flicked over Matthew to Otis. "You're standing mighty close to a lightning rod, pard. Just sayin'."

"I know where I stand," the large black man replied.

Lane shifted back to Matthew and tipped his hat. "Thank you for your hospitality."

The King M cowboys spurred their horses and pounded toward Matthew, a few brushing him as they passed, horse flanks causing him to sway a little, but he held his ground. Hoofbeats thundered on the wooden bridge like an erupting thunderstorm and faded just as fast. When they'd gone, a few miners, some disheveled girls, and Amanda ventured out of the woods to stand in the smoking remains of the Number Two's compound.

Hand on her hip, Amanda sashayed over to Matthew. "This

is gonna cost us a fortune. My girls need tents. And what are you going to do for a saloon?"

Matthew flexed his fingers and surveyed the charred mess. The important thing to remember at this moment was to keep a hold of his temper, because if he lost it...all hell would break loose on Defiance before he was ready.

But if McIntyre and his cowboys thought this stunt would shut him down or make him back off, they were unbelievably mistaken. Through a clenched jaw, he said, "Otis, go to the mercantile and get every tent and every piece of canvas I have in stock. And then," he turned to his aid-de-camp, "politely ask some of our neighbors to give up their tents for a spell. Move them across the creek here for the girls." He pivoted back to the remains of the Number Two. "In the meantime, I'm going to arrange a little retribution. Personally."

CHAPTER 50

*T*he moment Emilio told Naomi about Lane's incredible shot, peace had washed over her like a warm wave of tropical water. The enemy had tried to take her husband yet again, but God had sent a humble cowboy all the way from Texas to foil the plan.

Therefore, she knew without a doubt he would wake up. This was only the second day. He would open those eyes and smile at her. He would.

Waiting expectantly, she dragged a finger lightly over his jaw, tracing the trail of that jet-black beard. She'd come so close to losing him, though. *Oh, God, I don't think I've ever been that scared in my life. Not when John went over the cliff. Not when Rose had us all hostage in the kitchen. Not when One-Who-Cries kidnapped us.*

The image of Charles, rope around his neck, getting hoisted into the back of the wagon twisted her guts. It would haunt her for the rest of her life. Yet, the terror she'd felt then warred now with the bitter desire for revenge. Those men could have killed Charles. They could have killed their baby. She wanted to see every one of them strung up, too.

Father, forgive me. She squeezed her eyes shut. *We wrestle not with flesh and blood. I keep trying to tell myself that, but I'm human. Help us both find forgiveness for those men, for Matthew.*

She opened her eyes and studied her husband. He was struggling mightily with the desires of revenge, judgement, and control. *Don't let this push him into vengeance, Lord. It's not our place to take it. It's Yours. You will repay. Any control we think we have is an illusion.*

The thought of losing Charles to the man he *was* formed a knot in her throat. *No, no, no. He is a new creation and You have such a future in store for him, Father. Blessings, a long life, and children.*

Mentally squaring her shoulders, she forced cheer into her voice. "God has plans for you, my husband. You should wake up." She was only half-joking but when his eyes fluttered, she gasped. "Charles." All pretense of humor evaporated. She grasped his hand tightly between hers. "Charles, I'm here. Wake up." A relieved sob choked her voice. "Wake up."

His eyes continued to flutter, but finally they opened. Panic registered in them and he sat bolt upright yelling for Naomi, his voice raspy and weak.

"It's all right, Charles, it's all right." She leaped up and wrapped her arms around him. "I'm here." For an instant he fought against her until clarity came to him and he pulled her into such a tight embrace she nearly couldn't breathe.

"My God, Naomi—" He broke off and hugged her tighter. Then smothered her in kisses.

She had her husband back. *Oh, God, thank You. Thank You for sending Lane.* She let Charles' love and relief sweep over her.

"Well, it looks like our patient is feeling better."

The new—and slightly full of himself—physician in town chuckled. Naomi pulled away from Charles, but clung to his hands, not ashamed of her cheeks wet with tears. "Charles, this is the doctor you hired. Dr. Pratt." She quickly wiped her face. "I didn't know you'd found someone for the position."

Consternation warred with confusion on Charles' face and Dr. Pratt rocked on his heels, his shoulders bowing, the posture of a man guilty of something.

"I am not sure I did," Charles said, sounding bewildered.

"Mr. McIntyre, forgive my boldness. After our exchange of telegrams I decided to rush to Defiance. The town was in need of a physician and I needed to see Hope. It seems my timing was fortuitous." He then added quickly, "How do you feel?"

Charles, his brow wrinkled with skepticism, surveyed the man carefully. Naomi assumed he was not pleased by the doctor's brashness, but he also had a lot to take in here in these last moments.

He touched the rope burn on his neck. "This is tender, and my head feels like it was stomped on by an angry mule."

"Yes, you must have been flailing quite a bit. When the rope broke, I surmise the back of your head hit the ground first and took the full weight of your body. You could have broken your neck."

"Yes, that certainly would have been ironic." He looked at Naomi. "I don't remember. What did happen?"

"The rope didn't break. Apparently, according to Emilio, Lane took a shot with his Sharps that will make him a legend. Somewhere around seven or eight hundred yards." Naomi didn't miss the slight scowl that tightened Pratt's expression at the news.

"Praise God, that boy always could shoot." Charles grinned with satisfaction. "He was a sniper during the war." His brow dipped. "Where is he? And where is Two Spears?"

Naomi bit her lip. She didn't think Charles was going to like what he heard next. So she hemmed and hawed and started to pull away. "Two Spears is asleep in the other room."

Charles frowned and held on to her hands, not allowing a retreat. "And Lane?"

"Why don't you finish with the doctor before we get into that?"

His gaze hardened. He hesitated but then returned to the doctor. "So, Dr. Pratt. I had not made a decision regarding your credentials and I had two other candidates I was considering. Simply showing up in town before I had a chance to discuss things with Naomi, as well as Hope, and Hannah makes things awkward."

"You haven't officially hired him?"

Hope's voice from the door drew their attention. Charles and Naomi bounced their gazes back and forth between the nurse and the doctor. "Not officially," Charles said slowly, "I still have some questions for you, Dr. Pratt. As well as for you, Miss Clark."

"Charles," Hannah peeked around Hope. "Praise the Lord you're awake, but about Hope," she slipped into the room. "She didn't breathe a word to anyone about the baby. News has leaked out of this office via Mrs. Tunstall. She eavesdropped. Hope doesn't have any conversations anywhere near the front door now."

"That woman is such a pill," Naomi fumed. "She needs to learn to mind her own business."

"And I saw her talking to Uncl—I mean, Matthew's door man or bodyguard or whatever Otis is. I think he slipped her some money."

Scowling, Charles stared off into the distance. "That explains a few things." He touched his throat, obviously still in pain, and came back to Dr. Pratt. "My niece vouches enthusiastically for Miss Clark. I would not disrespect her service here by hiring a doctor without requesting her input. Especially since, apparently, you know each other. I'd best have her opinion on you forthwith."

All the eyes in the room shifted again to Hope. Naomi didn't miss the quick, pained flinch and tensed jaw before the woman seemed to decide on her next words. "I thought you'd hired him without my consideration. I—" She bit that off, moistening her lips, then forced a small, brittle smile. "Dr. Pratt and I were engaged. I can state unequivocally that is no longer the case nor do I desire for it to be so again."

Naomi watched Dr. Pratt's face for his reaction to Hope's comment. If anything, he seemed amused by it.

"That said," Hope continued, "professionally, Dr. Pratt is a highly skilled internist."

"Are you able to work with him, Hope?" Naomi asked, eager to keep the nurse she preferred to the doctor she hadn't warmed up to yet. And wasn't sure she would.

"Yes. Yes, I can," she said firmly.

Naomi smiled, hoping the woman could read the unspoken message: *good for you.*

Charles crossed his arms and studied the two medical professionals for several awkward minutes. "Very well," he said finally. "Miss Clark, if you are so inclined, continue living in Doc Cook's house. Dr. Pratt, if you'll stay at the hotel, I'll get some men started on your cabin. Now…" He bounced his gaze back and forth between Hope and Dr. Pratt, apparently using the pause to get their attention. "Let me be very clear on one thing. Naomi is going to have a baby. My baby. I will expect the highest level of professionalism and skill from the both of you." He reached out and took Naomi's hand. "You will treat her as if she were your own sister."

"Of course," Dr. Pratt said.

"Absolutely," Hope added.

Charles raised his chin. "I only have one other concern. When can I leave?"

"Barring any complications, I would prefer you not leave until tomorrow at least," Dr. Pratt said.

"All right." Charles and Dr. Pratt nodded at one another, then the doctor, Hope, and Hannah filtered out.

When the door closed behind them, Naomi smiled weakly at her husband. "I'm sorry, Charles, I lied about Two Spears. He left yesterday with Emilio and Lane."

"You lied?" Charles sounded incredulous. "What aren't you telling me?"

*C*harles was taken aback that Naomi had lied but had faith she had a good reason. He suspected it revolved around Lane. A lynching wasn't going to sit well with the man from Texas. It didn't sit well with Charles.

To say the least.

"I thought Two Spears would be safer on the ranch, Charles. Lane gathered up some of the hands, even a few men from the lumber camp. They tore through Hell's Half-Acre this morning. Pretty much burned it all. Lane said he wanted Matthew and the miners to know all of our hands ride for you. Will take care of you."

Charles took a deep breath. "The damnable Texas Way." Turned out, applying legal, political, and financial pressure on Matthew had not been the wisest strategy. That and the humiliation in the saloon had simply provided the drive to plan and escalate.

While Charles had sat on his hands.

The images of what could have happened to Naomi and their baby at the lynching had tortured Charles' brain as he and the fat man with the rope had squared off. The only thing he could think of—the only thing that mattered—was somehow keeping her and the baby safe. Now, all three of them were alive solely because of divine intervention in the form of a Texas Cowboy with uncanny shooting skills.

The miracle seemed a stretch, the kind of thing Charles couldn't—or shouldn't—count on again.

Time to be done with Matthew, Lord. Allow me...

"Did anyone get hurt in the raid?"

"No. Lane promised no one would."

"Then all he did was poke the bear. Now it's my turn."

Her voice rose with urgency, color flooded her cheeks. "Charles, the men who tried to lynch you are the ones who need to be dealt with—by the law. This vigilante approach will just make more trouble. Or get you killed. I can't lose you."

He laid a hand on her forearm, silencing her. "Naomi." He paused to choose his words carefully. "I made a mistake with Matthew. I misread him, gave him the benefit of the doubt unreasonably because I am trying to balance faith—trust in God —with handling certain things that I have the ability to handle."

"You know what the scripture says. Vengeance isn't yours to mete out."

His temper flared because he didn't want to hear those words. "Hanging me is one thing, but you were in harm's way." He tightened his grip on her arm. "Next time it could be Two Spears, or Hannah, or anyone he knows we care about. I have to stop him."

"No, Charles. This isn't the way."

"Unless God strikes him down with a lightning bolt, I am the avenging angel in this town." He tossed off the blanket and swung his feet to the floor, ignoring the cold air on his bare chest. His head thundered like a herd of buffalo pounding across the prairie and his throat ached. He reached up and touched the tender rope burn at his neck. A fine reminder why he was getting out of this bed.

"Charles," Naomi said, clutching his arm. "Matthew wasn't even there. You can't—"

"Oh, he was there. Make no mistake."

"You can't be judge and jury. It's not your place."

He endured the pounding in his skull for a breath, then pushed past it and stood. "I let Delilah get by with too much, Naomi, and a dozen men died. If you think Matthew won't do worse, you're wrong."

CHAPTER 51

illy pulled the supply wagon to a halt and nodded at the sawmill's yard boss, a Danish man named Bjorn Olsen. "Olsen, how's it going?"

A large-boned, towheaded fella sporting a bushy, white-blond mustache, he seemed always to be cheerful. "Fine, fine," he said enthusiastically. "I hope you are well, too."

Billy enjoyed coming up here. The sawmill was alive with the construction on the second flume. Hammers whacked away on lumber, wood thumped against more wood, and men laughed with the light hearts that come from working with folks you like. The saw in the mill shrieked like a banshee as it ripped through the lumber, and the gurgling of Little Deer Creek ran serenely beneath all this noise.

Olsen strode up to the wagon, eying the canvas-draped freight behind Billy. "Miss Naomi promised us some furniture for the Long House. The boys are tired of eating on the floor."

Billy chuckled and set the brake. "Yeah, there's some furniture back there. Along with more blankets, pillows..." He climbed down to join the man on the ground. "Even curtains.

She said she wants you to make your accommodations warm and homey."

Bjorn's pale blue eyes warmed. "She is a good woman, Miss Naomi. I would have been very upset if anything had happened to her."

"You heard already?"

"Yah. One of the boys from the King M came through late yesterday. Said we were invited to ride along and..." Bjorn trailed off, a guilty expression clouding his pale face. "I think I should not say more."

Billy narrowed his eyes. "The boys at the King M went looking for a little trouble over at Hell's Half-Acre, I heard."

"No," Bjorn said firmly, wagging his head back and forth. "I don't know nothing about no trouble."

Billy was inclined to push the conversation for details, but an explosion rocked the air somewhere over the next ridge, rumbling and vibrating in the ground like a dinosaur's footfalls. "Holy—" Billy stopped, he and Bjorn both hunkered down instinctively, and gazed off in the direction of the roar. A blue-brown plume of smoke and dirt was rising into the blue sky.

The men in the sawmill hollered, pointed at the smoke, searched their surroundings with confusion in their eyes.

"The creek," someone yelled. "The creek!"

The whole camp like one body raced to the foot of the flume. Billy pushed his way to the front of the crowd, to the edge of the water—which was receding. He couldn't make sense of this. "What's happening to the water?"

Right before his eyes the water level faded from a good three or four feet deep running in a creek thirty feet wide to mere inches in depth and width. As he watched, Little Deer Creek became a trickle.

Beside him, Olsen shook his head. "Dirty, rotten trick. This is a dirty, rotten trick."

"I don't understand." Billy looked at the grim faces milling around him. "What's happened?"

"Someone dammed the creek. No water. No flume."

"Hey, Tyree and Fitz were up there digging out the shore," one of the men said, stepping forward and scanning the crew. "And I don't see 'em now."

---

*C*harles had Lane and Emilio brought to his newly added library at the ranch. The pair sat in leather chairs on the other side of his grand and ornate walnut desk. He'd been proud of the way McIntyre cabin had transformed into a spacious, comfortable log home and the library was, for him, the highlight. His personal space of gleaming logs, shelves lined with books, and Civil War and Indian mementos decorating the walls and stone hearth.

Now it struck him as a trivial waste of time.

Lane and Emilio looked nervous, like boys brought before the principal. Their hats twirled and shook in their fidgety hands. Charles opened his mouth to speak, but Lane jumped in first.

"We didn't hurt anybody, Johnny Reb. At least a dozen miners have left town. They didn't want any trouble and let it be known they didn't hold with harming women."

"But they didn't leave," Emilio cut in, "until we delivered a message."

Charles picked up a small gold nugget from his desk. A paperweight now, once it had belonged to a man who'd thought to take the Iron Horse Saloon by force. Rolling it around in his fingers, he remembered the shoot-out. They'd faced each other over a table full of cards and beer mugs. When the smoke cleared, the interloper was dead, and Charles had calmly sat down to finish the game. He hated the man he used to be, but that man had accomplished things.

He'd kept Defiance under control.

That Charles McIntyre would keep Naomi and his family safe.

"I'll take care of Matthew. Stand down. No more trouble."

Lane and Emilio exchanged confused glances. "You think we put the nail in his coffin?" Lane asked.

"Not Matthew's, no. He won't scare. Even if all his men do."

Lane laced his fingers over his stomach and looked down. "So that's how it is?"

Charles plunked the nugget down on his desk. "I'm going to end this. No one else is going to die because of him, and he will never, ever put my family in danger again."

An urgent knock on the door interrupted them and Billy burst into the office. "You've got trouble at the sawmill, Charles. Somebody blew the creek. Dammed it up good." He lowered his voice. "There were casualties."

*C*harles, Emilio, and Lane were at the corral slipping into dusters and grabbing their mounts. The weather had turned, a gray sky threatening rain, when Naomi rushed up, jade eyes wide with fear, cheeks flushed. She grabbed Charles' shoulder and spun him around. "I can't find Two Spears."

Emilio looked up from checking the cinch on his saddle. "I saw him around noon. He was going to play over at his tipi."

"He's not there." She swung her panicked gaze back to Charles. "I've looked everywhere. He didn't come in for dinner. Something's wrong. I can feel it."

Her words hung in the air. Charles sucked on his teeth, debating. But Two Spears had a habit of disappearing. "Emilio, you go find him. I'll be at the sawmill." He felt Naomi's glare and shook his head at her. "There's been an incident there. I've no choice. But if Emilio can't find him, nothing else will be more important."

———

*T*he cougar was nothing if not patient. He had trailed the boy and the ugly wolf cub for a few hours, curious as to why they returned again and again to the ridge. Careful to stay downwind of the pup, the cat had moved silently, watching, looking forward to snapping his neck first.

Now, lounging on the ground in the low branches of a cedar, tail twitching with languid interest, he studied the boy doing the same thing: lying on the ground, peering over a rock, hiding, watching something in the hollow below.

The cat sniffed. No, the boy was watching someone. More men were in the forest. The cat did not want to lose the boy, but neither did he want to run into more humans. Some carried fire sticks and the cougar had seen the death they delivered from a great distance. Still, he could give things another moment. Perhaps the men would leave and the boy would be alone again.

Thunder, louder than the most powerful rumble the cat had ever heard, suddenly filled the world around him, rolling over him, rocking the ground, shaking pine needles loose from the tree, sending gravel cascading down the hill. The long, terrible roar hummed through his muscles into his very bones. Frightened, he surged to his paws and splayed them out, preparing to run—but the boy did not run. Though he had pulled back from the rock and was looking skyward at something, eyes round with fear. Behind the ridge, and high into the air over head, a great plume of dirt or smoke—perhaps a mix of both—rose upward like a giant, blooming tree.

The cat did not understand what had happened but was loath to leave his prey. Uncertain, he waited. The thunder fading, he calmed and remained still. The air smelled of fresh dirt, water, and something else. He sniffed deeper. A burnt smell and rotten eggs. The same scent that came from the fire sticks when they spoke.

Confused, but sensing the threat had passed, he settled once again onto the ground. He saw the boy reach out and snug the wolf up against him, while making a soft "Shhhh" sound. "We need to stay quiet and hidden, Cat Killer."

Curious, the cat thought.

A moment later, the cougar understood. He smelled the men again. Closer now. A twig snapped several yards away. He hunkered lower, flattening his ears as an extraordinarily large man with bright yellow hair slipped carefully toward the boy. Silent. Stalking.

The boy was totally unaware. The cat scoffed at the useless pup who was not even awake. He would definitely kill him first.

Or did his next meal depend on the approaching man? What was he going to do with the pair? The cougar gave thought to making a sound to wake the boy, give him a chance to get away, but decided he did not want to risk death. The fire stick on the man's hip was too dangerous.

Perplexed on the best course of action, the cat drew deeper into the shadows to wait.

The man stepped. Brittle leaves crackled and the boy looked up. The giant of a man swooped down and grabbed the child by his long, black hair. At the same moment, the man snatched his fire stick free, pointed it at the wolf; it roared, and the wolf dropped with a yelp.

The boy yowled with rage as the man hiked him up into the air. The cat held in a jealous growl. The big man raised the writhing child high with one hand. "Well, well, well. What have we here?" He shook the boy. "Looks like we got us a spy."

Another man emerged from the woods, slender, spindly like a bug, greasy hair hung over half his face, the other half etched with a long scar. "It's done and it was perfect—" He laughed at the sight. "Oh. He's too little. You gonna throw him back?" This man tossed a red stick in the air over and over.

The boy was grunting and twisting, kicking and reaching for his captor to claw him. The man laughed at the tiny efforts and spoke over his shoulder. "You'd best be careful with that. Dynamite sweats nitroglycerin."

The man with the red stick froze then examined what he held. Seemingly satisfied, he shoved it into his shirt. "What you gonna do with the minnow there?"

"You know who this is?"

"Yeah, I know. I see him at the ranch all the time. And now he's seen me."

The boy swung his fists and howled with rage. "I will cut out your heart," he yelled at the man holding him. And to the other man, "You, too, Buck. I will cut out your heart and scalp you."

Both men laughed, but then the man shook the boy hard. "You listen to me, you little runt." He set him on the ground and grabbed his shoulders. "McIntyre killed your father. I saw it."

The boy's flailing slowed.

"Yeah, I saw it. And now I'm gonna kill you. You know why? Because I think he has a soft spot for you. And so does she." He paused and squeezed the boy's shoulders. "And it would be so easy. I owe them. I owe them both."

The child winced, then set off kicking and writhing and screaming again. The man shook him, harder this time, and laughed louder—a booming, throaty sound that made the cat cower. This human was dangerous. Instinctively the cat knew he could die by this man's bare hands, torn in two.

"Settle down now, settle down," he commanded. The boy calmed once more. "Ain't you the little, bloodthirsty savage?"

"Let me go."

"So you can scalp us? Nah, I don't think so. I've got a better idea. A cat's been following us. Least ways, I thought it was after us. But now I think it might have been after you the whole time. So I'm gonna do him a favor."

The man reached out and struck the boy with the back of his hand. The child went limp without uttering a sound and the man dropped him like a dead bird. The cat's ears came up a hair.

"You just gonna leave him?" The second man asked.

The big man straightened and took a deep breath. "Oh, yeah."

The cat feared the big man and his booming laughter. He watched him and the other one mount their horses and ride off. Yet, even after the sound of the hooves had faded, he decided to wait just a little longer before dragging the boy back to his den.

CHAPTER 52

*H*annah readjusted little Billy on her hip as she strolled down the busy boardwalk. A hint of snow in the air made her wonder if she should have brought a heavier coat for him for the walk back to the mercantile.

Under normal circumstances, Hannah rarely brought Little Billy with her to Doc's office, but Billy had made a special run out to the sawmill today with supplies. Carrying the growing boy on her hip, her pace slowed considerably as she stared down at the top of her son's head, golden angel-hair bouncing in the breeze.

She shouldn't take him there at all. He was getting into everything now. Sighing, she cut down the street that crossed over to the doctor's office. "Maybe we'll just make our excuses today and go back to the mercantile or stop by and see Aunt Rebecca before dinner."

Viable ideas, but they made her a little sad. She always loved spending time with her son, but she loved being in the doctor's office. She was learning so much from Hope and, yes, even Dr. Pratt, though Hannah didn't care for the pompous man.

When the office came into view, she let little Billy down,

resigned to finish off the last hundred feet at a snail's pace. Holding his mother's hand with a death grip, the child swaggered and swayed drunkenly, his feet at times working against each other, but he persisted. And Hannah laughed. He wouldn't be this little forever. "Look at you go, my little man. You'll be running around town in no time."

The boy babbled something that sounded like happy agreement and persevered in his slow, teetering trek. Hannah shook her head and looked up, surprised to find Hope on the porch, hugging a post and watching them with a startling intensity. Hannah waved. Hope waved back, rather listlessly.

Eventually, the pair made it to the porch and Hannah released her son to toddle about the front yard of dry, golden buffalo grass. "Go on, honey. Momma will be right here watching." The child took a few steps and fell in front of a trio of hardy, late-blooming dandelions. Winking at Hope, Hannah stepped over and dropped to her knees beside little Billy. "Watch this." She plucked a dandelion and brought it close to his face. "Keep watching." Gently, Hannah blew on the weed and the downy-encased seeds broke free on the breeze. They swirled in front of them like fairies and the boy gasped, reaching pudgy fingers for them. "Everything's a miracle to them at this age," Hannah said to Hope. "It's so beautiful to watch. The awe, the wonder."

"Yes, it's...precious to watch."

Hannah didn't miss the distant tone in Hope's voice. Something had been bothering the good doctor for several days now. Hannah assumed it was putting up with Dr. Bossy Pants Pratt. She plucked another dandelion and gave it to her son. "You blow on this one. And do not eat it," she admonished firmly.

She stood back up and watched him attempt to blow a rather wet wind on the weed. Several times. Smiling, she stepped away from him, closer to Hope. "I didn't come to work, much as I would like to. Billy had to take a delivery out to the sawmill and had to leave Little Man there with me this afternoon. He's too active to have around the office now."

"Yes, a doctor's office is no place for a child."

More of the same cold, distant tone tweaked Hannah's heart. Her friend sounded as if she were trying to mask some pain. "Is working with him that hard on you?"

Hope blinked, pulled her gaze away from little Billy. "What? Oh, no, I can work with Edward. I think eventually he'll leave. Defiance is no place for a doctor who wants to make a name for himself."

Hannah turned to her. "Then what's wrong? If you want to tell me, I'll listen."

Hope sucked in a breath, then wandered down to the yard to play with Billy. Dropping to her knees, she plucked the last Dandelion and gave it to him. He took it but then clutched her hand and scrambled to his feet. Smiling, he touched her face with the dandelion, dragging it down her cheek, and giggled. Then a new thought seem to strike him. He dropped the dandelion and pressed his pudgy hand to her cheek. Voice full of cheer, he jabbered away about soft *fowers* and being *hung-wy*. Or at least this was Hannah's best interpretation and she started to laugh until she realized Hope's eyes had filled with tears.

Resolute now, she marched over, took Billy's free hand, and said, "Come on. You're both coming with me."

Hope stood up quickly, patting at her eyes. "I can't leave. Dr. Pratt will be alone."

"And Dr. Pratt will survive. We have an emergency."

*H*annah handed little Billy to Hope and unlocked the mercantile. Billy had the "Back Later" sign hanging in the door and she did not flip it to "Open." As the three of them entered the quiet store, she locked the door behind them.

"He has a crib in the backroom. Let me put him down for a nap and I'll be right back."

"Hannah, I really don't think I sh—"

Hannah squeezed her friend's hand. "You don't have to tell me anything you don't want to. But I thought the quiet might help you collect yourself. And if you need a good cry, Dr. Pratt will never know anything about it."

---

*H*ope drummed her fingers nervously on the counter and fought back the knot in her throat. For some reason, telling Hannah what she'd done was going to be harder than telling Lane.

Perhaps because of Little Billy. Precious, sweet, lively Little Billy.

Hannah's son.

She'd made her position on abortion clear. She was going to hate Hope if the truth came out.

And Hope truly did not want to lose Hannah as a friend. Though Hannah was quite a bit younger than she, the girl's wisdom seemed profound, beyond her years. Hope was drawn to her simple, dauntless determination to become a nurse, serve people, serve her God.

Be true to herself.

She would make a better nurse than Hope was proving to be as a doctor. Deeply ashamed, she dropped her head to the counter and hid it in her arms.

"It can't be that bad," Hannah said from the doorway.

Hope didn't move. She didn't trust herself, her voice, the waterworks in her eyes. The knot in her throat constricted a little more. She flinched and merely shook her head.

Hannah came alongside her and started rubbing her back. "I

grieve for you, Hope. Whatever has you so sad makes me sad, too. Please let me pray for you."

Hope shook her head. The tears gushed forth and she straightened up, embarrassed at her unstable emotional state. "If you knew what I've done, you wouldn't want to pray for me."

Hannah took Hope's hand and held it gently. "That's nonsense."

Hope shook her head. "Do you know what the Hippocratic oath is?"

"Yes. I mean, I've heard of it."

"Among other things, medical school graduates swear to put the health and well-being of the patient above their own goals. 'Whatever houses I may visit, I will come for the benefit of the sick, remaining free of all intentional injustice.'"

Hope pulled her hand free, wrapped herself in a tight hug, and turned away from Hannah. To her credit, the girl remained silent while Hope tethered her emotions. Finally, she could speak again. "I like you, Hannah. I respect your skills and your compassion. You'd never do what I did."

Still, Hannah kept her silence and Hope finally found the courage to face her. "I helped a woman from Tent Town terminate her pregnancy. And I hid it from you."

Hannah's eyes widened, her mouth moved and at first no sound came out. She laid a hand on the counter as if to steady herself. Her chin quivering, she asked softly, "Why are you so miserable?"

"Because everything about it was wrong." Hope's voice broke at the end, but she made a herculean effort to keep from sobbing. She could hardly speak past the inexplicable grip on her throat. "I did it because *I* was angry with Edward and Mr. McIntyre. *I* wanted to show them women have the right to make their own choices. I never considered *the patient*."

Hannah asked gently, "Did you consider the baby?"

"It wasn't real…until after. I tried to ignore the hands—" She whimpered and shook her head angrily, running from the images of dismembered hands, masticated legs, other parts swirled in a mix of blood. They couldn't become real. "The parts —" Parts weren't human — "the parts in the dish. But today when—when Little Billy touched my face…" No use. "Touched my face with his little, chubby fingers—" A wave of unstoppable grief crashed over Hope and she sank to her knees, sobbing. "Oh, please tell me, Hannah, what I did wasn't wrong."

Crying now, too, Hannah cradled Hope in a hug and rocked her like a baby. For several minutes she sobbed, and Hannah wept softly with her. Hope cried out all her fears, her uncertainties, her doubts, until only truth was left.

Eventually, Hannah sniffled and pulled away so she could look at Hope. "'Before I formed you in the womb, I knew you, before you were born I set you apart.' I can quote a dozen Scriptures like that, Hope. Life is God's to give. Unfortunately, He allows us the ability to take it away."

Hope shifted and leaned back on the bottom of the counter, wiping at the tears that simply would not stop. *Before I formed you in the womb I knew you.* The Scripture sliced at her heart. Seemed to be there specifically to cut her for what she'd done. She could still feel Little Billy's fingers on her face. Couldn't stop seeing the tiny, tiny remains diced and bloody in the kidney dish.

"Oh, Hannah," she wailed into her hands. "Forgive me. I'm so sorry. So sorry. I didn't know. I didn't know." Hope squeezed her eyes shut, wishing she could block it all out. Or be like Lane's mother and find peace. "Life is precious. It's—it's sacred." She didn't even know what she meant, but something had changed in her heart. She *knew* a truth that she didn't yet understand. "Oh, Jesus, I'm sorry," she whispered in a strangled sob.

A hand landed lightly on her shoulder. "Heavenly Father," Hannah began to pray, "they beat Your son, spit on Him, scourged Him, and then hung Him on a cross. Yet He asked You to forgive them because they *didn't know*. They didn't know what they were doing…until it was too late.

"Now Hope desperately needs You, Father. She needs Your forgiveness. Cleanse her of her sins. Bind up her broken heart. Lavish Your love and grace upon her." Hannah took Hope's hand and gazed on her with eyes full of mercy and compassion. "He loves you, Hope, more than I can express, and He wants to forgive you. Everything Jesus did, all that He went through, He suffered because He wanted to make a way for us to have peace with our Father." Hannah wrapped both her hands around Hope's. "You know, Hope. You know what you did was wrong because you sense Him. Only the fool says in his heart there is no God. You're not a fool, but you are in pain and He can take it all away. Will you let Him? Will you let Jesus heal your heart?"

Lane's mother surfaced in Hope's mind, the peace he said she had exuded, and Hope wanted to cry again, but now for a different reason. She had real hope. "Can He forgive even me?"

Hannah smiled. "He already has."

Hope burst into tears; this time born of joy. Love, pure and complete, invaded her soul. And she knew she was forgiven.

CHAPTER 53

*G*uilt weighed heavily on Emilio. He had not wanted Two Spears to hear the conversations about the raid against the miners and Matthew. Consequently, he had encouraged the boy to take his dog and go play in the woods in his makeshift tipi.

Now, staring into the shadowy forest of tall lodgepole pines, he knew he was alone; the little tipi of ragged blankets was empty. Emilio sighed in frustration and rubbed his jaw. "Niñito," he whispered, "where have you gone now?"

Leading his horse, he carefully surveyed the ground and found the tracks of a boy and his dog leading away...and up toward the ridge. He turned to his horse and mounted, urging the sorrel forward at an easy pace until Emilio was sure they were on the right trail.

Sometime later, coming to the bottom of the ridge, Emilio was surprised to see a set of hoof prints, right behind Two Spears and Cat Killer—no.

He got down for a closer look, surveying the ground carefully. *Two* riders had gone up the ridge before Two Spears, and apparently come back the same way, but *after* the boy had gone up. This wasn't a commonly used trail. And only a few people knew about it. The riders could have easily run into Two Spears. But who were they? Squatting and touching the cool earth, he was studying the tracks when something else caught his attention.

The silence.

He narrowed his eyes and slid his gaze around the woods.

Only two things would keep the animals silent: men or a predator.

Quietly, he stepped back up into the saddle and drew his rifle from the scabbard. He urged Bones forward but kept him at a walk. On the edge of the rocky ridge, where the forest gave way to slabs of granite, boulders, and scattered cedars, he dismounted once again and continued alone.

To his right, the rocky side of a mountain loomed over him. His nerves sang. His ears strained to pick up every sound. But all the birds were quiet. A cold, gentle breeze whispered a lonely song in the trees. His footfalls were too loud and he slowed his pace even more.

Was he looking for men or was the forest warning him of a bear…?

Or a cat?

The moment the thought entered his mind, he *knew* the cougar was here somewhere. Watching. The hair stood up on the back of his neck. The rocky crevices above him offered so many places to hide and ambush unwary prey.

He cocked the rifle slow and easy, softening the click of metal on metal best he could. He almost called out for Two Spears but inexplicably bit it back at the last moment. *Father, I pray that boy is safe. Please keep him safe.*

The last thing in the world Emilio wanted was to find Two Spears bloody and torn to pieces.

The trail passed between two mammoth boulders. His senses crackling with fear, but bolstered by determination,

Emilio raised the rifle to his shoulder and moved like a ghost soldier toward the opening. Scanning in every direction as he went, he kept the barrel tracking with his gaze.

Wary, listening intently, his eyes darting, he stepped out from between the rocks.

A great slab of granite, the size of the corral, rolled away from him. Two boulders bigger than Conestogas squatted side by side off to his right.

For an instant, it didn't register what he was seeing then his heart exploded in his chest.

Two Spears was backed up against the biggest rock, facing the cat who was poised, twitching, rippling, ready to leap. The boy held his knife in his hand, taking wild swings at him. Suddenly the cat screamed and lunged, landing on Two Spears in a blur of fur. Emilio squeezed the trigger but jerked the barrel at the last second. Two Spears and the cat were so entangled he had no shot.

Heart in his throat, he raced toward the pair, bellowing at the top of his lungs and fired the rifle in the air. The shrieking, yowling animal nearly drowned out the gunfire and his and Two Spears' cries.

The cat was on top of the boy, clutching him with razor-sharp claws. The child raged, writhed, and stabbed with his knife again and again. Emilio fired once more into the air. The second shot brought the cat's head up for an instant.

Long enough. In one fluid, perfect movement, faster than a blink, Emilio aimed and fired.

The thunder of the shot echoed over the granite floor, nearly drowning out the cougar's unearthly wail. The animal twisted and jerked then collapsed on Two Spears.

Emilio cocked the Winchester and aimed again, but the animal was dead. He bounded the last twenty feet and kicked the cat off Two Spears like it was a foul, disgusting thing. His breath hitched at what lay beneath. The boy looked as if he'd rolled in a bed of knives.

Blood glistened in his shredded clothes. His face was a mask of deep, razor-like cuts streaming blood. He stared up at Emilio through a torn eye lid, the other eye awash in crimson, his neck a rivulet of red. There was no fear in his expression, only anger and pride as evidenced in his clenched jaw. "I killed the cat," he whispered, his voice gurgling.

Emilio swept up the mangled child, desperate to outrun the panic growing in his heart. "Yes, Two Spears." He raced back across the rock, his boots making a hollow, futile sound on the rock as he flew. So much blood, how would he stop it all? "Now we must get you to the doctor."

If only he'd brought Bones closer.

Two Spears swallowed and tried, feebly, to squirm free, pressing a red-slicked hand against Emilio's chest. "No, now I have a white man to kill."

Emilio held him tighter, a knot of fear and grief forming in his throat. "No. You don't worry about that now, my friend." He had a cloth in his saddle bag. He would hold it to the boy's flayed face— or was the blood from his neck?—and he would get him to town in time. He *would* get him there in time. "You will be all right, Two Spears." He jogged through the boulders and down the trail.

God, please don't let him die...

---

aomi did not cook supper. Charles was gone. Two Spears was gone. A nagging worry sent her drifting around the cabin, clutching her Bible, praying and quoting Scriptures of protection. She was claiming a hedge of protection around her boys, but especially Two Spears.

Annoyed with herself for allowing fear any ground, she

slipped out to the back porch to watch the sunset over the valley. The sky was on fire with brilliant hues of red, oranges, and purples as the surrounding mountains cast their long, somber shadows on the land.

Flashes of the lynching cascaded through her mind. Reflexively, she cupped her burgeoning belly and tried to swallow the terror. She hadn't been herself since the incident. She felt jittery, fearful, and a sense of foreboding haunted her.

Yea, though I walk through the valley of the shadow—

Naomi shook her head, trying to turn away from thoughts of death, and clutched her Bible tighter. *I will fear no evil.* "I know I'm not supposed to worry, Father, but I can't shake this concern for Two Spears. Keep watch over him. Send Your mightiest angels to protect him, please. Wherever he is." Her concern shifted temporarily to anger. *Satan goes about like a roaring lion, seeking whom he may devour. I know the cougar isn't evil, Father, but I want that animal out of our lives—*

Fast moving hoof beats drew her attention in the direction of the corral and barn. An instant later, Luke Bodrey, a new hand, pounded around the corner, spotted Naomi, and spurred his horse toward her.

"Mrs. McIntyre," he hailed, reining in the sorrel hard, "I met Emilio coming down off the ridge trail. He couldn't stop. He said you need to get to Doc's office quick as you can."

Her grip on the Bible tightened reflexively. "Two Spears. Did he have Two Spears with him?"

Luke's face tensed. "Yes, ma'am. He looked cut up. How 'bout I saddle Buttercup for ya, quick-like?"

"Faster. And send a rider after Charles."

*D*arkness fell as Naomi was riding hard to Defiance, Luke alongside, her stubborn escort. He need not have feared for her. The night could have been black as pitch and filled with Indians or bandits, instead of lit by a frail finger-nail moon, and it wouldn't have mattered. She and Buttercup were unstoppable. Nothing short of heaven was going to keep Naomi from getting to Two Spears.

Her heart was in her throat the whole way, though, and her prayers never ceased. These were not prayers of begging, however. Something in her would not accept anything less than Two Spears living a long, blessed life. And she thanked God for the hope and the vision.

As they pounded into the doctor's yard, she swung from the saddle and hit the ground running, her shawl flailing off one shoulder. Hannah grabbed her before she could get past the waiting area. "Hold on, Naomi. Hold on."

At first Naomi wrestled with her little sister, until reason settled in. Hannah's blue eyes shined with intensity and Naomi stopped. Where she'd been trying to push past her little sister, now she backed up a step. "He's going to be all right, no matter what you're about to tell me."

Hannah took a deep breath and raised her chin. "And I've been praying. I know you have, too, probably all the way here, but he is gravely injured, Naomi. We're prepping for surgery."

"Surgery?"

The door opened and Doctor Pratt stepped out, drying his hands on a cloth. "Mrs. McInytre, I need to speak with you quickly."

"What's happening?"

"Two Spears has, among several serious lacerations, a verte-bral artery injury—"

"English," she demanded.

"The artery in his neck as has been nicked. It's delicate surgery because of the proximity to the spine. I want your permission to let Doctor Clark perform it."

"I don't understand, why are—?"

"All pride aside, Mrs. McIntyre, I must admit Doctor Clark is a better surgeon than I. However, I know the fact that she's a woman may—"

"I don't care if she's a moose." Fury erupted in Naomi at the idiocy of the delay. She shoved the doctor back toward the examination room. "If she's the better surgeon, quit wasting time."

Dr. Pratt's eyes widened but he nodded perfunctorily and slipped back in the room with Two Spears. Hannah squeezed Naomi's hand quickly and followed him.

When the door closed, Naomi let her fear and fury turn to praise, forced though it was. Yet she knew what she'd heard. *Doctor* Clark. "Thank you, Father, for knowing what we need. Thank you for sending us Hope." Two Spears was going to be all right. She couldn't entertain any other outcome. "This is why she's here. I just know it. Bless her hands, Lord."

Pulling her shawl tighter, Naomi wandered over to the window to stare up at the thin, silvery moon. *Oh, Lord, I wish Charles was here.*

CHAPTER 54

*T*wo minutes to midnight.

Matthew dropped the pocket watch back in his shirt and looked across the table littered with cards, coins, and bills to Tennessee Bob. "I need to wrap this up. Your call."

Buck usually rambled in about now and Matthew was looking forward to reports from the King M. He almost grinned at the chaos damming the creek had surely caused at the lumber camp. But leaving the kid for the cougar? That had been especially satisfying. He could just imagine poor little Naomi, wailing and sobbing with grief.

Tennessee, moderately drunk, folded and slapped his cards down. "Eh, too rich for mah blood." Alcohol thickened his already syrupy, hill billy accent. With a definite sway, he rose to his feet. "Ah need a drank."

Another miner walked up as Matthew was gathering in the money and cards. "Start a new game?"

"This table's closed," he grumbled absently. Where was Buck? The miner passed on by with an indignant scowl. Matthew commenced tapping the deck of cards into a neat stack when Buck finally dropped down beside him. He was haggard looking, a touch winded. A rosy blush colored his cheeks, highlighting the impressive scar. He pulled his black hat off his head and dropped it on the table. The man did not ask for a drink right off and Matthew stilled his hands. When Buck licked his lips nervously, Matthew knew something was wrong.

He settled back in the chair, dragging his hand across the felt. "You don't look like you have good news for me."

"I'm not exactly sure what I've got."

Matthew sneered. He hated men who beat around the bush. "Well, why don't you try explaining things," he said, not bothering to hide his condescension. "Maybe I can figure this mystery out for ya."

The sarcasm worked an indignant glare from Buck. "Near as I could tell, the lumber camp's in a mess. Two men were killed. And it'll be maybe two weeks before they're using the sluice again. Maybe longer."

Matthew waved a hand. "'Bout what I expected. Telling me that was hard why?"

"It's the boy. I wasn't sure how you'd take what I heard about him."

Matthew sighed and laced his big hands over his gut. "You're starting to annoy me. Spill it."

"He ain't dead. Least not yet."

This was not what Matthew wanted to hear. He closed his eyes, ground his teeth, but cautioned himself to get all the information from this pea-brained fool before he stabbed him in the throat. "Am I supposed to guess what you're not telling me?"

"Nah, I..." Buck shifted, as if preparing to move quick. "I heard he's sliced up pretty good. Cat did a job on him. Emilio rode hell-bent for leather to get him to the doctor. One of the hands escorted Mrs. McIntyre into town and I'm supposed to go find McIntyre. I don't know anything else."

Like a grizzly exploding from the shadows, Matthew

surged to his feet and flipped the table out of his way in a crash of mugs, coins, and cards. He slammed his big, meaty fist into Buck's chest so hard, the cowboy flipped over in his chair, boots and head swapping places, rolling end over end, till Buck stopped, lodged upright against one of the tent's support posts.

The saloon fell silent as a graveyard as the crowd, owl-eyed and swaying, watched the show. Matthew was on Buck in an instant, snatching the man to his feet as if he weighed no more than a rag doll. "You didn't warn me about that Texan's raid on my place—"

"I told you I didn't have time to, but I rode along to look loyal to McIntyre."

Matthew drew nose-to-nose with Buck. "Trust me, it's real important that you look loyal to me now. You understand?"

"Yes, sir. Whatever you need. That was our bargain."

"I need—" he softened his voice to a low, icy tone, so as not to broadcast his desire to the entire room, "I need that boy dead. Understand?"

Buck regained some of his confidence and shrugged out of Matthew's hand. "Killin' injuns and Mexicans is my pastime."

"Fine. Kill the Mexican kid, too." Matthew tossed up a hand, suddenly disgusted his plan wasn't producing the results he wanted. "Why stop there?" He'd let the words tumble out without thought but they brought him up short. "Why stop there?" he repeated slowly, the idea more appealing than ever.

Maybe it was time to end all this and get on with taking over Defiance. The lynch mob and the injured boy had inflicted enough fear on Naomi, surely. Besides, he was growing bored. McIntyre hadn't risen to the challenge. Maybe the man had gone so soft and religious there was no coming back.

Pity.

Buck drummed his fingers on the butt of the Colt on his hip. "I'll see what I can do. Mind you, no promises. I ain't hanging for nobody. But if I can make it happen…" He lowered his voice. "You care who's in the way?"

"Get McIntyre. He's the only one I really do want dead."

Buck's throat bobbed up and down. "McIntyre?"

The fear Matthew saw in Buck's eyes made him want to gouge them out of the Texan's skull. "He ain't God," he hissed. "Shoot him in the back. I don't care how you do it." He spoke slowly, as if to a daft child. "Just do it."

---

*F*lat-out, undisguised, bold *murder.*

Again.

Charles rested his hands on his hips and shook his head at the devastation here beside the creek. Pale moonlight painted an eerie scene. The splintered bones of the flume poked angrily at the star-studded sky. Shattered timbers, smaller splinters, chaotic mounds of dirt and rock littered the ground. Behind a berm of earth the size of a small building, Red Deer Creek had backed up and was meandering wildly in a dark, swampy flow turning the lower half of the valley into a quagmire.

No, maybe the two men at the lumber camp had not been shot or lynched, but someone had blown the dam sky-high. With an impressive amount of dynamite. Anyone within a hundred yards would have been killed by the shrapnel. The men in the camp were fortunate only Tyree and Fitz had been down here. Not so fortunate for the victims, of course.

"Dead man walking?" Lane whispered.

Charles nodded slowly and rested his hand on his gun. "This ends tonight."

. . .

*T*he only way to carry through with this was to close out the voice of God. On the way to town, rather than pray, Charles recalled each and every name of the men who had died in Defiance since the mine explosion. With each one, the darkness in his heart grew. He felt it, didn't like it, supposed he should pray. Then another name, maybe with a face, would come to mind and break the thought.

And if reason, love, peace tried to tug him back, he would see again the white-hot fear in Naomi's eyes as she'd watched the mob drop a rope around his neck. Would recall the fear in his own gut as he'd prayed she and his baby would get away safely.

Amazingly, he did not hate Matthew. For the same reason one did not hate a rabid coyote or a wounded bear. You just shot it.

Beside him, Lane did not speak. The two men rode in silence. They understood how things sat and what needed to happen.

I'll handle this one last situation, Lord. It's what You've equipped me for. The choice will save lives...

They rode into Defiance, not surprised by the quiet streets at this hour. The closer they drew to Water Street, the main track into Tent Town, the louder the sounds of sin and vice grew. Laughter, cursing, pianos, drunken voices, sirens singing their invitations.

When they made the turn on to the street, the muffled thud of approaching hoof beats cut through the night. Alert, Charles and Lane drew their guns and waited. Shortly, though, they recognized the shadowy figure riding toward them and slipped their Colts back.

"Boss!" Buck, the newer hand from Texas, called out. He slowed his pace, Charles assumed to make sure he wasn't about to get shot, then hurried up to them. "Luke sent me to find you. You're wanted at the doctor's office."

"Two Spears?"

"Yes, sir. My understanding is Emilio found him and he's pretty clawed up. I don't know any more than that."

The cougar. Charles didn't bother with pleasantries. "Yah," he yelled as he launched Traveller up into a gallop. Matthew would have to wait. All he could think of now was Naomi's last words to him:

Something's wrong, I can feel it.

———

CHAPTER 55

*H*ope stepped out of the examination room and smiled at Naomi, who immediately launched to her feet, hopeful expectation radiating from her.

"All right, you can come sit with him now, if you'd like." Hope held the door open.

Naomi hurried past her and Edward, tears sliding down her cheeks. She settled beside her son and clutched his hand. She flinched as she surveyed the bandages on his face, his neck, and his arms. Hannah was standing on the other side of the bed, wiping at her own eyes.

"Is he going to be all right?" Naomi asked hoarsely.

"I think he'll live," Hope said. "But we must be very careful with him. I'll let Hannah explain."

Hope slowly closed the door on them as Hannah took the boy's other hand and bowed her head to pray. The image stopped Hope for an instant, tugging at her heart. She almost went back in. This peace that she felt in her heart now, her surrender to Jesus Christ, had left her with a desire to be with people like Hannah and Naomi. She was hungry to know more. To be in the company of Believers.

The sisters, however, needed time alone with the boy and she pulled the door shut. She would never tell them how close the cat had come to snapping the boy's neck. Surely Someone had been watching over him. And she had been here to do the surgery. Her specialty.

No, that couldn't have been an accident. A Divine force had drawn her to Defiance. She was so grateful she wanted to weep, too, but was simply too exhausted.

Sighing, she trudged over to the dry sink and leaned on the counter, in need of the support. She sensed Edward behind her, staring, but she had no desire at all to speak. To him or anyone.

"Hope, I..." He faded off and she did nothing to encourage him to continue. In fact, she wished he'd go away. She was so tired...

She imagined laying her head on Lane's shoulder, his arms encircling her. The idea was so pleasant, she let it unfold in her mind. His strong, confident hand caressing her cheek, his gentle but firm kiss—

"Hope, are you listening to me?"

She frowned. Edward. "No, I'm sorry. I'm exhausted. What were you saying?"

He sighed but she did not turn around. "I was paying you a compliment. Your surgery. Masterful. Absolutely masterful. I dare say one slip of the scalpel and that boy could have been paralyzed, but your technique was flawless. For a woman, you are—"

She tensed at the ridiculous comment and he must have noticed.

"I should quit saying things like that. You are a gifted physician and surgeon. Philadelphia will welcome you with open arms."

She did turn then, rounding on him slowly. "As your nurse? As a doctor?"

"Now, now..." Edward stepped over to her and sandwiched

her hand in his. "Let's not go through that again. We'll start you off as a nurse. We'll need time to let patients build confi—"

The front door burst open and Mr. McIntyre and Lane spilled into the room, leather dusters swirling at their knees as they snatched off their hats. Both men immediately assessed the scene and Hope jerked her hand away from Edward. "Mr. McIntyre, Two Spears' surgery was successful. We have to watch him carefully for a few days, though."

"Surgery?" He was already crossing to the examination room.

"I have to admit, Dr. Clark did one of the most delicate procedures I've ever seen, and she did so with amazing skill."

Mr. McIntyre stopped with his hand on the doorknob and looked at Hope. "You performed the surgery?" She nodded and his gaze shot quickly to Edward, a troubled v forming in his brow. "Well, thank you." He stepped quickly into Two Spears' room and shut the door, muffled voices thick with joy greeting him.

Hope was quite pleased Mr. McIntyre had made it to his son's bedside, but she was more pleased Lane had come with him. However, he had seen Edward holding her hand, hadn't he? Hope took a deep breath and looked at him.

His jaw had a hard set to it, his gaze was cold, suspicious, and locked on Edward. Maybe that was good. Hope strode boldly over to him, forcing an energy into her step she did not feel. She laced her fingers at her waist and spoke softly. "I'm glad you're here."

Not the most eloquent, passionate thing she could say, but those few words held such import, at least to her. She prayed he wouldn't make her say more. Couldn't he understand what she meant?

He stubbornly pulled his attention from Edward to her, almost went back to him, but something arrested him. Hope saw understanding dawn in his warm, hazel eyes. "You're glad?"

"Very. And I'm very tired. Would you walk me over to my cabin? Edward and Hannah can handle things here. Isn't that right, Edward?" she said over her shoulder. She dared not look at him.

"Yeah, isn't that right, Edward?" Lane repeated, a wry smile on his lips.

His question was met with an icy silence, but it was short-lived. "I'll be happy to. You deserve some rest, Hope. Get some sleep."

"*W*ell, I reckon I could ask some questions about things," Lane said as he and Hope ambled down a dark, winding path over to the doctor's quarters, less than a hundred feet away. "I'll start with Two Spears. He's gonna be all right?"

"Yes. Barring infection, and we don't move him for a few days." The cool, mountain air sank through her shawl and she held on to Lane's arm a little tighter, drawing warmth from him. "And might I suppose you'd like to know why I was holding Edward's hand?"

"Uhmmm."

"*He* was holding *my* hand. Does that make it clear?"

"You're saying it wasn't your idea?"

"Not in the least. I wish he'd go back to Philadelphia and leave me alone. However, I'm afraid Mr. McIntyre looked rather put out that I did the surgery and not Edward."

They reached the porch of the little clapboard house and Hope took one step up before turning to Lane, eye level now with the lanky Texan. "I — I would like you to know that," she swallowed, nervous about what she wanted to say. "Well, when the surgery was done and I knew it had gone well, besides the McIntyres, you were the first person I wanted to tell."

Lane flashed a toothy grin, a bit cocky she thought, but

endearing in his Texas way. He leaned back on the handrail and chuckled. "Well, now, if I didn't know better, doctor, I'd say you're coming down with a case."

"A case of...?"

"And I'd say it might just be terminal."

Symptoms and diseases ran through Hope's mind—until she realized his joke. "A case, eh?"

"Yeah. Let's see if it's catching." He leaned in and pressed his warm, soft lips to hers. A thrill rushed through Hope, nearly took her breath away. He cupped her cheek in his hand and deepened the kiss. Heat and lightning arced through her and she kissed him back, amazed at the feelings, at what his touch could do to her.

Edward had never made her feel giddy or light-headed.

Lane pulled away and planted a gentle kiss on her forehead, still holding her cheek. "Yes, ma'am, I'd say I've definitely come down with it too."

But there was so much uncertainty stirring in Hope's life right now. She frowned and eased out of his hand. What was going to happen to her employment? What could she do to make Edward leave? What if he didn't want to? What if Mr. McIntyre wanted *her* to leave? Most importantly, what exactly was this case she had contracted?

"This ailment," she said drawing out the word, "I—I think we should give it some time to develop before we diagnose it. Put a name to it."

A sideways grin lifted a corner of his mouth. "That's all right with me. I've got plenty of time."

CHAPTER 56

*N*aomi did not care for Dr. Pratt personally, but he seemed efficient and knowledgeable. He touched Two Spears' forehead, looked in his eyes, measured the pulse at the boy's neck, careful not touch the bandage around the wound.

She once again marveled over the fact that God had sent such amazing medical personnel to Defiance. Just in time to save Two Spears.

She'd overheard Dr. Pratt tell Hannah the boy would have died if not for his and Hope's intervention. *Thank You, Jesus,* she prayed for the millionth time. *Thank You.*

"I expect he'll sleep for a while and that's good," Dr. Pratt said, stepping away from the bed to face Naomi and Charles, who were seated in two chairs beside the bed. "He needs to be kept as still as possible for a few days. If he wakes up excitable or antsy, calm him as quickly as possible."

"All right." Charles rose and extended his hand. "Thank you for all your help."

"Not at all."

When Dr. Pratt left, Charles sat back down, and Naomi took

his hand. "I can wait with him if you need to tend to things at the ranch or the lumber camp or…"

"Wherever the trouble is?" Charles shook his head. "I'm not leaving yet. What happened exactly, do you know?"

"Emilio found him up on the ridge, facing down that damnable cat—feet planted, a knife in his hand." Moved again by her boy's courage, Naomi laid a hand lightly on his bandaged forearm. "He killed the cat, not Emilio, or so Emilio believes."

Charles chuckled sadly. "He said he'd get him." He sighed heavily and raked a hand through his dark hair. "Seeing him here, like this, knowing what could have happened, I—" He swallowed and cleared his throat as Naomi squeezed his hand. "I feel like two men sometimes, Naomi. I want to stay in control of this town. We're safe that way. But the part of me—the part that can kill a man—is dangerous." He clenched his jaw, stared off into space. "I want to be a good husband. I want to be a good father to this boy. I didn't realize how much till this moment." He cut his eyes at her. "But he has to be protected. And so do you."

Naomi didn't like the tone she heard in his voice: cutting, flinty. She turned a little to face him better. "I've told you before you can't save Defiance alone. Quit taking the weight of the world on your shoulders." She didn't mean to scold him, but he couldn't keep stepping in for God, either, acting on his own.

"The moment you told me he was missing I should have gone—"

"Stop it. That does no good now. You said men had been killed. That was important too."

His countenance hardened and he regarded her with a disturbing iciness in his gaze. "He is more important. But, you see, that is my dilemma. If certain elements in Defiance still feared me, those men at the sawmill would not be dead. A mob would never have come after us. I would have been out looking for my son."

Dread squirmed in Naomi's heart. "You said thinking like that is dangerous."

He screwed his lips into a sideways grin and touched her cheek. "Don't you think it's possible God wants to use my skills? After all, what is Michael for?"

"An archangel carries out *God's* will. You're just a man, Charles. A man leaning on his own understanding. A man who is vulnerable to turning away from God because you're angry and you want revenge. *And* control of this town."

The smile slid from his face. "I have to stop Matthew."

"This is ridiculous, what you're saying. You're justifying taking control of Defiance again by whatever means necessary."

Charles surged to his feet and sliced the air as he spoke. "Matthew has to be stopped before anyone else dies. My God, Naomi, because of him I was nearly lynched and you were—you could have—" He tweaked his lips, as if biting off the thought. "That alone sealed his fate. Taking Defiance back is the least of it, but it is necessary."

"Lawfully." Naomi rose as well, feeling the anger heat her cheeks. "You've got to let the law deal with him." She clenched her teeth, furious at how he was twisting things to justify his desire for vengeance and control of Defiance again. "You can't lose your soul over Matthew."

"The big man with yellow hair."

Two Spears' breathy whisper stopped their argument and both Charles and Naomi leaned toward the boy. "Two Spears," Naomi said softly, trying to calm him and herself. "Two Spears, are you awake? Don't move. You've hurt your neck. Stay very still."

One fluttering eyelid, the other stitched and swollen shut, finally opened, revealing a deep brown eye, and a groggy gaze. "The big man. He killed Cat Killer. Left me for the cougar."

"What? Matthew?" Charles asked, sounding incredulous. He leaned in nearer to his son. "Matthew." The sound of death in his voice snatched Naomi's gaze to him. Her heart sank. She had seen that darkness burning in his eyes before.

"What do you mean he left you for the cat?" he asked.

"I think they blew up something. At the sawmill. The big one," the boy looked at Naomi, "Matthew. He shot Cat Killer. Said he wanted the cat to get me because you have a soft spot for me." His one eye went back to Charles. "Both of you."

Charles smiled at his son but the ice in it lowered the temperature in the room. "I do have a soft spot for you, Two Spears." For an instant the cold veneer thawed, and he touched his son's face. "I love you. I won't let anything else happen to you." The iron returned to his features; his gaze grew distant. "I will make this town safe for my family."

Naomi flinched at the prophecy. Trying to push her fear away and keep Two Spears relaxed, she reached out and tucked the blanket a little tighter around him. "We both love you and everything is going to be fine. The law is going to come in and round up all these hooli—" The slamming front door brought her upright.

Charles was gone.

CHAPTER 57

The sliver of a moon rose over the tops of the buildings on Main Street, giving off a laughable amount of light. Traveller seemed to know without being guided exactly where Charles needed to go.

Tent Town.

He and Lane rode in silence down the empty street, the ghostly hoot of an owl mixing somberly with the plodding hooves and squeaking leather.

"You hear that?" Lane asked.

Charles knew what he meant. "Tent Town. Hell's Half-Acre. They're both quiet."

That could mean only one thing.

"He knows you're coming."

"So it would seem."

"How?"

Charles scanned the darkness as they turned down the road toward Tent Town. "Buck." The name had come forth on its own, but he knew it was right. "I believe he was coming out of Tent Town tonight when we were on our way in."

"You think he warned—"

"You gentlemen should stop." A deep, velvety voice with a heavy Haitian accent spoke from the shadows.

Charles and Lane both drew their guns as they pulled their horses to a stop. But their target was invisible. "Otis," Charles whispered.

"He's planning an attack on the doctor's office," the man said flatly.

Charles peered into the shadows. He had a vague idea where Otis was standing. In the shadows of the Assayer's office. Squinting, he couldn't make him out. "Why are you telling us this? Why should we believe you?"

"I don't agree with killing women and children." He paused, then added, "I decided to move away from the lightning rod."

Charles and Lane exchanged tense glances. The doctor's office was a vulnerable target. Helpless patients. Women and a boy. For the first time, in a long time, actual hate did sprout in Charles' heart.

"You are supposed to be there, McIntyre. Buck, Tempe, a few others, they're going to use dynamite. Like at the sawmill. And the mine."

Good Lord, Matthew has truly lost his mind. "Where is Matthew now, Otis?"

"At the Number Two, waiting to hear the explosion. You have time to stop it, but you should hurry."

Charles heart hammered wildly in his chest. Everything was on the line. "I just don't know if we can believe him, but God help us if he's telling the truth."

Lane let out a long, heavy breath. "I think he is."

That was all Charles needed to hear. If Lane knew something, good enough. "Ride through, wake up the town, find Beckwith, Emilio, Ian, anyone who can set up a perimeter around the office. Two Spears shouldn't be moved but…"

Lane nodded. "And you?"

"I'm going to cut off the head of the snake."

. . .

*C*harles turned his horse and headed quietly toward Hell's Half-Acre. Behind him, Lane bolted back toward Main Street. He commenced to firing his gun and calling for men to turn out at the doctor's office. His ruckus lasted for several minutes.

Charles decided it was a fine distraction. He rode Traveller into the woods behind some tents, tied him up, then took a back way into Hell's Half-Acre, wading across the stream above the bridge at the shallowest crossing he could recall. Still, icy water nearly flooded his boots.

Gun drawn, he approached from the back. Some tents were dark, some lit with dim, amber lights, but all the lamps were turned suspiciously low. No one moved, no one made a sound. The Number Two, however, was lit boldly stem to stern. All the lanterns on the inside burned brightly; the tent glowed like a beacon, as if it was expecting a crowd of revelers at any moment. Only, it too, was silent as the grave. Charles found the cemetery-like silence unnerving. Were people asleep? Sitting in the dark until the word was given?

The *word* being an explosion from the other side of town that would kill Naomi, his unborn baby, Two Spears, Hannah? Charles grit his teeth. All doubts about what he had to do evaporated. Matthew was a cancer to be cut out of Defiance tonight, followed by all the little tumors he'd let in.

Slowly, quietly, he made his way to the backdoor of the Number Two and paused to listen. He heard the ever-so-soft thud of what sounded like someone setting down a glass. Was Matthew in there alone? Only one way to find out.

Moving at glacial speed, Charles opened the back door which led into the storage room. Nearly pitch black here, he let his eyes adjust but movement of a shadow in the saloon caught his eye. The bar's false wall blocked his view. He stepped in and shifted to the left, to peer around it.

A hand reached for and lifted a shot glass, then momentarily put it back down. Charles was sure the arm belonged to Matthew, who had to be sitting and looking at the front door. Carefully, Charles moved to the doorway for a full view of the saloon. The place was empty, save for Matthew nursing a bottle and staring at the entrance.

Feeling he did not have the right to pray and ask for help or protection, Charles resigned himself to the task before him. He stepped quickly out into the bar and pointed his Colt.

Matthew looked up but didn't turn. Charles heard him mutter a curse under his breath. "McIntyre."

"Raise your hands where I can see them."

"I'm not armed." Matthew shook his head. "And you aren't supposed to be here."

"Raise your hands," he repeated, and Matthew obliged. "Where am I supposed to be?" Charles asked, knowing the answer.

"Getting blown sky high with your wife and brats and whoever else was around."

Dear God, he is insane. To speak so coldly, so calculatingly about the deaths of innocent— "You've turned into a monster."

"Who's the monster here? You gonna shoot me in the back of the head?"

"What if I did? No loss to society. You kill a rattlesnake anyway you can."

Matthew chuckled, a dark, vile sound that bubbled up from the caldrons of hell. "I told you. I told you once: family men and preachers don't settle towns like this. Men like us do."

"Don't put me in the same—" Maybe he was right. *Trouble becomes us,* Matthew had said once. And he *had* come here to kill him. Even now? Knowing he was unarmed?

Charles shook his head, suddenly more troubled by this plan

than he had intended. He moved around to better see his nemesis but kept a dozen feet between them. "There is a difference between you and me. I would never—"

"Kill to get what you want? Step over bodies to climb to the top? Sure sounds like somebody we know."

"I changed." *Didn't I?* "Killing you is a matter of justice."

"Sure it is."

"The legal system is moving too slowly. I'm not going to let you kill anyone else." The truth bolstered his choice again. "Enough men have died because of you. I'm only sorry I waited this long."

CHAPTER 58

"We may have to move him, Naomi."

Hannah's rapid, breathy statement brought Naomi's head up from Two Spear' bed. She yawned, bewildered and groggy. "What?"

Hannah, her face flushed, stray blonde hairs fraying from her braid, grabbed the foot board, her knuckles turning white with her tense grip.

"What?" Naomi's brain woke and she stood up as Hope walked into the room. She addressed her concern to the good doctor. "You said we can't move him. You said it would be too dangerous."

"We may not have any choice." Hope went to Two Spears and laid a hand lightly on his forehead. "Lane said there might be some trouble. If it comes to it—"

Several pairs of boots tromping in the front room interrupted their conversation. Lane appeared in the doorway. "We've got the perimeter secured." His heated gaze scanned the room and then the women. "Put out the lights and just wait. Sit tight and don't make a sound."

"What's going on?" Naomi asked, her concern growing.

Lane looked over them at Two Spears. "I'd rather not move you, little pard, so we'll just make sure they don't get this far."

Anger sparked in Naomi over these vague comments. "Tell me what's going on right now."

"Matthew is sending some men to blow up the office, but we've beat them here. Now we'll be waiting for them."

Lane left and Hope doused the lights. Naomi heard her sigh, a breath filled with worry. *He was going to blow us up? Blow us up? And where is Charles? Oh, God, keep us safe. All of us.*

"*Y*ou boys need to wrap up this jawing."

Both Charles' and Matthew's eyebrows rose at the unexpected interruption.

Marshal Beckwith let himself in the front door and swaggered into the midst of their little party, his duster pulled back over his hip to reveal his revolver. His eyes riveted on Matthew, he spoke to Charles. "McIntyre, what are you doing here?"

"What am I doing here? Shouldn't you be at the doctor's office?" Surely he knew, surely Lane had asked him for help.

"Wade and half the town are there. It's all under control. You didn't answer my question."

He shrugged. "I came to have a talk with our illustrious mine-owner." Perhaps Beckwith was a U.S. Marshal now?

"Well, get in line. I've got business with him first. Miller," Beckwith tapped his chest, "here's a warrant for your arrest. You gonna come peaceable?"

For an instant, Charles saw the shock in Matthew's eyes, but he hid it almost as fast as it had appeared. "Warrant for what? Too many whores on the premises?"

"For the murder of Sam Bullock."

Matthew's face froze, but the reaction didn't hide the truth from Charles.

"I don't know anything about that," the man said blandly.

Beckwith shifted his lapel and revealed a new badge: U.S. Marshal. "I have jurisdiction now, Miller, and a witness who says you know a lot about Bullock's murder. He also implicates you in the murders of Barnes and Rubles, and the deaths of McIntyre's men at the sawmill and the lumberyard." Beckwith pulled the warrant from his breast pocket and tossed it to the floor. "The state's attorney general has offered the witness a deal for his testimony. I'd say you're in a heap of trouble."

Otis? McIntyre wondered. Had he turned?

"So, I'll ask again. Are you coming peaceably? I'd hate for McIntyre there to have to shoot you." Beckwith's statement sounded more like a lament than a warning for Matthew.

Charles' grip on his Colt tightened. With the weight of evidence against him, maybe Charles wouldn't get the chance to kill Matthew after all. He could surrender. Surely, he would—

The scene turned surreal. Matthew snatched up a sawed-off shotgun from beneath the table, rose and was bringing it to bear on either Beckwith or Charles—Charles would never know which for sure—when Beckwith's hand arced to his .44 faster than a lightning bolt. The gun belched fire and lead before Charles could even pull his trigger. The speed in the old man's hands was downright astonishing.

Matthew tumbled back, spilling over his chair and sprawling on the ground, spread eagle. Beckwith stood stock still in the swirling gunsmoke, crouched, his revolver hovering a hair's height from his holster. It had barely cleared the leather, but the shot looked to have been good enough.

After a moment of frigid silence, Charles holstered the Colt, his mind reeling. He'd come to kill Matthew. Yet, so had Beckwith, it seemed. "He's dead," Charles wondered aloud.

As if to argue, Matthew groaned weakly.

"Nah, he ain't, but he would be if you'd shot him." Beckwith slipped his revolver back in the leather. "That is, he ain't dead if we don't lollygag too long." He waved Charles away as he stepped over to the man and tugged his bandana from his pocket. "Go round up a wagon." Beckwith dropped to his knees and pressed the cloth to Matthew's chest.

Still shocked by the lethal speed in the marshal's hand, Charles backed away toward the door. Something had transpired here he didn't understand and it vexed him. "You shot him to save his life?"

"Nope. Shot him to save yours. Now go get that wagon."

Charles moved, was at the door pushing it open when he had to stop. "But I would have taken him."

Beckwith made a grumbling noise. "The wagon. Now!" he barked.

CHAPTER 59

*I*n the dark examination room, Naomi tried to focus on the quiet breaths coming from Hope, Hannah, and Two Spears. She tried not to think about the explosion of the Sunnyside Mine only a few months earlier, and it's painful, vivid memories. The blood, the mangled bodies, the grief. She closed her eyes against the images and sat down beside Two Spears. It couldn't happen again. It couldn't.

"Hannah, let's pray," she whispered softly in the dark.

Her sister moved carefully around the bed, dropped to her knees beside Naomi and took her hand.

"May I join you?" Hope asked, hesitantly.

Stunned into silence, Naomi took a moment to work her way through the request. Hannah squeezed Naomi's fingers, jolting her brain back into motion. "Yes, of course," Naomi managed. "Of course."

Hope took hold of Naomi's other hand.

"Dear Heavenly Father," Hannah began, "we praise You for who You are. You are King of Kings and Lord of Lords. You are our shield and our refuge, Father. We thank You for watching over us. We thank You for the angels that are encamped around us and our loved ones tonight as something—as darkness— makes its assault on us. But we are victors in Christ, Lord. We are overcomers and we know no weapon formed against us will prosper. Thank You for victory tonight, Lord. In Jesus' mighty name we pray."

Naomi added her own short words, but her heart was heavy wondering where Charles was at the moment. The women fell silent, but Naomi continued praying in her heart. She knew Hannah was doing the same. Maybe even Hope was as well?

A few moments later they heard muffled voices over near the alley that crossed to Main Street. Several men were yelling, and the tone quickly escalated to anger. Guns erupted and the girls gasped, clenching hands and praying again. *Oh, God, Oh, God, Oh, God,* Naomi begged, *Please keep Charles safe...*

More yelling, but different now, calmer. Then only one voice, from the front room. "Naomi!"

Naomi could have fainted with relief. She leaped to her feet and ran into Charles' arms as he opened the door. He hugged her mightily, kissed her, whispered in her ear, "Two Spears?"

"He's all right, he's all right."

"Praise God." He raised his voice addressing Hannah and Hope. "We need you to get ready. An injured man coming in. Well, two if you count the scratch on Lane's arm."

"I heard that, Johnny Reb." Lane's voice from the waiting room.

Hope gasped and clawed her way past Charles and Naomi like a drowning woman scrambling for a life preserver. Hannah lit the lantern next to the bed and cleared her throat. "Charles, have you seen Billy?"

He pulled away from Naomi enough to face her. "He's on his way with Emilio to get Matthew and bring him here."

Naomi stiffened. Matthew was the injured man. What

happened? Had Charles given in to his thirst for vengeance? *God, don't let Matthew die. Don't let that be on Charles' heart...*

As if he'd heard her prayer, Charles looked at her and smiled. His dark eyes glimmered with peace. "Beckwith saved me the trouble of shooting him." His gaze softened. "Saved me in more ways than one, I think."

---

*H*ope saw the shadow of the tall Texan barely silhouetted in the front window and ran to him, all but leaping into his arms. He staggered on his feet and wrapped one arm around her.

"Whoa, there, missy," he said, laughter lacing his voice. "I'm an injured man."

She gasped, shocked at herself. But she was so relieved... "Sit down," she ordered, directing him into the chair. She grabbed the matches from the stove and, as she lit the lantern overhead, Hannah came out of Two Spears' room.

"I'll do that and get everything ready for Matthew." She stepped up and watched Hope untie the shirt tied around Lane's arm. "Tend to the cowboy and his life-threatening wound."

Hope pushed away all thoughts of Lane as a man and focused on him solely as a patient. She carefully peeled back the bloody shirt from his bicep and immediately a definite trickle of blood followed. Stanching it with the shirt, she called to Hannah, "Make up the sutures and surgery trays."

Moments later, Lane was sitting on the examination table, shirtless, while Hope cleaned the wound. He hadn't taken his eyes off her the whole time and it was beginning to unnerve her. "I wish you'd stop staring at me."

"Rather stare at you than that hole in my arm."

"It's not a hole." She spun to the instrument tray and picked up the suture. When she turned back to Lane, he was wearing a broad grin.

He glanced at the needle in her hand. "I'm mighty tired of getting sewed up."

"Yes, well, if this is the worst injury you get going forward, count yourself fortunate." She angled his arm out, revealing the underside of his bicep. "The bullet only grazed you." Considering the proximity to vital organs in the chest, it could have been much, much worse. Easily lethal. She whispered her own prayer of gratitude. "Tell me what happened," she said, beginning to suture the wound.

He shrugged. "Once we were sure they hadn't been here to plant any dynamite, we left Emilio, Ian, Corky and Billy to watch your office. Figuring they were on their way, the deputy and me went looking for 'em. Found 'em coming through a back trail, one running behind the Sunnyside Mine."

"How did you know where to look?" When he didn't answer right away, she glanced up.

He scratched his nose. "That big, strapping black fella that works for Matthew. He told us."

"Interesting," she commented as she finished the last stitch. Of five. Indeed, Lane was fortunate. "How did you get shot?"

This time the pause was longer, and she sensed she shouldn't push. Finally, he said, "Buck and Tempe. They started shooting. We shot back."

Hope heard it in his voice. The two men weren't here in the office being treated. And Lane, from what she'd heard, was quite the marksman. "I'm sorry. I'm sure that was difficult."

He sucked air through his teeth and nodded. "Better them than me, I guess."

She wrapped a bandage around his arm and smiled tenderly at him. "Yes." The jangle of a wagon cut into their moment and she straightened. "Hannah, is everything ready? I hear a wagon."

And it's coming in fast. She cut her eyes back to Lane. "I hate to ask. Would you mind getting Dr. Pratt? Hannah is skilled, but…"

Lane stood up with a sigh and touched the bandage. "I guess I'll find him at the hotel?"

CHAPTER 60

*B*illy yawned and stretched and exhaled long and deep, trying to exorcise the stiffness from his bones. Enjoying the warmth of the stove here in the doctor's office, he was ready for a nap. First, he had to shift Mollie from working at the hotel to watching the mercantile, get his son from Rebecca and then, hopefully, take him and his new bride home. Tired as he was, he wanted to spend some simple, quiet time with his family, maybe just sitting on the floor talking and playing with Little Billy.

He'd sat out in the cold last night for two hours until it was confirmed Buck and Tempe were dead; Matthew had been brought to Hope to remove the bullet; and the threats—for the time being—had passed.

For the time being.

He dragged a weary hand over his scruffy face as he watched Hannah finish off cleaning and tidying the office. Maybe Defiance was no place to raise a family. Billy himself had been shot once, fought in the street like common riffraff, Hannah had been kidnapped by marauding Indians, a saboteur had killed twelve men in an explosion, and Matthew had ordered the same tactic be used on Hope's office.

Sitting in the cold, Billy'd broken into a sweat thinking about what he would have done if the monstrous plan had succeeded. His wife and everyone he cared about blown to smithereens.

The possibility made his guts twist.

A nice, safe, civilized town in Pennsylvania with a medical college—the idea was growing on him. He swept his hat up off the floor and ambled over to her. She had her back to him, washing dishes. Trying not to startle her, but evoking a little gasp from her regardless, he slipped his arms around her and kissed her on the neck—well, on the braid more precisely. She paused in her chore and leaned back on him.

"Tired?" he asked.

"Exhausted."

"But you love it?"

He could sense her smile. "Yes, I do."

"Hannah, every place in the world has its dangers, but I'm thinking I could use a little break from the Wild West. Go back east for a spell. Maybe some place nice and tame like…Philadelphia."

She shook the dishwater off her hands and spun around in his arms. "I was thinking next fall. If you were agreeable."

"Well, Mrs. Page," he plopped a kiss on her lips. "I was thinking, with Dr. Pratt and Dr. Clark in town, why not the spring? It'll be a new adventure."

Hannah laid a hand on his heart. "An adventure for Pages. All of us together. Yes, the spring might be fine."

---

*E*milio cut and side-stepped his way through the busy dining room to the only open table—one near the fireplace. And he was pretty happy to take it. He'd dang near frozen to death last night making sure no one came to blow up the doctor's office. He'd had enough of explosions. Nearly lost his hearing in the one that took down the Sunnyside.

Peeling out of his coat, he shivered at the thought of what could have happened and thanked God the disaster had been stopped. Too bad for Buck and Tempe. They wouldn't exactly be missed, however.

Casting around the room looking for Mollie, he absently thought if Lane didn't miss a shot every now and then, he was going to get a dangerous reputation for gunslinging.

There she was. Pouring coffee for a customer, Mollie looked up and their eyes met. In that instant, an amazing fact dawned on Emilio—he couldn't imagine Defiance without her. He couldn't imagine her traveling to Kansas—or anywhere—without him either. She needed protection.

She finished off with the customers and hurried over. "I heard. I heard about Two Spears, the shooting last night." She shook her head and swallowed, the blue of her new dress reflecting magically in her eyes. "Billy was just here. Said everyone's all right."

"Sí, except for Buck and Tempe. Matthew, I don't know if he's going to make it, but Two Spears is going to be all right, I think." Emilio shook his head. "Going to be pretty scarred up though."

She sagged a little and sighed. "Never stops coming in this town, does it? Trouble, I mean."

"Sí, yeah, I know what you mean."

"Listen, Emilio," she glanced around quickly then sat down, "I just want you to know, I'm leaving next week for Kansas. I want to go before the snow starts. Spend Thanksgiving with my mother. I—I want to say, I'd love your company." The words started rushing past her pretty, pink lips. "You don't have to stay. Just maybe come see Kansas and meet her. Maybe I won't stay either. I don't know exactly what I want. Other than, I mean, I want to see my mother again before I decide what I'm doing with my future."

Emilio pursed his lips, thinking hard. Maybe a little too hard. Mollie's hopeful expression drooped and she rose to her feet. "Anyway, think about things. What can I get you for breakfast? I'll get your order in but then I have to go over to the mercantile."

This time he didn't take near as long to come up with an answer. He gave Mollie a huge, toothy grin, then leaned forward and curled his index finger, beckoning her to join him. Brow furrowed, she leaned down as well, whereupon Emilio clutched her chin gently and pressed a long, firm kiss to her lips. "I'll have a big, thick Kansas steak, por favor."

CHAPTER 61

*H*ope quietly closed the door behind her and leaned back on it. Matthew was going to make it, she was quite sure now. He'd passed the dangerous mark. Fourth day here and his vitals were getting stronger. He'd spent more time awake today, though in short, sulky bursts. Marshal Beckwith had shackled him to the bed. The action struck her at this point as overly cautious, but she understood the reasons for it, of course.

Now, her day was at an end—a little earlier than normal and she smiled. "Dr. Pratt," she called, practically gliding across the waiting room. "Dr. Pratt, I'm leaving, as we discussed earlier. Good day."

As she was reaching for the doorknob to let herself out, Edward surged from the patient's room. "I did not agree to this. You do not have my permission to leave. We still have—"

"Agreed?" She rounded on him. "I didn't ask you to agree to it. You. *You* still have three appointments today."

Hope had dinner plans.

. . .

*S*he cooked a pork tenderloin and filled in the side dishes with canned tomatoes and okra, and fresh-baked biscuits. She built a fire, set the table with nice china borrowed from the hotel, and looked around her simple, warm, inviting home with pride.

Home.

The word brought her to a standstill.

She liked the hard-scrabble, earthy life here in Defiance. She was needed here. She had purpose. But with all that had happened, it hadn't quite been *clarified* she was a doctor. And Edward was still trying to run over her. Make her miserable. Make her give up.

She smiled. She was quite sure she could outlast him here in town, if Mr. McIntyre let her stay. Would he let a woman doctor in Defiance?

A gentle rap on her door loosed butterflies in her stomach. When she opened the door, a few snowflakes unexpectedly followed him in. "Looks like we might get a little snow toni—"

He was peeling out of his coat but stopped when he saw the table set with the steaming food. "Your timing couldn't be more perfect, Mr. Chandler." She heard him swallow.

"Yes, ma'am. A doctor and a cook." He inhaled as he slid out of his coat and handed it to her. "Smells mighty good."

She hung his coat on a hook by the wall and motioned toward the table. "Join me?"

They settled in to dine and suddenly Hope stopped as she was about to take her first bite. Lane's eyes widened with concern. "What's the matter?"

Hope set her fork down. "We should say the blessing."

Lane set his fork down and laced his fingers together. "Yes, ma'am."

Hope shook her head. "I don't know what to say exactly. Lane, I wasn't raised in a Christian home but, you should know,

I—well, I wanted the peace you were telling me your mother found. I accepted Jesus as my savior. I—I don't want my mistakes to haunt me, define me." She cleared her throat, embarrassed. "I'm sorry, I didn't mean to get so serious."

But his brow dipped, and she wondered what concerned him. Did he not want to be around someone who was pursuing a relationship with Christ?

She was about to ask, when he said, "I ain't a Believer like my ma. You should know that." His gaze drifted. "If I was, I think I might feel differently about what I did, I mean, with Buck and Tempe. As it stands right now, it don't bother me too much." He came back to her, the candlelight at the table highlighting a stubborn set to his jaw. "I think justice is a simple thing sometimes. They deserved it for trying to kill three women and a kid. And they did shoot first."

Hope didn't know what to say. Jesus, moral decisions led by a Higher Power, not leaning on her own understanding...it was all so new to her. But Hannah had said God gave us grace instead of what we deserved. "I don't understand it all, yet, Lane. I can't judge you. There have been some terrible things done to people in this town. I was stabbed. The man who did it—all I know is if he's dead he'll never have a chance to meet the Savior."

That deep, troubled crease returned to Lane's forehead. "You think what I did was wrong?"

She reached across the table and touched his hand. "No. You didn't set out to kill Buck and Tempe. I think what makes me a little sad is you don't seem to regret their deaths. I believe, however, you did what you had to do."

A heaviness hung between them. It confused Hope and she didn't understand it. Eager to move past it, she pulled away. "The food is getting cold. Um...thank you, Jesus, for this meal."

A simpleminded prayer, perhaps, but neither of them

mentioned it. They ate in silence for a few minutes, the only sounds the clink of silverware and the popping of the fire.

"You are a fine cook," Lane finally said.

Hope appreciated the compliment. "Thank you. If Mr. McIntyre won't let me work as the town doctor, perhaps I can work in the kitchen at the inn."

He looked up. "You want to stay in Defiance that much?"

His eyes pierced into her soul. Part of her wanted to blurt out, *I'd go anywhere you are.* She managed to refrain and offer a more rational answer. "Practicing medicine is my life, Lane. I want to do that more than anything…"

"But," he goaded.

"But you certainly add quite a bit of charm to the town."

That maddening sideways grin pulled his mouth up. "You know, not every decision in Defiance rests with Charles McIntyre. You're a good doctor and you want to stay. So stay."

"Is it that simple? What about Edward? If he won't leave, I'd be competing against him for patients. And in Denver, people wouldn't come to see me, Lane, because I'm female." Her voice rose with her passion, "But I am a better doctor than Edward."

"And I can tell you every man at the King M is chompin' at the bit to get hurt. They don't want to see ol' Edward for their stitches, that's for sure." She shook her head, laughing softly at his facetious observation. Then he reached across the table and took her hand in his. "If it's worth anything, I sure would like you to stay. You see, I've got this terrible case of something right here," he tapped his heart, "and I think you're the only one who can get me through it."

She fell into those mesmerizing, mischief-filled eyes of his and nodded. "Yes, I think I may know just the right treatment."

Lane tossed his napkin onto the table, stood, and brought Hope with him. His gaze, boring into her like a ray of sun, stole her will, her thoughts, her breath as he pulled her into his arms. He sighed heavily and trailed his thumb down her jaw, over her lips. His touch left a trail of electricity over her skin. "You know, come to think of it, I'm not sure I want to be cured, Dr. Clark."

Hope's pulse raced to dizzying levels. He kissed her, kissed her again, and she felt faint, absolutely weak with desire and something better...

Peace, like coming home.

CHAPTER 62

*N*aomi found her beloved husband on the back porch, staring out at a gray wall of flurries, a steaming cup of coffee in his hands. She slipped up behind him and wrapped her arms around him. "Snow is starting early this year."

"This is just a taste. Won't be more than a few inches." He turned a little and gathered her up against him. "Though I won't be surprised if there is snow for Thanksgiving."

She snuggled, breathed in the scent of fresh laundry, coffee, and him. She hugged him tighter, delirious to have him back. She sensed he had returned from a dark place.

"I was thinking about Beckwith," he said, as if she'd asked, "and what he did. Why he did it."

She waited, assuming he would explain.

"A law man takes on certain responsibilities. Namely, killing, if necessary. The badge sanctions it, if it's done within the parameters of the law. I was following my own law, Naomi. If I had killed, Matthew, it wouldn't have been..."

"Legal?"

"Righteous, I think is a better word."

She thought she understood. The guilt would have either consumed him...or hardened his heart.

He took a sip, considering things, then said, "I tried to pretend it was justice. It wasn't. It was a thirst for vengeance and control. Maybe I am no better than Matthew."

"Who you are in Christ makes you very different from him. You said you had doubts before Beckwith intervened. Your struggle was a cry for help."

The idea seemed to surprise him. "You think so?"

"I do. First Corinthians ten thirteen, says, God *is* faithful, who will not suffer you to be tempted above that ye are able; but will with the temptation also make a way to escape, that ye may be able to bear *it.*"

He raised his head, as if taken with the idea. "Beckwith was my escape?"

"And I think he knew it."

Charles didn't respond and she let the thought rest with him. He was quiet a long while before he finally said, "He is the fastest gunhand I have ever seen, and he is uncannily accurate." He shook his head. "Uncannily."

"Will he be leaving us? Now that he's a U.S. Marshal."

"I understand the governor will station him in Denver, but not until January."

Naomi would miss Beckwith. He'd married Ian and Rebecca, then Billy and Hannah. He'd ridden with Charles to save Naomi from Indians intent on selling her and Hannah to slave traders. And he'd saved Charles from himself the other night. He was a good, decent, fearless lawman who added such stability to the town.

"He and Wade will be moving Matthew in a few weeks, to the territorial prison to await trial."

"Matthew," she whispered his name like a sad prayer but could find only an ember of compassion for the man. He'd made such awful choices and inflicted so much pain. "He asked to see me. I declined."

Charles nodded subtly. "He's going away to prison for a very long time, Naomi. Otis has made a deal. He knew everything the man did. I doubt we'll ever see Matthew again in Defiance or anywhere else."

Naomi shook her head. "Enough of the darkness." She wanted to speak of happier things. "I'm excited for Hannah and Billy."

"Won't you miss your sister?"

"Terribly, but my grief is overshadowed by her joy. She'll be the best nurse Defiance has ever seen."

"And what are we to do with two doctors?"

"You heard?"

"Lane told me. And I know that she performed the surgery on Two Spears."

"I suspect Dr. Pratt will leave of his own volition, once he realizes there's no competing with your swaggering, sharp-shooting ranch foreman."

Charles chuckled and lifted his coffee cup in a toast. "God bless Texas."

She pulled away and lifted her chin. "And God bless Defiance."

EPILOGUE

*B*illy wiped away one last smudge and then stepped back from the mercantile's new window. He smiled with satisfaction, pleased at the installation—so much better looking than the boards he'd used to cover the gaping hole. Yes indeed, tickled to have his storefront back, he couldn't resist wiping away one more, possibly imagined, smudge.

It had taken nearly a week to get the glass delivered and then another month to get the two carpenters to repair the frame and do the installation. The lengthy delay was courtesy of the MP&G. The conglomerate had not missed a beat on operating the mine. They'd had a new manager up here within a week of Matthew's arrest. Hence, the building boom continued without a hitch, and carpenters were as valuable in Defiance now as doctors. Nearly, anyway.

Billy shrugged off the wintery chill and turned to head back inside to open for the day. The sound of boots muffled by the early December snow pulled his gaze to the end of the porch and he stopped.

A stout fella in a sheepskin coat and a stained, white hat

jogged up the steps toward him. "You wouldn't be Billy Page, would ya?"

Billy nodded. "I am. What can I do for you?" He shrugged a hand toward the door. "I am about to open. Come on in."

The two stepped inside, the stranger heading over to the stove. "Chilly morning," he said, reaching for the warmth.

"Yeah, and just the start." Billy flipped the sign to open and raised the blind on the door. He took a moment to survey the street, filling quickly with early-morning traffic. "So…" he strode back to the counter and picked up his apron. "Need some supplies or…?"

The man removed his hat and shook out his wavy, blond hair. "Name's Toby Johnson. I'm a friend of Eleanor's. She said you could give us the lay of the land."

"Eleanor?"

The man approached the counter, sapphire eyes alight with a mysterious intensity. "She said you met in Dodge."

Eleanor! "She's here?"

Toby nodded.

Billy shook his head, grinning with the memory. "Boy, I owe her. A rough crew beat the hound out of me in Dodge. Eleanor gave me breakfast, a dollar so I could get my horse out of impound, and then she even squared things with Marshal Wyatt Earp so I could slip out of town."

Toby chuckled, but somberly, Billy thought.

"Yeah, that sounds like Eleanor," he said.

"I offered her a job a while back. To manage my hotel, but she didn't want to leave Dodge. She was waiting—"

Waiting on her wayward daughter, Victoria, to return home.

Victoria.

Alias Delilah.

Billy's heart sank into his stomach.

This was the last place Eleanor should be now. He let out a long whistle. "Listen, I would do anything for Eleanor. Only, I don't think it's safe for her in Defiance. If anyone found out she was Delilah's mother—" He patted the air. "These miners have already tried to lynch my brother-in-law Charles McIntyre. Eleanor should not be here."

The man swiped a hand over his face and sighed. "Yeah, I didn't think this was a good idea."

A more concerning thought occurred to Billy. He had told Delilah—Victoria—her mother was alive, back in Dodge, waiting on her to come home some day. If Eleanor was here—

Billy swallowed against a mouth going desperately dry. "Tell me Eleanor's alone."

Toby dropped his fist on the counter. "Victoria's here. She wants to turn herself in."

<<<<>>>>

*D*ear Reader, if you liked Book 4 in my *Romance in the Rockies* series, may I ask you to leave me a review? I would be sincerely grateful. Thank you, thank you, thank you for the sacrifice of your time. I know it is one of your most precious treasures!

AFTERWORD

Dear Reader,

Did you know the character of Dr. Hope Clark is based on a true, Colorado historical figure—Dr. Susie Anderson? Here's the the blog I wrote on her back in 2018, "The Doctor Who Treated You, Hell or High Water."

The women who built this country did amazing things to make America a better place and rarely complained while they were doing it. They just rolled up their sleeves and jumped in. They didn't whine or cry. They didn't call themselves victims when they weren't treated fairly. They just kept working at doing good for the country or their little corner of it. AOC and Omar could learn a thing or two from these gals. Case in point, meet Susie Anderson.

Born in Indiana in 1870, she moved with her family to Cripple Creek Colorado at the beginning of the town's gold rush. Deciding she needed more of a challenge than the rough and rowdy mining town could provide, her father encouraged her to attend medical school. In 1893, she entered the University of Michigan medical school. Little did she know how difficult the journey to put two letters behind her name would be.

She graduated in '97, but while in school, was diagnosed with tuberculosis. The illness would plague her for the rest of her life. She returned to Cripple Creek and tended to the miners there for three years, but the pretty, petite doctor was jilted by her fiancé in 1900. That same year she suffered the loss of her little brother.

In need of a change, she relocated her practice to Denver. Surely, the bustling, modern city would provide a steady flow of patients. Not. Anderson nearly starved to death. Patients were very leery of a female doctor, especially when there were already several male doctors in town. Frustrated, she moved again, this time to Greely, and took work as a nurse. How frustrating that must have been for this gutsy, stubborn gal. Probably the stress had something to do with her TB flaring up. Sick and weak, Anderson moved to Fraser, Colorado to recuperate or die. She breathed not a word of her vocation.

But word got out, as it always does, and her health improved. I wonder if the two events are related? At any rate, the citizens of remote Fraser were delighted to have a doctor. They didn't care if she was male, female, or a different species entirely. Everyone from lumberjacks to ranchers to pregnant wives came to see her. She occasionally even treated a sick horse.

In her career as a doctor, "Doc Susie" was paid with everything from firewood to food. Cash was an extreme rarity and her living conditions reflected that. Nearly destitute, sometime around 1915 or so she was appointed the Grand County Coroner and the regular paycheck helped ease some of her financial concerns.

She never owned a car but always found a way to visit her patients. Most often she walked, sometimes in hip-deep snow. Mostly, though, friends and family members of patients provided transportation. Anderson was not rich financially, but she earned an esteemed reputation as a fine rural doctor and diagnostician. Her life was not easy but I think that's how she would have wanted it. She liked fighting for her accomplishments.

She conquered a frontier, both real and emotional, leaving behind a path for other women who dared to dream big. Anderson practiced in Fraser until 1956 then retired to an old folks home in Denver. She died four years later and was buried with her family in Cripple Creek.

SNEAK PEEK - DAUGHTER OF DEFIANCE

This novella came ***between***
A Promise in Defiance and
A Destiny in Defiance

CHAPTER ONE

— the Box Set Victoria Patterson stared at the saloon's batwings and took a deep breath. It did nothing to still the butterflies in her stomach or restore the strength to her wobbly legs. A knot formed in her throat and she swallowed it down.

Victoria was terrified to see her mother again after all these years...and, yet, *desperate* to see her.

She pinched away sweat from her upper lip with a gloved hand and looked down at her simple, blue cotton dress. Brushing her fingers over the paisley patterns at her stomach, she smiled bitterly. She was no longer the satin-draped, diamond-encrusted, rouged-up Delilah Goodnight. The party was over.

Used up, empty, and broken, she had returned to Dodge

City. Would her mother care to see the prodigal return? Victoria squeezed her eyes shut and felt around in the mental darkness for a shred of courage.

I have to go in there.

But what if she knows about me? All that I've done? What happened in Defiance? She'll hate me.

And if she does, you can just keep right on moving east.

The same two warring voices in her head that had been arguing since leaving Colorado. But Victoria had to know. Had to see if there was any hope for love...for sanctuary...for peace.

She raised her hand to push the batwing out of the way but paused when she heard humming. Coming from the alley beside the saloon. Victoria knew her mother's voice instantly, even after all this time.

Shocked that she had to fight back a sob, she drifted unsteadily over to the edge of the porch and peered down the alley. Eleanor Patterson, a heavy-set woman with her mostly-gray and brown hair pulled into a bun, stood on the stoop, shaking out a rug. She was older and bent a little, most likely from work like this. Still humming, she draped the mat over the rail, went inside, and returned a moment later with another. Snapping it back and forth, she paused quickly to mop her brow with a corner of her apron.

Victoria's heart was firmly lodged in her throat. How many years? Fifteen? All that time thinking her mother had sent her to a house of prostitution on purpose. The results of the action—well-intentioned or not—were still echoing in the universe.

If only things had turned out differently...

Victoria pushed away from the darkness of the thought and forced her legs to move. She descended the steps to the alley as if she were walking on glass. She approached Eleanor slowly, silently, came to within a few yards, and stopped.

Finally, the woman looked up. A bland curiosity glimmered

in her eyes, then slowly something else dawned there and her face went slack. She moved her mouth, but no sound came out.

Her shock freed Victoria to speak. "Momma, it's me. Victoria. I'm back."

Eleanor remained incapable of speech for another moment, but, finally, tears sprang to her eyes and the rug slid from her hand. "Victoria?" she whispered hoarsely.

Victoria gave up her own fight and let the tears flood her eyes and spill down her cheeks. "Yes." It came out as jagged croak.

Eleanor shook her head, as if finally realizing the moment's import, and ran down from the stoop. She flung herself at Victoria and hugged her daughter with a desperate, vice-like grip, her sobs shaking both their bodies. Aware this affection probably wouldn't last—not once Victoria told her mother her story—she still gave in to the moment. She returned the hug with the desperation of a human starved for affection, kindness, and, most of all, love.

"Oh, Momma, I have missed you so much."

The two women held each other for several minutes until Eleanor finally backed away, sniffling. Her ruddy cheeks were slick with tears. "Oh, Victoria." Hazel eyes glistening, she patted Victoria's cheek. "My daughter, my daughter. I feared I'd never see you again, but I knew you were alive. I knew it."

"Momma," Victoria wiped one of her mother's cheeks. "I'm alive. I'm back. But I have so much to tell you and—" her voice broke and her own tears returned. "And most of it's awful about me."

Eleanor's expression of weepy joy changed. Her round, slightly-weathered face softened with love and mercy. She tilted her head and took her daughter's hand. "Oh, baby girl, it makes no difference. You're home. That's what matters to me."

Victoria watched her mother prepare a simple breakfast of eggs and bacon. The cramped quarters of the little kitchen in the back of the saloon barely gave the woman enough room to shuffle about. After setting two plates of fried eggs on the table, Eleanor poured them each some coffee and finally sat. Victoria had drifted, staring into the black, steaming cup, but she could feel her mother's frank stare like a hand on her shoulder.

Where to start? She supposed at the beginning. Fifteen years ago. "When you put me on the stage to Stillwater that day, where did you think you were sending me?"

"You know. I had a job for you at the Stillwater Inn. Cleaning rooms. I told you I did that to get you out of here, away from some of the things I was doing, get you around decent people. Away from…"

"Away from Logan." Victoria laughed softly, bitterly. "You sent me to a brothel."

The blood drained from Eleanor's face, her expression changed to a mask of horror and pain. "What?"

"It was a bordello. The man—Sam Collins—he was a pimp. I thought you sold me. He said you sold me."

Eleanor's ample bosom rose and fell like it belonged to a winded horse. Her chin trembled. Right before Victoria's eyes, the woman seemed to age a decade. "God as my witness, I didn't know," she whispered. "I would never have done that. I only wanted to keep you away—I mean, give you something better." Her words came in a rush. "I thought I could trust him. He never—he never came to see me for that. He said he had a wife and family…No wonder you never wrote—" Visibly shaken, Eleanor sagged in her chair.

Victoria didn't exactly have pity for her mother, but at least the hate she'd harbored for the woman all this time was gone. "It doesn't matter now, Momma."

Eleanor pressed a hand to her mouth. Her eyes flooded

again. "I just wanted you safe. He said it was a nice hotel. There would be opportunities for you—"

Victoria reached across the table and took her mother's hand. "All water under the bridge now. No matter what—" a knot drew tight again in her throat and she had to fight past it. "No matter what you did or thought you did, I made the decisions from there. Horrible ones."

Eleanor seemed to sense her daughter's desperation and changed the grip, taking Victoria's hand in hers. "Tell me." She nodded, clearing the way. "Get it said. Whatever it is."

Victoria couldn't stop the fresh tears. They came suddenly in a scalding flood. "I don't want to," she said, the words tangled in a sob. "I'm afraid you'll hate me and make me leave." Oh, how had she come to this sniveling, disheveled mess? The old Victoria had never cried. Because she'd never cared about anything but power. Shame heated her cheeks.

"My darling daughter, I will never make you leave again." Eleanor squeezed Victoria's hand tighter, almost desperately. "I'll never lose you again, Victoria. No matter what you've done, no matter where you've been, I love you. And I've been waiting right here for you all these years."

That sounded just like something Logan would have said about God. The pain of missing the man twisting in her heart, Victoria lowered her head to the table, hid her face in the crook of her elbow and tried to get the debilitating, life-sucking grief under some kind of control. Her auburn curls, once piled high and pinned with gem-studded jewelry, spilled messily around her. "I changed my name. You probably heard it and never knew it was me."

"What did you change it to?"

She hesitated, but knew delay was pointless. "Delilah Goodnight." Her mother's gasp was soft, barely audible, but Victoria heard it just the same. What was worse? Her reputation as a decadent, no-holds-barred madam, or the devastation she'd wreaked in Defiance? Resigned to facing the music, she sat back up.

Eleanor's eyes were wide with surprise and revulsion. The last vestige of hope for anything good in Victoria's life seeped out of her.

"Are those things they said about you—they can't be true," Eleanor said, sounding hopeful the rumors were merely lies.

Victoria wished she could deny it, all of it, but there was no way. She'd shed the moniker of Delilah Goodnight in Defiance. The fancy clothes, the scandalous acts, the upstairs girls, the pink champagne, the life without limits belonged to someone who no longer existed. Folks would never let the reputation die, though, and Victoria knew it.

"It's all true," she said flatly. "If it's any kind of excuse, I thought you'd sold me. Logan saw me one night a few years later, but was so drunk he didn't recognize me." And he'd beat her in a drunken rage. That was the night Victoria Patterson had slipped beneath the surface and Delilah had risen in her place. She remembered it well.

Eleanor rubbed her forehead, as if a headache was stirring. "Oh, God. This is all my fault. If I hadn't interfered. If I had just left you and Logan alone. You woulda wound up pregnant but he would have killed anyone who touched you."

Hearing his name out loud squeezed Victoria's heart and for a moment she thought she might just curl up in a ball and stay that way till she died. She'd never ever been so devoid of hope, so overwhelmed with gut-wrenching guilt. God, would it ever go away?

And what of their daughter in Stillwater? The girl certainly could never know the truth about her mother.

Victoria flicked a glance at Eleanor—she didn't need to know about Elise. The woman had enough heartache thrust upon her by a wretch of a daughter. News of a granddaughter would only add to it.

"Why are you here now? After all this time."

"Something happened in Defiance." She looked at her hands. She could still recall the feel of Logan's blood on them, hear his last words to her, as he lay dying in the street. "Logan found me there. And I loved him every bit as much as I did when I was seventeen. Maybe more. And we were talking about a future." Her voice turned cold with bitterness. "A drunk stabbed him and he bled to death in the dirt and the horse manure." She closed her eyes, unwilling, unable to bear her mother's stunned gaze. "And because of me, twelve men are buried at the bottom of a mine in Defiance. I paid a man to blow it up."

There. It was all out now. No secrets. Her mother knew the harlot and murderer Victoria Patterson had become.

Silence fell. The Regulator clock on the wall ticked away the minutes. It was a long time before Eleanor spoke. "Do you want to change, Victoria?" she asked softly. "Is that why you're here?"

"Change?" Change meant a future, some kind of way to move forward. That didn't seem possible. But she wasn't Delilah Goodnight anymore, either. "I have changed. The weight of what I've done...those men shouldn't be dead. Logan shouldn't be dead. I should be." There was no holding back the sobs. They raged through her body, shaking her violently, punitively. "I don't know why I came here. There's no place in the world for me." Oh, God, she wondered if she'd ever get through a day without succumbing to this guilt and the grief.

Suddenly her mother's arms were around her and Victoria cried harder. Eleanor held her, stroked her head, rocked her little girl, and whispered soothing words. For just a moment, Victoria pretended she was eight years old again and nothing terrible had happened in her life. She couldn't hold back the flood of horrible memories for long, though.

"I tried to kill myself once," she whispered to her mother. "If I'd succeeded, Logan and all those men would still be alive."

"Oh, no, no, no," Eleanor said, sounding shocked, compassionate. "Don't talk like that." She rocked Victoria and hugged her. "You need to understand something." She waited for Victoria to look up. "Your tears, your guilt, won't bring Logan or those men back. And I'm not gonna to let you crawl into a grave right behind them. You hear me?"

"What am I going to do, Momma?" Pain choked her voice, her soul.

"Start over. Start living again."

"I can't. All this death—I can't. It's too much."

"Shhhh." Eleanor laid her cheek on Victoria's head. "We're gonna take this one day at a time. You're home. You're safe and we'll get through this together."

One day turned into ten. As the gray light of dawn began claiming the night, Eleanor peered in quietly at Victoria. Her daughter lay sleeping, tangled in a shift, most of the covers kicked off. Tendrils of long, auburn hair shot out crazily in every direction. It looked as if she'd been wrestling a bear all night.

Or ghosts.

Eleanor sighed but was empty of tears now. Her and Victoria's pasts were riddled with huge, vicious mistakes and there was no arguing the consequences had been nearly soul-destroying. But they could get through this. They had to.

God help us...

The newspaper clasped behind her back rustled with her tightening grip. She backed away from the door and once again opened the month-old paper. A headline screamed, "Dozens Dead in Defiance Disaster."

The first time she'd read the article she'd thought only of the men buried in the explosion. She paid scant attention to the references about the event being a criminal act instigated by Delilah Goodnight. *A horrid woman*, she'd thought, *to put someone up to a heinous act like this.* But her sympathy had quickly drifted back to the missing men, most likely entombed beneath tons of rock.

She'd thought little of the infamous madam's involvement. Murder wasn't such a leap from the other things the woman had reportedly practiced.

Only, *the woman* turned out to be Victoria.

Struggling to take all this in, Eleanor stepped over to their little dining table and dropped onto a chair, shoulders sagging. Thanks to an army of notoriously graphic cowboys, the name 'Delilah Goodnight' was as well-known as Custer or Hickock in the scandalous circles. Thanks to what had transpired in Defiance, it would be synonymous with Satan for the next century.

It?

Didn't she mean *her*?

Eleanor's gaze drifted back to the bedroom door. She'd only had the best intentions for Victoria by getting her out of Dodge. To a decent job. A brighter future than what Eleanor could offer. The pretty picture Eleanor had kept tucked away in her heart.

The broken, hopeless thing in there bore little resemblance to that picture. But neither was she the godless, decadent, cold-hearted human train wreck known as Delilah.

Eleanor and Victoria had to try to move on, make something good of the years they had left. If a person dwelt on nothing but regrets, giving up on life was inevitable. Eleanor feared Victoria had come home because she *had* given up and was on the verge of succumbing to those regrets.

A hopeful thought sparked to life in Eleanor's heart. Perhaps Victoria had returned to Dodge because she was ready to be *remade* into something better? Maybe *that* was why Eleanor had stayed put all these years—God knew her daughter would need her one day.

And Eleanor would not lose Victoria again. A fierce sense of protection rose up in her. *I won't, Lord. Please tell me I won't have to. I'll do anything to help her, to keep her safe, see her get her life back on track.*

She folded her hands and bowed her head. "So many mistakes, Lord," she whispered. "Oh, if only I hadn't interfered with her and Logan, maybe none of this would have happened in the first place." The guilt pierced her heart once more.

There is therefore now no condemnation for those who are in Christ Jesus.

The scripture eased some of her regret and she smiled, grateful for the Lord's compassion. The words reminded her their mistakes were a part of a bigger plan. She had to believe that, or she would go crazy. "Guide me, Lord. Help me to know how to help her."

Victoria gurgled, a strange, sad sound, and rolled over. She did not wake up.

She slept. She slept quite a lot and Eleanor had been giving her some time, but maybe what Victoria needed now was a reason to get out of bed.

The idea felt right. Eleanor would ask around about a job—something that would keep her daughter away from people. Or at least men. She couldn't be recognized. She would need to hide for a long time yet to come.

Perhaps they should move. Living over a saloon was the worst possible place for Victoria. Eventually someone would recognize her.

One step at a time, Eleanor cautioned herself. *Get her a job first. Give her some place to be, something to do with her time while she heals.* Resigned to taking this slow, she went downstairs to make their dinner.

To keep reading, get your copy of *Daughter of Defiance* today!

Or would you like to start at the beginning and read ALL the Defiance books? Then grab your copy of *Romance in the Rockies —the Box Set today!*

ABOUT THE AUTHOR

"Heather Blanton is blessed with a natural storytelling ability, an 'old soul' wisdom, and wide expansive heart. Her characters are vividly drawn, and in the western settings where life can be hard, over quickly, and seemingly without meaning, she reveals Larger Hands holding everyone and everything together."

MARK RICHARD, *EXECUTIVE PRODUCER, AMC'S HELL ON WHEELS, and PEN/ERNEST HEMINGWAY AWARD WINNER*

A former journalist, I am an avid researcher and endeavor to skillfully weave truth in among fictional storylines. I love exploring the American West, especially ghost towns and museums. I have walked parts of the Oregon Trail, ridden horses through the Rockies, climbed to the top of Independence Rock, and even held an outlaw's note in my hand.

I grew up in the mountains of Western North Carolina on a steady diet of Bonanza, Gunsmoke, and John Wayne Westerns. My most fond childhood memory is of sitting next to my daddy, munching on popcorn, and watching Lucas McCain unload that Winchester! My daddy also taught me to shoot and, trust me, I can sew buttons on with my rifle.

Currently I reside near Raleigh, NC, on my farm with my three boys and lots of dirt, some dogs, and a couple of horses. Oh, and a trio of cats who are above it all. And did I say dirt? #FarmLife

Heather Blanton

Please subscribe to my newsletter by visiting my website at
authorheatherblanton.com
to receive updates on my new releases and other fun news.
You'll also receive a FREE e-book—
A Lady in Defiance, The Lost Chapters
just for subscribing!

ALSO BY HEATHER BLANTON

A Lady in Defiance (Romance in the Rockies Book 1)

Charles McIntyre owns everything and everyone in the lawless, godless mining town of Defiance. When three good, Christian sisters show up, stranded and alone, he decides to let them stay—as long as they serve his purposes…but they may prove more trouble than they're worth.

Hearts in Defiance (Romance in the Rockies Book 2)

Notorious gambler and brothel-owner Charles McIntyre finally fell in love. Now he wants to be a better man, he wants to know Christ. But all the devils in Defiance are trying to drag him back to the man he was.

A Promise in Defiance (Romance in the Rockies Book 3)

When scandalous madam Delilah Goodnight flings open the doors to the newest, most decadent saloon in Defiance, two good men will be forced to face their personal demons.

Daughter of Defiance (Thanksgiving Books & Blessings Book 6)

When you hit rock bottom, you have a choice: seek the light or live in the darkness. Victoria chose the darkness. Can someone like her find redemption?

Hang Your Heart on Christmas (Brides of Evergreen Book 1)

A marshal tormented by a thirst for vengeance. A school teacher desperate to trade fear for courage. They have nothing in common except a quiet, little town built on betrayal.

Ask Me to Marry You (Brides of Evergreen Book 2)

Here comes the bride…and he isn't happy. With her father's passing, Audra Drysdale accepts she needs a man to save her ranch. A mail-order groom will keep her prideful men working and a neighboring rancher at bay. What could go wrong?

Mail-Order Deception (Brides of Evergreen Book 3)

Intrepid reporter Ellie Blair gets an undercover assignment as a mail-order bride and heads off to Wyoming where she discovers her potential groom isn't what he appears to be, either.

To Love and to Honor (Brides of Evergreen Book 4)

Wounded cavalry soldier Joel Chapman is struggling to find his place in the world of able-bodied men. A beautiful but unwed woman may be his chance to restore his soul.

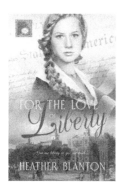

For the Love of Liberty

Novelist Liberty Ridley experiences an ancestor's memory from the Autumn of 1777. Stunned by the detail of it, she is even more amazed to find she's intensely drawn to Martin Hemsworth--a man dead for two centuries.

In Time for Christmas

Is she beyond the reach of a violent husband who hasn't even been born yet? Abandoned by her abusive husband on a dilapidated farm, Charlene wakes up a hundred years in the past. Can love keep her there?

Love, Lies, & Typewriters

A soldier with a purple heart. A reporter with a broken heart. Which one is her Mr. Right? A Christmas wedding could force the choice...

Hell-Bent on Blessings

Left bankrupt and homeless by a worthless husband, Harriet Pullen isn't about to lay down and die.

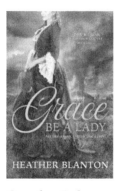

Grace be a Lady

Banished and separated from her son, city-girl Grace has to survive in a cowboy's world. Maybe it's time to stop thinking like a lady…and act like a man.

Locket Full of Love (Lockets & Lace Book 5)

A mysterious key hidden in a locket leads Juliet Watts and a handsome military intelligence officer on a journey of riddles, revelations, and romance.

A Good Man Comes Around (Sweethearts of Jubilee Springs Book 8)

Since love has let her down, widow Abigail Holt decides to become a mail-order bride, but with a clear set of qualifications to use in choosing her new husband. Oliver Martin certainly doesn't measure up…not by a long shot.

Made in the USA
Las Vegas, NV
18 August 2024

93994864R00236